Deferred Prejudice

Doug Booth

Deferred Prejudice

Most thoughts of wrongdoing are tempered by fear of retribution,

Which doesn't exonerate us, or make us better. We are what we are.

D Booth

Deferred Prejudice

1
November 30th of this Year

Anita Juárez strode into The Boss' office. She never strolled in, or sauntered. She strode in, as she did everywhere, with elegant confidence. And as did everyone everywhere, he stopped what he was doing to acknowledge her. She was captivating. Except this time something was wrong.

"Cacique… perdón."

"Anita, ¿perdón? We are alone. Since when do you excuse yourself to me at such times? Am I in trouble with you again, in our last month together?" He feigned alarm. "You know that I will not survive very long without you."

She had no whimsical reply. She answered with her eyes. Of late she found little or no humour in his cavalier bearing, the inherent charm that so many others continued to see and would soon miss.

He leaned forward onto his elbows. "What is it, Anita? Tell me."

"I do not know. This letter, there is not one word in these three pages that does not frighten me."

"What does it say?"

"No. You must read this immediately with your own eyes, Cacique. Security has told me that a young boy was asked to deliver this letter to you personally. He was paid well, he told them. Of course, whoever wrote this must have known that such freedom of access to you is not possible.

They followed him outside, to confirm that he was alone. They saw no one else."

"Tell me what the letter says, Anita? You begin to worry me."

She knew that wasn't true. The Boss never worried, but for those rare occasions at 11:53 PM when his phone would ring at what was truly the eleventh hour. The phone call was a formality, of course. He never faltered in what he believed. He was not a man given to clemency.

"The letter is cryptic, clearly written for you alone to understand, for no one else."

She put the open letter on his desk and left him, closing the door quietly behind her. He would tell her in due course, or not. Yet in her heart she knew he would not.
*

Dear Sir,

Please understand that I cannot and did not assign my name, or yours, to this missive which speaks to an undeniable and prolonged regret, a deep and tormenting wound that has caused both you and me incalculable distress these many years.

I send to you now this letter which I have written in my heart and in my mind countless times. To assign a quantitative value would serve no purpose. I speak of my dreams each sleepless night, filled with evil spectres haunting me without compassion for the knowledge which I alone possessed, of my every waking thought pitilessly invaded and appropriated without the slightest reprieve by reason of my complicity and guilt.

Mercifully for me these constant, dark and malicious companions, which for me were vivid memories relived, are ended. I am now passed away, and with me, I sincerely hope and pray, your deep torment and private spectres that surely must relentlessly haunt your empty days and sleepless nights.

I remember clearly the words you spoke that day so many years ago, when last we met at her grave. I remember your breath, the cold hate in your dark eyes. But who were you then to speak such words, and who was I to believe you. However I came to know the truth which I have harboured unto myself for a very long time. For that I shall never cease to grieve, even in death. Yet I came to believe that my first and callous disregard for you, and my righteous fear of what would come to pass had I then embraced your truth, was right for you, and for him, if not just or morally correct for either one until this day.

You were correct to believe that he lives, though he does not in any way deserve such luxury. He does well in Key West onboard a luxury fifty-foot yacht which serves as his livelihood, the registered name scrawled in red is as repugnant to me as it will undoubtedly be to you. I saw him one month ago, though he did not see me despite our closeness. This I write without the slightest lament, that he would not have recognized his own mother. He is no longer my son to protect. Neither can I any longer protect you by virtue of my silence, which, you must believe, grew to become my gravest concern. You were, until this day, my life's work. That I waited until well beyond that grievous day is my life's lament. I beseech you to believe that we, she and I, were not wicked in our hearts but narrow in our minds by virtue of our epoch and our history.

When once you did not, you now have my utmost regard. Beware of him. Such vile contempt as his for life does not diminish with time. I urge you to approach such evil with equal and malevolent indifference. However, those cruel words you once spoke came from a heart that was not then, and is not now, malicious. You are not that man. You must search beyond your grief. His crime was not against your heart alone. He hides not just from you. Let others do easily that which you cannot. Find them. Be their guiding hand, lest you be condemned to everlasting anguish. You will not discover salvation in whatever you devise alone, rather certain misery for you and for others, those who have shared your life and those who have not, and might never should you choose to discount me.

Walk into the dark, find those who will with great joy and gratitude take the sword from your hand. They share your grief as they do your hate. They are skilled where you are not. They will not cower. Nor will they forsake you. You will not walk alone. Although your first steps will be cautious and uncertain you will not falter at this the precipice of your new genesis, your rebirth.

Detective Drew Carling of the LAPD has proven himself an honest man, beyond reproach, his integrity is well-established. His service record to-date is commendable and meritorious. He is highly regarded and does not stoop to the lowest of ideals. He is unmarried, with no family beyond his parents who are inconsequential to you. You and he have much in common. He will embrace you. He will help you find your way into the dark once you confide in him all that you know and all that you feel without contrition.

Deidre Commons is a corporate executive. She is well-positioned and very wealthy for her young age. She is also an only child, orphaned by tragedy when still in school. She is very beautiful and very smart. Those who know her are proud of her, as I am certain you shall be. She is open-minded, very level and in no way pretentious. My belief is that she can be of great assistance to you, and you to her. Her main preoccupation beyond her success in corporate America is yachting. She works and resides, you will be interested to discover, not one mile from where you sit at this very moment. I have met with her formally on several occasions, though she knows nothing of me or of you.

I have no doubt you will like and admire one another.

She owns a second residence in Miami, an escape to leisure where she docks her Life's Compensation not 200 miles from him, a pleasant day cruise which I am certain you will enjoy together.

Sadly, Darcy Wilson is quite another matter indeed. Her parents fell on hard times which regrettably forced her to leave and find her own way at an early age. She has not fared well by your strict standards or mine. However she is well regarded by the male patrons of a gentlemen's' bar in New Orleans where she earns a good living by disrobing completely for their entertainment. She does not, I hasten to add, extend the baseness of their pleasure by any imaginable degree. Her stage name is Demure and whatever else I know of her you will discover for yourself when you feel the time propitious to contact her. And I pray that you do so quickly so that you might save her as you have saved so many others.

I have spoken with her beyond the sordid walls of her workplace. She is blessed with a natural beauty and kind heart, deserving without question of what she does not know to expect.

In closing, I look forward to once again being by my son's side, in my new world, so that he will at last discover the extent of my scorn and repugnance towards him for the evil he has done. His new name I send to you under separate cover to your home in the event this letter might be read by others.

I have done my best to absolve myself of my first disbelief and indifference, alas I cannot. I am truly sorry. Be assured that I leave whatever wealth and comfort I undeservedly possess to those more worthy and in greater need by way of charitable hearts and dispositions, as you will soon discover. I can do no more.

With sincerest regret for that which I have done, I remain eternally in your debt. Forgive me.

*

The tiny green light on her desk flickered. She stood and strode in.

"Anita, cancel my agenda through to Monday. Tell anyone who cares that I am tired, sick or on vacation. Tell them whatever you please."

She wanted to ask, but didn't. She knew him. "You do not look well, Cacique. You have no colour." She saw the letter scrolled in his hand. "I will call your doctor."

"No, you will not. You will call my driver instead. I am going to the mansion, alone, and must not be disturbed. Anita, I need to be alone. ¿Comprendes lo que digo?"

He was The Boss. Whether or not she understood didn't matter.

"Cacique, the letter, what does it mean?"

He clenched the three sheets. What he had read filled him with dread, made him feel sick. He didn't need another haunting memory. He read the names once again, went to the cross shredder by his credenza and destroyed the letter.

"It is better not to hear the truth, Anita, than to hear a lie. Come by for me tomorrow, though not too early. I anticipate a greater need than ever before of your delicious omelettes. And this time, I promise, I will not frighten you as you come through my door."

Yet at that very moment he did frighten her. She was visibly distraught, her own face drained of its warm colour. She'd never forgotten the day so long ago or his venomous words.

"I will go with you. You must talk with me, Cacique, and tell me about that letter."

He didn't smile. He seldom smiled.

"There is nothing to tell, other than I expect to be very drunk this evening, Santa Anita, and very hung-over tomorrow at long last."

When he'd gone she remained in his office. She sat in a

leather sofa by the large bay window overlooking Sacramento, watching as the limousine passed through his private gate of the State Capitol. She was numb, her mind a kaleidoscope of irrational thoughts and images. When finally she stood, lost in time, her face was streaked with coloured tears.

2

He hadn't called her Santa Anita since that day. He never said he was going home. He had no home to go to, no wife, no children to call his own, to call for any reason. Instead he had a beautiful mansion, a condo by the sea which he never used, three offices, two chauffeurs and a personal assistant who seldom left his side until he went to an empty house alone each evening near midnight.

She possessed a key to each of his doors, enjoying exclusive right of entry regardless of the hour, the day or the reason, with an open invitation to use the seaside retreat whenever she wanted. Her job was to maintain him, to put him where he had to be, to brief him on strangers who were cleared to meet with him, to ensure that his files and speeches were always at hand, and to bring him coffee that others would first bring to her. And soon he would be lost without her.

He worked seventeen-hour days, she worked eighteen. She knew everything about him and was well-paid so that no one else would. She was his defence, his shield, though in her dreams and most private thoughts she was so much more in a way she could never express. She was Anita Juárez, unofficially the second most powerful person in the state, his confidante and sounding board.

She was thirty-eight. She had the face and body of a twenty-eight-year-old and had been with him since the first agonizing days of his total collapse twenty-one years earlier when she first stepped into his storefront office at 4:55 one Friday searching for work, barely able to speak English, wearing one sister's sweater and another's skirt, her legs bare, her shoes scuffed from the rubber mats in her father's ancient Winnebago.

She was young and should have fled at once into the swirling violence of wind and rain, seeing the glare in his eyes, the aura of seething hatred enshrouding him like a forbidding mantle, standing her ground despite her fear, her clothes soaked through, her black hair plastered to an innocent face in thick, unruly strands. She was desperate. She didn't want a life of waiting tables for nickels and dimes. She didn't want to clean rich peoples' toilets and she didn't want to open her legs to unclean strangers to make ends meet.

He was drunk; his life shattered. He took one look at the windblown waif and screamed at her to go, to get out. And she did, for some reason returning undaunted with black coffee and a day-old sandwich which she earned with a few minutes of menial work. He was slow to react, immersed in a selfish whirlpool of regret and pity, mounting rage and desperation, staring into the empty space between his desk and the door. She was gone, the same words pounding over and over again in his head.

"You'll remember Pichilingue, dusty dirt roads and sleeping on the floor, though not the way you might believe. You'll remember this place, your beginning here and your end, which will come one day too soon. That's life. We move on. It's the natural order of things. And one day you'll come across someone who'll be in the right place at the right time, someone who needs a break. He or she will be in your place, chavo, in your space and time, wherever and whenever that might be, some desperate kid who needs a job, a chance to change his or her life. I'm not talking about dimes in a tin cup. I'm talking about real help. Not everyone, chavo, has parents like yours."

He pressed his palms hard against his temples and screamed.

She wasn't afraid, she was sad. She felt sorrow for him because her father was a drunk and the bottle she'd seen on the young man's desk was a single drink from being empty. She hadn't seen a glass or a cup and the cardboard liquor box on the floor was also empty, the centrepiece of a careless montage of the blue vodka bottles she recognized and food wrappers. Files were strewn across his desk and the floor, strangely juxtaposed to an otherwise orderly room. She didn't understand. Though what she didn't see would have frightened her. To see a man that imposing, his face contorted with such fury, standing, staggering and kicking away his chair, hurling the bottle into his framed credentials, exploding the glass. At that moment he wanted to kill, and he hoped that one day he would.

Had she seen him lurch through his doorway onto the wet street she would have run. But she didn't see him. He saw her, pulling herself into the dilapidated van as though suddenly robbed of her youth, one foot drowning in a torrent of rainwater.

He didn't stumble or fall, preferring instead to destroy his shirt and damage his left shoulder against a half-block of blurred windows, doorways and brick walls. He wanted to vomit, when before her intrusion he'd felt perfectly fine. What did she think she was doing? And what was he doing, making a spectacle of himself? He saw them watching, staring, all of them oblivious to the storm, afraid of him, of what he might do or say. What made them so perfect? If only they knew, if they could feel what he felt, had lost what he lost. He needed to empty his guts onto the street. But he wouldn't. What was done was done.

He inched his way to the front of the van, their faces not three feet apart. She was right there in front of him, her

14

hands gripping the steering wheel, her face frozen into a despondent mask, the source of her green tears the blackest eyes he'd ever seen. She squeezed her eyes shut several times more than blink, he couldn't do either. He simply stood there, his left sleeve pink with blood, trying to focus, trying to master his breathing, wondering whether he should smile, laugh or cross his arms decisively and hope not to fall. Instead he leaned onto the windshield and brought up his hands in prayerful search of forgiveness.

The next morning he woke late, his torso twisted into a woollen blanket, his head pounding. He could feel his heart beating erratically, on the verge of exploding through his chest. The sound of blood pumping through his veins made him nauseous. His teeth were thick with plaque, his eyes glued together with salted crust. His clothes were damp, made wet by the previous day's rain and the cold sweat of recovery and horrid dreams. He'd poisoned himself with alcohol for too long, oblivious to those who loved him, punishing them for the atrocity which they also endured. He'd disgraced his mother, dishonoured his father and had cruelly rejected the warmth of his closest friends. He felt less than human, beneath the vilest of creatures.

The broken glass was gone, so were the empties, the remnants of stale food and the broken frame. His current files were organized in neat piles by client name and rich Columbian coffee permeated the room. Anita came to work in a new skirt and sweater, new shoes and stockings. She'd gone to the hairdresser the night before and had bought designer cosmetics she might never have afforded. She'd splurged, spending her entire signing bonus, an unexpected generosity she didn't quite comprehend.

She wasn't at all what he remembered, seeing her first with one eye, then both. She was a pretty little thing, so young and so innocent. Her hair was obsidian black. Her skin was pale amber, her teeth blinding white and he would discover that her dark eyes would more than once convey a succinct message when mere words might be less meaningful.

She was five-foot nothing. Her A-line skirt came to just above her knees, her sweater conforming to every perfect curve. Her skin was flawless, her breasts neither large nor small. Her waist and her hips would be the envy of most women, he believed, and the sheen of her stockings in concert with her low-heeled pumps made her seem immovable, untouchable, too good for him, beyond him, poised quietly with a coffee cup in her hand...waiting.

She didn't expect him to comment, and he didn't. He couldn't. She was a vision to behold; he was a dishevelled mess. She smelled of pears or apricots; she smelled fresh. He smelled of booze and sweat and had fallen asleep on the couch the night before instead of vomiting. Something foul had died or defecated in his mouth. His stomach was sour, its revolt not entirely quelled. His attempt to free himself and to sit straight was exaggerated, clumsy, his arms finally flailing in the air, throwing the blanket to the side.

His hair was matted into pasty strands, his face dark with thick stubble not yet a full beard, his usually bright brown eyes covered over with a yellow film. He'd made the tear in his shirt worse, pushing in a facecloth to stop the bleeding, he thought. His shirttails were pulled out from under his belt and stained. With what, she didn't know. She didn't want to know. His pants were twisted, one leg bare to his knee, his executive socks were pushed to his ankles and he'd forgotten to remove the second of two shoes.

She proffered the coffee, hesitating, which he took with both hands. He had nothing to say. Her transformation was incredible, and he had no words, insisting to himself that he would not under any circumstances apologize for his pathetic condition. Yet, that's not what he'd seen in her eyes. He saw curiosity, and he saw hope.

16

He was still drunk, and disadvantaged. He didn't like people standing over him. He never had. Yet he had a beautiful young girl whom he knew nothing about standing in front of him, waiting, her eyes cast down. He remembered the money, if not exactly how much. Though he was conscious enough to consider whatever amount he'd given her as a cash reward for saving him when he most needed help, which he still did, to stand.

He asked in a drawl whether she was honest. She was. Had she ever been to jail? No. Did she take drugs or have a boyfriend who sold drugs? No, never, she promised. Was she legal? Yes she was. She had papers. Did she speak English? She shook her head. No, not very well, but she would very soon. If he left her alone, would she be there later in the day when he returned? Yes, she would, she promised. She had work to do. What work? She didn't know. He hadn't told her, but she would not make him sorry for his kindness to her.

Kindness to her? She had it all wrong. Why the hell did he chase after her? What had he done?

Why hadn't he locked the door? He needed to get out, to get away from her, to figure out what to do with her and why he should do anything. He'd probably already given her more than she'd earn in a month. Not a bad salary for a half-day's work.

She wasn't letting go of his arm. He told her that he was fine, really, that he was leaving for a while and that he'd be back…sometime. Still she held his arm, not believing him. She guided him to the desk, letting him transfer his full weight onto his arms, his palms anchored between the short stacks of neatly placed files.

Where were his damned keys? He looked at her, then at her new leather purse. She closed her hands across the top edges; she knew what he was thinking. He gurgled a laugh. Someone had to give in. How more ridiculous could he make himself? He let his head drop, defeated, asking whether she could at least call him a taxi. Did she speak that much English? She nodded innocently that she could, though even in his deteriorated state he wasn't blind to feminine guile. He knew she wanted to smile from ear to ear, bathing in her victory. Santa Anita had won the day.

On his own he made his way to the door and stepped out, inhaling deeply without feeling any appreciable improvement in his condition, glad to be away from her. Nothing in his office was worth stealing. His car was insured and she couldn't be any worse than the few of his pro bono clients who preferred jail to school. Besides, perhaps she was a saint sent to redeem him, which would mean the presence of a God he'd once believed in, the same God that had forsaken him, robbing his body of heart and soul.

Later that afternoon he did return to his office matter-of-factly, after a serious workout that to-date, he told himself, was his worst abuse, after a meal that would make a vegetarian think twice, after swearing never to drink another drop until the promise he'd made at the funeral was honoured. He'd lost everything he once lived for and could do nothing about it, not then. But one day, yes, he would. One day he would kill.

"Te lo juro, mi corazón," he whispered, stepping through the doorway. "He will not escape me. Until then, let him live in a fantasy world of demons and ghosts. Let him think of me, as I will think of him. On my honour, he will die before me."

Anita Juárez heard the final few words. She jerked backward, visibly shocked, her wide-open eyes and mouth almost making him smile. But he didn't. He seldom would again. His suit was tailored and black. His shirt was starched, white as the purest cloud and his tie was a deep burgundy, the colour of blood. The crease in his pants was razor-sharp and his loafers had the dull shine of expensive Italian leather. His face was clean, his brown eyes bright and alert, his hair thick and lustrous, the deep red-brown of mahogany, tousled by the wind as though he'd been sailing. His face and hands were the colour of cinnamon and for the first time she noticed the single ruby in a silver setting, a symbol of achievement, and a simple silver band with the deepest green emerald she'd ever seen, a symbol of a shattered life, identical to the one she'd seen hanging from the silver chain at his neck the night before as she cared for him before leaving.

He spread his arms, dropping his gaze slightly as though appraising himself. "I thought my renaissance should be as complete as possible, señorita." He smirked. "Everything else went into a laundry bag." He inhaled deeply, taking in all that she'd done, the newly repaired frame mounted on the wall. "This is the real me, señorita. Or the best I could accomplish in such a short time. I hope you see a difference."

She said, "Lo siento, Cacique."

"For what, Anita? I am the one who should be sorry. And I am. I did not expect to see you upon my return. Truly, I did not, for the despicable way in which I treated you." He put a hand to her cheek. "Mi Santa Anita, you have come at the right time to save me."

She shook her head. She was sorry. She hadn't made a mistake. This was a good man, she knew. He was not like her father. This man was strong and brave, not weak and pathetic. She would stay with him. She would work hard to please him and one day she would have such a gallant caballero of her own.

The office closed early, not that he was ever open for business on a Saturday, which would soon change. They went to dinner and learned a little about each other. After dinner he drove her home, disheartened by what he saw. He took her hand, forcing a smile, and she saw in his eyes the hope that he'd earlier seen in hers. With her other hand she took the tiny gold cross hanging from her neck between her fingers and kissed the meaningful pendant. She knew she hadn't simply gone to El Cacique's office on a whim, when all others had turned her down. She was sent to him.

He went with her into her father's house where he spoke privately with the man who clearly understood that Anita would never again, for the short while she would remain in his house, feel worried or threatened. Not many days later she moved out.

When she came in early on the second day wearing the same ensemble he gave her a month's advance, the rest of the day off, and from then on he paid her on the first of each month. Now the state paid her, and had for eight years.

He'd put her through university, went with her to her father's funeral, her mother's wedding, and to her graduation. She was first in her class, that year's valedictorian. Anita Juárez could have commanded the best salaries in the best communications or public relations firms. Instead she stayed by his side, helping the wrongly accused or those who couldn't afford to pay exorbitant fees to minimize the after-effects of their errant lives.

She listened to him, to his plans, his ideals, and never laughed, never thought him a dreamer.

To Anita, in private, he was always Cacique and when his dream was realized she went with him. In public he was The Boss and no one stood in his way, or got past her. He was at the end of his second term. She loved him and she adored him. She knew all that there was to know about him, save the reason that at long last he would keep his promise, and that he would kill.

3
Thirty-five Years Ago

His mother and father raised Scott Gibson to become an upstanding citizen. His friends and neighbours believed that he was. His law professors believed that he would one day become a prominent trial lawyer and a brilliant strategist, as did Scott Gibson himself. His family minister who would marry him believed he was a good Christian. Others believed he was an immoral egoist, a man self-infatuated, driven by adoration, lust and greed.

He gave the disparate views not a moment's consideration. Those who thought most disparagingly of him were those who'd lost in love, licentious college women or naïve and playful diversions vying for a place in his promising life with their eager bodies and of their own volition without any remarkable or sustainable degree of satisfaction on his part. Never once considering what he gave them in return: lasting memories of fine restaurants, admission to an exclusive nightlife, jewelled mementos of their time together and, of course, his expertise in all things carnal.

In the early years Scott Gibson was the all-star boy, a collegiate wonder with brains equal to his brawn, the world believed. He was the golden-haired boy: perfect in every way. His hair seemed permanently combed to perfection, his teeth were Pepsodent-perfect, his eyes the perfect shade of blue, his athletic body tanned precisely to within the exacting tolerances of glossy magazines. He was a glamour boy.

To the endless parade of girls eager to leap from a girlish precipice feigned or real into womanhood, he was an ephemeral trophy worthy of their virginity; to the male contingent he was the one to emulate, to admire, or to loathe in moments of quiet depression and festering jealousy.

His family was old money, dug from the ground in the form of gold, much of which over time had been diversified into preferred shares, mutual funds, real-estate, venture capital, political campaigns and IOUs. His father, long since dead, was then Senator Arthur Gibson: wealthy, a Democrat, a lobbyist, well-connected, a broker of favours and very proud father.

He was corrupt, in the moral sense, to the extent that the law allowed. He gave no quarter and asked for none. He didn't have to. If you screwed him, you were screwed. If he screwed you, you got on with life, or not. Either way, he didn't care. He had learned from an early age that he was above most others. He was sophisticated, good with the ladies and he'd taught his son well that to receive is better than to give.

Scott's mother, Mrs. Claire Gibson, was thirty-nine and attractive. She was from good stock and a child bride, though not of necessity at the time. She wore expensive dresses fashionably short and her shoes fashionably high. She wore fitted décolleté sweaters and loose silk blouses provocatively unbuttoned to entice when other women wore two-piece suits with blouses buttoned to the neck and a string of pearls. She liked men. She dressed for them, enjoying their undisguised attention. She always had, believing that many of her girlhood boyfriends fondly remembered her body, her insatiable appetite and need for change. When what they remembered more were their prayers that Arthur Gibson, and not one of them, had succeeded in getting her pregnant.

She was also a socialite and obedient, a woman more endowed with etiquette and grace than knowledge of the world beyond her closely knit circle. She was eleven years younger than her husband whose pragmatic love for her he displayed in public despite his frequent dalliances with proactive interns or the wives of up and coming junior Representatives who either didn't know or didn't care. Of greater importance were their shared futures.

For Claire station and decorum, or its façade, were paramount. Men such as her husband deviated as they must, as was expected, a function of preservation and control, lifting the puppy from the floor as it were. Love didn't enter into the equation. Conversely, decent women, proper women of rank, did not despite their inclinations. Such was not their place. Their sole purpose was to maintain appearances and never acknowledge their adventurous past. The social penalties were too severe.

Claire's single achievement in life was the birth of her one child whom she doted on from his birth to the day she sat proudly watching him swagger across the stage of the main auditorium at his alma mater to grasp written proof of his excellence. He was twenty-one and three months away from his first year of law.

On her right sat her husband, his face flushed, his average shape belying his proclivity for fine food and drink. On her left sat Mr. and Mrs. Franklin Duval and their daughter, Francine. Mr. Duval was senior partner of the city's most prominent law firm. He was wealthy; he enjoyed the good life and didn't cheat on his wife. He was on a first name basis with most members of the state's judiciary and sat on the Executive Committee of the very exclusive club co-owned by him and Arthur Gibson.

If you weren't the Honourable Mr. or Mrs. Someone or

Mr. President, you would complete a membership application, pay two-hundred-thousand upfront to be held in escrow and pray you'd be spared the shame of refusal. Or perhaps be denied an invitation by someone who at some point had stood before you in a court of law, your courtroom, waiting for you to pass sentence, waiting to base his decision on yours, disappointed. Such were the politics of society.

Mrs. Duval was the same age as Claire, albeit much less promiscuous in her youth. However, much like Claire, she'd never worked a day in her life. Women of quality did not. They held benefits and attached their names to important charitable work. She was aristocratic, standoffish and prudish. She was Mrs. Franklin Duval, mistress and overseer of the Duval estate, sought after guest for luncheons and garden parties and devoted mother of Francine Duval.

Francine was fifteen, in the final year of her secondary and private education. She was a virgin, possibly by virtue of her schoolmates being girls, or possibly by virtue itself. She didn't know which. She had no available barometer by which to judge herself. She'd spent her young life cloistered with nannies, nurses and governesses, chauffeurs and trips to Spain most summers to live with her no-nonsense and loving grandparents who understood the need to give her balance.

She was blonde with peaches and cream skin, petite, daddy's little girl with big green eyes and her mother's pride and joy. She wore a ponytail, bobby socks, plaid skirts and V-neck sweaters. At the ocean with her girlfriends she wore one-piece European designs, rose-coloured glasses, wide-brimmed hats, and sipped lemonade through a straw. She was nothing like those girls on Venice Beach, their skin glistening with baby oil, flaunting their almost naked bodies in slutty bikinis that left nothing to the boys' imaginations.

24

She watched Scott on the stage. He was handsome, tall, athletic and charming. She'd met him twice before and had to admit that each time her vivid imagination succumbed to an eventual physical release. All the girls in her class did, dreaming of their teachers, inventing, making them suave gigolos or daring buccaneers, highwaymen sweeping them off their feet or sophisticated polo players, those who didn't dream of taunting their parents' chiselled pool boys, sweating gardeners or gentlemanly chauffeurs.

But soon she wouldn't imagine. Soon she would become Mrs. Scott Gibson because she was expected to do what was right for the family. She'd known for some time. What choice did she have? She owed her parents that much after all they had done for her. She would complete her high school in two years and spend another year away at prep school learning what was right and what was wrong, what to say and what not to say, learning to be a proper and dignified wife. In the meantime he would study law for three years and be given every opportunity to visit with Francine during his brief summer recess. In his fourth year he would clerk for her father and she would travel to Spain to perfect her Castilian Spanish so that she might later better understand her domestics. Mrs. Duval considered the various dialects of Latin America somewhat vulgar, not unlike the rude variation of English spoken by the coloured community.

That last summer they would court. They would come to know each other, fall in love and in the autumn she would become Mrs. Scott Gibson. She would be a wife and then a mother. She would have a beautiful baby to adore, maybe as many as three if it didn't hurt too much. All the girls worried about that. And their bodies, what about their bodies? She would not, she had already decided, be like those women at her father's club. She would stay young and flawless. Yes, she would, and she would have the most perfect babies in the entire world.

She studied him as he bounded proudly from the stage, his arms held high. She inhaled deeply and smiled. She wanted badly to go home to her room where she could curl into her pillow, close her eyes and be with him as man and wife.

The men had discussed the pragmatic union many times previously at the club. Scott would be a fine addition to the firm of Duval & Associates once in possession of his LL.M. degree after which he would prove himself and succeed according to his determination. Of course the agreement inferred the fathers' continued friendship as well as their business relationship and their children's continued harmony. They would soon be family, and family took care of family.

The mothers agreed, which was expected, meeting several times each month in the gardens of either mansion to further solidify the men's alliance while sipping tea or sherry. Scott and Francine were simply ideal for each other. He was charming, handsome and caring. She was beautiful, pristine, and would graduate from the finest prep school in the state reserved for the privileged few, a place of learning that most young girls could never hope to attend, practiced in all facets of being a perfect young woman. She would be nineteen, mature for her age. He would be twenty-five, his wild oats sown, ready for life's responsibilities, a career, his Master of Law, and in due course Duval & Associates would become Duval, Gibson & Associates.

That she would deliver whole and healthy children free of imperfections was a given.

What Scott saw in her was a virgin bride held in reserve for his pleasure, his guaranteed future, the daughter of San Francisco's most prominent and influential trial lawyer and guarantor of a young man's dreams. That she dressed like a 60s store window mannequin wasn't a concern. He would make the necessary changes quickly, at least making her appear as a woman. The big question was: what would he do with her after the first night? He didn't want a girl for a wife when he'd grown accustomed to temporary, mature women familiar with the concept of social bartering, being wined and dined in exchange for their bodies. On the plus side she was young, impressionable and mouldable.

To Francine, Scott was her future, her father's dream. She would marry him, bear his children and raise their family. They would be happy together. She would do lunch with close friends, become a much sought after hostess for him, an adoring wife, and in a few years history would repeat itself. He would become a senior partner destined to one day own the firm and she would be Mrs. Scott Gibson and her name would appear on the most enviable guest lists.

4

Hidalgo Arquero never allowed himself such fanciful dreams. He believed with each passing year that he would never leave Pichilingue. He would die there. He'd completed his schooling a few months earlier; he had nothing else to learn. Or his teacher had no more wisdom to impart. At fifteen his education was over and he'd begun searching for work, except no one was hiring.

Many days over the summer he walked to La Paz, leaving home early to meet the first American tourists disembarking the ferry from Mazatlán, holding out desperate hands filled with tiny seashells for them to buy. Most did not, though some did, later tossing them into the street, feeling they had done something worthwhile, something humanitarian. And each evening Hidalgo returned home late, never waking his mother, waiting until yet another morning to give her the few pesos he'd earned.

He would be no better than his father who one day would come home unannounced once again, never staying longer than the time he needed to mend what was broken or old in the house.

Then he would leave. He would embrace his wife and shake Hidalgo's hand, promising both that things would one day be different, better. He would disappear onto the local bus and they would not see him for months. Hidalgo hadn't liked his father for a very long time.

He'd heard the promises of a better life from his father over and over again, twice each year when his father returned home, never believing the man. He had no reason. He barely knew his father and what he heard each night, sitting on the floor in front of their small black and white television, in the shack that was their home at the edge of a dusty road in the low hills of Pichilingue, told him that his father was either a thoughtless liar or a careless dreamer. Hidalgo knew what would happen to Mexicans who tried to cross the border.

Señor Arquero was not a man to admire. In his son's eyes he was a failure. He was illiterate, unskilled, a man who could never find even the most menial work cleaning floors in the local factories or casting nets onboard barely seaworthy trawlers. Instead he preferred to abandon his family and grovel for a minimum wage in America. And one day he would not come home. Hidalgo knew that also. He would abandon his family forever.

But this night was different when Hidalgo walked through the door to the dank smell of wet cloths strung across the cramped living space, anxious to fall onto his cot, to relieve his tired feet. His mother was not sleeping. She was in her chair, rocking, hunched over, tears running between her fingers. She put a finger quickly to her lips, her eyes darting towards her bedroom door. He was not to make a sound. His father had come home. He was in bed asleep.

Hidalgo asked what the man had done to make her cry. Nothing, she replied. He'd done nothing. She signalled her son closer, kissing his cheek. She saw in his eyes how weary he was. She wanted him to sleep also. He would know everything in the morning.

"Y querido," she added, "mañana, no trabajarás en la ciudad. Quederás aquí en la casa."

Something was very wrong. Often he would hear his mother whimpering softly in her room late at night, though never had he seen her weeping so openly. What was she thinking to say such a thing? She knew that he must go into town each day, to be a man for her, to be strong, to earn what money he could. Why must he stay home?

He did his best not to sleep, forcing one bad thought into his mind after another, wondering what his father might have told his mother to make her cry, imagining the worst. Yet eventually he did drift into a better world, one he would never know, oblivious to his mother's footsteps, the rising sun and the first of several soft taps against his shoulder.

He dressed slowly. He wasn't anxious to see his father. He had nothing to say and nothing that he wanted to hear. What could he say? Perhaps hola, papá. Then what? We missed you. Did you pick many grapes while you were gone? Is a bushel heavy upon the back, worse than walking into La Paz each day, worse than scrubbing your knuckles to the bone, like my mother? Did you have a good bus ride, papá? Do I care?

His father was seated at the table. They exchanged glances; his father's only welcome a curt nod. Nothing was said, and not for the first time. Usually during such visits many hours would pass, if not a day or two, before father and son would speak.

When the wooden plates were cleared, Señor Arquero folded his arms, leaning his chest into the edge of the table. He cleared his throat. This time he would promise them nothing, promises spoke to the future. Instead he told Hidalgo to leave the house and remain nearby. When Hidalgo hesitated, looking to his mother, his father repeated the command silently with another curt nod.

When Hidalgo returned for lunch his mother was crying, her golden-brown cheeks glistening with more unstoppable tears. He felt rage towards his father who sat with her silently, watching her without holding her, doing nothing to console her.

Hidalgo wanted to strike out at his father, but he was fifteen. His father was twice that age and more and Hidalgo was no match for a body hardened by manual labour or the sinewy arms and callused hands of a heartless man.

Hidalgo did as he was told. He sat, his mind racing, his heart beating wildly, quietly watching as his mother went into the corner of her home reserved for cooking, her shoulders drooping with despair. She prepared a meagre meal, though no one was hungry. She brought her husband a drink of lemon water mixed with spices and, for Hidalgo, a cup of goat's milk from a ceramic jug.

Hidalgo listened to his father as they picked at their meal, not believing him. What he was hearing wasn't possible. His father hadn't come home this time to relax after so many months of hard work in the field. No. He'd come for his family, to take them away. Hidalgo was not to leave the house. He was to speak with no one. No one was to know. He was to spend what remained of the day making himself ready, gathering his belongings, bathing; making certain he was well-rested and clean. His mother would tend to the washing of their soiled clothes and prepare their meals for the journey ahead while he, Fernando Arquero, made certain that nothing of value remained in their home for others to find once they were gone.

They were leaving Pichilingue with his father who would once more break his back in the Gringos' vineyards. And Hidalgo was certain that now he would never be better than his father. He would spend his life stooped over, always seeing the feet of his American masters. He was scared. He was scared because his mother was scared and he was afraid for her, for what might happen to her. Or worse, what would not happen.

They woke early the next morning, closing the broken door of the one home he'd ever known and went away together, his father with one bag, his mother with another,

Hidalgo with his bag and his most precious possessions: yellowed and worn books brought home a long time ago by his father.

Hidalgo never did read Code of the West or West of the Pecos. He wasn't able to; he didn't know what the words meant. He didn't speak English and could barely read Spanish, once hoping that one day he would master both, that one day he would attend a real school, that one day he would become a fine caballero. Then one day he stopped dreaming. The pain of knowing the truth was too great.

He would marry, leave his mother, grow old with regret and die. The only way he would ever leave his small world. Now they were stealing away well before dawn, stepping quietly from the porch onto the dried dirt of the narrow street, hurrying past neighbours' windows and doors like thieves in the night. His father didn't want to be seen. They would walk to La Paz. He didn't want the bus driver to know. Pichilingue was a small place, curious and talkative. They walked in silence, Señor Arquero several paces ahead of them, leading the way they all knew so well. Hidalgo followed behind with his mother, hand in hand.

The eleven-mile trek lasted a few minutes shy of four hours, Señor Arquero not once glancing over his shoulders. Halfway there Hidalgo took his mother's bag, disregarding her pursed lips and furrowed brow, giving her the lighter books to carry instead. He knew her feet ached through her thin sandals, under the weight of her cumbersome load, because his did, and he promised that one day she would live in a wonderful hacienda with a beautiful garden and many servants. She would wear fancy dresses and drive expensive cars made in the United States of America. He saw all of this on television. He knew. He knew also that he would never be like his father.

When they arrived at the bus station in La Paz they sat to eat a breakfast of tortillas stuffed with shredded chicken and chopped lettuce sprinkled with jalapeño sauce. Only once did the father caution them not to worry, that all would be well. They would see. They would soon believe all that he had ever promised. Maria Arquero nodded a meek reply; Hidalgo said nothing, squeezing her hand. He saw her doubt, her fear, even if his father did not. The bus left an hour later.

The 800-mile journey from the southeast coast of Baja California Sur to the northwest coast by bus was a hot and arduous eighteen hours, the temperature rising steadily to a scorching midday high of 98°F. There was no fresh air to breathe; the seats were better suited to a detention centre and the smell of sweat and cigarette smoke wafting about their heads made Maria and Hidalgo feel ill. They stopped twice for fuel, nature's relief and to stretch their legs, sharing one meal of cold stewed beans and diced jalapeño from a glazed jar and another of hardboiled eggs and pickles mashed onto the last of their tortillas. All they had to drink was water from a tap.

His father slept most of the way, his mother didn't. Her troubled heart wanted to feel joy, yet she'd heard the stories of families turned back, of men imprisoned for what they were attempting to do. And her son was now a man.

In her heart she wanted to believe, yet she could not. She no longer knew this man who was so often away, who had once beguiled her, charming her heart, causing her father to disown her, to throw her onto the street like a common street whore. She had disappointed him by giving herself to the man she loved, who had promised her the world, and for that she was no longer his daughter.

So then, how could she trust him? She did not know. Yet she was his woman, his wife, and a woman did what she was told.

She had no sense of time. Watches were a foolish luxury in such a place as Pichilingue. The sun rose and the sun set.

That was all anyone had to know. She thought she'd been thinking, worrying for her son. Instead she was sleeping, transported to another place where her son was a prosperous and important young man, dressed in fine clothes, his heart filled with joy and kindness. She woke in a daze, to Hidalgo's kiss upon her cheek and a sudden cacophony of excitement and confusion. She leaned across her husband and peered from the window, shrieking. Not in her wildest dreams did she ever imagine so much noise, so many cars, trucks and buses, so many people, so many lights, so many men with guns and unsmiling faces searching into windows.

She twisted to see through the door behind her son and saw the grim face, an armed man dressed in black standing behind the bus. Along the side she could see others like him.

"We have arrived, mamá. Over there, that is America."

She studied the armed border guards once more, wrapping her arms around her son. "Yo me arrepiento de lo que he hecho, hijo." She kissed her cross. "I am sorry for letting him bring us here. We should not have come. Forgive me for what I have done to you."

She was shaking.

"I am not afraid, mamá," he lied. "You will see. One day…"

His father stirred. "One day, Maria, your son will be all that you wish him to be. He will not have to see in his woman's eyes what I see in yours."

"Fernando…"

He reached into his shirt pocket. "We have papers, Maria. This is what you wanted, is it not, Maria, a better life for your son?" He brought his watch close to his face. The time was 4:35 AM, the day was August 31st. He handed her the visas. "Feliz cumpleaños, Maria."

"Fernando…"

He went back to sleep. Maria was thirty-years-old. Hidalgo stared past the window, deeply ashamed. He had nothing to give his mother but his love.

They remained on the bus for three hours. Not once did the man behind them smile. Then more confusion. Two men came onto the bus, armed with threatening weapons pointing upward. One stayed at the front, speaking words that neither mother nor son understood. One went to the rear and stood beside Hidalgo, his back pressed against the emergency door. He had no expression; Maria saw no life in his eyes. Where had they come, she worried? How could they live in such a place? What had she done to her son?

The bus emptied quickly. Most of the passengers were men, migrant workers. They knew what to do. Maria did not. Then Hidalgo felt the guard's hand nudging his shoulder. He looked at his father who flicked his head as a sign for him to stand, to follow the others.

They were the last to disembark, the early morning air outside at once fresher, cooler. Hidalgo's father took the papers from Maria, holding them out for the guard to examine. The man nodded, pointing to the immigration building, traces of a thin smile incongruous amidst dark glasses, Kevlar vest and automatic weapon. He signalled them to walk ahead, he followed behind.

Inside was a man, a big man with thick yellow hair under a well-worn straw hat that drooped in the front and in the back. He wore silver sunglasses that hid his eyes and made him seem sinister. His skin was dark brown from the sun; his face was scarred with deep crevices chiselled by age, hard work and worry. He wore boots that glistened from the lights on the ceiling, low-cut, faded jeans and a wide leather belt studded with turquoise stones that was held together with a silver buckle depicting an Aztec shield and a blue denim shirt with the sleeves rolled to his elbows. He wasn't smiling. She didn't think he could, shocked when her husband left her and Hidalgo with the border guard as he went straight to the man.

They shook hands and spoke for a brief few moments before the two came to where Maria and Hidalgo stood waiting. Then the big man pulled away his glasses and spoke with the guard who nodded and left. The man was John Canyon. He was filthy rich, a man who didn't mind getting his hands dirty, a humble philanthropist and owner of Canyon Estates, the largest and privately held vineyard in the Napa Valley. He pinched the tip of his hat, tilting his head towards Maria, acknowledging her. Fixing his glasses in place he turned his attention to Hidalgo without saying a word.

Why would such a frightful man know her husband, Maria wondered? She had never seen such a huge man and she'd never heard her husband speak English. John Canyon raised an arm, glancing at the watch on his wrist, nodding. She didn't understand a word he was saying, but when he turned and walked away with Fernando she and Hidalgo followed behind, hand in hand, into a small room where they waited what was, for Maria, a lifetime. No one said a word. Maria had never been in a room that made her feel nervous, yet she was nervous, because of the room. The big man must be very bad, she believed, not to be nervous in such a place. She squeezed her son's hand.

In real time, a few minutes later, a woman came through the door, a Mexican woman, dressed in black like all the other guards. She did not wear dark glasses or a hat, though her gun was black and ominous and seemed much too large for her small frame, Maria thought.

She was not friendly. She didn't look at, but scrutinized father, mother and son with eyes that Maria doubted would ever blink. Mr. Canyon she ignored. She knew him, or knew of him. Everyone at Immigration knew John Canyon. The woman began to speak, first to the father, Maria leaning forward instinctively, listening, not believing what was happening, and suddenly the woman was staring right into Maria's eyes, the trace of a smile flashing across her face.

"Feliz cumpleaños, Maria."

Maria nodded, her lips quivering. The woman didn't know her at all, yet she was wishing Maria happy birthday. Then the woman glanced at Hidalgo.

She asked his age, and he answered. She seemed not to care. Then she asked what he had bought his mother for her birthday, and he didn't answer. Again she appeared not to care, standing, gathering the documents she'd been stamping. When she stood in front of him, appraising him, he was afraid, even his father felt consumed with worry.

"Then give her these, Hidalgo," she smiled, "and welcome your mother to your new home. Bienvenido a Los Estados Unidos, muchacho."

He stood, as his mother would expect of him. The agent shook his hand, nodded to Maria, acknowledged the two men and walked out.

Hidalgo stared into his hands, at the documents and the lapel pins. He didn't know what they were, but he gave one to his mother. She did know, although the only jewellery she'd ever worn was her cross. She pinned the tiny flag to her blouse, kissed his cheek, and sat waiting with her hands in her lap.

John Canyon had nothing much to add. He'd been in similar rooms many times before. Some families had disappointed him, most did not. He'd spent the twenty minutes leaning against the wall, not moving so much as an inch, watching Maria, studying Hidalgo. He knew good people when he saw them.

Maria didn't know of the Napa Valley. All she knew of America was what she'd learned from pictures in out-dated magazines she'd borrowed from the library. She knew of

New York and Chicago, Washington and Miami. Yet exactly how near or far the cities were she didn't know. And now she didn't know her husband.

John Canyon shook her hand. He wasn't a man given to excessive expression and hadn't hugged a woman other than his daughter in years. He shook Hidalgo's hand, slapped his back and led him out past the door and into the glare of the morning sun. He'd travelled 500 miles by air to meet them, from his vineyard to a private airstrip a twenty-dollar cab fare from the border, to ensure everything went smoothly. He would return home the same way once the Arqueros and the others were settled onboard the bus. He had no time to waste by sitting with them. Time was money. He was gone by 9:30.

Maria thought she'd died and gone to heaven. Her seat was in the first row to the right of the driver, by the window. She felt as though she was sitting on a cushion of air. Her sweat had evaporated and her skin was cool. She had nothing to carry. Another man, American, had taken their bags and had stowed them under the bus. She sat in awe. She wanted to feel overwhelmed with excitement, still afraid, uncertain. She couldn't let herself believe. She had never seen such luxury; not quite knowing what to say when yet another man leaned into her, drew a tray from inside her armrest and placed a breakfast of fresh fruit, cereal, warm toast and honey in front of her. He asked whether she preferred milk or cream with her coffee. She shook her head, worried that she had no money with which to pay him. He smiled and gave her one of each.

He did the same for Hidalgo who said 'gracias' for his mother. He didn't know what was in the small carton container, and didn't want to ask. That man didn't speak Spanish either, but he understood, seeing the unopened carton once he'd finished serving the other Canyon passengers. Hidalgo watched as the man peeled back the sealed edges and removed the straw from its paper sleeve, inserting it into the opening. Hidalgo had never seen or tasted milk in a box, especially cold milk.

At ten the bus closed its doors.

Fernando Arquero had remained outside all the while. He had a reason. He knew what his wife thought of him; how his son believed he was a poor husband and father. And he was. He wasn't worthy of them, he knew. And when he boarded he didn't sit with them. He sat beside them, across the aisle, behind the driver where he belonged, causing his wife's mouth to open wide when he stood to face the other migrant workers and speak to them through the PA system. He'd practiced every word over and over again. He would not make a mistake.

Many of them knew Fernando, a few did not. However none was aware until then that he was the new assistant to the vineyard manager. He would be their capitán, their consejero until the end of the season when they would once again return home to their families.

When the applause and raucous comments broke out Maria and Hidalgo exchanged curious glances. These men liked Fernando? But what Fernando did not say was that Maria would never see Mexico again. She had one more birthday gift to see. Yet she saw nothing in his eyes, not even a glance their way.

The bus arrived at Canyon Estates Vineyard at 4:00. John Canyon had already arrived though he wasn't on site to greet them. That wasn't his job. His reason for being at the border was Fernando Arquero, though they wouldn't see each other again for a week.

Maria had never been to the circus. Yet she remembered seeing pictures when she was a little girl. Now she thought she was at the circus. But she wasn't. The tent was humongous, large enough for a bullfight, she thought, or to cover the entire farmers' market in Pichilingue. Inside were rows of tables and chairs and to one side of the tent a buffet of food she thought mustn't be real. What was this place? Was this where they were to live with all these other people? She wanted to ask, but couldn't. She was too afraid to hear the answer.

Fernando was first in line. El capitán always went first into the tent. The tradition was a matter of pragmatism, an easy way to show newcomers what they should do. Maria was second, the only woman, Hidalgo was third. When they took their seats Fernando's plate was full, Maria's and Hidalgo's were not. Neither wanted to be greedy when there were so many others behind them and they knew that more men would arrive shortly from the border. Besides, their stomachs were full from breakfast.

Maria looked at the glass of red wine, then to her husband. He nodded permission. The last time she'd tasted wine was when he'd taken her from the chapel in La Paz to the diner as his wife. She remembered the bitter taste. Yet this wine was sweet and filled her mouth with such wonderful flavour. Then she looked at her son, nodding approval. "Sí, hijo mío, this is my birthday."

When the last man was seated, the meal finished, a group of men arrived and stood on a small platform erected near the entrance. The first man nodded to Fernando who had no reason to stay longer, he'd heard the introduction so many times before and, besides, he was now part of the management team.

He stood, acknowledged them, took his family and left.

They walked a while without speaking. Maria had never see a vineyard, or anywhere so lush and green. The two days had been filled with so many surprises for her, and the next was a mere arm's length away. She gasped.

"Sí, Maria, this is my car. It comes with my new position here with Señor Canyon."

¡Ay! Fernando, ¿Es verdad?"

"It is true, Maria. Come." He opened her door. "Hidalgo, you will sit in the back. Maria, do you remember my promise to your father when he shamed you in the street in front of me, for all our neighbours to see?" He knew the answer. She did not. "Never have I forgotten, Maria, not one moment. Now, Maria, the shame is gone."

"I do not understand, Fernando."

He smiled for the first time since arriving home in Pichilingue, and said nothing, closing her door, hurrying to his side, climbing in behind the wheel of the shiny new SUV.

"Where are you taking us, Fernando? I am already afraid. What will happen to my son?"

"I am an educated man now, Maria. The others, they drink beer on the weekends and spend each night playing cards, taking each other's money. I did not do this. I went to school, Maria, one night each week, and twice each week I sat in Señora Canyon's class to learn more. His young daughter is a very good teacher. This year, Maria, I have my eighth grade. I have the paper to prove this, Maria."

"Fernando …"

He was too excited. "Maria, I can now read and I can write in their language. Without this I could not be El Capitán. This I did for you, and for our son. And I have more to tell you, much more. The others, they will stay in simple houses, ten of them together. We will not do this. You will have a home, Maria, a real home with water for drinking and cooking. No longer will you fill your bath with a bucket of cold water from the well, Maria."

"Where is this house, Fernando? I see no house here other than the great hacienda."

"Soon you will see your home, Maria. You will see that what I told your father is true."

Forty minutes later they drove up to their new home. Fernando drove slowly. He'd waited a long time for his one

41

fleeting moment of glory, but for the little that Maria could see clearly they might have been driving in a torrential downpour. Her eyes were flooding with tears. Hidalgo sat quietly in the backseat, absorbing all that he was seeing as though his head were mounted on a pivot, not certain whether he should hate or love his father for making his mother cry. What he was seeing could not be true. He was first from the vehicle, opening his mother's door. Fernando stayed where he was, watching them, giving them time, proud of what he'd achieved for them, his long years of deception, never certain that he would succeed, now worth every moment.

He was no longer a migrant. He was Mr. Fernando Arquero.

The street was paved, lined with sidewalks, magnificent trees and streetlights. No two houses were the same, each with a lawn of lush green grass bordered by a white picket fence, trimmed hedges and colourful flowers.

He joined his family and together they walked to the front door where he gave Hidalgo the key, garnering a quizzical expression. No one in Pichilingue locked their door.

Inside the living room was sparsely furnished, which would soon change. The kitchen cupboards were empty because he hadn't known what to buy. That didn't matter. Maria dropped onto a chair by her new table, staring in awe at her new stove and fridge. Hidalgo stared through the window at their new backyard, the first he'd ever seen. Then he asked his father in which of the corners he would sleep. He saw no mat.

Fernando said nothing, leading the way upstairs where Hidalgo saw his room which was four times the size of his mother' private space in Pichilingue. He sat on his bed; the mattress was soft and smooth. He bounced, and pressed down hard with his hands, feeling not a single spring that would dig into his back. When Maria saw her bedroom she felt faint. The walls were freshly painted, decorated with picture frames, and the floor was carpeted from one wall to the other. Then he took her into the bathroom. He flushed the toilet with a smile, the thin gold outline of his front teeth glistening under the bright light. He leaned into the bath, opened the faucet and they stood together watching the steaming water rise.

No longer would Maria heat her bathwater on a wood stove.

He ordered his son downstairs, waited until he was gone and kissed his wife. She deserved her time alone, he told her. She was not to be nervous and when she was finished her bath, she was to enjoy her new closet. She would be safe in the house alone. He would not be long. He had to leave for a little while with his son.

When they did return, Hidalgo could not believe that his father had a special place in the house for his car, or that they could walk from the car through to the kitchen. He could not believe that his mother could be so beautiful. She was dressed in a thick fleecy robe, her feet covered in soft velvet slippers, her skin glowing with a pinkish hue. She was a princess. But what he really wanted was to eat the all-dressed pizza, drink his Coca-Cola and to watch her blow out the candles before he sank his teeth into the thick, sugary coating of her birthday cake.

He also had a robe, which he didn't wear that night. Instead he kissed his mother, hugged a father he would have to rediscover and went to bed early. Mr. Canyon had given his father a bottle of wine to enjoy with their pizza and Hidalgo wanted his parents to finish the wine together. They had much to learn about one another.

He fell asleep quickly, not expecting to dream. He was too exhausted. He knew now that he would be as good as his father. One day he, too, would be El Capitán. He was fifteen, and in a few years he would marry the way all the boys did in Pichilingue with girls who lived next door because there was nothing else to do and to be a man with a woman who was not your wife was a sin. But who would he marry now?

5

The next morning Maria was overwhelmed. She hadn't slept. How could she? She had so many questions. She was anxious to work in the field with her son, anxious to no longer rely on her neighbours who would pay her what they could for mending or washing their clothes. But above all, how could she live on an American street with neighbours who would not understand her? They would not like her. She did not speak English. What education she did have ended with Hidalgo and what she knew of the world was Pichilingue. They would laugh at her.

No, Fernando contradicted. They would not. They would laugh with her, upon hearing the musical sound of her laugher. They would see her warm smile, and they would smile. He'd already spoken with a few of them from across the fence. They were anxious to meet her, to meet Hidalgo. She would see that he was right. Surely, now, she must believe him. Still, she was nervous.

He hadn't touched her the night before, not that way. He would in time, when she was ready. But when he woke with the sun filtering through the curtained windows, she was spooned into his arms. What had felt wrong to her for so long now felt right.

She looked good in her new slacks and sweater, years younger with the dust of Pichilingue scrubbed from her face. Fernando had done well with sizing and colours. Hidalgo wore new jeans made in the USA, a tee-shirt and running shoes with thick soles.

He saw a difference in his parents. They were talking excitedly about the future, about their day off when his father would take them to San Francisco across the Golden Gate Bridge. They would be higher in the sky than they could ever imagine, he told them. Or he would take them to the ocean that was vaster than the Sea of Cortés where they would swim, eat hot dogs and ice cream and Hidalgo could watch all the pretty girls. Or he would take them shopping for new clothes with their first paycheques. Or…whatever they wanted.

Hidalgo let his father talk. This was his first day as a man, his first day of work when he would prove himself. He would fill the most baskets, carry the heaviest loads. He would make his father proud and with his first paycheque he would buy his mother a pretty dress and shoes with high heels like the American women. Yes, with his first cheque he would begin to keep the silent promise he'd made to himself.

The workday began each day at seven and the vineyard was a hive of activity through to seven each night. The morning and afternoon breaks were brief, meant to refresh the men with fruit and water or ice tea. Lunch lasted one hour under the huge tent where they could talk about life, play cards, backgammon or stretch out on a hammock to straighten their backs.

Men and women did not work together. What they did on their own time, on Sundays, was their business. He wasn't their keeper. Weekdays, however, belonged to John Canyon. He paid the highest wages in the county and in return he expected the highest yield.

Men worked the fields, from sixteen to sixty-years-old, the oldest men often outdoing the youngest. Hidalgo was an exception. He wasn't on the payroll and wouldn't be for six months. In the meantime his pay would come from John

Canyon's pocket, in an envelope.

Maria would not be working by her son's side, as she believed. She would not spend her day bent over picking grapes. She was assigned to the bottling and labelling departments where she would spend her day with American women who spoke some Spanish and Mexican women who spoke good English. None were migrant and were fewer in number than the men, with separate facilities for their breaks and lunch and, at day's end, they all went home to their families. Maria would not.

Those who wanted more from life ended their Tuesdays and Fridays an hour earlier with Jennie Canyon. Most of the men did not. They did their time, worked an honest day, spent or saved their money and went home to their families in Mexico at the end of the season. Fernando Arquero wanted more. He knew that one day he would tire of the long journey home twice each year, and that sooner or later he would have no home, no wife.

He'd worked for Canyon Estates since Hidalgo was five, and for six of those years he attended night classes in Santa Rosa and studied with Jennie Canyon twice each week to improve his English and discover more about wine, each year guarding his secret with increasing shame until he felt the time was right to tell his wife, to prove her father wrong. He, Fernando Arquero, was not a beggar to spit at on the street. Never would he wash away the urine of other men from the floor of factory toilets or come home to his woman reeking of gutted fish. Neither would his son, with Miss Canyon's help. The son of Fernando Arquero would one day be a great leader of men.

John Canyon's daughter taught high school in Santa Rosa, harbouring a secret passion for writing, never quite able to begin the first page. On Tuesdays and Fridays between 6:00 and 7:00 she worked for her father. She taught the workers to read and write English as well as Spanish and, in doing so, a little about wine which, of course, necessitated wine tasting.

She was eager to greet her newest student. Fernando had told her much about Maria and Hidalgo. She understood that Maria would need time to adjust, time to acclimate to her new life and new friends. No one ever came to her class during the first week, often times not until years later. Many were too proud to admit what they didn't know, like Fernando. But Hidalgo would not be part of her class, she was told. He wouldn't fit in with those twice his age and John Canyon would tell Fernando personally, in due course.

6

At the end of their first full week John Canyon summoned Fernando to his office just past noon. The occasion was Fernando's first working lunch. He was proud as he strode towards the grand hacienda, hoping that his wife and her new co-workers would notice him. He believed the meeting was the first of many weekly meetings to discuss various production and performance issues. He was wrong.

John Canyon greeted him at the door. Fernando suspected that Señor Canyon spoke good Spanish because his daughter was fluent, but had never presumed to test those waters. Señor Canyon had nothing to prove. He was already a great man.

Fernando's strong grip was lost in Canyon's massive paw, yet despite his size John Canyon's easy manner made all but the very meek and humble feel equal. They walked side by side, making small talk: How was Maria? Was she fitting in? Does she like her new home? Does she enjoy working at the Estates? Will she find happiness in America?

Maria was fine, he replied. The neighbours like her very much and each night she walks from room to room in her new home. Already she has made a list of things for him to do. And the other women at work have been very kind to her. Yes, her happiness shows clearly on her face. She now sees a bright future for her son. Canyon nodded.

Lunch was laid out on the kitchen table. Fernando could not believe this was happening. Canyon filled matching tumblers half-full with a deep, burgundy-coloured Cabernet Sauvignon. He wasn't much into fancy glasses and didn't bother with the formalities. He didn't stick his nose into the glass, smell the cork, hold his glass to the light or swirl the wine. That was for the fancy pants. He knew his wine was excellent. Instead he touched the rim of his glass to Fernando's. Salud. And he drank, savouring the wine in his mouth mere seconds before swallowing. He was pleased. Fernando did the same.

Lunch was simple: a hearty soup and roast beef sandwich with all the condiments cherished by the Latin palate. Fernando sipped his wine once for every two of Canyon's and soon the meal was over, synchronized to end their discussion.

Fernando stood to leave, bowing slightly. Then Canyon stood. He refilled both glasses, took his and walked through the door leading to the patio. Fernando was uncertain, aware that he mustn't show self-doubt. Better that Señor Canyon should scold him for being impertinent, for remaining longer than he should, than dismissing him for walking out from a meeting. He followed through the door.

Canyon was leaning against a wooden pillar, unsmiling, gazing out over the southern quadrant of the Estates, his silver glasses reflecting the sun. Fernando remembered how Maria at first was afraid of him. Now she wasn't. She'd been told so many times by others how kind the big man was.

Fernando wanted to make small talk, but he couldn't. What could he say that wouldn't sound stupid or trite? He waited. Canyon pushed away from the pillar, sitting side-saddle on the veranda's wooden railing.

"Thank you, Fernando, for accepting the job. It's hard to find good men. I'm pleased, and I hope that you are. I'd be hard-pressed to replace you."

"Sí, Señor Canyon, claro, I am very pleased. I have

much to thank you for. My family, nothing is more important to me. And now they are with me. My wife, she will work very hard. You will see. Tonight she begins her lessons with your daughter and once each week she will go with me to school to learn more. And our son will go with us." Fernando beamed. "Already his baskets are the heaviest, with the fattest grapes. He is proud of me now. He was not before. Tonight he will sit with his mother in class and one day he will be better than I am. A son must always surpass his father. Now I know that he will."

"My granddad started this place not long after the big war with a few vines brought over from France. He didn't speak a word of French. He wasn't gifted that way. My grandma, she had to learn English, but he spent a couple of years working for them, like you, in the fields. And, like you, he learned. He came back here with his bride, did some planting, and what you see out there is because he didn't mind hard work. He saw light at the end of the tunnel. But, Fernando, he was also educated. A man needs more than prayers and good luck."

"Sí, señor, and this year I begin my ninth grade."

"I know, Jennie, talks about you often. And I hope you follow through to the end. You wouldn't be the first man to earn a degree later in life. However this isn't about you."

"Señor?"

John Canyon sipped his wine. "Hidalgo, you described him very well. He's a good-looking boy and strong for his age. His eyes are clear and his mind is alert. He's got a brain, like his father and his mother. Still he's young, Fernando, too young to work in the field."

"Señor, I will speak with him. Soon he will be sixteen, like many of the others. He will work harder. You will see. He will be one of my finest workers."

"The others return home to Mexico after each season with their fathers, some because they want to, others because they have no choice." He sipped his wine. "Hidalgo's fifteen. His time in the field would be wasted, not to mention illegal. If anyone were to discover that oversight I'd be in a pretty deep mess without a paddle…and I wouldn't be swimming in water, amigo. I don't need Child Protection Services running around here waving their Boy Scout badges in my face. That wouldn't be good for either of us."

"Señor, you knew of his age."

"You're right. I did know. I thought before seeing him that he could work until Labour Day, then on Saturdays, part-time and fully legal. However now I don't see that working as a viable plan. The boy won't be happy here, Fernando, not for long. He'll see that he's different from the other boys on your street and he'll choose a direction that's different from what you and Maria have planned for him. We can't let that happen. I've given this matter a lot of thought. I want today to be his last." He focused on Fernando's glass. "Something wrong with the wine, compadre?"

7

Later that afternoon Maria sat alone at the front of the class. She'd asked her supervisor for permission to leave a few minutes earlier than the usual six PM class time. She needed time alone to talk with Jennie Canyon. Fernando had stopped by the labelling plant earlier, after his meeting with Señor Canyon, and in a quiet corner together they cried for their son.

Jennie wasn't much younger than Maria, truly her father's daughter right down to the jeans, boots, denim shirt and glasses, albeit much prettier. Her smile was contagious; the joy for life that echoed in her voice was sincere, not contrived. She called Maria by name as she walked into the room, her arms loaded with reading material, writing pads and boxes of pencils and erasers.

Maria all but leapt from her seat, wrapping her arms tightly around the surprised young woman, squeezing her, clasping the shocked expression in her warm hands, kissing her cheeks, promising she would never forget such kindness. Her son, Hidalgo Arquero, she promised, would for all his life never stop being a good man.

Wow! Jennie squeezed back. She had another 'A' student in the making. She had known about Hidalgo, she also knew about Maria, but first things first. Too much of any good thing too soon was never good. And she knew that Fernando would not be joining them. He was with his son by the edge of the field.

"Does your back hurt, my son?"

"No, papá. My back is strong. I am already anxious to work again tomorrow."

Fernando hung his head, smiling, crossing his arms. "After my first day, niño, my first week with Señor Canyon, I believed that I would never stand straight again. And you tell me that you are ready for another difficult day. That is good, hijo. How quickly you surpass your father."

"Papá, we can talk later at home. I should go to class with mamá. Now, papá, I will be able to read my books."

"No, hijo. She knows not to expect you. And tomorrow there will be no work for you in the field. Today was your last day of work, despite your strong back. Now you must strengthen your mind. Señor Canyon, he does not stop his kindness towards us. He has brought you from Pichilingue with your mother, not me. You must never forget this, hijo. We owe what we can never repay. He is very wise and knows many important people. He is a great cacique in this land and today we spoke together of your future. Now you must listen carefully to me, hijo."

8

The next three years passed quickly as Hidalgo left childhood behind. By eighteen he was fluent in English, eloquent in both languages, excelling in all that he studied. He grew tall, his hair grew long, and his mother was pleased by how the girls in the neighbourhood began more each year to swoon over him. He was fast becoming a handsome caballero. He was well-mannered and gracious, humble, and kind to those less fortunate.

During that first meeting at the hacienda Fernando understood John Canyon's reasoning. Hidalgo was years behind American boys his age and would likely never catch up, certainly not in time for college. ¡Universidad! ¡Dios mío! he remembered crying. And for two years Hidalgo studied with a private tutor at the Estates, entering a private school at seventeen to graduate at year's end with honours.

Fernando also had a certificate to frame: his tenth grade, mounted beside Maria's in what had become the family study room. Maria had attended Jennie's classes faithfully and, in her first year, she attended many of her son's private classes, at the end of which she took an equivalency test and passed her grade nine. She and her husband were equals and Hidalgo was accepted into Golden Gate University on his own merit.

John Canyon understood when Fernando turned down dinner at the hacienda to celebrate Hidalgo's success, quite taken aback when Maria reversed the invitation. He and

Jennie would come to their home. Fernando presented his son with a fine leather belt crafted with a special buckle; his mother's gift was a pair of kid leather pants and boots, which she insisted that he model for her and Jennie to see. He was indeed a handsome caballero. Jennie gave him a book, her first novel about a young Latino who beat the odds. However, she joked, no one would truly know for quite a few years whether the story was fiction…or fact. That, she smiled, was up to Hidalgo.

John Canyon stood, apologizing for the champagne. The better wine he assured them, his, would come later with the meal. Maria stood to hug him, her tears flowing easily. She'd been crying all week. Hidalgo stood to thank his mother, his father, Jennie for all she'd done, and Señor Canyon for believing in his family. He would not disappoint any of them.

"Bastante, chavo," John Canyon replied, surprising everyone except Jennie, "before we all cry. We're not quite done here." He tossed Hidalgo a set of keys. "Time is money. Understand that. We can't have you wasting your time on a bus, when you could be studying, making something of yourself. We expect great things of you. We also expect you to work at the Estates' store on Saturdays to help your parents pay your way…and to stay level. There's no free lunch here. We can't have your head getting any bigger than it is."

He nodded to the window.

Fernando, Maria and their guests went into the dining room. Hidalgo was left to stand at the window staring at his new Mustang GT red convertible. He needed a moment, and went outside not only to sit in the car and grasp the wheel. He was overwhelmed, suddenly very anxious to read Jennie's novel.

They were moving to Vallejo. His parents would be closer to their work and he would be closer to the university, but never had he imagined that he would arrive in such style. He would be the envy of everyone. When he went inside he stood beside John Canyon and the two men shook hands. Maria cried.

*

Scott Gibson's three years at law school were more demanding than his easy ride through four years of university. However he was a man well-versed in social studies and, despite the burgeoning female population of the school being considerably more intent on their own success in law than his in bed, he was never alone very long.

He'd met with Francine and her family regularly over the three years at Thanksgiving, Christmas and at the club's New Year's ball. She was developing nicely. At eighteen she'd discovered stockings, foregoing bobby socks and the brassiere under her dress no longer appeared to be manufactured from army surplus. Her shape was changing. She was still a prude, a little too prissy, a daddy's girl, and other than dancing together occasionally, struggling for conversation, he still hadn't touched her in any significant way. Not that he cared. Touch one, touch them all. Only the faces changed and most times any real conversation was completely impossible, if at all necessary.

She would be the wife, no different than his mother, a figure head. While he, like his father, would be the man, charged with ensuring the continuance of the family's good name and reputation. They would have two-point-one children, a white fence, life insurance, a dog, a two-car garage and a mortgage all paid for by him. She would do charity work to give her life meaning and sip tea.

*

Claire and Mrs. Duval did their best to make Francine's coming out a memorable occasion. But what was she coming out from? She was a child of the seventies, a true child, and a virgin when most girls gave no thought at all each morning to who the father might be. Not only was love free, love was rampant, except for her. She was daddy's little girl, a prisoner in the family mansion.

She was eighteen. Her body was changing. She had breasts and she had hips. Her shapeless lines and baby fat were gone and increasingly she envied those other girls at Venice Beach in their skimpy and sexy bikinis. She saw the way the boys ogled them, she saw the lust in their eyes; she knew what the boys were thinking. As for Scott, she knew the way he felt about her. She wasn't that naïve. She knew what men wanted. He was anxious to take her hand in matrimony, to declare his vows before family and friends, to be hers alone, to fulfill his desire and take her to their bed. Their love would be real and everlasting.

In a few weeks she would travel to Spain alone, to spend a year chaperoned by four ancient and fun-loving grandparents who, years earlier, had made a decision to exchange the burden of family with the romance of Madrid while romance still had meaning.

She remembered them fondly; though she hadn't seen them in over two years.

9
Thirty-One Years Ago

Hidalgo did read Jennie's book. But he knew such fantasies weren't his to one day live. He would never be that man. He would never decide the fate of men. All things being equal, he was Mexican, born into the poorest of the poor families despite their new life. Still, he knew as he read each word that Jennie was writing about him as much as she was for him. She had more than a little faith in the boy from Pichilingue.

What Hidalgo knew for certain was that he didn't want to earn his living with a scalpel or a drill. He didn't want to mend broken bodies or extract rotten teeth. He knew what he didn't want to do. The problem was what he did want to do. That, he did not know.

In Mexico his mother had told him constantly that one day he would be a noble young man and that he could do anything he desired. But they each knew then that wasn't true and he had convinced himself that he would one day be a noble young man who could do nothing, until his father and John Canyon together had made all his dreams possible. He just didn't know which one to choose. All he knew was that he would help people as he and his mother had promised John and Jennie and, he thought, make lots of money while doing so. He would make lots of money and buy his mother that beautiful home with many servants.

His parents refused to get involved, though they would listen to his arguments for and against and support any wise decision he made. Nevertheless the future was his alone, they told him. Hence, the choice was his alone.

"Mamá," he declared one evening, "my decision is made. I will study to become a social worker."

"And how will you make money doing such commendable work, my son?" Fernando wanted to know. "The hours will be long and the pay very low. How would you drive your expensive car or wear these clothes that make the pretty girls chase you as though you are the last young man on earth?"

"Did not mamá chase you, papá, so many years before she saw you in a suit?"

Fernando shrugged. "I was the best of the few men in Pichilingue, niño. Her choice was not a difficult one and not so many years ago as you believe. And your mother was the prettiest girl and desperate for me. How could I leave her to another?"

Maria smacked her husband.

"You and mamá live well, papá. Why would I need more to make me as happy," he glanced at his mother, "than a beautiful bride?"

"Be a social worker if that is what you truly want, Hidalgo," his mother answered, "if you are certain. This is not a time to worry about women. Yes, we are in a different world." She put an open palm to Fernando's cheek. "But when you are ready even here you will find many women who will love a poor man, if they do not find you first. Money is not everything. What is in your head and in your heart is more important than what is in your pockets."

"What your mother says is true, Hidalgo. We see how the ladies gather around you at the store. Señor Canyon tells me that his profits are up very much over last year because of you. Even the grandmothers are taken with you."

"Sometimes, at night, I do not believe what has happened in such a short time, papá, because of your hard work and Señor Canyon's kindness."

"We are both repaid many times over, Hidalgo, as is your mother. You are the very best in each of your classes; you are blessed with your mother's good looks and charm. What I have given you is nothing. This, you have done on your own."

"I will be a social worker, mamá, papá. Es lo que quiero."

Saturday Hidalgo drove his mother to work. He enjoyed being with her, helping her with her studies, not to mention having a stunning Latina in his car for others to envy. Maria no longer wore woven sandals, loose-fitting skirts and peasant blouses. She was no longer a peasant. She was assistant manager of the bottling and labelling division. She wore rich leather boots or low-heeled pumps, fitted slacks or skirts, silk blouses or cashmere sweaters and anyone seeing mother and son together would believe that Hidalgo had lucked out in love with a woman not much older than himself, which he did. He loved his mother very much. He was proud of her. In two years Maria would graduate from high school. And each day the celebration he was planning for his mother and father drew closer. Hidalgo was not the only Arquero with a dream.

*

For a man whose ego was more expansive than the football field he once starred on, Scott Gibson's twelve months of clerking at Duval & Associates were a prolonged and unpleasant experience in humility. He'd never stood on the bottom rung of any ladder, and he despised not being first and foremost. He was, in fact, ignored most of the time by those whose success he most coveted, male or female, whose attention he most desired. He felt demeaned, each day deliberately balancing atypical restraint which was requisite to his temporary place in the world with measured quantities of arrogance towards the men who worked as messengers or in the mailroom and bravado towards the younger females who were secretaries, copy typists or some higher-up's pretty daughter or niece.

The latter were the easiest. He didn't require that they aid and abet him in his future success. Both were guaranteed. He was first in his class, after all, and gifted. They had more need of him, as Mr. Duval at fifty-five was past his prime and naturally eager to appoint the son of his closest friend as heir apparent.

The older women saw through him. He was there to assist them, not the inverse. Whereas the younger ones nursed him throughout the brief indenture, seeing him as a target, an essential part of their careers in the firm if not a partner in life, bartering their warm beds for their futures, which he willingly accommodated, although he never woke with them or stayed for breakfast. Life was good.

Neither father assumed Scott would be a saint. After all, a collegiate football hero, an academic achiever, handsome, athletic, from an enviable family, what could anyone expect beyond the utmost discretion? And he was discreet. Each young woman had her turn, some short-lived, others lasting a month or more, all left abandoned to their memories and dreams or disappointment and regret on the eve of his departure when he left the firm to complete his final year of studies that was a prerequisite to any hope of his becoming the Gibson of Duval, Gibson & Associates.

That evening he dined in the company of his parents and the Duvals and, for the most part, Francine's narration recounting her year in Spain was a matter of polite indulgence. No one cared. Mr. Gibson had heard the stories from Claire, the Duvals a dozen times over the past week from Francine with little variation to make the telling more interesting and Scott was strictly interested in how her body had changed and whether her innocence had changed as well.

She was tanned, at least what he could see of her which was more than he ever had. Her heels were higher, her skirt shorter and apparently she'd discovered the feminine concept of displaying her cleavage. He wondered what she'd done in Spain that she hadn't told her parents. Her transformation was too drastic to have accomplished on her own during a single year away, he thought, certain she'd left behind at least one Spaniard with memories of teaching her more than Castilian. Not that he cared in the least. Virginity was fast becoming an antiquated notion synonymous with deficiency in some apparent physical or intellectual way, homeliness or some misguided belief that one's body was an altar to be regarded as sacrosanct. Bodies were bodies. If some Carlos or Juan had paved his way, so much the better, she would know what to expect. The last thing he wanted on his wedding night was a prima donna, feigned tears and darkness. He wanted to see what he was getting. Sadly, he wouldn't confirm his suspicion until then. He was curious, though. He would know immediately and had less than a year to wait.

He called her name, raised his glass and invited her to a dinner alone the following night. She looked at Claire, who nodded. Then to Scott and said "yes, thank you."

The primary conversation was between the men, focusing on Scott's expected graduation within the year and his pursuant junior position at the firm. The wives and Francine sat and listened. The men had no interest in specific wedding plans. Such was the domain of women and best discussed in their own environment. Of greater import, if not their sole concern, were the mergers of family and firm, mutual gain, the privilege of collective rank and the next junior partner of Duval & Associates.

Summer was at an end. The upcoming study year would

be Scott's most demanding, the most critical. However he would be expected to attend family functions, Francine's birthday party and begin to see as much of her as his agenda would allow.

As for Francine, she had several months of meetings with caterers and her seamstress ahead of her, invitations to prepare, a menu and proper seating arrangements. Certain friends, she would soon learn, were more important than others. She was living in a whirlwind of excitement. She was going to be a wife and a mother. She was going to make love and be with a man, her husband. Until then, however, she would be the dutiful daughter. She would meet with the minister in private, if for no other reason than decorum, and the doctor so that she would know what to expect from her first experience.

She would, she agreed, meet the minister as a matter of propriety, social correctness, though she'd never given religion a second thought. She went to church because her mother did. Her father went to church to shake hands with current and prospective members of his club, his belief in God one of self-interest. Everyone, she believed, went to church for decorum with the possible exception of the minister who probably went for the money. How else could he afford to drive a Mercedes and preach in tailor-made suits, she once asked her mother?

As for the doctor, what could he tell her that she and her girlfriends didn't already know? Mrs. Duval simply patted her cheek and called for the appointment.

10

At the Canyon Estates' annual party a week before Christmas Hidalgo was a hit with all the ladies. Jennie reserved the first dance, Maria the second. Fernando was a less graceful partner and spent most of the evening sitting with John Canyon commiserating with each other over a glass of wine regarding their prime years now in the past.

Christmas morning, gathered around their tree, the Arqueros sipped hot toddies and opened their gifts. None was extravagant. Despite their newly earned affluence Fernando and Maria insisted that they remember their humble beginnings. Good fortune was not to be taken for granted, despite the coming year.

Fernando was entering into his fifteenth year with John Canyon. He'd gone from picking grapes to overseeing the vineyard and teaching others. He was the first to drive the new harvester, responsible for production and quality. He'd learned all that he could about wine and often he would conduct informal tours. Now his office would be a mere few steps from John Canyon's. He would begin the year as Operations Manager. He'd come a long way.

Secretly Maria knew what he was thinking, but she wouldn't allow a single bitter moment so long ago in their past to spoil the celebration. Her father was dead. He died the very moment he threw her from her modest home onto the street. And with him her mother who wept not a single tear, standing unmoved in the doorway as though Maria were a stranger and not her only daughter being sent away. Since that moment only two men dwelled in her heart.

Hidalgo was midway through his second year, working two days a week. He knew almost as much about wine as Fernando and Maria and had convinced John Canyon that opening the store on Sundays would give the Estates a competitive edge. He was right. More importantly his income doubled allowing him to lessen the burden of his education on his parents who, for his nineteenth birthday, surprised him with a slim Cartier watch with a black face, silver numerals and rich, black strap, something that a few years earlier would have been a cruel extravagance to even imagine.

As for the money, as much as he pleaded, his parents steadfastly refused.

*

Francine's birthday came a day before Valentine's. Scott gave her a gift for one, not the other, which everyone chose to ignore. The diamond engagement ring was the size of a marble, paid for by Arthur Gibson, a reward for his son's academic achievement. He was also aware that his son lacked the means to then afford such extravagance at a time when appearances were paramount.

Scott gave her the bauble during an intimate dinner at the club. Of course the parents looked on from across the room, ending the evening with champagne, firm handshakes and proper hugs after which Francine went home ecstatic, counting the days, whereas Scott went to a strip bar. He was twenty-five. Time was running out. He was already losing many of his bachelor friends. No one wanted a married man hanging around, diluting the male dynamic, especially one who would likely be a father anytime soon. Nor did he have any married friends, for those very reasons.

When he was finished with the bevy of nude bodies he couldn't touch and wouldn't remember, he stopped at a phone booth and called one that he could. When would that stop, he wondered? He knew the answer and when he left her later that morning before the sun rose he wished her Happy Valentines, showered her away and went home.

She was Francine's age and hadn't needed more than a few glasses of wine to set the mood. He'd known her for three weeks and wasn't ready to stop seeing her. She was different. She was Asian and exotic. She was aggressive and immoral, wearing her sexuality the way other women wore perfume. She had no problem talking about past lovers, or her future. She was in second year law and wanted to be the best. She knew where she was going and how best to get there. Certain professors and fourth year students who could one day be helpful insiders knew that and she saw no difference in one man helping her achieve success or ten, twenty or thirty.

And now she was working at being recognized by Duval & Associates. Whether he dumped her the next day, in a month or the next year, she was making certain that he would never forget her. When she was ready, when the time was right, he'd be easy to rekindle. Life was all about acting; her immediate world was a stage, her body a spectacular prop. She knew she was everything that white, prim and proper Francine was not and before he'd even closed the door she rolled over and went back to sleep. Guys like that had too much money and ego to ever be faithful.

He would complete his LL.M in May, marry Francine in June, take her away and begin practicing law in July. His home was being built in Oakland, equidistant from the parents, paid for by Mr. Duval, Mr. Gibson agreeing to match the amount in cash so that the children might begin their life together without financial worry.

As for the women, the church was set, the caterers selected, the menu decided and the final fitting was a week away. Francine would be a gorgeous bride, despite snubbing convention, if not modesty entirely. Her gown was the one aspect of her wedding that was hers alone. She had no intention of appearing in public strung up like a nineteenth century dressmaker's dummy. She was a modern woman, a woman, no longer a girl. She would wear white, which is all they could expect. Nor did she want Scott standing by her side like a frumpy old man in a waistcoat and pinstripe tails. She wanted him in a dark blue or black suit and a plain silk tie.

Her parents' gift to her raised eyebrows, Mr. Duval's most of all, but she always got what she wanted and he came packaged in a bright yellow Camaro convertible, Adidas shorts and a tee-shirt that was a size too small. She had a personal trainer, hired to ensure that with all the pre-nuptial parties she would fit perfectly into the size five. She would be the most beautiful bride ever and Scott would never again even think to glance at another woman.

He called her once each week, every other week inviting her to dinner. He was anxious to see her naked, to see what he was getting, hoping that would be the 'for better' and not 'for worse'. They were living in an era where women traded sex for almost anything they couldn't afford, from a dinner to rent-free apartments, and he still hadn't so much as seen or fondled a bare breast believing she would either faint or run home to her mother blowing a simple grope into deviant fornication.

She was certainly nothing like China, he mused, sitting in the car, knowing he had to kiss her. In fact she was a prissy little bitch who should have had her panties ripped off years earlier. No one expected to marry a virgin and he certainly wasn't about to start mauling his fiancée through sweaters or blouses like a clumsy teenager. He hadn't been that desperate in years.

Instead he kissed her, though not the way he would have kissed China. He stepped out, opened her door and walked her to the porch. He said goodnight. There wasn't much else to say, and he left.

He knew the answer. Many more Chinas would come and go in the years to come. He would balance diversion with duty. He would be the quintessential husband when need be, and a perfect lover, just not with the same woman.

He was Scott Gibson, all-star. He attracted girls like a magnet. He couldn't remember his last dry spell. Becoming like his father or old man Duval wasn't an option. He wouldn't spend each day of his life politicking, sucking up to the wealthy for the betterment of a private club. His father couldn't give a damn about social issues; he wanted high-profile members. And Duval hadn't tried a case in years. That wouldn't happen to him. He chose criminal law for a reason. Defending high-profile cases would in turn make him high-profile. He wanted his face on the front page, he wanted the glory, he wanted to be seen, and he wanted to defend those who could afford to pay top dollar for their continued freedom or reduced incarceration.

He wanted people to whisper his name; he wanted invitations into the homes of the state's elite, not because he was a senator's son, because he was Scott Gibson the best criminal lawyer in the state. And how could he achieve that from behind a picket fence. He couldn't. High-profile meant exposure, living up to one's image. People, his clients, would have high expectations. They would want to see him in a fast car, leaving fine restaurants in the company of a beautiful woman like China, any woman as beautiful, not a four-door sedan, a prissy wife and a herd of brats in a family restaurant.

He was royally screwed. He wanted all of that and more, yet to get there he needed Francine. Duval & Associates was the premier law firm in the state. He needed them and, for that, he needed her. There was no escaping. As well, the club was at stake. Any rift between the families would cause inevitable bad feelings and Duval was a major contributor to the Democratic Party. And the mother's secondary roles as wives, fund raisers and hostesses were no less important to the status quo. Any ill-feeling between them would have an immeasurable and catastrophic effect on his future.

He chortled, not from any degree of humour in what he was thinking. His first lay was when he was barely fourteen. She was cute. She was the housekeeper's daughter who helped around the mansion during the summer months by maintaining the pool and the patio or filling in for other staff who required a week's vacation when she would do the laundry and ironing. She was seventeen. She wanted extra money and one day when her mother went to do the groceries they cleaned the pool together. She was his first. He barely understood a word she was saying, but she was good. She set the bar high in accordance with what she expected in return which was half his weekly allowance. Grocery day became his focus and the bar never lowered.

But what if he'd given the señorita more than a good time in a heated pool with a few drinks from his father's poolside bar and as much money as her mother earned from drudgery? What then? Senator Gibson would have paid the mother handsomely to shut her mouth, he would have paid the hospital bills and perhaps the girl would have given the kid up for adoption. Better yet, no kid. No kid, no media, no risk. And the senator would have paid handsomely for that as well, which never happened. Not with any of them. If it had the Duvals would have thought twice about strategically trading their daughter to their advantage. Old man Duval would have seen past his poor judgement. He would have forgiven a good friend's son and Francine would never have entered into the equation. Men were men. That was understood, which didn't mean Duval would give his daughter away to a man who had once fathered a

Mexican bastard.

Of all the girls that had recently come and gone, most of them vying for a more permanent place in his life or in his career, in particular the girls at the office, he hadn't once thought of how he might fully employ them to his advantage. And now time was against him

11

Fernando and Maria completed the eleventh grade in May. They celebrated with John and Jennie Canyon at the Estates. Hidalgo was the acting sommelier. He often went into Señor Canyon's private cellar with specific instructions as to which bottles he was to move, where he was to place them and how. That evening he was instructed to select a wine appropriate for dinner. His choice was a '65 Cabernet Sauvignon. John and Jennie served the meal.

John Canyon had servants because he needed them for specific purposes. Serving his meals wasn't one of them. When he entertained he relied on his daughter to add the finer touches. He'd been a widower since the year he first hired Fernando and had never found another woman to love. He wasn't interested and Jennie understood why. She understood that some wounds never heal.

He was proud of Maria and Fernando, proud of Hidalgo, proud to call them friends. They had come so far in such a short time, but he just didn't see Hidalgo as a social worker. The boy was becoming too refined. He would have to trade the lush countryside for the barrios of Los Angeles where he would never fit in. He was too smooth, never ruffled, and elegant with an air of sophistication that was inherent to his nature, qualities not often found or cultivated until much later in life. Whatever was intended for him in life, he wasn't meant to walk dark streets or alleyways searching for homeless runaways under cardboard blankets, empathizing with incurable drug addicts or trying to persuade teenage girls away from their pimps. That was not his destiny.

Neither was his father enthusiastic about the idea, but the boy wanted to please his mother. He wanted to do good things, to repay their good fortune which wasn't good fortune at all. They'd worked hard as a family to achieve their place in life. But his life was his own. He would learn in his own way and time that he could do good in many ways. The concept of self-sacrifice for the sake of helping others was in itself self-serving. No better or worse than achieving a high position with financial success and using that personal triumph for the betterment of others. However his life was his own, he couldn't be told what to do. One day he would discover that his chosen path was too narrow in scope, that he had much more to offer.

John Canyon raised his glass. He smiled at Maria, making a simple toast to her and Fernando. His eyes were ice-blue and penetrating, yet warm and kind. Then he turned his attention to Hidalgo. The young man had seen the piercing look many times before, in the early years, when he believed that simply asking was preferable to developing critical thinking and problem-solving skills. Señor Canyon was sending him a message, telling him to think for himself. John Canyon raised his glass again. No words were needed.

In two years Hidalgo would graduate from university, his parents from high school, though for the next three months he would work at the Estates, in the store where his knowledge of wine and the vineyard wouldn't be wasted. John Canyon had every confidence in Hidalgo's ability when dealing with walk-in clients who might buy several cases for various occasions. That said, the Duvals were different, more than a step above. They were, privately and as co-owners of a posh members-only club, amongst the Estates' most valued clients.

Hidalgo knew of them. He knew what they preferred and what they paid. He wasn't impressed. He didn't believe they knew much about wine. Jennie was always with them by appointment to make the selections for them. Deliveries were made to the club once each month and to their home twice a year. He had seen them once before, two years earlier, and he didn't like them. He saw in their eyes that he was a Mexican, one of Señor Canyon's migrants. And their daughter was… what was the word? Oh yeah, stuck-up. He remembered thinking that not even a hurricane could muss her hair. She was too perfect, like a plastic doll and, he remembered, she mimicked whatever her mother did like a shadow.

Mrs. Duval and her daughter would visit the Estates that coming Saturday for a private tasting. The young woman's wedding was in a month's time and John Canyon wanted Hidalgo to assist Jennie with the pretentious formalities.

In spite of himself, Hidalgo did realize the honour and the gravity of Señor Canyon's confidence in him. Yet he couldn't imagine a wedding of 500 guests or 1000 bottles of the Estates finest reserve. He was in a daze, unaware that he'd wondered out loud who would marry such a shallow and rude girl.

John Canyon answered matter-of-factly: "Someone just as shallow, and," he added, "just as important to us. ¿Comprendes, chavo?"

Hidalgo did understand, which didn't mean he approved of their current expectation of him.

A telling smirk etched across John Canyon's weathered face. He told Hidalgo to consider the difficult task as part of his life's learning curve, leaving the young man feeling despondent at the thought of what he was about to endure. Not even Jennie was commiserating with his unexpected misery, covering her grin with the palm of her hand as Fernando gave his son an admonishing glare and Maria couldn't believe her son had said such a thing, her eyes open wide.

John Canyon poured more wine, slouched into his seat and chuckled at the freshness of youthful honesty.

Hidalgo decided for the best that he would sit quietly for what remained of the evening.

12

A stationary system hovering over the Pacific Coast wasn't abating anytime soon. Jennie phoned the Duval residence to confirm, suggesting another less violent day. Mrs. Duval would have rescheduled, however with so little time left to her, what choice did she have? She and her daughter would arrive at one o'clock and Jennie knew better than to argue, giving Mrs. Duval directions to the loading dock where she could park inside and not arrive windblown and drenched.

She wasn't surprised, and didn't object when Hidalgo, arriving early, parked his pristine red Mustang in the second of three bays, curious that her Latino lover-boy as she called him had come to work in sneakers, jeans and a sweatshirt. She wasn't expecting much client traffic on such a miserable day, which was no excuse…until she saw him drying, waxing and polishing his prized possession. Even her father would have to chuckle at that. He was up to something. He was too nonchalant, doing his best to ignore her when she knew very well he was bursting at the seams.

Then she saw him next in black boots polished to a mirrored finish, black leather pants, his oxblood belt buckled with a discreet silver H, a collarless black silk shirt with billowy sleeves, the top three buttons undone, his rich reddish-brown hair combed into a long, straight ponytail and knotted with an oxblood leather thong. He belonged on a romance book cover. All that was missing was a cape, a rapier, a wide-brimmed hat and mask.

The kid was making a statement, saying everything by saying nothing.

She could easily imagine him standing under a window, by a tree, ready to scale a wall to rescue a pretty señorita in distress. As it was he was leaning against his car directly under the one 500-watt light he'd turned on, waiting, at 12:55, his arms by his side to avoid even the slightest crease to his shirt. The last time he'd been stocking the shelves wearing jeans, a tee-shirt, hiking boots and a suede baseball cap. Not this time, and Jennie thought she'd never seen him so serious…so Latino.

Hidalgo peered through a single window into a day that was dark as night, he felt the thunder reverberate through him, bursts of white light alternating the pane of glass from a silvery mirror to a blank canvas.

He knew Señorita Jennie was eyeing him, pretending to wait for their guests. She'd gone from being a good teacher and mentor to a good friend. Unfortunately she was ten years older. Were he ten years older they would already be married. He would have stolen her heart, though she would never know that and he was content to spend his weekends and summer days with her.

The Mercedes sedan was invisible behind its high beams. The worst thing to do in such bad weather, he scoffed in a mutter, garnering a friendly cough from the corner. His deep breath was imperceptible. He stood straight and began walking toward the bay doors. Jennie waved him back. Why spoil perfection, she thought? The kid had guts.

Door number three rose silently amidst the thunder and Jennie waited as long as she could, long enough for the Mustang and her young caballero to shine under the single flood light. She was as bad as Hidalgo, feeling a tad disappointed when at last she flipped the switch to illuminate a second lamp directly over the sedan.

Mrs. Duval drove in slowly. She was uncertain. She'd

never seen a loading dock. She felt uneasy and the door came down. She wasn't comfortable, he could tell. Thank goodness, he thought, that mother and daughter had him to focus on. They were staring at him, talking, fumbling with their seatbelts, talking about him, taking their time because of him.

He counted to five, in Spanish, and strode to the driver's side, each step a precise action, authoritative though not intimidating. He waited for the mother to first open the door, putting his hand to the handle, swinging it back and proffering his hand.

"Buenas tardes, Señora Duval, y bienvenida a nuestra casa. We are pleased to see you, once again. Our time here passes so slowly between your visits."

She took his hand or, better said, she let him take hers. He barely touched her, and she barely saw him. She dressed like an old woman, he thought, and her perfume was too thick.

"Good afternoon, Jennie. How nice to see you again. What a frightful day."

"Mrs. Duval, as usual, we're so happy to see you and Francine. We were so worried..."

Hidalgo closed the car door and put up a hand, though he needn't have bothered. Francine Duval was too fixated on him to think of stepping from the car on her own. He crossed in front of her, purposefully, letting her take in every inch of him. At her door he paused for affect, and very well, before reaching to open her door.

"Buenas tardes, Señorita Francine. Me llamo Hidalgo. Miss Canyon and I thank you for coming to our Estates on such a terrible day. Our hearts were heavy with concern for your safety."

She didn't take his hand, stepping out and smoothing her dress. "Me llamo Señorita Duval."

"Sí, claro, and soon you will be la Señora Gibson. Your

future husband is a fortunate man. He is certainly the envy of so many others you have disappointed in his favour."

She ignored him and walked to her mother.

He is also a poor man who will need extra blankets at night to stay warm in a bed of ice, he mused, or a flashlight to find his way.

Jennie and Mrs. Duval walked side by side, followed closely by Francine who didn't want to miss a single word, hating that the annoying Mexican boy was behind her, ogling her, leering at her with his dark eyes. The reception room was reserved for the most serious buyers. The ambiance was intimate with comfortable seating for six around a low table, of which John and Jennie Canyon normally occupied two. There was no window, but the lighting was bright, imitating daylight. This was a place of business. At each place setting was a glass, a napkin, a note pad and pencil. On display off to the side were six vintages: two Cabernet-Sauvignons, a Pinot Noir, a Fumé Blanc, two Chardonnays and a collection of many more clean crystal glasses.

Mrs. Duval had made quite clear weeks earlier that the bridal party and the more important of their invités should enjoy a more exclusive label, which Jennie interpreted as fine wine for the few, swill for the masses, yet Canyon Estates only produced fine wine. Therein lay the problem; therein lay the reason John Canyon wasn't at the table. Mr. Duval he could tolerate, Mrs. Duval was a royal pain in the ass.

They began with the white. The Fumé Blanc, certainly, was the unquestionable choice for the bridal party and preferred guests. Either one of the Chardonnays would satisfy a less refined palate.

Hidalgo watched the mother swirl, hold the glass to the light, swirl again as though washing the glass, stick her nose too far into the glass, inhale, exhale too quickly, swirl once more, sip, swish the wine from one side of her mouth to the other almost with a gurgling sound and swallow. Not quite certain, she swirled and sipped again. Then he watched the daughter who, not quite certain, also swirled and sipped again, apparently not very comfortable with a Mexican sitting beside her whose every second sentence was irksomely spoken in Spanish telling her how best to hold her glass to the light, swirl, sip and swallow.

He was the most vexing young man she had come across in her entire life. She hated him instantly and why was he dressed that way, like the Cisco Kid. And his accent was atrocious, not at all like hers. She barely understood a word he was saying. Were it not for watching him, she would be completely lost.

Hidalgo stood to clear the glasses as Jennie wrote notes. Mother and daughter didn't bother to do either.

The red was next and Hidalgo uncorked the first Cabernet-Sauvignon with expert ease. And again he annoyed her, despite Jennie conducting the tasting and talking for the most part with Mrs. Duval. He was asking her what she thought. What did she think of the clarity, the nose and the textures? What textures? She wanted to smack him. What did she know about robust or delicate? Apparently nothing, he thought, reading her mind as she read his. She wanted to yell at him, to kick him, to remind him who exactly she was. How dare he presume to treat her that way? And why was he smirking? She wanted to wipe the grin from his face. She wanted to hurt him, to put him in his place. What was that? Pardon me?

"Señorita, todavía no has tragado tu vino. Does the wine not please you? Would you prefer a bucket, rather than swallowing, or a piece of bread to cleanse your palate?"

She gulped hard, coughing, wanting to spit at him for his unmitigated impertinence.

He stood once more to uncork the second red. Again,

either one would do. Mrs. Duval had noted no appreciable difference between the vintages. And the Pinot Noir, although delightful, would certainly satisfy those guests whose personal wine cellars were stocked more modestly.

Jennie agreed, whereas her father would have escorted the woman to her car, the one she would have parked outside.

Hidalgo stood, tilting his head out of respect, thanking Mrs. Duval for her time and her selection. Jennie and Mrs. Duval stepped into the office to prepare a list, arrange for delivery and settle the account. John Canyon believed that folk should drink what they can afford. Drink now, pay later wasn't an option. He didn't give credit. He didn't have to. Rich folk went broke as quickly as poor folk and Mrs. Duval had just ordered $90,000 worth of wine. The cheque would clear on Monday, which wasn't Francine's business.

Hidalgo had cleared the table of the glasses, the last bottle and the napkins, once again neatly arranging the note pads and pencils. Then he brought clean glasses for each of them, the first Cabernet-Sauvignon, and sat beside her.

"This is the one you liked the most, señorita. ¿no es verdad? I saw this in your eyes. When we drink wine our eyes will tell us what our tongue does not. However we must always swallow or spit into the bucket." He paused, smirking. "I prefer to swallow. This is so much more polite."

She wanted to throw the glass at him. How vulgar to assume he could sit and talk with her as an equal. "No, it is not true. I preferred the other, in fact. Yes, I know I did."

"¡Ay! You are right. Either one will do. Now I remember. Yes, this is what you and your mother said. Please forgive me." He stood and went to the counter for the other red. He filled their glasses and sat. "May I toast your future happiness, señorita? And may I compliment your Spanish. Your Cuban teachers have taught you well."

Hidalgo sipped his wine. Francine's eyes practically bulging from her head. Her Spanish was good, yet far from excellent, she knew. She wanted to kill him! She had taken one course each year in high school and during her twelve months in Spain just half that time was spent with her private tutor, wanting to spend time with her grandparents. She struggled to find the words, the more she fumed the fewer she found. She composed herself and she switched to what she did speak well.

"Something is wrong with your ears. I speak Castilian, Spanish the proper way. I was in Spain for an entire year with the best private tutors."

"¡Ay! An entire year. Truly I am sorry. Te pido perdón. I am not well-travelled, señorita. I am a simple man who has recently come from Mexico to work and to study."

He was an idiot, and he was arrogant. He was simple, she told herself glaring at him, and he certainly didn't know his proper place.

"Mr. Canyon is so kind, is he not, to help you people escape your poverty?"

He switched to English. "Yes, what you say is true. We are very grateful. He is a kind and benevolent master."

She studied him from head to toe. He was mocking her, slouching just so in his seat, trying to appear so suave and sophisticated.

"You should be grateful." She paused. He was smirking. "Knowing you must return to Mexico each year when your visa expires must be horrible, leaving all this behind."

"I do not, señorita. Each night I return to my home in Vallejo. During my summers I work here with Señorita Jennie. The rest of the year I study at Golden Gate. I have just now completed my second year." He put his nose to the rim of his glass, inhaling. "The red Mustang is mine." He paused, studying her from head to toe. "Sunday evening is my time to relax, but perhaps your mother would pay me to help you improve your Spanish. Os and vosotros are not difficult to master and with her generous help I could escape my poverty and my service to Señor Canyon much faster."

She thoroughly despised him. "To buy gas for a car you can't afford to drive? Do you even have a licence or insurance? It's illegal not to, you know."

"So you can teach me to dance the flamenco, so that I might appear less clumsy to beautiful women such as you, when we are finished with your lessons of course. You must have bought castanets to hang on your wall, señorita, when you were in Spain?"

She didn't answer, her deep crimson cheeks much darker against her pale blonde hair. Then: "So what if I did? What business is it of yours?"

He shrugged. "One cannot dance the flamenco without them."

"Me, dancing with you." She snorted. "How dare you?"

Her glass was empty.

"More wine, señorita." He wasn't asking. He poured a small amount into her glass. "You do not remember me, Señorita Francine. Perdón… Señorita Duval, do you? I remember you. We met two years ago."

"We did not." She sneered. "I would have remembered you."

"But we did. You came with your mother. I was stocking the shelves." The teasing had gone far enough. He tipped his glass towards her. "My name is Hidalgo Arquero. I come from Pichilingue. I am studying Social Sciences at Golden Gate. My parents are managers here at the Estates." He sipped his wine. "Perhaps you are right. This is the finer of the wines, and you are much lovelier than what I remember from two years ago when I was a poor Mexican peasant. Perhaps you were as lovely and I was too afraid or too shy to see you as I do now."

83

She sipped her wine. She needed something to do, to moisten her throat, time to think.

"My Spanish is very good. Thank you. And my schedule does not allow for more lessons. I will improve by reading. I would be more concerned, if I were you, about how well you speak English. And why are you dressed like Zorro? You're ridiculous."

She felt instantly stupid. His English was excellent, even though she was certain he was exaggerating his accent for affect, to make himself sound sophisticated and erudite when he wasn't.

"Ah, El Zorro. Sí, Señor Guy Williams, the actor. Yes, I know of him, now that we have a television and electricity. Thank you."

"Thank you, for what?"

"For thinking I am so handsome, like El Zorro. Was he not adored by every woman? Was he not charming and debonair? Did he not make women's hearts flutter with desire? Was he not brave and daring? Thank you. To know that you think I am all of these things, I am left without words."

Yes, he was, she mused, and so very handsome. She gulped her wine. "I told mother not to come here today. Now I know why. You are a completely silly and rude young man."

"When I woke this morning, climbing from my luxurious and warm bed, I was anxious to come here. And now I know why." He leaned discreetly forward. "No longer must I sleep on the hard floor with the cats and the dogs. However, I must also work." He glanced at his watch. "Con permiso, allow me escort you to your mother."

She nodded. She had nothing to say. She felt like a stupid little girl. He stepped behind her seat, helping her to stand. Scott never helped to pull her seat from a table.

"Gracias, Señorita Duval. I have enjoyed our time

together. Allow me to offer my congratulations once more."

"De nada, Señor Arquero, y gracias."

She walked ahead of him, never glancing over her shoulder. He was behind her; she heard the soft sound of his footfalls. He was purposely annoying her.

Jennie and Mrs. Duval were standing at the entrance to the loading dock. If anything the weather had worsened. Jennie suggested they stay for dinner, but Mrs. Duval wouldn't think of imposing. She had so much to accomplish in so little time. Instead they shook hands and Hidalgo opened her door, bowing slightly. He didn't think Francine Duval could have walked more slowly to her side of the car. When he joined her, she proffered her hand, which he took in his, kissing it gently.

Yes, he was making her heart flutter. No, she didn't like him at all. She ignored him, glancing at Jennie who waved goodbye. She stepped in and he closed the door. When next she chose to notice hime he was leaning against the red Mustang under a bright light with his arms and legs crossed.

Mrs. Duval backed out as nervously as she'd driven in, waving to Jennie without seeing her, disregarding Hidalgo entirely. When the oversized door rumbled downward, sealing out all but the cacophony of the tempest, Jennie signalled him over and took his arm. They couldn't let such good wine go to waste. Could they?

"Say it."

"Say what, SJ?"

She was no longer Señorita Jennie, or Jennie. One was too formal for friends, the other made him uncomfortable. SJ felt right for both of them.

"The mother has a big stick up her ass. Say it."

"I do not know. But I do think perhaps that could be the reason she does not smile."

"Or maybe she's found her Mexican caballero too late to love her."

"Many years too late, SJ. The damage is done and, I believe, irreversible."

"And the daughter? She paused. "Tell me lover-boy, you like the girl."

"What I like does not matter. She is promised to another and one day she will become like her mother. She will have a big stick up her ass, a very big one I believe. I feel sorry for her."

"She likes you, lover-boy. Big time."

"Then she will live her life never knowing the heated love of a Latino caballero." The rims of their glasses clinked together. "She will never be happy, SJ. I see this in her eyes."

Jennie agreed. She allowed him another glass of wine, gave him something to eat, let him drive her to the hacienda with the half-case of opened bottles and sent him home. Sunday was another day and Hidalgo wanted to earn as much as he could over the summer.

Monday the Duval cheque cleared the bank, Tuesday Jennie's phone rang at the opening of business. Francine Duval was calling on behalf of her mother. The wine was to be delivered in a week's time so that the bottles might properly rest.

Jennie was quite certain she had previously discussed the delivery with Mrs. Duval for that very reason. In fact, she had.

13

Francine Duval spent the next seven days working with her trainer, doing push-ups and sit-ups three times each day after he was gone, each afternoon driving to the beach to sunbath and jog. Now she didn't have to envy those women who dared to wear such tiny bikinis. She owned her own. In Spain she had occasionally worn a string bikini at her grandparents' pool when they were gone, and by the end of the week she didn't mind how the boys at the beach stared at her. But Scott would never permit such a lack of propriety in public. He would expect his wife to act in a dignified and proper way.

By her wedding night her tan line would still tell all, which she would explain by telling him that she had sunbathed by the mansion's pool in private, away from the help, that she'd tanned for their first night of love. She'd spent the morning between her room and the pool, first in the red, followed by the blue, the bronze and the silver. The blue won out. The one dilemma remaining was how much of her buttocks and breasts to reveal. Whichever way she stood, sat, twisted or tugged, much more of her was hanging out than in her two-piece.

She was nervous. Her mouth was dry and her hands were shaking. Her heart was fluttering. It had all week. She couldn't pull her bottoms down or up and, perfectly centred, she was showing more than the girls she'd once hated at the beach. She should have bought the next size up but the sales clerk hadn't let her and her top was just as bad, or good. Most of her breasts were bare, thin blue strings framing them, emphasizing them. God! She should wear a tee-shirt. No, she wouldn't. She would look stupid. The temperature was at least 90°. Besides, the padding would stop him from seeing anything more and she wouldn't give him the satisfaction.

God! Why did she phone Jennie in the first place? She really hated him. She hated everything about him, the way he spoke, the way he leaned against his car, if the car was really his, which she doubted. Why did she ask for him to deliver the wine? And why did Jennie agree so quickly?

This would not end well. She would jump into the pool, she decided. He wouldn't see a thing. He didn't deserve to see her undressed. Why should he? Then he could lay awake all week thinking of her, dreaming of her. But if he didn't see her, how would he know what to dream? What if he imagined that she wasn't as tanned and as beautiful in her bikini as she was?

She had a better idea.

*

The wedding was three weeks away and Hidalgo wasn't pleased. He asked Jennie how he would look driving a van.

She replied, "Better than you'll look…unemployed, lover-boy."

He grumbled. He knew why the girl wanted him there.

"Hey, lover-boy, I speak Spanish. Remember?"

"SJ, she wants only to see the poor Mexican kid knocking at the back door of her fancy house. She wants to laugh at me, SJ. Where is your heart? I thought you liked me. How can you do this to me, your best friend?"

She went to him, wrapping her arms tightly around him. "You are so right, Hidalgo. You are my best friend. And I hate myself." She kissed his cheek. "Now go load the van. You're expected at noon." She chuckled. "You'll impress her just as much in those tight blue jeans and snug white tee-shirt." She leaned in closer, breathing in deeply. "No wrinkles…and so clean. Isn't that interesting? Is this a new one?" She patted his cheek, walking away shaking her head. "You guys are so pathetic."

*

The Duval Oakland mansion was brownstone and square with no particular flare. The window casings painted black on both floors were trimmed with white shutters behind wrought iron bars, the property was behind wrought iron fencing lined with tall, manicured hedges and trees and the front lawn appeared more like a lush carpet. The stairs were fashioned from precisely cut slate, the front door was painted in a black glaze, trimmed with panels of frosted glass and the door fixtures were polished brass.

He hated stepping from the van, but the intercom was placed for the convenience of rich people with low-profile cars like a Mustang, not deliveries. The voice spoke to him in Spanish, giving him directions to the side of the house where he would find a service entrance. He was to place the wine by the pantry, one case at a time to prevent possible breakage. The household staff would transfer the cases to the cellar at a later time.

One case at a time, he repeated, in this heat, eighty-five cases?

Yes. The gate swung open and when he saw the distance from the van to the doors he knew he would die of heatstroke. He would require at least two hours.

"¡Son muy locos esta familia!"

The side doors were intended for the household staff, contractors, tradesmen, general deliveries and, Hidalgo was certain, young Mexicans. The doors were also in line with the south end of the patio where the deep end of the pool and the diving boards were clearly visible.

The heat struck him instantly. Despite the sun resting at

its zenith and the hard work ahead he was determined not to break a sweat. Nor would he once glance at the pool, linger in the air-conditioned home or run the van's air for relief. He was from Pichilingue; 95° was nothing to him.

*

By one o'clock he had transferred half the cases into the house. He was leaning against the van, drinking the ice water that he wanted to pour over his head, but she didn't know that. She simply saw him slouching and she was becoming angrier each moment. He hadn't once glanced her way. She was covered in baby oil, glistening beads of water clinging to her body, accentuating her tan. She had never been so perfect, not once in her life that she could remember. And not once did he see her dive from the low board or leap from the higher platform, each time her smooth entry into the heated water pushing her bikini mischievously this way and that. Any normal man would find a reason, or lie about why he was peeking at her. What was wrong with him? What reason did he have to think himself God's gift to the world?

*

By1:30 Hidalgo was pacing himself, taking more time to place the boxes inside, less time to carry them from the van to the doors. Not like her, he thought. The van had windowed sides. He saw her perfectly from his vantage each time he reached in for another case of wine. She must be tired after all that climbing and jumping. How could she not be? How often could a girl adjust her bathing suit, untying and tying her side strings, tugging her bottoms a little downward, tugging them a little upward, always one side of her bum exposed to the sun more than the other. He wasn't surprised. He'd suspected as much. She had lured him there to tease and taunt the Mexican kid. Well, he could play the same game.

He'd decided that watching her through the van's

windows wasn't the same as gawking. She didn't know, and she wouldn't. Worse, thinking he wasn't interested was killing her. She couldn't be more obvious. Why couldn't she just admit that she liked him? And Jennie thought guys were pathetic. No way, José.

*

She was adamant. He was not leaving without seeing her. The way he treated her like a little girl at the Estates was inexcusable, mocking her with effusive attention, staring at her with those deep brown eyes, leaning against his car as though he owned the place, acting so superior when he wasn't. He was just a rude immigrant boy who hadn't learned his place.

She dived in again, first standing where she'd stepped so precisely, so intently onto the board. She was focused, inhaling, holding in her stomach, exhaling, pushing out her breasts, adjusting the triangles of her top, her arms outstretched at 90° to her torso, standing on her toes, her legs taut, springing forward, vanishing from sight, plunging.

Surfacing she drew herself from the deepest water onto the deck, standing where he could not help seeing her sweep her cupped hands from her face to the nape of her neck, combing her hair with her palms into a flat and golden headdress. Then she disappeared, nonchalantly, behind the mansion.

*

Hidalgo watched the entire spectacle, chuckling when he first saw the beach ball arcing his way from nowhere. He quickly grabbed a case and hurried through the doors, his eyes straight ahead. Again at the van, he knew what was coming. She was being so obvious. Something was about to happen, he was almost finished. Only a few cases remained, and just as he cleared the van's rear doors the ball struck the side of his face.

"Oh! I'm so sorry, sir… Oh… it's you."

"Sí, Señorita Francine, perdóneme otra vez, Señorita Duval. Soy yo, Hidalgo Arquero."

"I know who you are. What are you doing here?" she snarled.

He placed the case on the ground, reached for the ball and held it out to her.

"I am here to deliver your wine for the wedding." He tilted his head. "Señorita, as lovely as you were under the bright lights of the Estates, under the brilliance of this unforgiving sun you are a Maya princess to my eyes, a vision bathed in gold."

She swept up the towel she'd been dragging to cover her breasts and her belly which, he noticed, she hadn't stopped sucking in. "And you imagine yourself as a Maya prince, I suppose."

"No, señorita, de ninguna manera. I am El Zorro. Remember?" He was enjoying this. "El Zorro came many centuries later, which makes me much younger than you. I am, for that reason, your humble servant. May I carry the ball for you to your pool? I see that your hands are full."

"You're gauche and uncivilized. A gentleman would turn his head. You're obnoxious and undignified, not a gentleman at all. This is the second time I want to smack your face."

"Nor would a lady ever think to present herself to such an uncivilized man while looking so radiant, señorita, tempting his heart to stop beating. And you already have smacked my face, with this ball. So we are even, ¿no es verdad?" He furrowed his brow, studying the ball. "How unusual that such a light ball has travelled such a great distance when the air is completely still."

She was struggling. She despised him. He was horrible and infuriating. She peered into the van, avoiding him, seeing the few remaining boxes, staring at the ground.

He stood his ground. They were at an impasse. She

pursed her lips, wanting to wipe the smirk from his face. She was vulnerable, naked but for a few slivers and bits of shiny fabric. And he was…so damned flawless, his tee-shirt painted onto his chest, his jeans so long and straight, and not a speck of dust on his boots. He was loathsome.

"Why are you leaving the wine in the sun? Don't you know anything? You can bring me the ball when you've finished your work, if you can remember that much. And I'm not moving an inch until you're inside."

He dropped the ball, reached for the box, tilted his head towards her and strode away without saying a word. When he came out she was gone. When he finished moving all the boxes he reached for the ball and leaned against the van, gazing towards the pool. He was not a deliveryman. Of course he could go to the pool. He was Hidalgo Arquero, doing Jennie a favour by being there. But he knew he was right. Francine wasn't happy, and she never would be.

He pushed himself from the van, ready for whatever. He didn't know.

*

She was sitting at a patio table under a parasol. Her towel was strewn across a nearby deck chair. She was ignoring him.

"Señorita Duval, here is your beach ball." He saw the two glasses on the table. "I see that you are expecting company. I must tell you that seeing you again made my day more pleasant than I could have wished for. Adios, señorita."

He spun more quickly than she imagined. He was leaving!

She blurted. "Me llamo Francine."

He turned from the waist. "¿Perdón?"

She glanced up. "I've decided that you may call me Francine." She hesitated. "I've made lemonade, for myself, though I suppose you can have some if you want."

"That glass is for me?"

"Do you see anyone else?"

He smiled. "I thought you didn't like me." She didn't reply. "Thank you. The day is very hot. May I also fill your glass?"

"Yes, you may. And why are you standing in the sun when you can sit in the shade? Are you that stupid?"

He beamed as he sat. "Confronted with such beauty, señorita, what man would not act so uncertain?"

Seconds passed as slowly as minutes. Why wasn't he saying anything? She felt more undressed with each controlled breath, abruptly aware that with her hands in her lap she would appear completely naked to him. She grabbed for her glass. God! He was so aggravating.

"I expected to see you in your red Mustang. Did you have to return it?"

"My car is for carrying beautiful women, not cases of wine." He paused. "Perhaps the next time you visit the Estates, you will allow me to drive you through the vineyards."

"Is my lemonade good?"

He shrugged. "I do not know. However mine is excellent."

She chortled, her face coming alive. "Thank you. You did look like Zorro, you know."

"And you to me were a Maya Princess." He sipped his lemonade. "Did you like Señor Zorro, Francine, even a little?"

What! "I suppose he was charming, in an arrogant sort of way." She sipped. "Were all Maya princesses visions bathed in gold?"

"I can only speak of the one that I know…yes. I cannot imagine how lovely she will be in the years to come. She can only grow lovelier with each passing year."

His words resounded over and over again in her head

until she lost her smile. This wasn't going her way. "I can make some sandwiches, if you're hungry. I'm very good in the kitchen."

"I am not, thank you." He was starving. "But perhaps I can enjoy a bit more of your delicious lemonade before I must return the van to the vineyard."

She filled his glass. She didn't want him to go. She wanted to know more about him. She wanted to know why she shouldn't despise him for making her feel stupid. They spoke for an hour, and when he left she felt as happy as she did sad: happy that he'd come, that he'd seen more of her than any other man, and sad that she'd treated him so badly. Yet now they were friends. She knew much more about him, about his dreams and his future. They hadn't spoken about hers because secretly she felt, listening to him, that she didn't have one. She envied him, envied the girl who would one day fill his arms, when she would soon merely fill a social void. She knew that.

For the rest of the day, and in her bed that night, she could not stop thinking of Hidalgo Arquero, how he'd kissed her hand and gazed into her eyes before leaving her. She told herself that he didn't want to leave, as much as she wanted him to stay. She couldn't be wrong, but then she had been so wrong about him. She wanted to believe that something had happened: a spark, a fleeting thought, anything, albeit much too late.

She was going insane. She was getting married in three weeks. Why was she thinking about making love to a Mexican boy? She screamed into her pillow. What had he done to her!

14

Late Sunday afternoon, one week later, Hidalgo was at the ocean. He loved sitting by the sea, gazing across the horizon, dreaming. Jennie had sent him home early. Even eager Latin lovers needed alone time. He was working a seven-day week, and she knew why. However, even though he wasn't breaking his back toiling in the field, all work and no play wasn't a healthy ethic for anyone, especially for a kid his age.

He wasn't into shorts and baseball caps didn't go with the leather thong knotting his mahogany ponytail. Sitting by himself dressed in black boots, black jeans and a black tee-shirt, he appeared untouchable to most guys passing by and intriguing to all the girls.

"Hola, Zorro."

He turned. "Hola, Francine. What are you doing here?"

He stood.

"You told me that you come here to think. And I remembered that you owe me a glass of lemonade. Actually, you owe me two."

"You are beautiful, truly a vision." His face lit with sincere appreciation. "Clearly you dressed this way to steal all the attention from me."

She smacked him. "You are so conceited, completely incorrigible."

"I do not know this word."

"It means you're stupid, and I came here to tell you

why."

"You could have phoned me, at the Estates."

"But then you couldn't take me for a drive along the coast in your red Mustang."

He beamed. "Your parents, do they know you are here?"

"Do yours?"

"May I take your arm, señorita?"

"No, you may not." She took his hand, and didn't say a word until she saw the car. "So this really is yours. You didn't borrow or steal it to impress me?"

He coughed a laugh. He liked her. "All that was stolen is my heart, and you are the thief."

She was gorgeous. Her hair was combed into a ponytail, like his, her dress was mid-thigh, her shoes low-heeled pumps that he carried in his other hand, her face half-covered with dark glasses to match the red of her dress. Everything was brand new, bought the day before.

But the ocean wasn't his favourite spot. He was there because he'd told her so and he was waiting for her as he did the Sunday before, curious. They hadn't finished talking that day at the pool, each one knew.

He let her hand go to open the door. He watched her climb in, curl into her seat and look at the blacktop roof without saying a word. Sitting behind the wheel, not gawking at her legs required inhuman restraint. Driving would be almost impossible with her sitting that way. He lowered the roof, laid her shoes on the rear seat and shifted into reverse.

The twenty miles northward along the coastal highway were quiet, for them. The wind made talking impossible. He wanted to take her hand, to touch her knee, her thighs, refusing to dare. Instead she read his mind and took his again, facing him, breathing in the sea air, feeling free and not letting go of his hand when he turned off the road with only the ocean before them, the dull thunder of crashing waves 150 feet below.

When he reached to open his door, she stopped him.

"I'm sorry, Hidalgo."

"For what reason, Francine?"

"For everything, for being so rude to you when I didn't want to be rude, for not meeting you sooner, for being who I am and for you being who you are. I'm not really a prissy bitch. I'm a nice girl," she sighed, "with not so nice parents. Maybe they were nice once, before I knew them, which is pretty moot."

"I don't understand, chica. Remember, I am a poor and stupid boy from Pichilingue."

"And I'm a rich girl from here."

"The ocean, Francine, does not know the difference between us. Neither do the sun or the moon." He squeezed her hand, forcing a smile. "I will always like you, even if you are a nice, rich girl. This is not your fault. We will always be friends," he paused for affect, "now that I know you like me."

He thought she would smack him again, tenderly. She didn't.

"He screws around."

"¿Perdón?"

"Scott, he screws around with anything in a skirt. He's been doing it since he was in high school. He thinks I don't know, but I do. First he did pom-pom girls, now he does anything that moves, including the girls in the office. I've known for a long time, trying my best to imagine that he doesn't. I can't believe my father doesn't know."

"But he will stop when you are married. What man could love anyone but you?"

"No, he won't. He'll be like his father and I'll be like my mother, drab before my time. Not that his mother's any better. The only difference between them is that Claire keeps herself young and mother didn't sleep around. I heard her telling my father once that Scott probably isn't a Gibson." She smirked. "Apparently Claire was a bit of whore in high school. Like mother like son."

"Then don't marry him, Francine. Marry me instead."

"That's not funny." She kissed his hand. "Two years ago I didn't know better than to think badly of you, Hidalgo. I was being like them. Then two weeks ago, when I saw you, I thought you were the most beautiful man in the world. I acted the way I did because I was nervous. I felt stupid. Then you started speaking Spanish to me. I thought I was going to die, that you were making fun of me in front of Jennie."

"I'm sorry, truly I am. I was teasing you because of the way you stared at me two years ago. I wanted you to know that I was not that boy, not a migrant worker, that one day I will be someone. I was wrong to do so. My mother would be ashamed of me to know of this."

"No, you were right. I was wrong. Last week, at my home, I was trying all afternoon to get your attention. I was so angry with you for not noticing me."

"I know. I watched you from the windows of the van each time you were ready to dive into the water, wondering 'how often will that girl adjust her strings and try to cover her bum with so little material'."

"You saw me!"

He nodded. "And I saw the first ball." He chuckled softly. "But I felt the second. What took you so long? And, last Sunday, I waited for you at the ocean. I was disappointed when you didn't come. But I knew why you did not."

"Because of the wedding?"

"Sí, claro. You are promised to another man."

"Now when I think of marrying him, I feel sick. He's not who he once was. He possibly never was. I was fifteen when I was told that I would marry him. He was much older.

It all sounded so romantic. Now, Hidalgo, I don't want to marry him."

"Then why will you? Walk away. Are we not in the United States of America?"

"Because I'm a girl from a wealthy family and wealthy people do things to stay wealthy."

"No comprendo."

"He's going to work for my father, as a lawyer. In a few years he'll become a partner and eventually he will take over the firm. If he doesn't, because of me, my father will lose many of his most important clients because of the senator, Senator Gibson will lose my father's financial support and the support of his close friends, and our mothers will lose prestige in each other's social circles. I can't begin to think what would happen to the club, not to mention Jennie and John Canyon. If my parents or his ever found out about us being together like this, their precious daughter and future daughter-in-law sitting in a convertible at the ocean holding hands with a Mexican boy, not only would they have strokes, Mr. Canyon would lose a fortune in wine sales. Between the club's cellar and the private cellars in the mansions Mr. Canyon would lose 2,500 cases a year, and possibly much more because of me. That's well over three million dollars."

"This is my fault, for wanting to impress you."

"No, it isn't. It's my fault, for seeing in you what I believed I once saw in him. And I never will again. When I was fifteen, he was twenty-one. I was naïve, he wasn't. Now he's twenty-five, travelled, educated, experienced with women and doesn't know me at all. And I don't know him. We're marrying each other's family." She took a deep breath. "Hidalgo, I feel sick."

"Because we are sitting here with this console between us when a lush blanket of grass covers the ground around us. Come, chica."

100

They left the car. She watched Hidalgo spread a blanket as though casting a soft woollen net across a green sea in a single fluid motion. They sat facing the vast and sparkling expanse of a black and silver sea, neither one anxious to speak, each one struggling to contain a maelstrom of inconceivable and identical thoughts ravaging their minds.

Then: "You did not tell me why I am stupid. I know why I am, but why do you think so?"

"Hidalgo, you will not be happy as a social worker. What are you thinking? Mr. Canyon and your father are right. That life isn't for you, spending your days filling out forms, always begging agencies for more money, never feeling good about what you do. The work is important, yes. But you can do work that's just as important and help so many more people."

"I have chosen my path, chica. My education is half over. I must finish what I have begun, as you must."

"Become that great lawyer they see in your future. They're not wrong about you. Help those people who cannot afford my father or others like him." Her smile was weak. "Perhaps I could learn to type and be your secretary and we could have an affair...at least until you marry someone else. I wouldn't want to see that." She looked out over the ocean. "You can do it, Hidalgo. What's another three years of school? You could have your law degree in five years. Hidalgo, the way you speak, the way you search people's eyes, the way you stand, the way everyone watches you. I stopped behind you at the beach to watch how everyone was taking notice of you, before I made all the young girls jealous." She smiled, at last. "When you're older people will come to you for help, or run from you because they're afraid of you or know that they're wrong and you are right. Don't spend your life helping a few when you can help many. When I saw you for the first time on your car in the garage I practically stopped breathing. I didn't want to leave the car. I did remember you from before. Imagine how you will be five years from now, an officer of the court."

"But my courses are already selected for the coming year."

"Hidalgo, I'm Francine Duval. My father has connections you can't begin to imagine. If you want to be a lawyer in five years, you will be. I promise you. If I can't do anything else for you, please let me do this." She stroked his hair. "If I can never be anything in your life, let me do this for you. If I'm wrong, you can hate me forever, but I'm not wrong. Neither is your father or Mr. Canyon."

"My heart feels crushed by the earth itself."

"Because of me."

"Sí, debido a ti. What good does it do to crave a precious jewel within my grasp, one I can never possess? I have thought of nothing else since I last saw you. Now I am cursed for wanting to impress you. Now I will never see you again unless I am carrying boxes of wine into your new home." Then he realized what he'd said. "This I will never do. After today we must not see each other."

"Hidalgo, the senator and his wife have separate bedrooms. They haven't slept together in years. Neither have my parents. It's all about show, being seen, writing cheques and saying the right thing to the right people. They've never divorced because of reputation. The fathers would be ruined and the mothers would be left with limited bank accounts and no one to impress. I won't let that happen to me, and I certainly won't give myself, married or not, to a man who screws around with other women before he comes home to me, if he does come home. I'm too special, because of you."

"My head is aching."

"Then let me put it this way…chico. With you or without you, he's not touching me. I have to go through with this or I will ruin the club, two families and two people you love very much, Jennie and her father…not to mention your mom and dad who would probably lose their jobs. And you, you have to become something and someone important. My father and his father can stop that from ever happening. They could ruin you because of me, and they would. The one reason I'm not jumping off this cliff right now is you. You think your head is aching. Last week I could barely breathe while I waited for you. Then I hated you for not seeing me, because I wanted you to see me, to watch me. I haven't slept for two weeks because of you, because I'm afraid I'll wake up two weeks from now with nothing to remember you by." She grabbed his face between her hands, smothering him with an ardent kiss, stealing his breath. "And you will see me again, often, because we're friends and because I need time to discover how much I love a poor Mexican boy from Pichilingue who must become a brilliant lawyer. That's you…stupid."

"Do not speak such words, Francine. Your love would be wasted on me, chica. We've only known each other a few hours and you will soon have a husband to care for. The last girlfriend I had was nine-years-old when I was ten. What would I do with a woman as beautiful as you in my hands or in my heart? What would you do with me? I am poor and will remain so for a long time. It is wrong for us to feel this way. You're afraid of being a bride as much as I am afraid of not seeing you again. But what we have done is wrong."

"All I've done is to kiss a handsome and gallant caballero; I'm still a virgin…and single. I haven't broken any rule." She kissed him again, pressing a warm hand against his heart. "So you tell me. What would you do with a woman as beautiful as me, Zorro? Or has the fox lost his gallant tongue?"
*

The warm blanket became a cloak as the sun sank more quickly than they wanted into the sea. Yet to Francine the darkness was as welcome as his body's heat. She hadn't spoken for an hour. Not so for Hidalgo whose mind and body waged a cruel battle, one defending her honour, the other wanting to ravage her innocence, the silent night air and star-filled universe unfeeling co-conspirators to the weaker of the two. He had never touched skin as smooth or as warm, peered into eyes as green or kissed lips as soft. He knew they had to leave, before his inner conflict was lost, missing her warmth instantly as he pulled away, his body suddenly chilled by what he feared and the strength of her grip at his wrist. She wasn't ready to say goodbye.
*

The drive to the oceanfront was quiet, the top left down because Francine wanted to see the stars. At her car the evening was over, with nothing more to say. At her home she stepped from the car at the gate and went to the curb to see him one last time.

"I know now that what I once foolishly believed was his love for me that I saw in his eyes, wasn't. I was fifteen. I was too young for what they expected of me. I'm too young now. That isn't love. That doesn't require a wife. Tonight, what we shared, that was love, Hidalgo. That's what I will always remember. That will be my wedding night, my dreams and my memories of you. His will be whatever else he chooses and have whoever he chooses, just not me. I promise you." She leaned over his door, pulling him closer, kissing him. "You must be the one to tell me, Hidalgo. And I will know whether you are lying, or not, by what I see in your eyes."

She left him to the dark night.

15

"Your mother and I were worried, hijo. Where have you been so late to frighten her so?"

"I was at the ocean, papá. Mamá, I am sorry. I had much to think about."

His mother put down her book. "And were you thinking all this time by yourself, Hidalgo?"

"Mamá, you know that you and papá are always in my heart, where always I can find the difficult answers I seek."

"Sí, yo sé, but what is her name?"

He kept his breathing shallow. "Francine Duval, she was with me to decide an important matter, one we have already discussed."

"The young girl who is to be married. ¡Ay! hijo."

"It is not what you think, mamá, but I thank you for believing that such a wonderful girl would be attracted to me."

Fernando cut in. "Chico, when you first saw the girl she was annoying; you spent hours making yourself into a Don Juan and waxing your car to impress her. Last week you came home with stars in your eyes and air beneath your feet. Now you come home in the dark to tell us she is wonderful. On what matter did you both decide? Another man's woman in the dark, hijo, this is not a good thing. Es muy peligro."

"Papá, she made me see that you and Señor Canyon were right. I will tell him also in the morning. Mamá, I will become lawyer. When I am finished with my university, I will go to law school. This I will pay for myself. I will ask Señor Canyon tomorrow if I can work with Jennie three more years. That is how much time I will need. If I cannot, I will find a way. Francine also said that her father will help me." He faced his mother. "Mamá, I have not forgotten my promise to you and to Señor Canyon. I will help many people."

She nodded. "Fernando, our son will one day be an important person. I knew this. I told you."

Sí, mi amor, if he is not first called into the street by a jealous suitor or husband." He looked to his son. "And how is Señorita Francine?"

"She is well, papá. However I will not see her again, for the reason you say. She came to the ocean to meet me, to advise me that you and Señor Canyon were right. That is all." He kissed them both. "Por favor, I am very tired. Con permiso, I will go to my bed now."

He left them. When they heard the door to his room close Fernando rubbed his face hard with his open palms and turned to his wife.

"Maria, may God forgive me, I do not believe him."

She moved closer to him, squeezing his hands. "Sea lo que sea, querido. One day in my lifetime he will be a great man. I know this, Fernando, in my heart. If she is meant to be with him, she will be. That is what God knows."

16

Francine Duval lay in her bed, her face streaked with silent tears. Not so much because of Hidalgo, not because she would never have him, not because she had once acted so terribly towards him, because she was being bartered for prestige. Her parents were giving her to the highest bidder, serving their own best interests. What was worse, before meeting the most aggravating man she'd ever known, she hadn't known better.

She could not, would not metamorphose into her mother: neglected when not in the public eye, acting older than her years. She wanted more from life than tea parties, organizing benefits, smiling at the precise moment, saying the right thing on cue or saying nothing at all, speaking when spoken to and never being happy.

All this began festering in her mind the day at the Estates when she realized she didn't like Hidalgo Arquero because she did like him, very much. And that evening, at the ocean, the way he listened to her every word as though she was important, as though she knew what he did not. For what was life without dreams? But when he asked her about her dreams, she had no reply worth speaking. She fell silent, pensive, infused with shame. Held in his arms, feeling his hot breath, hearing his sweet voice, she realized she had not a single dream.

But now she did. She would dream of being held close, by him. She would dream of the way he combed his fingers through her hair, the way he smothered her face and mouth with warm kisses, of the way he made love to her without touching her, his whispered words, the way she begged him to consume her completely with heated passion. Each night in her dreams she would relive the delicate touch of his fingertips tracing every inch of her bare skin as though she were a rare porcelain doll, to awaken and titillate every nerve-ending, to never let her forget.

She wiped her face. Perhaps she'd known all along that she was a prisoner of her birth, whose one purpose in life was to be a gracious hostess, a perfect mother and obedient wife with no mind of her own.

She rolled onto her side, hugging her pillow, smothering her sobs, regretting she'd ever met the boy from Pichilingue, regretting she was rich; regretting that her memories of him would one day fade. She could never see him again. How could she? He wouldn't bury his face in his books much longer. Soon he would meet girls; he would date beautiful girls, get married and have beautiful children. No, she would never see him again. He was gone from her, forbidden to her.

She wanted to rip her pillow apart. She wanted to hurt something as much as she hurt.

She was wealthy in her own right, or would be in two years. For her fifteenth birthday her grandparents jointly opened a trust fund worth half a million. By her twenty-first, she would have twice that much and her current annual allowance was well beyond what any woman her age earned in the workforce. Yet she knew without being told what extensive damage she would wreak, were she to disregard her obligations, and that she couldn't do.

It wasn't fair.

*

The next morning she lay in bed ignoring her mother's persistent calls. She hadn't slept a wink. There wasn't time.

Not once in her life could she remember thinking for herself beyond what clothes to wear or what lipstick best complemented those clothes. Even then her mother often intruded. Yet of two things she was now certain: the first being that Hidalgo Arquero would become a famous lawyer. Secondly, she would do nothing to impede his future.

When she did rise, the clear sky and warm breeze off the Pacific meant nothing to her. Her first order of business was to frustrate her mother. Her wedding gown could wait a day, so could everything else for that matter. She wanted to spend the day alone, which caused her mother to involuntarily convulse.

Mrs. Duval was frantic, she couldn't understand. Less than two weeks remained.

Francine replied, "That's okay, mother. You don't have to."

She went to her room with no real idea where to start. She knew what she wanted to accomplish and in what timeframe, but she needed someone to guide her. Someone she could trust, someone in her father's office with street smarts.

She liked the woman, and the woman liked her. They'd spoken previously on the phone and at various office functions Virginia Meadows had always taken the time to make Francine feel comfortable. She knew everything that went on in the office and Francine was certain, without ever having enquired, that she did not like Scott Gibson. The last time they'd spoken Francine was in Virginia Meadows' office, the day Francine happened to discover that the cute redhead in the short dress who'd brought them tea was the last girl Scott Gibson had entertained outside of work. Of course the girl left her employment shortly after for what was termed 'greener pastures'.

Virginia Meadows was also in charge of Personnel and Recruitment.

The phone conversation was brief. Virginia Meadows was experienced in getting to the point, switching to Spanish when she understood Francine's concern. The switchboard operator spoke only English. She gave Francine the man's name without the slightest hesitation, his phone number and his business address. She would make the arrangements herself, she insisted, for three PM that day. She had experience with such men, Francine did not. She would explain to him in brief what was expected, Francine could later explain in detail and in her own words.

If for any reason the timing was inconvenient, she would return Francine's call immediately without fail. Otherwise Francine was to present herself at the man's place of work that afternoon. On time, she repeated.

*

Francine wasn't good at this, she was simply determined. She asked the woman what she should wear to the meeting, uncertain. The woman replied: a dress, sandals and a hat...or jeans, a sweater and sneakers. He wouldn't care either way. She should know; the man was her husband.

She arrived at 2:55. She was expecting she didn't know what, Peter Gunn or Broderick Crawford. He was neither. He was tall, slim, well-dressed and didn't wear a big gun strapped to his chest or his belt. He was relaxed, confident, not someone easily intimidated by men like her father. He offered her a coffee, although he didn't have a secretary. When she declined he poured something thick and black into his cup. He added yellow cream that she thought was clotted more than glutinous, stirred once, left the stick in the cup, sat behind his desk, reached for a notepad, leaned forward and asked her to fill in what he didn't already know.

Why did she want her future husband followed, in her own words? How far back should he investigate? What was his time frame? And what if she didn't like the answers? No one hired private investigators to discover good news.

She knew that. She wasn't expecting good news. She was expecting accurate information that would help her understand her future. That was her reasoning. As far as possible into Scott Gibson's past four years would suffice and whether or not she liked the news didn't matter. She knew she wouldn't. What she needed to know was how many, who, and, in particular, who and when was the last woman he slept with.

Before she left his office Meadows knew everything about Scott Gibson that she could think to tell him, which wasn't much: age, schools, friends' names, achievements, SI number, what he drove, where he lived, where he worked, why she didn't know him at all. And finally, she needed the absolute most current information in her hands the morning of her wedding. She would later expect an extensive written report, though she must have a brief summary of the week and night before her wedding. He was simply to come to her house where she would be waiting for him.

She stood, placing an envelope on the edge of his desk, a thousand dollars. They shook hands and she left. In the corridor by the elevator, she thought she'd done well. In his office, his feet on the desk, so did he. He'd seen a lot of suspicious wives and husbands in his time, but this was a first.

And more changes were on the way. The next day she would go shopping. She chortled, what else could one expect of an affluent young woman with no skills?
*

Hidalgo drove his mother to work. Fernando either left earlier most days, or trailed behind. He was proud of his wife and their son. Often he would remember his last trek from Pichilingue, the bus ride from La Paz and how he could barely contain his excitement while pretending to sleep as though he didn't care. He'd never stopped loving them, working for them while fearing in his heart that she would one day leave him for another, and now they were weeks away from becoming American citizens.

At the Estates he took back his wife from the one other man she would ever love. At work he showed Hidalgo no favours. Hidalgo would speak to Señor Canyon alone, man to man as he must.

John Canyon listened intently. Finally, he didn't know. He would have to discuss the matter with Jennie. They would advise him at a later date. But, for the time being, didn't he have work to do?

When Hidalgo left the office John Canyon created a rare smile on his face, stifling a chuckle. He called his daughter and filled her in. Mum's the word. Keep the kid on his toes.

The next morning John Canyon's phone rang. Mr. Franklin Duval was calling. Please hold.

The niceties were brief. Both men were busy. Duval wanted to know everything there was to know about some Mexican kid called Arquero and how his daughter had come to know him.

At the end of the conversation, Hidalgo's future was assured. He would attend law school, assuming he maintained his academic grade point average. Franklin Duval would see to the technicalities. He would contact Golden Gate and the law school; however the kid would have to get in on his own merit. No free ride, and if the kid was any good he'd have a job clerking after his third year. If he demonstrated excellence, and fit the mould, he could be welcomed at Duval & Associates as an entry level. After that, he would pave his own road.

Finally, what about the kid's finances? Law school didn't come cheap. John Canyon told Duval not to worry. The kid was good for the full amount.

John Canyon put the phone into its cradle, stretching back with his feet on the desk. Something was going on that he knew nothing about. First the kid asked to work three more years, so he could afford law school without help from his parents. That he understood. He had no problem with that. Then out of the blue Duval calls to check-up on the kid, saying he'll be making the necessary arrangements, practically offering the kid a job. He called his daughter.

That Tuesday Jennie invited Maria and Fernando to join her and her father for lunch at the hacienda. By the time Jennie served dessert Maria was crying and hugging everyone while Fernando swore that he would repay every penny and that his son would study and work hard to make them all proud. At which point John Canyon set matters straight.

There would be no debt to repay. Fernando Arquero was producing the finest crops in the Estates' history and Maria Arquero was proving herself talented in marketing. She had already redesigned labels for three of the vineyards' leading vintages, which, he believed, accounted for sales exceeding any previous expectation. The matter was closed. However he did think Hidalgo should sweat a little, and Maria squeezed him all the harder.

He looked to Fernando for help, then to Jennie, but he got none.
*

The following Saturday at dinner Hidalgo heard the news. He heard about the bursary that would relieve any anxiety over the coming five years, and about the appointment at Golden Gate to arrange for the changes to his third year semesters. Maria and Fernando could see the happiness in his eyes, great joy cloaked by deep sadness. They understood the reasons for both, yet could do nothing to assuage his heartache. One of the few times Maria felt useless as a mother.

113

She and Fernando knew very well that Francine Duval had done this wonderful thing for their son, and why, and that her wedding day was one week away. Maria's heart was filled with grief that she could feel such happiness while somewhere a young girl could not. Jennie had confided to Maria how such weddings of convenience were expected between certain well-established families, which did nothing to lessen the sorrow she felt for the young girl.
*

Monday morning, Hidalgo also knew that he must be a man. John Canyon would not expect less of him. On the Monday before the wedding he went to Señor Canyon's office to thank him, after requesting a formal meeting through Jennie. He wanted to know how he could ever repay such a gift. He would not accept charity.

"You'll have a job here as long as you need one, chavo. Seems my daughter believes you're good for business. The call was hers, not mine."

"This I know is not true, señor. I will work very hard to repay you. Muchísimas gracias. Your gift is too great."

"You'll be rich one day, chavo, no doubt very rich. Then, at some point when all your money doesn't mean very much anymore, for whatever reason, you're going to wonder why you possess so much when so many others, who so deserve, have nothing. You'll remember Pichilingue, dusty dirt roads and sleeping on the floor, though not in the way you might believe. You'll remember this place, your beginning here and your end, which will come one day sooner than we wish. That's life. We move on. It's the natural order of things. And one day you'll come across someone who'll be in the right place at the right time, someone who needs a break. He or she will be in your place, chavo, in your space and time, wherever and whenever that might be, some desperate kid who needs a job, a chance to change his or her life. I'm not talking about dimes in a tin cup. I'm talking real help. Not everyone, chavo, has parents like yours. I don't much believe in God. Don't have much reason to. There's too much bad around. I leave all that nose-pinching church business to Jennie. Then someone like you comes along and reinforces my belief that I'm here for a reason. And you're no different. I can see that, and now so should you. We're here for a reason, you and me, and it's got nothing to do with squeezing wine from grapes. We're here to do some good. So your debt, if you want to believe you have one, is to someone you haven't yet met. But the day will come and, if I'm any judge of character, I suspect more than once before you're done. Don't let them down. Be the guy who can get things done. Just stay level. Rich and obnoxious doesn't work. Walk quietly. Keep your eyes and your ears open, your mouth shut. You won't ever learn much by listening to yourself." He checked his watch. "As far as I'm concerned the matter's closed. Paid in full. I don't want to hear another word about it. The rest is up to you, chavo." He pushed himself from behind the desk. "Do us proud, chavo, and why are you sitting here when my daughter is doing your work?"

They stood.

"Gracias, señor. I will always be humble and never will I refuse those who may need my help. Se lo juro."

They shook hands across the desk. When Hidalgo was at the door John Canyon's voice stopped him. "Chavo… some things in life we have no control over. Don't let sadness blur your vision. No one's life is free of sorrow, not yours, not mine. You will have much more grief to battle throughout your life, and that's a fact. Many of your days will not be easy. But remember this above all: The most important are the dark days of despair that you must struggle to overcome. These are the times that will make you strong."

When the door closed John Canyon went to his private reserve. He poured an ample amount of Pinot Noir into his favourite glass and wondered why the hell his daughter had to tell him everything.

*

Monday afternoon, five days before the wedding, Francine's personal phone rang in her bedroom. The man wanted to see her that afternoon noon, urgently. He wanted her key to the new house in Oakland. He preferred not to say why over the phone.

In fact, they met at the house and went in together. They saw a pizza box in the kitchen with two wine bottles; another bottle stood empty in the living room and they came across a fourth in the bedroom. Dirty glasses were strewn everywhere. The photographs would be part of his final report. The bed was unmade. He threw back the covers and took another photograph. He photographed the bath, the shower and the soiled towels. He peered into the step-on wastebasket where he saw tissues stained with lipstick, soap wrappers, still-moist remnants of bars, not seeing what he was searching for, which gave him cause for hope.

When he was done they sat on the stairs in the hallway and she listened to his preliminary report. Things weren't looking good. When she asked his opinion, he answered that her life was more important than disrupting the Saturdays of 500 rich and famous who needed a place to be. But he wasn't being paid to act as her spiritual advisor. He'd come prepared to do the finest work possible and Francine stayed with him to observe, gleaning certain pleasure from each photograph he snapped.

When he asked whether she could afford an additional thousand dollars, she said yes. Then she asked him why. The money wasn't for him; he'd been well-paid in advance. The money was intended as a cash bonus for someone who wouldn't make that much after tax money in a month. And for that reason she wouldn't be getting a receipt. That was all he wanted to tell her at the moment.

They left when he was done. She went home completely stunned, incapable of rational thought, bombarded by the myriad of new truths she'd discovered.

Tuesday she went alone to the seamstress with a special request. Wednesday she went to a travel agent and Thursday she went to a lawyer who assured her of the utmost client/attorney confidentiality. She needed someone to act on her behalf. Despite her age of majority, she had recently become all too aware of her shortcomings. Despite that fault, she knew what she wanted. The date of her marriage would be the date of her rebirth.

Friday she sat in her room and cried, struggling to remember his smell, the warmth of his arms and the gentle pressure of his lips. The only photograph she had of him was in her mind.

*

Friday Hidalgo did work hard, to forget. He wanted to phone her, but what would he say? He hadn't seen her in twelve days. Each night in his room he remembered John Canyon's words. The man was right. Grief and hardship were integral to life. Without them, how could one determine one's true strength?

Friday night Fernando took his wife to dinner. His son was told in no uncertain terms that he was to stay home. Hidalgo needed time alone to think, to reflect, and Fernando didn't want his son driving when his mind was unclear. He was permitted two glasses of wine, not more. Self-pity was not an enviable trait, Fernando told his son. He had come too far to wallow in selfish lament. What was done was done, he must understand. He'd lost a love that he'd barely found. This was not the end of his world. His path was now clear to him, a path which many more women would cross. This because of la Señorita Francine whose kindness was beyond words to initiate her father's interest in him. She saw in him what he could not see in himself. Did he not owe her in return what she would expect of him? Would she want to see him this way, dejected and forlorn? Did she do such a wonderful thing for a common peasant from Pichilingue or for a fine caballero, el Señor Hidalgo Arquero, Attorney at Law?

He kissed his son and left to join his wife who knew to step outside and wait by the car. These were not words for a mother to hear.

17

Saturday Hidalgo awoke feeling no less miserable to the smell of fresh coffee and Maria's soft voice. His father sat stoically at the table, unsmiling, not happy with how he'd spoken to his son the night before. Hidalgo kissed his mother lightly on her lips and hugged her; no morning was complete without her high-pitched squeal or her light smack on his cheek for his insolence.

He went behind his father, gripping the man's strong shoulders in his hands, squeezing lightly, rocking Fernando back and forth until his father's face brightened into a reluctant smile.

"Thank you, papá, for shaking me. I still have much to learn. I will always need your wise words to guide me when I do not see clearly."
*
In Oakland, Francine was up and dressed in a bathrobe. The morning would be her last in her parents' home. Her breakfast would be the last that a domestic would serve her. In a few hours she would become Mrs. Scott Gibson. Her bedroom was bare, all her worldly goods boxed and ready for shipment to her new home. She would call the cartage company herself, she told her mother, after the honeymoon. The new home's interior decoration wasn't yet quite to her liking. In fact, the house wasn't quite to her liking.

Mrs. Duval understood. Her daughter had spent her entire life in a stately and luxurious mansion with servants and the finest amenities, now she would have to adjust to a more modest home she didn't know, new neighbours of perhaps a lesser standing and a husband.

At 10:00 AM Francine answered the door. Of course her mother couldn't understand why the man was there, or what business he could possibly have with her daughter. Not knowing what else to do, not understanding her daughter's uncharacteristic behaviour of late, she called her husband from his study.

Francine led the investigator to the pool area and, by the time coffee was served, Mr. Duval stood by the table, his composure close to obliterated when she advised him that the man had come at her invitation and on business that did not concern him. She was about to become a married woman and, as such, would no longer tolerate her father presuming any degree of involvement in her personal affairs.

Mr. Meadows reiterated as much in less emotional terms. She was of age and very much entitled to manage her private affairs, although he realized that he was in Mr. Duval's home, not hers, and they might just as easily discuss their private business in his car parked on the street, should Mr. Duval so prefer.

Mr. Duval most assuredly did not, and walked away on the verge of apoplectic trauma.

"Sir, tell me first about last night."

"This morning is more telling, Miss Duval, unfortunately." He reached into a 10X12 Kraft envelope. "I took these Polaroids three hours ago. The woman stayed the night. I went in when they were gone. They had quite a party, I must say. You'll have those photographs very shortly with my full report."

The snapshots showed Gibson with a young woman, her hair colour a pure white, her skin an unnatural yellowish-brown. Her legs were long and bare, her skirt was short and her low-cut sweater left little to the imagination even from across the street. In one they were kissing, in another he was locking the door, the last showed the woman groping her own breasts and pouting. Francine contorted her face.

"It doesn't get any better, Miss Duval. However I believe you'll find these the most condemning." He reached into his briefcase. "The first tape is from the bedroom, the second is from the living room. I'm afraid not much was said on the second."

The first tape played for sixty seconds before Meadows pressed STOP, Francine resisting the urge to vomit.

"Who is she?"

"She's a law student, and not a very good one."

"My guess is that she's thinking of him as an entry level position at Duval & Associates. We both know that won't happen. She's the last in a very long line that's getting longer. For my money, she'll drop out when she has to read a book or she'll do a couple of professors to get a passing grade. The best she'll do in life is bailing out ten-dollar hookers and requesting time-served for first-time offenders. She's not very good."

"And regarding the thousand dollars, were you successful?"

"Yes...I was."

"Miss Duval, you have no reason to go through with this marriage. I do understand your concern, but..."

"Sir, people I care very deeply about have too much to lose if I don't. I'm not talking about the Duvals and Gibsons. They're filthy rich and always will be. I'm talking about people they can hurt badly. My father knows a lot of people in the Southwest and Mr. Gibson, so I hear when I shouldn't be listening, can be a real piece of work."

"I know him by reputation."

"I know him by association. He's not very nice when he's not standing directly in front of you. When he's not, you don't exist. I think if he weren't in politics he'd be a pretty bad man."

"Being in politics doesn't make him good. But now you know something he doesn't, something he can't controvert when he hears the truth, if he does."

"The reason you needed the thousand dollars."

He nodded. "Yes."

"And what exactly does a thousand buy these days from a detective?"

Meadows put the files on the table, closed. "I strongly suggest that you let me keep these until such time as you have a safe place to hide them. The first file, Miss Duval, is your way out."

Francine put her hand to the inch-thick folders. "What exactly am I seeing here?"

"The top folder is Gibson's complete medical history. The bottom is a comprehensive psych evaluation which was somewhat easier to obtain. Anyone seeking to be a high-priced lawyer with your father has to prove beyond reasonable doubt that he or she doesn't have a soul. I took the liberty of tagging the more pertinent pages in both files."

When Francine finished reading the highlighted data, she returned the file. She gave the man another envelope and asked that he continue his service to her as of the day Scott Gibson would return from his honeymoon. He agreed, discreetly sliding the envelope into his jacket.

"Mr. Meadows, I would also like you to do something very important to me this afternoon at three o'clock, precisely. Please, take this package to the Canyon Estates and deliver it to Mr. Hidalgo Arquero, no one else. Do you understand?"

"I do. Do you have a message to deliver as well to Mr. Arquero?"

"No, just walk away. And I don't want to know anything about him."

"Miss Duval, this isn't my business. You're paying me for information, and that's fine. I'll tell you this because my wife thinks you're a nice kid. So do I. And by the way, she's not aware of any of this. Do not under any circumstance tell anyone about this information, including Gibson. After tonight this file will be the only reason the courts will issue a judgement of nullity in your favour before things go too far. You have your reasons, and that's fine. But if I were you, I would spend tonight in lock-down mode. Any corpse I've seen in my time was warmer than Gibson. I'd say there's a very fine line between him working for your father, and becoming a client. There's not a chance in hell I'd let this guy near my daughter. I'm just saying."

"That's precisely what I intend to do, Mr. Meadows."

Meadows returned the file with the tapes and photos to his briefcase. He accepted the small package and left by the side of the mansion. They would talk again soon.

18

The groom was at the church with his father and best man, enjoying cognacs with the minister in his antechamber.

The bride was at her parents' home, in her room, at the window, contemplating the limousine that had just arrived. Her mind and her heart were in the Napa Valley. If only she could have told him.

Her mother and father were downstairs, waiting anxiously. Not even Mrs. Duval had been privy to the bride's preparations. Nor did Francine have a bride's maid, all that had changed much to her mother's alarm. The girl's mother would never forgive the last minute affront and Francine had lost a friend. Both mother and daughter had removed themselves from the guest list, but with all else she'd lost what did a shallow acquaintance matter? Anyway, single friends never lasted very long after all the hype and glitter of a wedding faded into matrimonial monotony.

She'd bathed, pampered and dressed herself, her mother quite put off that she hadn't seen the wedding gown once since the first fitting. Francine had gone to the seamstress alone the night before, after her appointment alone with the hairdresser, and had carried the slim garment bag to her room without the slightest fanfare where she spent what remained of the evening doing her nails and selecting her wardrobe for her vacation.

She examined herself in the mirror, she was satisfied. She left her room feeling empty.

Her father heard her door close and went to the bottom of the stairs, his 16mm movie camera already in focus. Francine had summarily refused to have a photographer anywhere but the church. Mrs. Duval had decided to wait in the parlour until her daughter stood by her husband's side. She wanted the fullest impact of the moment that, in her mind, was fast becoming tainted by a spoiled child's selfish antics. She didn't wait long. Her husband's loud intake of air and violent gasping sounds brought her scurrying to his side.

Mr. Duval barely had time to drop his camera and grab her, preventing his wife from collapsing. His face was purple with rage, hers a portrait of shock and horror.

The bride was gorgeous, her blonde hair braided into a popular French fashion. Her eyes sparkled a liquescent green. She wore no veil. Her simple silk sheath dress was strapless, bright red and mid-thigh. She wore no stockings. Her low-heeled satin sandals were the same shade, decorated with discreet satin bows. Her only adornments were emerald earrings and a matching pendant. She was beauty personified.

Conversely, her mother was gasping for breath, her face a live mask of grief, shame, disgust and fright. She burst into unstoppable tears, begging her husband to do something, anything.

Mr. Duval ordered her to her room, to change into the proper wedding gown. What was she thinking? The family would be a laughingstock. How dare she attempt to disgrace them?

This was her gown, Francine replied without the slightest tension in her voice. She had given the other that she'd designed herself to the mission, not quite happy with her work. This was who she was, not Cinderella. Now, she asked them, were they ready or was she going alone to the church with only the chauffeur to give her away?

125

She'd seen no need for a rehearsal. She'd been to the church a thousand times, to a dozen weddings and the funerals of those dearly departed whom her father had decided would be as important to him after death as much as in life. She knew where to stand, what to say, when to turn and when to run the gauntlet of 498 faux-smiling faces. No one cared that she was getting married. The day was all about Senator Gibson and Mr. Franklin Duval of Duval & Associates.

*

The Duvals took what time they needed to compose themselves. Soon she wouldn't be their problem. Mrs. Duval went ahead of them in one limo. Francine and her father followed not long after, neither one speaking a word.

At the church Mr. Duval let the chauffeur earn his fee by helping the bride from the car, her father waiting to offer his arm until they stood at the arched doors that were the main entrance. He didn't care what the ushers might think. At that very moment he didn't care whether he lived or died as long as the day would end quickly.

Scott Gibson turned at the waist at the first resounding chord of the wedding march. She didn't know the man standing beside him, other than his name. They were whispering, staring at her, if not unabashedly ogling her.

There was no practiced march; she walked like a modern, independent lady, not a pampered doll parading in an antiquated costume. At the altar her father stepped aside and sat by his distraught wife. What must everyone be thinking!

The minister smiled, she didn't. She knew very well that he was eyeing her up and down peripherally. She looked as though she'd come from an elegant cocktail party, whereas Gibson looked as though he'd stepped off a cake. Precisely what she didn't want, what she had specifically asked him not to do. He was ridiculous, she thought, given that nine

126

hours earlier he'd been screwing the white-haired bitch.
*

Jennie Canyon gave her Latino lover space. She knew the reason for his sombre mood. She also knew she had nothing to say that wouldn't sound trite. He was nineteen. He would get over her, though she watched him through the corner of her eye. The kid had it all: good looks, smarts, humility and an air of je ne sais quoi. Exactly what, she didn't know. He was the sum total of exquisite moving parts and enviable traits that most girls could only read about in romance novels, those who could read. He never walked quickly, never slowly, always straight, but never stiff. He never ran. The way he spoke showed that he was certain, never brash or over confident. His clothes were never trendy, always Hidalgo Arquero. He didn't care what others thought. He wore leather as well as he did denim. He was his own man, not remotely like a thousand others. Once, on her birthday, he'd taken her to dinner dressed in a black suit and yellow silk tie. She'd almost lost her breath and she didn't think her father was joking when he told the young caballero to have his only daughter home by eleven. They were, without the slightest doubt, the evening's celebrities.

When he spoke English, which they seldom did together, his words flowed like melted butter. When he spoke in his native tongue his words had a musical quality, as though he were singing a quiet lullaby.

Everyone who came to the store liked him, even the men, though particularly the women. Francine Duval would pass. She had to, to make room in his life for a dozen other women who would vie for her and Maria's favourite man.

But this man wasn't smiling when he came into the store. He'd driven into the vineyard at 2:50 and hadn't stirred until a minute before three. He hadn't come to buy wine. She took him more for a scotch drinker, or bourbon. He was dressed in a suit, walked straight to her and asked in a flat yet not unfriendly tone to see Hidalgo Arquero.

Jennie Canyon pointed. She didn't ask why, or who he was. Somehow she knew. Guys like that had a presence. They stood apart. They didn't take crap and didn't answer banal questions that were no one's business.

He went to where the young man was stocking shelves. He'd been instructed by his client not to talk, and he wouldn't. He'd been sent to deliver a parcel, which didn't mean he couldn't have an opinion. Scott Gibson was trash. This kid was everything that Gibson was not. What had Francine Duval been thinking?

Meadows didn't speak Spanish.

"Mr. Arquero, I've been asked to deliver this package to you, precisely at this time."

Hidalgo took the package. "This is from…"

"Suffice it to say, until you see what's inside, from a very unhappy young woman."

"Señor, please, did she give you a message for me? Please tell me that she did."

"She did not, which doesn't mean there isn't one."

"What do you mean?"

"I mean that at times like this I wish I were a car salesman. She's not doing the right thing, kid. Or maybe she is and I don't have all the facts. Either way, she's one unhappy little girl."

Hidalgo glanced at his watch. "Am I wrong to think that right now…?"

"My advice, don't think. Just open the box."

Meadows turned and walked to the door, acknowledging Jennie with a genteel Southern tilt of his head. This was one of the times he wondered why he didn't drink more, not that Virginia would let him.

*

"And do you, Francine Elizabeth Duval take this man, Scott Ellery Gibson, to be your lawfully wedded husband till death shall you part?"

"I do."

"And would you now declare by the vows written by you, your everlasting love?"

"No, Reverend, I would not. This man, who stands by my side, knows the extent of my love for him, a love that I know we share equally in our hearts and in our minds. What is in my heart cannot be spoken or declared to those who do not comprehend or do not feel the depth of my true love. My words, composed last night from deep in my heart, with all my love and all my devotion, he will read with his own eyes. And he will know that I truly love him.

*

Jennie walked slowly. He saw her coming. This wasn't a time for warm endearments, tender words meant to console a broken heart, empty words that would make the pain that much worse.

She hugged him, told him to go home and not to do anything stupid. She loved him too much to lose him. They all did.

His eyes were glassy, though nothing else about him had changed. He was a true caballero, the best, Francine Duval-Gibson's loss. Jennie changed her mind instantly. He wasn't going home, not until she could drive him. Instead she pushed him gently towards the empty reception room where, once inside, alone, he remained standing.

He tore away the ribbon, then the wrapping, staring at the folded paper and black velvet box. He couldn't read what she'd written, not then. He opened the tiny box. Inside was an emerald ring set in silver. He'd never seen a ring as beautiful, never a green as deep or as mesmerizing. Peering into its glitter was to see into her eyes, to see the depths of her pain. The inscription was simple: Zorro.

He unfolded the letter, not wanting to, not wanting to breathe or to see another day. Yet she would expect more of

him.
*

Hidalgo, mi corazón, cómo te amo tanto. Do not believe for a moment what your heart tells you. Our hearts often deceive us when we feel weak.

And when you sleep alone in your bed tonight, know that I am alone in mine thinking of you.

Remember instead what you know is true.

Remember the tears you kissed from my green eyes.

Wear this ring for me as long as you can, until you meet another.

Mine reads: Maya Princess. And you must believe how your Maya princess loves you, how she misses you. We have known each other for so short a time, but for how many heart beats?

Francine.
*

"You may kiss the bride."

Scott Gibson beamed twin rows of perfect teeth, penetrating the green eyes of his virgin bride. He cupped her face, closed his eyes and…kissed her cheek. His blushing bride smiled demurely. She was unaccustomed to performing on cue, displaying her love and affection in public. The audience, congregation, friends, or whatever they were to her, applauded. The bride was lovely, innocent, as yet untouched, albeit inappropriately attired, as though she could give a beggar's damn. They could all go to hell.
*

Hidalgo slipped the ring onto his finger. His mind was numb. How could she marry a man she did not love, a man who would never love her? How could she not sleep with her husband, and what of the honeymoon and their new home? She was so young and naïve. And she was lost to him. The ring, he was certain, would be a constant torment, a cruel reminder of a dark night still fresh in his mind, a star-filled sky, her warmth and soft whimpers.

At that moment all he longed for was the dusty streets of Pichilingue, where once he knew no pain, where once he knew not to dream. How would he face his mother and his father? How could he walk out and face Jennie and Señor Canyon? They all knew.

He scanned the room, at the low table and six seats where he sat teasing her four weeks earlier, where she sat wanting to believe that she hated him. How would he ever again go to the ocean and not remember her warmth, her body, her sweet breath? He studied the ring. Señor Canyon was right. At that very moment he knew that his life would be filled with heartache and grief.

*

At the reception very few of the guests noticed the bride, other than those seated closest to the head table. She did what she had to do, her way. She stood and sat on cue, to the tapping of silver spoons against the rims of expensive crystal goblets, each time bashfully depriving him of her lips until out-dated clinking gave way to the one thing she couldn't avoid: the first waltz.

She did, and she got through the ordeal. Then she danced with her father, Senator Gibson and the best man whom she knew nothing about. Nor did she care to. Nor did she escape to her hotel room with the groom to change from formal to casual when Gibson did.

Most of the guests were gone by ten. Her parents and the Gibsons departed at eleven. A few minutes later Francine left the hall with her husband. Those who remained either didn't know or didn't care. At the fifteenth floor she held the elevator door open. She told him to go ahead. She had a last minute surprise and would see him in a few minutes. She wouldn't be long, she promised.

He waited alone in the room until midnight when she rapped her knuckles abruptly once against the door. He stepped back and gawked. Her hair was combed out, her make-up was fresh and she was dressed in jeans, a sweatshirt and boots with a designer handbag draped over her shoulders. She was leaving. Her plane was scheduled to depart at 6:00 AM and the bellhop had already taken her luggage to the lobby. Something he didn't yet know.

"Finally, so where's the big surprise, apart from the fact you're dressed more for a rodeo than a nervous bride on her wedding night? And while I'm asking questions, where did you change and where the hell's your luggage? I called down to the desk and all I got from them was bullshit. The jerk made it sound as though you have your own room."

She said, "I do, and my luggage is downstairs because I'm checking out. But the surprise I promised you is the annulment of this ridiculous sham of a wedding that's coming your way in three weeks."

He thought he hadn't heard right. "What?"

"I'm filing for an annulment as soon as I return from vacation. I still have a few things to work out. However, what I do know is that you're history. I want you as a husband as much as you want me for a wife. This whole thing was a charade because your father wants votes and you want a job you couldn't otherwise dream of because you're not all that bright when your father's money can't buy good grades. And my father's no better. He wants certain perquisites that come from knowing a well-placed senator as much as you want something squeaky clean that you can be the first to screw, label, and call your own. Guess again."

He burst into a raucous laugh. "You're not serious. Or is this why you came to your own wedding dressed like a high-priced whore? And by the way, I've kissed warmer ice packs."

"You kiss whores, like the one you were kissing and screwing last night and this morning in my new home. How high-priced was she, or was she putting out again for an all-dressed pizza or the promise of that once-in-lifetime job she'll never get?"

"What are you talking about? I was at my parents' getting ready for you."

She slid a hand into a pocket to retrieve the ring, eyeing the over-sized diamond as though it were a cheap curio she'd found by chance.

"Bullshit. You were fucking her brains out and I've got the tapes to prove that you were." She smirked, flicking the ring into the air for him to catch. "Maybe she'll want that. I prefer emeralds. I am curious though, what exactly did you do to her to make her yelp that way?"

"You're drunk. What tapes? You don't know what you're talking about."

"Yeah, I do. This is where you go your way and I go mine, Scottie."

"You're out of your mind. We're leaving for Tahiti at noon. Get real. The Ice Queen act was pretty cute for the audience, but this is ridiculous. We're married. Get undressed, now, like you're supposed to. This is your frigging wedding night."

She snorted. "I don't think so. I'm not into sloppy seconds and, yes, you are leaving for Tahiti…alone. I'm going somewhere else."

"This is bullshit," he snorted. "Where could you possibly go on your own without getting lost?"

"Not your business, and when I get back we're getting that annulment. So here's the thing, Scottie." She paused, smirking. "That is what she calls you, isn't it, when you're screwing her in what was supposed to be my bed? Or am I wrong? How many times did you do her in my bed?"

"What are you…?"

"Don't even think to bullshit me. I know all about her, the one with the white hair. I know when she left and I know how she left. I know everything about her. Could that dress have been any shorter? Did she even have to take it off before you screwed her? Or didn't she bother wearing anything underneath? And does she always scream like that, Scottie? You know, from what I heard, you're not that good. She must want something pretty badly to play it that real."

"You're crazy. We're married."

"I've got photographs of her, and you. I've been in the house. I've seen the wine bottles and her girlie leftovers. So why don't you shut your mouth. I also have pictures of the maids leaving this morning. How often did they come in to clean up after Caligula of California? Don't know? Don't worry. The question was rhetorical. I'll have those details added to my Scott Gibson file by the time I get back."

He blew a long breath through pursed lips. "Okay, okay, I admit it. She was a final fling, Francine. It's over. Now I've got you. So let's stop all this. Get undressed. This is behind us now. If you do have tickets to somewhere else, we'll cancel them in the morning. We should be thinking about other things, not arguing about a nothing fling. Shit, I don't even remember her name."

"Her name is Lucinda, and she's dumb, very dumb. I'm pretty sure she'll make a living on her back long before she has a career in court and you're the one that's cancelled."

"Get undressed Francine. I won't ask again. You're my wife for Christ's sake. Do what you're supposed to do. I've got rights."

"Go get another whore. Stop me from leaving and you won't work another day in the State of California or anywhere else in the Southwest. Remember who I am and who you work for... so far. Without me you're dead in the water, so is your old man. In case you don't know, the Duvals trump the Gibsons. That LL.M you're working on won't land you a secretarial job without me."

"My father's a senator. Think I'm worried?"

"Think I care. Front page, read all about it. Senator's son arrested for rape on wedding night." She went to the mini-bar. She took out two miniature vodkas and sprinkled the minute amounts into a single glass. "Something else, husband. We're moving. I won't spend another minute in that whorehouse. The short time I spent there last week was long enough. So when your honeymoon's over in three weeks it's going on the market and we'll split the profit or the loss fifty-fifty. We're accepting the first offer. There's no way I'm living between the two of them, or with you, playing the loving wife trapped behind a picket fence. Really, how long did you think that was going to last? I don't need their money, and I don't need you. I've bought my own home in Vallejo and put a deposit on an apartment in Santa Rosa for you. You'll be happy to know it's a one-bedroom loft with an ocean view, big enough for a big-time bachelor lawyer and concrete, which means she can scream all she wants. Furthermore, and more importantly, the place is way too small for entertaining our parents together. For that you owe me five grand and I want it in cash. Granted, for the next few years we will have to play the happy couple, and we will because it suits me, just very separately and not wedged between them. I think twice a year should do. You'll be busy enough keeping rich scum out of jail or impressing more titanium bimbos with your corporate Mercedes and expense account. How unfortunate you'll never get them into the club. And I'll be too busy studying. Twice a year, which is about all I can stomach. Not a bad deal. Besides that I don't want you anywhere near me. And when the time is right, five maybe six years from now, I'll make it known that I'm divorcing you on grounds of incompatibility. That way you keep your job and I don't have to live a lie with a pig. You also get to keep 250 wedding gifts, which should keep you busy for a while. Have fun with that one."

"Divorce me in six years, after your old man made a big deal at the wedding about Duval & Gibson in ten years. Are you insane? That's not going to happen. We're married and we're staying married. Period, get used to it. And there's not a fucking chance in hell that I'm driving from Santa Rosa to the bridge every day. Anyway you're forgetting your parents…and mine. They want us close, in Oakland, in case you forgot. You remember, a little something about grandchildren, Sunday dinner and family vacations. They won't stand for us moving away."

"Be a man, which brings us back to the grounds for the annulment. Exactly when and how was that little something supposed to happen, an immaculate conception, perhaps a cosy visit from your best man while you, what, sit there and watch us? Is that what made you so popular with the girls, that you were sterile, shooting blanks?" She drained the glass. "Yeah, I've got your full medical history. I know. And how were you going to break that news to your parents? I also know about your grade point average and what goes on in that egocentric head of yours. Tell me, was it all about the number of touchdowns you scored, or was your father really stupid enough to believe you were actually worth all that money?" She put down the glass. "We're done."

"You bitch!" The impact of his open hand sent her tumbling backward. "Aren't you forgetting something, those words you composed last night from so deep in your heart, with all your love and devotion?"

"They weren't for you." She put an open palm to her cheek.

"Nice ring. His?"

"Yes… his."

"You frigging bitch."

"Yeah, I heard. You are a big man. Aren't you? Good thing for me you punch like a girl." Francine took a moment to catch her breath; she'd never been struck in the face.

"I'm leaving. I'll see you in three weeks. Bring a notepad to the diner across the street. You'll need it. In the meantime enjoy Tahiti. Just think how lucky you are. How often does a groom get to fuck around on his honeymoon? Play smart and you'll do well. Be stupid about it and you're screwed. I'll make certain you are. Don't doubt me for a minute." She rubbed her cheek. "And I won't forget this anytime soon. The wedding was your first mistake, this was your second."

"Francine, I'm sorry. I'll make it up to you. This is all so new to me. I'm not like this."

"You're not sorry. And how would you make up for punching a girl in the face? You're too pathetic. Just remember this; there is one thing that I am that you can never be."

"Like what?"

"Like daddy's little girl, and that never changes. Hit me once more and you are totally fucked."

He sprinted towards her, his hands outstretched. "Francine, this isn't happening. I'm telling you, it's nerves. I promise, never again. I've waited years for this day, so have you. Don't tell me you're not scared."

She pushed him away, standing on her own. "No, I'm not. And you've waited four years only to suck up to my father. How long that lasts depends on me, not you. You got what you really wanted out of this and I did what I had to do for my own purposes. And you weren't one of them. So enjoy your honeymoon, and I want that five grand when we meet across the street the day after you get back." She grinned. "Shall we say noonish, before we meet the agent and the lawyer?"

He coughed a gasp. "That's it. You're telling me my wedding night's over in five minutes? Done?"

She looked at her watch. "Four minutes, thirty seconds. Not bad. That's got to be a record for a man beating his wife."

She turned on her heels and walked out.

19

When Hidalgo Arquero woke that Sunday morning, of two things he was certain. He would never see her again. Nor would he ever stop loving her. Of that he was the most certain.

His bank account was beginning to burgeon. Not one person his age in Pichilingue could hope to become as wealthy in a lifetime. He was truly blessed. And he knew what he must do.

At the breakfast table, he knew there would be no better time to make the announcement. The night before, sulking in his room, his mood sombre with no appetite for Maria's usual Saturday night feast, he'd come to a decision after his mother had twice knocked at his door wanting to feed him and console him. Francine Duval was now a married woman, while he was still living with his parents down the hall from their bedroom.

"Mamá, I am too old for you to come to my room to see whether I am well and to feed me like a child. I am no longer a boy. And papá," he continued, "with a woman as lovely and as young as my mother, I know I am cramping your style, hombre." He forced a wicked smile, winking, his sadness showing through. "You do not have her to yourself often enough. Always I am in your way, sharing her. And this must stop."

"Fernando, your son is about to say something I will not like. Stop him from upsetting me."

"No, mamá, I will not. Yes, I am leaving your home. This I have decided on my own, yet not so far that I cannot delight in your fine meals many nights each week. However I will phone first, before I come, so that I will not disturb you or hear papá speak those words you do not like."

Maria smacked then rubbed his cheek. "You will remain where you are, in my home, and your father does not require help from his son in such matters. Fernando, say something."

"He is right, Maria. Sadly, this boy often ruins what in my mind I know will soothe your young woman's insatiable heart. He is right. He must go, and he must go quickly."

Her mouth snapped open wide. "You encourage each other. I will not hear such words in my home."

Hidalgo's hearty laugh was real. "What papá says is true, which is why I must go, mamá, before your husband grows too old and frail to speak the words to your insatiable heart that I am too young to hear."

Fernando punched his son's shoulder. "Niño, the boy is not yet better than the man." He looked to his wife, not certain, in a way only mothers and fathers know. "We should hear the boy, mi querida. Should he not practice independence for when he is a famous lawyer and soon forgets his humble beginnings?"

"I have no interest in hearing such silliness, mi quer-i-do, ¿Comprendes lo que digo, mi marido?"

Fernando wore a shroud of defeat familiar to most married men: a simple matter of defence when the enemy's strength was greater. Yet his son was no longer a boy.

"No, I do not understand a mother's love. How could I? What I understand is that my son has become a man before our eyes. In Pichilingue he would now be married with two small mouths feeding from his woman's breasts. Maria, listen to your son. See how he is. Is this a man who wants to hurt his mother, the same man who carried your heavy

140

burden as a boy from Pichilingue to La Paz? We must listen to what he will tell us."

They did. The plan was simple, and wise, which didn't stop Maria from ignoring them until breakfast the following morning when she surpassed her usual Latina culinary expertise and waited for the appropriate and well-deserved accolades before relenting and almost forgiving them. Yes, Hidalgo could move out if that is what he truly wanted. She was only his mother. Of course she didn't matter. Why would she? What did a loving mother matter to anyone?

Both men knew not to interrupt, move or breathe.

Hidalgo might be a man, she conceded, but he was her son and would always be her boy, one who currently knew nothing of survival in the kitchen or in the laundry room. There was more to living than washing a fancy car and wearing handsome clothes washed and ironed each week by a mother who mattered very little in their conspiracy against her. At least she was needed for something.

As for Fernando's fate, that was a different matter entirely. He knew all too well that his son was too young despite his search for independence to fully understand the intricacies of the female mind. Mending Maria's broken heart would require several nights of effusive and servile attention. And that his son saw even the slightest humour in his predicament was a mystery to him.

When breakfast was over Hidalgo went to his mother who stood at the sink washing dishes, humming. Not a good sign, Fernando knew. He turned her by the shoulders, guiding her reluctant eyes toward his with a finger pressed gently to her chin. He asked her to smile. She didn't. He asked her again, and she tried not to. When she ignored his third request he swept her feet from the floor and held her in his arms until she did.

When Fernando stood and went to her with open arms, beaming a white smile with his new front teeth, she snubbed him with raised eyebrows and a sneer before returning to her dishes. At least she was now singing. That was good.

The work began later that week and would last a month. The loft over the garage would be his home away from home, separated from the house so that he might enjoy his independence, his private place to eat, sleep and study, his hideaway where he could be alone to remember her, create in his mind images of what might have been, to one day forget her because to remember her meant sharing her with another.
*

Francine arrived in La Paz late Sunday. She was elated. She was going to discover another part of Hidalgo. Monday she equipped herself with water, a sandwich from the hotel kitchen, a map, and set out on foot to Pichilingue wearing thin sandals and not her comfortable boots that she'd buried in her knapsack. She wanted to feel what he felt that first day of his journey towards a new life, towards her. How afraid and uncertain he must have been as such a young boy on his way to a strange new world.

She'd never seen such a barren countryside; the soil baked to a chalky white, the few plants and shrubs a lifeless shade of green. She'd never seen such an unceasing and blinding sun. She'd never felt such dry heat, suffocating, making her breathing difficult, her throat and chest burn and her skin prickle, rising from the ground and through the thin leather of her sandals to burn her feet. She'd never felt so weary or depleted, stopping often to kick or finger small pebbles from between her feet and the brittle leather soles.

She knew where to find the house and when she arrived she sank onto the dried and cracked earth in the shade, against the stucco wall of a dilapidated structure across the deserted street from a humble home she could never have imagined had she ever tried.

Her back ached, her feet were swollen and bleeding, thin white blisters rubbing between her toes and at her heels. She drank what was left of her water greedily, staring blankly for what must have been an hour, alone.

No dogs were barking; no cats curled into a ball against the midday sun. The air was rippled with oppressive heat. No children were playing. She heard not a single sound. She glanced at her watch. What had taken Hidalgo and his parents four hours to walk had taken her six.

She wanted to knock on the door, afraid. She wanted to see inside, to see the floors and the walls, and yet she was afraid of what she would see, or would not see.

Hidalgo had travelled to a foreign country and mastered a foreign language. Now she was afraid to simply knock on the door to his past, the reason she'd come all this way, to learn as much about him as she could, to understand him the way someone who loves him with all her heart should. She pushed herself to her feet and crossed the street, scolding herself.

The woman who answered the door shocked her. She was neither young nor old. She was short with bowed legs and seemed much fatter than she was because of her billowy peasant dress and the full apron she was wearing whose pockets were overflowing with wooden spoons and dish rags. The single tooth at the front of her concaved mouth was chipped and yellowed, framed by thin purple lips. Her wrinkled skin was sun-baked without the sheen of a natural glow and her eyes that had probably once been black were cloudy and grey.

She knew of the Arqueros and could not disguise that she was instantly worried. Francine remembered how Hidalgo had described his family's departure, cloaked by the darkness of early morning, and that his father had wanted no one to see them leave. She could see by the woman's condition that she wouldn't want to hear of the family's comfortable new life in California. Instead she explained that she'd met young Hidalgo and his parents while travelling on vacation in northern Mexico a few years earlier and that she'd promised to one day visit them in Pichilingue. She didn't realize the family had moved on. She was sorry for the intrusion and disappointed in not seeing them. The woman wasn't interested. She wanted to know whether Fernando and Maria were returning to take away her home. She had been living there for almost four years and didn't want to move. She had nowhere else to go.

Francine assured her that if the family hadn't returned in four years, they never would. They were probably content to remain in the north. She remembered that they seemed very happy there. But, since she had come so far, could she please see where Hidalgo had once lived?

The woman shrugged. Why not? What could the harm be, if first she could have twenty American dollars?

Francine immediately wished she hadn't stepped from the sun's scorching heat into Hidalgo's past. The entire place was the size of her bedroom in her parents' home, with two slatted doors besides the one she passed through. She opened both. The first was the woman's bedroom that was small and dark. The smell throughout was heavy and unpleasant; the air filled with a blend of pungent spices and the dankness of wet clothes strung across what she supposed was a living area, the floor littered with half-woven blankets and half-painted pieces of pottery. And true to what Hidalgo had told her, she saw the thin sleeping mat still on the crude wooden frame in the corner close to the floor where the woman's eldest son slept unaware of them, or uninterested.

The second door led to an outhouse, no different than a dozen others she saw dotting the rear alley. She opened that door and wished she hadn't. To one side were a mop and a broom, on the other hung a scrub board and wash bucket for washing their clothes, which once each week Hidalgo would fill for his mother to bathe in the kitchen while he waited outside until she was finished and he could refill the tub for his bath.

She thanked the woman and hurried out with directions to the bus stop. She'd seen enough. She wanted to cry, fighting the urge. What right did she have? She had three weeks to kill, a lifetime, when even in Spain she hadn't been alone for three days. Then she chuckled out loud, remembering her grandmothers confiding in her at the wedding, once they'd stolen her away for a few precious moments to themselves, that neither one liked Scott Gibson very much, both their mouths agape when Francine declared in a whisper that neither did she. But that she did have a very secret and handsome lover. What she didn't say was that in just a few weeks she would be single again and free to live her life.

So why wasn't she going home to Vallejo where she had so much to do? She would be free of Gibson very soon and, more importantly, she had kept her promise to Hidalgo. She would return to him pure in body and soul.

20

Each evening after work Hidalgo met with the builder, anxious for the day he would invite his mother and father to his new home, each day Maria softening a little bit more to the idea of her only son moving out. Until the day the washer, dryer, fridge and stove arrived. Fernando and Hidalgo hadn't told her about that detail and neither man escaped unscathed. The air that night over Vallejo was somewhat tinged with the frosty blue of an arctic ice field.

Be that as it may, by the July 04th weekend her son was moving out and the 100-foot trek across the lawn was longer and more painful for Maria than her march from Pichilingue to La Paz, Hidalgo several times expressing heartfelt regret to his father for the suffering the older man would inevitably cope with that evening because of a selfish son. Once again Fernando failed to see the humour in his son's lament that was noticeably lacking in sincerity.

Maria felt out of place sitting in his small living room while her son prepared dinner, even more so when he refused to let her clear the table and do the dishes, while Fernando tipped a bottle of wine into her glass a few extra times in the hopes of a more peaceful night. He also insisted that, if his son was not in the house for breakfast, he would come for Hidalgo himself and carry the boy down the stairs and across the yard bouncing across his shoulders.

Hidalgo walked through their unlocked door at seven, squeezed his mother as always, lightly kissed her lips and sat by his father, asking with a smirk how their evening ended, if they had slept well after their visit to his new home. Maria laid down her spatula. She went to her son, smacked his cheek, smiled and winked at Fernando, and returned to her stove.

Hidalgo wasn't working that Tuesday. He had a 10:00 AM meeting with the Assistant Dean at Golden Gate to arrange necessary curriculum changes to his upcoming school year.

*

By month's end Francine's new home was in order. The walls were painted, the furniture was in, the front and back lawns were laid, the landscaping was complete and the safe was installed where she now kept certain personal files and tapes. She'd read each file thoroughly and listened to each tape until she felt sick, wondering what unfortunate woman would one day marry such a contemptible man. Or would his true personality one day begin to show through his thin veneer?

As planned, she met with Scott Gibson on the Sunday afternoon at the diner to discuss strategy, get her five grand in cash and give him the shock of his life. She didn't care about his tan or what he'd done. She knew perfectly well what he was doing throughout his honeymoon.

"I'm pregnant."

"So little Miss Duval isn't that pure and innocent after all...or was it immaculate?"

"You'll never know. That said, this does change things."

"Meaning what?"

"Meaning, don't be stupid. You can hide your bimbos and one-nighters. A baby, that's something a little more difficult to cover up."

"Get a cross border abortion. They're a dime a dozen in Tijuana." He chortled. "Get a tattoo at the same time. I'm thinking 'Bitch' would be a good one."

"That won't happen. What will happen in another month or so is that I'll make the big announcement and you're going to be the man of the hour. Wow, another Gibson in the world, yippee. Won't mommy and daddy be so proud of their potent son for getting things done so soon?" She beamed. "Only he or she will be christened Duval...and speak Spanish."

"You screwed a spic. No shit." He took a moment, as though he didn't believe her. "That pretty much makes you a whore in anyone's book, and you have the nerve to talk about me. At least I stay with my own kind. Who was it, the guy with the ring?"

"He makes you look like something that crawls."

"When did he get lucky? Or, better yet, when did he do you once too often?"

"You'll find out soon enough, with our parents."

"What colour is this thing going to be?"

"I suppose he or she will be born with a non-Gibson Latino glow. I hope so."

"If I had a gun in my hand right now, putting a bullet in your head would be really easy." He snorted. "A new groom finding out that his bride spent her honeymoon banging the hired help. With the right Democrat judge on the bench, if anything, I'd be out in a few months with a slap on the wrist. So I wouldn't push too far."

"Thank you for saying so. You've just admitted on tape to wanting to kill me, and that your father's crooked. Isn't that a big surprise? And let's not talk about whores unless we're talking about your mother. The difference between her and me, I love the father of my child. So, yeah, I'm filing for that annulment and you're not contesting unless you want me to add threats of violence to your lying, cheating and infertility. Guys like you should be stamped on the forehead."

He ignored her. "Our parents would never go along

with this."

"With what?"

"Christening it as a Duval."

"They're not invited. Neither are you. My child, my choice of names. The father wouldn't like you, and you know what they say about the Latin temper. How did you refer to him a few minutes ago? Remember, after today we're not married. The paperwork won't take long to process. As far as your parents go, I couldn't be less interested in what they think. As for mine, I'm less interested each day. They did this to me, meaning you. They should have known you were a prick, which means they either didn't do their due diligence or they didn't care. Which is worse? Either way, they swapped me for personal gain, and you're no better." She put aside her coffee and opened her purse. "So, first the five grand, followed by the For Sale sign and the annulment, after which I'm going home. You're on your own for the apartment."

"Yeah, about that, I don't think so. You're insane if you think I'm commuting from Santa Rosa to the bridge every day. In case you forget, I'm still in my LL.M. We're keeping the house, so get used to it. Do what you have to do."

"Okay, you keep it. Explain to my father, after I invite him to dinner next Sunday, why I'm not there." She waited. "Good. We understand each other. What's another eighty miles a day to see your name in lights one day? So be smart and do what you're told for the next six years."

"Ten years, remember?" He ran the fingers of both hands through his hair, wanting to choke her. He passed her the envelope. "Ten years, that's the deal."

"Six years, and we'll meet for a review."

Francine counted the fifty new bills and stood. He asked for her address, she told him to wait for next year's phone directory. He asked for her phone number and she refused.

When and if she needed to talk with him, she would leave a message at Duval & Associates. She would also be contacting her mother to make very clear that the newlyweds had no intention of doing the weekly church thing or Sunday dinners. They would develop their own social circle over time; create their own social commitments with people their age. And neither set of in-laws should expect to visit the new apartment without an invitation. Ground rules: 101. And he was free to screw as many white-haired bimbos as he wanted.

Claire and Arthur Gibson were his problem. As far as the house was concerned, he could say whatever he wanted. From her perspective, she didn't like the neighbourhood.

His eyes were a window to his soul. He wanted nothing more than to pommel her, strangle her with his bare hands. A good enough reason, she thought, to have chosen a public venue.

The house she never liked was on the market an hour later. An hour after that their annulment was in the works without the slightest contest on his part. He just wanted to get away from the lawyer's office; certain Francine had chosen a woman to intentionally humiliate him. She was the only other person in the world who knew he was a sterile liar, the only other person in the world with a copy of his medical record and a comprehensive sense of his mental health.

What he wanted more than seeing her dead, more than anything, was a drink, several drinks. He would discover soon enough where she lived and who the Mexican was.

21

Francine knew what she was doing. Not only was her son being born, she was being reborn in a purely familial sense.

Remarkably her parents had never become an issue, as though they were quite relieved that their envisioned family relations had been arbitrarily reduced. As for the pregnancy, neither Claire Gibson nor Mrs. Duval were gifted mothers. Of course they were delighted to the extent that Scott would have a son, as opposed to them acquiring a grandson, quite pleased that Scott and Francine had opted for a nanny, though quite perplexed as to how the couple could possibly survive in such a small apartment. Indeed, they could not.

By springtime Scott would have to acquire a larger apartment for appearance sake, Francine told him, unless he relished the prospect of confessing his way out of a job.

By Christmas she was seven months along and called Canyon Estates, placing an order for delivery at the end of business the next day, hoping her address and the proximity to Hidalgo's home wouldn't go unnoticed. The order was substantial, the best wine, which she knew would be handled with priority care: Twelve cases that would fit nicely into a Mustang convertible.

Two days before Christmas her doorbell rang. She had spent the entire morning bathing, doing her make-up, combing her hair, crying, laughing, talking to her unborn baby, dressing and undressing until she was pleased with her outfit.

She was terrified, her eyes blurred to blindness as she opened the door. Hearing the car's engine, she'd squeezed drops into them, to dry her tears, succeeding in making them worse. He stood dumbly, saying nothing, seeing her hugely rounded belly, imagining all the wrong things, she knew. Her lips were quivering. Why wasn't he saying anything?

When he could finally speak he wanted to smack himself: "Buenos días, Francine. How happy I am to see you once again. I believed you were living in Oakland. Never did I believe you were so close."

"Hola, Hidalgo. No, I live here now. I have for some time. Come in."

He didn't know what else to say, where to begin.

"Where should I put the boxes, Francine?"

"In the pantry by the kitchen," she replied. "I don't have a real cellar. And could you please place them for me, any way you wish? I'm not supposed to lift anything."

He nodded, graciously. From the car to the doorway, and from there to the pantry, he carried the twelve cases without saying a word as she watched his every move. When he was done stocking the modest cellar he faced her, wanting to stay, to kiss every part of her, to kiss her wet eyes, to leave, to run, to forget he'd ever seen her that way.

"Your eyes are so red, Francine. Why are you crying? What can I do for you?"

"It is nothing, Hidalgo. Before you came I had a spasm. That is all."

"Then I will wish you Merry Christmas, Francine. Congratulations on your baby. Jennie will be truly happy to hear of this joyous news, to know that you will soon have a child. I will call her tonight to tell her." He paused. He was on foreign ground. "May I ask......?"

"It's a boy, Hidalgo, a healthy boy. I know he will grow to be strong and brave like his father. He will have his father's name, Hidalgo, so that he will never forget who he is."

The stab to his heart could not have been deeper or more searing. "Sí, claro. It is right that you do so. His father will be very proud to be presented with such a son by a mother as lovely as you, Francine."

She wanted so badly to force even the weakest smile, unable to. "His father doesn't know yet, or that his son's name will be," she gulped, "Diego Hidalgo Arquero-Duval."

The earth stood still.

"¡No es possible! This baby, he is mine?"

She nodded excitedly. "Así es, if you want him. If you do not, I will understand." She wiped her face. "Perhaps you should have a glass of wine, Hidalgo, unless you must go. I know Christmas is important to you. I will understand if you have someone waiting for you, maybe a girlfriend you're taking to a party."

She searched his hands for an emerald ring. He hadn't forgotten her.

"Yes, I will have a glass of wine, a big one I think. And no one is waiting for me, but your husband will soon be home. No?"

"No, Hidalgo. I have no husband. Did you not believe what I wrote to you in my letter, Hidalgo? I left him the night of the wedding, while others were dancing." She held out her left hand, the emerald glittered. "I told you, Zorro, I am your Maya Princess. Hidalgo, the very next day I went to Pichilingue by myself … to see for myself. I wanted to know everything about you. I walked to your home from La Paz so I could know what you felt. It was horrible. And when I came home, to this place, I ended the marriage permanently. Officially I was never married. This is my home, Hidalgo; no one else has ever been here, except you tonight. No other man has ever touched me but you. Te lo juro. This child is yours."

He brought his ring to his lips, kissing the green stone.

"Not an hour has passed that I have not stared into my beautiful ring to remember your beautiful green eyes, to imagine your soft lips pressed against mine. Why did you do these things, Francine? I should be your husband. This is my son...our son."

"Because my father and the senator are dangerous men, because they had a plan and men like them don't like their plans being compromised, not by anyone." She patted her belly. "And we did a pretty good job of that, hombre."

He wrapped his arms around her. "Each night my heart has been sick to think that I would never see you again. When I saw you at the door, I believed my heart would explode and that I would truly never see you again."

"Can you stay with me tonight, Hidalgo? Would you stay with me tonight?" She giggled, cupping her belly "I'm not the sexiest girl in town, though I'm pretty sure we can work something out."

"How can you think that I would leave you? I have so much to tell you, and to hear. I will stay, and I will prepare a fine feast for us. I now live alone and I am becoming an excellent cocinero, although my mother does not...¡Ay!"

He grabbed his head, to help contain the shockwave.

She switched to English. "She won't like me, will she, your mother? She'll hate me, won't she?"

"My mother will love you. It is me she will kill many times for what I have done to you, for keeping her from you since our first night. I'm sorry, Francine. By tomorrow I will be dead. I am sorry."

"I think you'd better call her...after a glass of wine."
*

Hidalgo didn't sip or savour his wine; he gulped the first mouthful and swallowed what remained with equal finesse.

He first spoke with his father, explaining that he was

154

spending the night with…a very special lady, but that he couldn't say more. With Fernando's permission, he would invite the young lady to spend Christmas in his father's home. The air was still for a moment, Francine's heart pounding the loudest, wondering why Hidalgo wasn't saying anything, why he seemed so dejected. Then he nodded, and asked whether he could please speak with his mother. Francine was on the verge of tears, afraid to say a word.

That conversation with Maria seemed to go on forever, Francine imagining the pointed questions to Hidalgo's careful yet truthful replies. Finally, would his mother allow him to bring a guest for the weekend, a young and beautiful girl? Francine stopped breathing. Yes, he said, nodding his head, he did understand.

When the conversation ended he gulped another glass of wine, apologizing silently for his lack of subtlety to Jennie Canyon who had taught him so much about finesse and decorum, apparently for naught. Both parents had refused his visit with the girl, he explained. And both had used the same excuse: they had no room. Yet Francine knew very well that they did have room. What she couldn't understand was why Hidalgo was smiling so sheepishly, not in the least upset, albeit not quite over the anxiety of the conversations or the sight of her rounded belly.

When she asked him, he replied, "No te preocupes, mi corazón. We will find another place to stay, somewhere where they will take us in and love you very much."

She wasn't consoled. She was worried and she wanted to punch him, but how could she hurt him after she'd just found him? And what other place was he talking about when she already had a nice home? He loved his parents, she knew. He would never think of spending Christmas away from them. Perhaps, she tried; they could come to their home. The Arquero home wasn't ten minutes away.

He should call them, to invite them for Christmas dinner.

"Don't worry, mi corazón, this will be your best Nochebuena ever. I promise. You will see that what I say is true."

Francine soon forgot Christmas, anxious to hear about everything Hidalgo had done over the past seven months.

For dinner he made the best Mexican pizza she'd ever tasted, the only Mexican pizza she'd ever tasted. They talked and they listened, they talked more and went to bed where they talked and made tentative love, neither one certain. They fell asleep resisting, murmuring, and woke Christmas Eve morning to a new life, this time Francine wanting to talk and she needed Hidalgo to listen carefully.

She was wealthy in her own right; the house had barely put a dent in her portfolio. He would stay in school and, yes, he would continue to work at the Estates. She understood that, but she expected him to be important one day. That was his single priority; he and their son would be hers. She would return to school when the time was right. She wanted a career in teaching. But first he would attend law school, so that one day Diego Hidalgo would be proud of his father. By then Diego would be ready for school, as would she.

As for the other matter, her family was all about money, society, nannies, chauffeurs, limousines, being seen, being envied, and never being needlessly inconvenienced by errant daughters or children. Children best belonged in nurseries, preschool, private school away from home, prep schools or on extended trips abroad when having an extra body at home became intrusive. Such was their way of life, adhered to by all parties. Twice each year for a just a couple of hours, she promised, not a day or minute more.

That was her commitment, and she would marry him anytime he wanted. But he had to understand that, without his commitment to her, she could never marry him. And she would not. She would never endanger him or his future that way.

Hidalgo knew enough about feminine resolve and combativeness by studying his father not to surrender at the first sign of defeat, rather to placate them by appearing to accept their terms and conditions as logical and pragmatic. Although of greater importance, paramount importance, was the element of surprise, the need to escape unscathed, which Hidalgo did.

He tapped his Cartier watch. His parents would be expecting them.

*

On the way Hidalgo explained Posada. As homeless travellers, pilgrims searching for a warm place to stay for the night, they were denied twice, however this place, the third inn at which they have called, will take them in with warm hearts. She wasn't to worry. And they were not to exchange gifts. That would come later, on the sixth of January. Instead they would eat, drink and dance. They would attend la Misa de Nochebuena at midnight where he would thank God for blessing him with such loving parents, a beautiful girl who would soon be his wife, and his son. Nor had he once since coming to America omitted John Canyon or Jennie from his Christmas prayers.

When they arrived Hidalgo knew better than to sneak quietly into his loft. His mother had ears like navy sonar. There was no avoiding her, not with a Mustang GT breaking the morning quiet.

He patted Francine's cheek and parked at the top of his parents' driveway by the Nativity scene set in a miniature barn built by Fernando and decorated by Maria where later that night they would lay the baby Jesus in the nacimiento and gather to sing traditional Mexican Christmas carols around the peaceful setting with their closest neighbours and good friends. They would drink Fernando's homemade Ponche, a fruity and sweet alcoholic drink made with sugar cane and cinnamon, and eat Maria's prized buñuelos, succulent fruit fried in lard and coated with eggs, flour and sugar.

The real feast would come after church, with more dancing and more Ponche, except for her and their baby. And they would wake to yet another day of more cooking and more eating. At Christmas Maria could only be found in the kitchen and that curious interlopers were forbidden was a given.

"Is she Señora Arquero?"

"No, she is not. She is Maria, my mother," was all he could manage, his mouth dry from talking.

Maria appeared as though by magic, Fernando trailing behind. She stood poised at the end of the walkway, waiting with her arms by her side, dressed as though she were going to an elegant event.

Francine had never seen Maria.

"Hidalgo, your mother's gorgeous. Really, she could be your sister."

He blew a stream of warm air through pursed lips. "Sí, claro, she is, and like most women she is the most lovely when she is happy. Do nothing, mi corazón, to change the way she looks. Te imploro."

She gurgled a laugh, kissed him, and slid from the car. Nothing would spoil her Christmas. And she already loved Maria. She could feel in her heart that she did, that they would be best friends and that Maria would love her.

Maria was by her side in a blink, shocked to see what she wasn't told to expect, leaving Fernando to examine his son, the same son who kept secrets from his mother and had not changed his clothes in thirty hours. Father and son watched the women disappear into the house, believing it wise to remain behind a little while.

"Hidalgo, hijo," he whispered. "What are we in for, the two of us? What dangers now lurk within my home?"

"She is Francine Duval, papá. She was never really married as I have always believed and have regretted with such sadness in my heart." He inhaled a deep breath, such words weren't easy. "Papá, Francine loves only me, and the baby is mine."

"She loves you more than merely to have a father for the child. You are certain of this, hijo?"

"She will tell you herself, papá, and you will know by the glow in her eyes."

Fernando draped an arm across his son's shoulders. "You are saying that you and I, we have no reason to fear your mother? She has not been easy since you called. You owe me, hijo."

"We do not; neither should we leave them alone much longer. Vamos ¡de prisa!"

*

Hidalgo had never changed his clothes as quickly, spurred on by the unknown, by what he was missing. Or, better said, what he wasn't privy to. When he returned to the house he and Fernando played secondary roles to Francine who, Maria insisted, would not spend the night sleeping over cars. Francine would stay in the guestroom where she belonged, where Maria would be close by…in case.

Francine had never been kissed and hugged as much over the two days. What she thought was particularly curious, she told Hidalgo, was that she hadn't once thought of her parents. She called them, of course, a few days earlier, as Scott Gibson had called his parents to explain the couple's impromptu ski vacation with friends.

The difficult part for Francine was Christmas morning, she confided to Hidalgo. She had come to his parents' home without gifts. She had nothing for them. That was her tradition. Hidalgo took advantage of his native tongue and spoke lightning-fast to his parents so that she wouldn't fully understand. Fernando added his Spanish comment with a sly smile and Maria came from the kitchen to scold them both in a blur of words. She turned to Francine, scolding her in Spanish as well, slowly, so that she would understand each word.

To think that she hadn't brought a gift was unspeakable when, in fact, she had brought to their home the most precious of gifts. What did it matter that the wrapping would remain intact several weeks longer?

For the rest of the day father and son lay on the floor watching Mexico play off against Italy. Maria and Francine cooked in the kitchen the entire day, a rare immunity, talking endlessly, jumping from Spanish to English, laughing, sometimes stepping outside for fresh air, away from the curious ears of men who couldn't possibly be interested in a soccer match they'd watched twice before.

But one thing men did know better than any woman, Fernando informed his son: when women come in from a quiet walk together, arm in arm, their eyes wet with tears, don't stop watching the game.

Christmas Day dinner was festive and jocular with a vast array of food, fine Estates wine, tequila, and many more hugs and kisses, Maria gradually understanding that her son was an idiot, that he'd teased the poor girl about Posada, making the poor creature believe that she was not welcome in her home.

He was on his own, temporarily shunned by the women and disowned by his father who knew the benefits of silence and decisive separation from the guilty.

The day after, the men were satiated, lethargic, and Maria was busy in the kitchen when Francine asked her privately if she could stay in Maria's home a day longer, without knowing that her simple words were the highlight of Maria's Christmas. Francine had a few things to talk about, woman to woman, perhaps when the men were gone if they could ever pull themselves away from the television.

Maria smiled and patted her cheek. She took Francine by the hand and walked with her into the living room where Fernando knew his day was about to change, whereas his son did not. They were gone most of the day. They could watch their foolish replays anytime, they were told. And the women talked endlessly.

Francine loved Maria's son, and she knew Hidalgo loved her. She didn't want her baby born to a single mother, despite Diego's name. And she didn't want Maria or Fernando to hate her for stealing their son away. Francine explained what she had said to Hidalgo about his education, which Maria understood. However, Maria assured her, Hidalgo's future was not a concern. He would become a lawyer without the weight of his wife's generosity pressing down upon his shoulders. Francine's single concern should be little Diego and, perhaps together, they could work to improve Hidalgo as a husband.

At supper that night Fernando said grace, thanking the Lord for the bountiful past few days and His divine creation of such breathtaking women, and that they should come together in his humble home was truly a miracle. Maria, with a sigh, her black eyes searching skyward, begged that her husband be forgiven his waywardness, waiting a moment before blowing him a kiss from across the table.

But Fernando continued asking God as an addendum, what had these two devious women done that day to conspire against unwary and guiltless men, men of sound heart and good intention. He was teaching his son well, which included when to sit and listen.

"Francine, already Fernando and I love you as a daughter. We understand what you have done and we understand why you have done so, even if my silly and handsome son does not. He is young and must be forgiven certain aspects of his becoming a man. Yet we are proud of him because he is a man, a good man. And he will be a

161

good father, like the other one sitting beside him with his tongue tucked neatly into his mouth," she flashed a smile to the only man she had ever loved, "waiting to hear from us what they must do."

"Gracias, Maria. Yo…"

Maria patted Francine's hand. "Hidalgo, this young woman and I have spoken all day about you. I never realized anyone could talk so much about one boy." She smiled at Fernando, "with possibly one exception. And together we have come to a decision for you."

Fernando said, "Be brave, my son, here it comes. This is the reason we were instructed to leave. Together they have worked against us."

"This girl must be a bride before she is a mother, and together we have decided that El Día del Amor y la Amistad will be a perfect time, February 14th. We could not think of a more appropriate day." Mother and daughter hugged. "That is enough for now, except this, hijo."

Fernando gripped his son's shoulders. "We stand together, hombre. Be strong."

"Fernando, ¡cállate! momentito. Gracias. Hidalgo, this girl whom you rightfully adore will not live alone as she is. For that reason only I will allow you to rip my heart from my chest and leave my home to be by her side for one month. In her last month she will live here, with me and your father. However you will not. Nor will you live over the garage. She will have proper care with us, and you will call on her as a man should call on the woman he loves. And you will continue to study hard. This you will promise all of us here."

"I do promise, mamá." He stood. He went to where she sat and kissed her forehead. He kissed Francine and smirked. "Never will I think to disappoint… the four of you."

His father waved him away, feigning disgust. His son had made the evening another one of wet faces.

Francine began crying, and Maria cried with her. Fernando pushed himself from the table, took his son aside quietly and poured double tequilas for each of them. That's how men got things done: A proud father saluting a prouder son.

22

John Canyon never refused Fernando and Maria the day of January 06th. The day was one of celebration and gift-giving and he never missed sending Jennie to their home with something special, not that Jennie ever needed to be reminded. She never refused one of Maria's superb meals, though John wasn't much into hugs and kisses and Christmas which, for him, was a quiet time of memories. At New Year's he just went to bed early.

This year was different; John Canyon went with his daughter after Maria's and Jennie's combined threats not to leave his office until he agreed to join them for El Día de los Reyes when the three kings traditionally came to homes bearing gifts.

Francine was ecstatic; she finally had a real family. She'd never celebrated New Year's the way they celebrated Nochevieja with dancing and singing and laughing. She had always believed that New Year's was a time for old men to shake hands and talk business while old women smiled and listened without saying much. Most of all she was anxious for the sixth, anxious for Maria and Fernando to open their gifts.

On the evening of the fifth she went alone with Fernando to stand the three kings in the barn. How else could they come the next day, Fernando questioned? She listened intently as he explained why that night of all nights, how he'd carved them and why, Francine stopping him when she didn't understand. He never spoke English to her. How else would she learn?

She liked him very much, intrigued when he began showing her how to start a campfire.

She'd never seen one, let alone feeling its heat on her toes, and they sat quietly watching the flames and the three silent kings. When Maria and her son came out to join them no one thought to break the quiet.
*

John and Jennie arrived midday. He'd heard the news a few days earlier and had given Jennie strict orders to do things right, insisting with raised eyebrows that it was all her idea, waiting until she agreed that, yes, it was.

Of course he always came to their home with a bottle of the vineyard's finest wine, but when he pushed his way through the doorway behind a baby carriage filled to the brim with clothes and other things he knew nothing about, not even Maria could disguise her shock.

He went directly to Fernando and Hidalgo, taking the tequila that was waiting for him, figuring Jennie would be good for at least an hour with her girlie business oohing and aahing, until Francine came from behind to reach as high as she could to tap his shoulder. When he turned from the hip she hugged him as hard as she could, being that her arms scarcely made it halfway. She had a favour to ask, which he'd been given no heads-up about, and when his eyes implored the other men he got no help whatsoever.

She knew all about him from Maria, Fernando and Hidalgo. He was a saint for what he'd done to help Hidalgo. However since he was coming to the wedding anyway, could he please give the bride away? And could he wear something besides his boots, jeans and denim shirt, for once?

He was thinking, or pretending to, sipping his drink. He normally didn't like surprises, and he sure as hell had no use for Franklin Duval. Hidalgo thought Señor Canyon should hear the entire story from the source. He also knew that John Canyon would know the importance of keeping a secret. Maria and Jennie stepped in. Hidalgo and his father stepped away. John was on his own, and certainly big enough to deal with three small women.

Okay, he would do it, and he would wear a suit, but here was the deal. No honeymoon until the groom completed his school year, and then only two weeks. The kid still had to earn a living. The trio moved in closer. He was trapped. There was no avoiding the flood of tears, kisses and hugs, John promising Fernando that, if this was the way he could expect to be treated, he was never coming back.

He held his glass high over the women's heads, he needed another drink.

The meal was a Mexican feast to remember, complete with Maria's Rosca de Reyes, a sweet bread sprinkled with fruit which Francine helped to bake, surprised when Maria stood a small figurine into the batter. She was learning something new each day, including why to laugh when John discovered that his slice contained the hidden gift. Now he really wasn't coming back, he assured them. He didn't know a damned thing about going to church, besides, he was Protestant.

And a poor example of one at that, Jennie added, taking the figurine from his plate and patting his cheek. She would go to church in his place, and pray for him. He needed all the help he could get.
*

Throughout January Maria stopped at Francine's home each night after work when she wasn't at school to help in the kitchen and teach the young girl how to prepare Hidalgo's favourite Mexican dishes, which her son later washed and dried before leaving them alone to talk more about him while he studied.

Each weekend the women spent time together, planning a small wedding and becoming more like sisters while Hidalgo worked at the Estates, but when he returned home his mother was there to show her son how to use a vacuum cleaner, broom and duster.

Fernando stayed home most weekends, claiming his son's agony was too painful for him to witness.

On February 01st Hidalgo drove Francine to his parents' and reluctantly left her there. He would see her once before the wedding, Sunday afternoon, which made his weeks interminable and his nights unbearable.

Francine's thirteen days flew by. The priest understood that she wasn't Catholic and that she wanted a simple ceremony. Maria understood that she didn't want to walk down the aisle in a dress from a bygone era. She wanted short and green satin to match her ring, and a little décolleté. She didn't have the biggest breasts in the world, but she needed something to detract from her belly, although she didn't have a problem with wearing a silk scarf during the service. And she wanted green satin shoes, not so fancy that she couldn't wear them again.

For their honeymoon she wanted to see Las Vegas. She'd always wanted to go, never allowed. Such places weren't proper for young girls. She also wanted a suitcase full of sexy lingerie that didn't have stretchy waistbands. As for the rings, she wanted to exchange the emeralds they already wore. Besides, she giggled, Hidalgo was not yet a wealthy lawyer.

She also wanted a small reception with a few of their neighbours and hers, the Canyons and the few friends Hidalgo had at university. She had no friends and no one invited knew of the Duvals or of her connection with Senator Gibson. Of course there would be no formal announcement. Apart from the fact she believed such public statements were pretentious, the backlash would be catastrophic. In any event, no one outside of those invited cared in the least how much she loved Hidalgo.

23

February 13th Fernando paid for adjoining rooms at the Hilton in San Francisco so that his son would end his evening safely with his three friends. Although he was still young enough to enjoy a good time, he declined to join them. There were certain things a father didn't have to know. Instead, as his best man, he gave Hidalgo 500 dollars and told him to have a good time. He would arrive at the hotel promptly at seven the next morning to drive the groom home and make certain he was fit to stand by his lovely bride.

*

Francine's bachelorette party was planned by Jennie. Francine had asked her to be her maid of honour since Hidalgo thought so much of her.

The half-dozen women invited to the wedding would meet at her place for some pizza, some good wine and some girl talk. She knew this great pizza place that delivered. Not as much fun as ogling a bunch of young, naked women, she told Francine and Maria, but she'd ordered take-out from this place a few times before and wasn't disappointed. In fact they specialized in bachelorette parties.

Maria agreed. The idea was perfect. The last thing she wanted was Francine getting excited. She was excited enough and big enough to destabilize the polar axis and make California the new South Pole. Maria would see to inviting the women, Jennie would see to the pizza guy, and everyone arrived at eight.

At 8:30, with the first glass of wine gone, Jennie went to the phone in her kitchen. When she came out she told them thirty, maybe thirty-five minutes, more than enough time for another glass of wine.

*

In San Francisco things weren't going so well for Hidalgo. The gorgeous girls on stage were naked by the end of their three dances, the waitresses serving were half-naked and no less beautiful, and the girl standing on a stool, twisting, gyrating, doing things he'd never seen a girl do, her face twelve inches from his face, was getting naked very quickly. He'd never seen so many naked women and his friends had already invited four to the table. He'd never tried so hard to see into a woman's eyes, and she was talking to him.

No, he answered, he wasn't a salesman from out of town. Yes, he was getting married. He was a student. Where, she asked? At Golden Gate, he said. Hey, so was she. Wasn't the world so small?

When the dance finished she thanked him. She hoped that he liked her. She would love to dance for him again. He thanked her for dancing so well, but he was Latino and knew very well that she hadn't danced at all. Yes, he said. She could dance for him and his friends again. Though the evening was young and they hadn't yet eaten. And when the meals were brought to the table, that girl might as well have been naked. And his beautiful bride, his lovely Francine was eight and a half months pregnant. Life was truly filled with misery.

His friends tried to empathize, two of them reminding him that he wasn't sleeping alone that night.

"Ah, hombres, I am Latino. ¿Comprenden?" He squeezed the shoulder of his roomie for the night. "Thank you, but as handsome as you are, I will find another way?"

which brought on more raucous laughter.

By midnight he was down 300, his friends were down a hundred each, their throats and clothes were thick with cigar smoke, their heads were somewhere, they weren't quite sure where, and they were becoming colour blind. They began seeing no distinguishable difference between red, blonde, brunette, auburn, ginger or black. They needed to regain their senses, get some fresh air.

So they left, stood outside long enough for the cab to move from the curb to the door, drove to the Hilton five blocks away and went to the bar for cognacs and gentlemanly conversation during which they would decide which of the colours they liked the most.
*

At 9:00 PM precisely Jennie's doorbell chimed. The man at the door didn't appear as though he needed extra income from making late-night deliveries carrying in an extra-large and twin six-packs of Coke. What got Maria chattering was the ghetto blaster strapped across his shoulders.

He didn't look like a pizza boy at all. He wasn't wearing a silly cap, striped shirt or shiny polyester windbreaker with geeky slacks and running shoes. He was wearing a loose, crisp white shirt over a tight white tee-shirt, leather pants and soft Italian leather slippers. He was a good 6'2", slim, tanned, blond, blue-eyed, and pretty much Adonis' double.

He wouldn't let Jennie take the pizza or the drinks; he was more than happy to carry them into the kitchen. In fact, he would be delighted to serve each of her guests personally. His restaurant was full service, he told her, adding that he'd even brought music to set the mood while he worked. Who was the special lady, he asked? Jennie pointed to Francine. She did like Latin rhythm, didn't she? She nodded.

Jennie had made certain that all the wine glasses were filled. He served Francine first, then Jennie, Maria and the other ladies, each time arranging napkins across their laps.

He worked efficiently, not quickly. Not that anyone cared. Even Maria was enjoying the 'service'. But before he left he had a special gift for the bride, a memento of the evening before her very special day. When she opened the small box inside was a four-inch figurine of a flawlessly proportioned blond-haired man wearing a gold-coloured thong and a smile, at the very moment the music changed from melodic to upbeat dance.

Maria's eyes went from the ornament to the man, and back to the ornament. She had no idea, but the man was dancing, moving as well as any Latino, she had to admit. She was so happy that Francine was getting so much attention on her special night. The girl was blushing, and Jennie was sitting cross-legged on a sofa, leaning forward, eating pizza, not blinking and making loud sounds as though she really liked the pizza. So were the other women. Some were rocking back and forth, others swaying their arms or clapping to the music. ¡Qué pasaba! Yet somehow she knew this wasn't the time to ask questions.

The man's shirt was on the floor. Then he kicked away his slippers, which Maria thought wasn't any worse than the boys at the beach. And she also had to admit that he wasn't hard on the eyes, realizing that her feet were tapping and that she was smiling. Most of all she was happy for Francine who was receiving all his attention. No one, it seemed, was eating pizza.

When he pulled away his tee-shirt, slowly, purposefully, away from his tight, sculpted abdomen, across his tanned, steel-like chest and over his head, she gulped her wine once, twice. He was saying something about the bride's mother. ¡Dios! He was standing in front of her, almost touching her. Never had she seen such a scandalous thing. She crossed herself. Never would she tell Fernando that she was singing and swaying in her seat like a giddy young girl.

She could feel the heat of her flushed cheeks, her

quickened pulse, half delighted, half disappointed when he blew her a kiss and moved on to Jennie. All the women had their turn, but the night belonged to the bride. He put his back to her. His pants were tight and shiny, his back perfectly smooth, tanned and glistening with a fine coating of perspiration…sweat. He was gyrating in perfect rhythm to the music, his movements provocative and enticing.

Maria had stopped sipping her wine. Her mouth wouldn't close. The women were all talking to Francine, yelling at her, but what were they telling her? ¡Dios! She was reaching for the young man's waist. ¡Ay, no! She was reaching into the back of his pants. His hips were swivelling so, so…¡Ay, Francine!

The dancer moved suddenly away, tugging at his waistband in sync with Francine, and Maria was left gawking at tanned and tight buns. God would forgive her, Fernando would forgive her. She would say an extra prayer and light an extra candle the next morning at church.

He was turning, slowly, not an ounce of fat on him, she noticed, her eyes joining a crowd of others focused on glittering gold. Never had she seen a man wearing anything as tiny. How could he even…? Truly, he was a fine specimen. ¡Ay! No es posible. His thumbs, he was reaching under the strings. Now God would never forgive her.

Instead, the music ended. The young pizza guy leaned forward, kissed Francine's hand, stooped for his clothes and went into the kitchen. When he came out moments later he was dressed. He beamed a bright white smile, thanked them, took his ghetto blaster and left, glancing back with a gallant wave. Most of the women were pleading for an encore, Jennie was pouring more wine and Francine was waving her napkin at Maria to cool her.

*

Maria and Francine arrived home at midnight. Fernando had just fallen asleep after an evening of studying. She waited for Francine to change, made certain the bride-to-be was tucked in, told her with a giggle to be careful who filled her dreams that night, and went to her bedroom.

Fernando stirred at the soft patter of feet and the rustling of silk and satin sliding to the floor. He never missed an opportunity to watch Maria undress.

"So how was your Ladies' Evening? I suppose you spoke about babies, the benefits of breast milk and the miracles of life."

"We did not, you foolish man. We ate pizza, we drank a little wine, listened to music and later spoke of such fine men like you, of how strong, handsome and virile you are."

"So you enjoyed."

"Sí, claro, I enjoyed very much."

"And the little girl, who sleeps in our home, was the night special for her?"

"I believe she will never forget the night. I believe that, as we speak, she is dreaming of our Hidalgo dancing with her tomorrow."

"That is good." He patted the sheets. "Come to bed, you must be as beautiful tomorrow as you are to my eyes this very moment."

She stood as she was, smirking devilishly; her lingerie and dress her exotic pedestal crumpled at her feet. "But, Señor Arquero," she pouted, lowering her eyes submissively, "I am not very tired."
*

Fernando woke feeling more tired than when he went to bed. He leaned over and kissed his wife. He chortled, stroking her cheek. He had no idea what went on at Jennie's the night before, though he could imagine that some young wolf had been lured to the henhouse to delight them and make them cackle. He'd heard of such entertainment. Whether his suspicions were correct or not, of one thing he was certain: Maria should attend such parties much more often. He patted her bum and left her. The early morning sky was still dark.

He arrived at the Hilton promptly at seven. His son and three other bodies were waiting for him in the lobby, slumped four abreast into a lush sofa; their arms crossed, their chins pressing into their barely moving chests.

He shook each one by the knees, inspecting them from head to toe, doing his best not to inhale too deeply. Outwardly he appeared dismayed; inwardly he wanted to burst into a raucous laugh. How they must each be suffering. Had Maria come with him to see her son so much the victim of his own choices she would have called for an ambulance...or, at the very least, terrorized him with her black eyes to the point where his beleaguered soul would beg to seek refuge in a safer place.

"So, these are the fearless Titans of Golden Gate that I see before me."

"Papá we got to the hotel late. There is much to see in San Francisco. ¿Comprendes?"

Fernando chuckled. "Sí, comprendo, but are not all these exquisite attractions at the same location? Caballeros, you smell like smoked hams and appear somewhat abused, albeit self-inflicted. It is a ritual I understand and I am certain that your punishment has begun. The four of you look like lost puppies in the rain, abandoned by those who once loved them."

"Papá, the evening was long, we had much to discuss between us. Our evening was one of difficult decisions and debate."

Fernando belched out a laugh. "Si, yo sé. I am aware of these difficult decisions when so many beautiful options confront us, soon made more difficult by a curtain of thick blue smoke and a few toasts to the groom who, by the way, must be married in eight hours that will soon seem to him as eight minutes."

They tried to move, more than one passer-by smiling compassionately.

"Muchachos, I salute you. You have survived an arduous undertaking. Yet you are now faced with another which is all the more demanding. You must appear to be alive! You are not the most handsome of men at this very moment. You require urgent maintenance. You must eat well to fortify yourselves against the day ahead. I, on the other hand, will enjoy a tall and delicious mimosa while you struggle with black coffee, knowing that I commiserate with your misery and that I will protect you from Maria Magdalena Arquero at the cost of my own discomfort. Believe me or not, this is not the worst day of your life. However I see by your blurred eyes and pained expressions that you do not believe me. ¡Andemos!"

*

The groom arrived at 2:30. Fernando had allowed his son one cognac before leaving home, since Hidalgo appeared to have restored his constitution to its pre-celebratory condition with enviable resilience. And to their mutual surprise, Hidalgo wasn't the least bit nervous standing before his guests with Fernando at his side.

"This is what I want, papá. This is what we want, Francine and I. I will be a good father, as you have been to me. And, Francine, she will be a good mother, as my mother has been to me."

"You make me proud with these words, hijo. Your mother would weep to hear them, as she does freely these days with happiness for you, though never once did I imagine that she would be a grandmother at such a young age." He squeezed his son's shoulder. "Let us be wise in this matter, muchacho, and never remind her of this. Our lives will be much happier for our silence."

"Papa, Diego, I did not..."

"Bastante, Hidalgo. You will one day make this a better

world. And your son will follow in your footsteps. Diego will be to his father, what my Hidalgo is to me, a constant reminder of how I first loved your mother. I cannot imagine a better gift in this life. The moment is as vivid as my last night's dream of her."

"My mother makes you the envy of many men."

"Amigo, at times I envy myself."

The organ's first chord of music burst from within the walls, startling them both. Fernando turned from the hip to see Maria taking her place in the first row. Hidalgo turned as well.

"You see, hijo, already she weeps."

"She will not be rid of me so easily, papá."

"She knows that. She weeps with joy for her new daughter." The second chord echoed loudly. "This is your only moment, hijo, this very second when you see your young bride's glow. See how they all ignore you in anticipation of her." He slapped his son's back. "From this second forward she will come first in everyone's eyes but her own."

Jennie was first through the arched doors. That she wasn't married, Hidalgo thought, was an unthinkable crime against mankind. Few women were as charming or as lovely, as warm or as kind.

*

Standing with her hand resting on John Canyon's arm, the bride might truly have been a little girl; a flower girl at someone else's wedding, innocent, as yet untroubled by worldly matters. Her ensemble was stunning. The green satin gown was flared from under her breasts and cut to just above her knees, a green silk scarf lending modesty to an otherwise glamorous evening dress. The scarf, Hidalgo recognized, was one of the first gifts he'd given to his mother in keeping his promise to himself.

Her hair was styled into a tight Latin bun highlighted

with a silver and emerald pin. Her green satin sandals appeared so small to him from where he stood, her skin glowing with discreet silver sparkles accentuating the amber hue of a light tan.

Francine had told John exactly how he should walk, and she'd made him practice as though going into a business meeting with a bit of a swagger. He wasn't the type to act pompous, she told him. In another life he might have been a ruthless buccaneer, a debonair highwayman or a handsome desperado, definitely not a man of the cloth or an aristocrat.

He did his best to live up to her expectations, with Jennie's help. He looked sophisticated in a dark blue suit accented with the red tie and the pocket hanky Francine had bought him. He was clearly proud. He was proud. And the thought wasn't lost on him that somewhere, whatever he was doing, playing golf or rubbing elbows at the club while drinking wine from the Estates, Franklin Duval had not the slightest idea that his daughter was being married to this kid from Mexico who'd come so far in such a short time.

She whispered, "You're doing very well, John, just like we rehearsed."

"Thank you, Francine. I'm doing my best."

Jennie had thought it ridiculous that, given the circumstances, Francine should call him Mr. Canyon. Especially after he discovered he was going to be a godfather, despite his insistence that he was too old and knew nothing about kids. He'd forgotten all that he once did know, and wasn't about to start over.

At the altar he placed her beside the groom and Jennie. He gave her a gentle squeeze and stepped away to sit with Maria, hoping that she had an adequate supply of Kleenex in her clutch.

*

Hidalgo Filipe Arquero placed the familiar ring onto her finger. "Within these rings our hearts will forever beat as

178

one. Never will I let you escape my heart, Francine."

Francine moved slightly towards Jennie who stepped in closer, letting Francine take Hidalgo's glittering green jewel from the tiny velvet box, remembering the day she'd given that very box to Mr. Meadows, the day before she travelled alone to Pichilingue.

Jennie smiled warmly. She'd never seen a happier bride.

Francine's vow was simple, whispered in Spanish that she'd practiced a few hundred times, wanting each word to flow seamlessly. "Te amo, mi amor. Never will I give you a reason to remove this ring from my finger, the pathway from my heart so filled with joy to your heart, not until the day I die."

24
December 01st of this Year

The boss' second limousine pulled into his guarded property at 10:30.

Anita Juárez had been up for hours. Her workday began the moment she eased from her bed and padded across her bedroom floor to the bathroom. She didn't use an alarm clock; her wake-up call came each morning at five from the security detail posted at her door. Her first priority was her treadmill and universal for a full-body workout, her second was a rich Columbian coffee and steaming shower, her third was a wake-up call to El Cacique. This morning she didn't bother. If what she believed was true, he would need his sleep. If in fact he'd slept at all.

Her one constant pleasure was dressing each morning. She loved being a woman. She adored the sensations of silk and satin lingerie against her body, silk dresses and satin slacks with silk blouses. She dressed in a way befitting her position, though none would deny her inherent sensuality. Very few men would pass her by without glancing over their shoulders to appreciate her stunning beauty a while longer, those who did not were more likely to be visually impaired or in dire need of a testosterone refill.

She was at her door and ready at 5:55. That never changed. She liked to spend a few minutes each day speaking with the men assigned to her security detail. They were well-trained and chosen personally by El Cacique. Face to face they called her Señora Juárez, to her back they called her La Bonita, but she knew that, and she loved them for the endearment. For the officers, guarding her was an honour, for The Boss, her well-being was an imperative.

His second limousine, used almost exclusively by her, arrived at 6:00. She first went to her office to reorganize his agenda and gather certain papers that required his signature, his current state of mind notwithstanding. His signature was the one thing she could not do for him.

She didn't make excuses to the staff. As much as they were devoted to him, Anita Juárez was their boss. What he did or didn't do wasn't their concern. They rarely saw him, though when they did he would take the time to ask about their families or significant others. He was human, warm and kind, and very popular. What they didn't know was that, without Anita Juárez, he likely would have perished in abject misery years earlier.

She simply issued instructions to them and left.

Arriving at the mansion, she didn't knock. She never did. His security detail opened the front door for her.

She didn't know what to expect. But she knew what not to expect. However, if she were wrong, she would never forgive him the weakness.

"Good morning, Cacique. ¿Cómo vas?"

"¡Buenas! Santa Anita." He brought her a cup of coffee. "You usually say what you mean, Anita. My head is fine, if I am reading correctly the question that lingers behind your beautiful and dark eyes. Last night I very quickly rediscovered my long-forgotten contempt for hard drink," he sipped his coffee, "or possibly its contempt of me. I suppose a wise man once saved from drowning in the misery of his personal and deep sorrow should know better than to purposely return to the blackest depths of the same menacing sea. I hope I did not scare you, Anita. But for my memory of you that one Friday night I might feel very ill this morning. And I suppose that is why you are much later than usual. You thought the worst. You suspected that my ugly mood might have revisited me," his lips curved into a thin and humourless smile, though his eyes remained sombre, "and you worried that I might chase you away again, albeit in a luxurious limousine this time."

"You are quite incorrect, Cacique. First, you instructed me to come later than usual. However I did understand that you required time to yourself this morning, as did I. What I read in that letter yesterday terrified me. I did not sleep well because of it."

"The letter, Anita, was filled with mystery and intrigue. I understand that you were unnerved, and I apologize for your distress. That you continue to worry so about me warms my heart."

"But you understood the content, and you know the author who has recently died."

"Yes, I know what was intended for me to decipher, as well as the author who waited these many years to tell me what I must know."

"Since the time we first met."

"Yes."

"I was so young, so frightened, as I am again today."

"Was so young, a woman whose beauty forces men to stumble and other less fortunate women to openly envy such flawless perfection? Were I not so old and tired I would... When was the last time I took you to dinner alone?"

He wasn't old. He was young and handsome, his youthful body belying his midlife years. He was strong and resilient. And he was blind. She knew now, she'd known for some time that leaving him was a good decision, the right thing to do. She'd wasted her life hoping.

"Alone, with the four-man security detail seated around us? Two months. We went to Casa Madrid directly from the office. I was wearing a business suit. We both were. We had a secluded corner where we discussed business across the table from each other. There was also music and I recall that people were dancing." She paused. "Yes, they were dancing. They seemed to enjoy themselves."

"Ah, yes, but your suit was more curvaceous, more demanding of attention than mine. A man's suit is designed to disguise his flaws, a woman's is meant to enhance her charms. Your suits in particular, Anita, excel in their purpose. Though I daresay the inverse is more the case."

Increasingly, since her decision to leave him, she found him annoying, difficult to talk with.

"As I recall we spoke of your pending retirement and my upcoming position as VP at Trans-Pacific Marketing. I do not recall that you once mentioned my charms and I certainly do not recall enumerating your flaws, which are many...in certain areas. As for my curvaceous suit, I was sitting where no one could see me."

"Their loss, my gain, and two months is much too extended a time to deprive myself of your very delightful company. Unfortunately I have one short month remaining in which to honour my mandate and see my promises through to completion, Anita, after which we will dine as friends without guards or prying ears, and without talk of business. And perhaps you will allow me a dance with TPM's newest and most captivating senior vice-president, although I have not danced for many years. However we now have more serious matters to discuss and, Anita, this is no one's business but ours alone. I must also add that, once we leave this office, each of us to secure a new life, the oath of this office remains in force regarding this particular matter."

Sometimes she wanted to smack him. How could such a

brilliant man be so stupid?

"You do not appear well-rested for a man who chose his bed over a bottle. In fact, you seem worse than you did yesterday. I really believe I should call your doctor. Your health is not your concern alone for the next month."

"The last thing I need or desire is being poked and prodded for no reason and told to work fewer hours by someone who works six-hour days, five-day weeks and plays eighteen holes most days with blood-clotted millionaires who can scarcely swing a club without collapsing. No. I do not require a physician, Anita. I need you to sit and listen."

She sat. "I know that I will not like this. I remember that day, the hate in your voice and in your eyes because then you did not know what you learned yesterday from that letter."

"I want you to obtain the most complete information on Detective Drew Carling, LAPD. I want to know everything about the man. I also want to know what kind of man he is, where he lives, where he went to school. I want to know why he chose to become a police officer, if he can be trusted, if he is truly beyond reproach. Few men are completely beyond reproach and temptation; I want to know why I should believe he is one of them. If there is the slightest malice in his heart, I want to know. And I will. Evil is easily camouflaged by one skilled in subterfuge, possibly a street-smart cop by way of example. Unless, of course, confronted by someone whose heart is equally tainted with sinister intent."

"What will you do with this information, Cacique?"

He didn't answer.

"The woman whose name you read, Deidre Commons, find her. Find out everything about her, her entire background. Leave no stone unturned. I want to know where she works and what she does that she can afford two homes and a yacht in the highest priced markets of this country. I want copies of her bank and credit card statements. I want copies of her phone bills; I want to know who she sleeps with, where she has lunch, what she eats and where she buys her clothes. Anita, I want to know why she was mentioned in that letter. And, for that, I must know her completely."

"Should I arrange for a phone tap?"

He ignored her, his mind too congested.

"Darcy Wilson, what could a stripper possibly have in common with a city cop a thousand miles away? And what connection has she with Deidre Commons, or is Commons the reason she is in New Orleans?" he thought aloud. "Anita, I want to know why a young woman determines to live in a desperate city baring her soul on a footstool for the pleasure of drunken lowlifes. She had to come from somewhere. Find out from where. I expect she will be the most difficult to research. Find out where she works, who owns the club, whether she is being paid or paying off a debt for something she did or did not do, perhaps a dealer or a pimp. From this one I expect the worst. I want to know her education, if she is on drugs, if she drinks, if she can even spell her name."

"Perhaps she is doing this to finance her education. Dancing for such a reason is not uncommon. Or perhaps she went there when so many others left, in search of a new beginning. I understand that many of these women earn very good lives. And, Cacique, on that Friday so many years ago, were it not for your belief in me, possibly her story would have been my own."

"I don't believe that for a moment. Stripping is the beginning of the end most often. You were much too beautiful and intelligent to even contemplate such a career. You and I were destined to find one another at a time when we believed all was lost. And do not think for a moment that I will not miss seeing you each day." He shook his head to clear his mind, shocked to discover he'd been staring at her crossed legs. "Anyway, regarding this Darcy Wilson, I want photographs of this woman. I want to see her condition for myself. I want to see the joy or the sadness in her eyes. I want to see whether she saunters with happiness or treads heavily from the weight upon her shoulders."

"You will have the information as soon as possible in the order that you have given me their names. I will keep you informed."

"Assign our best people."

"I would, of course."

"I want this information before the end of next week so that I might have sufficient time to react appropriately. Use my influence in whichever way you choose. "

"Yes, Cacique. Is there anything else before I go?"

"Yes. Christmas is closing in on us quickly. I would like after-hours access to the mall this Saturday and Sunday."

"Should I request that a restaurant remain open for your convenience as well?"

"Thank you, no. To what end? Eating alone is dismal at best, which I can do at the mansion."

"And your tailor, for New Year's, should I arrange a private fitting?"

"There will be no gala this year, Anita. At least none that I will attend. I have decided to leave office on the 31st, not the third. The decision is recent, made since yesterday. I did not mean to leave you in the dark, for which I apologize. On my own I have discussed the matter with my successor. He and his staff are in agreement, prepared to take over from us on the first."

He might just as well have slapped her face. She tilted her head graciously. Over the past eight years she'd been the one to attend the official New Year's celebration by his side, while others arrived with women on their arms, or hand in hand. Her gown could be returned, as she was the exclusive boutique's most favoured client. At that moment she wanted to stab his heart, the way he'd stabbed hers.

"I understand."

"I regret not having told you earlier. I did not know myself until recent events abetted my decision. Perhaps you might yet arrange to celebrate your new beginning with your future colleagues at TPM." He paused, letting his mind travel briefly to a distant place. "I believe that my coming year will be the most rewarding in many years. I look forward to our evening together when all this that we now see around us is behind us, and hearing of the new challenges that face you."

She smirked. "And what will you tell me as we dine somewhere quiet and intimate where we can discuss our new lives and watch others dancing? Am I to believe that letter will be behind you, Cacique? That is what you mean to imply, is it not?"

"That letter, Anita, is of value to no one except me. That I am aware of, no one other than I can derive pain or guilt, happiness or satisfaction from its content. That letter was meant for my eyes alone and was, for me alone, not so much a confession from a dying woman as it was permission to do what must be done." He inhaled deeply. "But for now, please, leave me to my thoughts. My calendar in the New Year is open to whatever evening you arrange for our dinner."

The man, she thought, was an idiot. She had no friends, because of him. She hadn't danced in years, because of him, and in a month's time she wouldn't have a life because of him because she had forgotten how to live because of him. At that very moment his inherent charisma was fast evaporating and she wanted to leave. She also knew he was at the precipice of committing the unforgiveable, and then how would she ever tell him if ever she could ever find the words? Or would she even want to?

She nodded, knowing full-well those would be the only instructions she would ever disobey. He would no longer be The Boss, El Cacique. If he wanted to sit with her and watch others dance, he would have to call her, he would have to ask her out.

"I will call you later. And, Cacique, your heart is not tainted with evil, this I know."

"Thank you, Anita. I will see you Monday. Come for me at the usual hour. I want time alone until then to condition myself for what remains of the trying month ahead."

She stood. "No. You misunderstand me. I know this because your heart is as pure as your heart is empty. That letter has rekindled your hatred, Cacique, not your love. The man I see standing before me is not the man I once knew. I will pray for you. I will pray for your soul."

Any pretence at indifference was impossible.

"Anita? Pray for me, and pray for my soul? What have I done to make you judge me so unkindly? I can think of nothing I have done to earn such pity, and I need no one's prayers but my own."

"You have not been to mass once since I have known you. Those three people, the ones in the letter, the ones you wish to know so well, I began the investigation before I went into your office yesterday. That letter had a single purpose, and the purpose is not yours. Who are these people who will take the sword from your hands, Cacique? That letter was not for your eyes alone, but for them to share with you."

"That is not for you to know. That letter, Anita, came to me for one purpose. And you are quite incorrect. It came to me because I alone was able to interpret its meaning."

She said: "Then I was wrong as a young girl to interpret 'Te lo juro, mi corazón. Until then, let him live in a fantasy world of demons and ghosts. Let him think of me, as I will think of him. On my honour, he will die before me'."

She disregarded his undisguised astonishment. She gathered the papers she'd brought with her and walked out not saying a word. He knew better than to stop her. Instead he went to the wine cabinet. She'd made her point. She wasn't pleased with him and hadn't been herself for several weeks, not since the confirmation of her new position at Trans-Pacific.

She didn't understand. Why would she? How could she? She'd never been privy to his real anguish of which she was so great a part. How could he dare to tell her after so many years of friendship that he loved her? But that he could never love her. Neither could he ever tell her why, or that his head turned as did so many others each time she entered a room, that he dreamed of her, that for so long he'd searched for the right words to speak. That so many times he'd wanted her to stay over, to be with him as a woman with a man, to feel her warmth next to his, to hear her whisper his name, not Cacique, not The Boss, not to cook his breakfast every once in a while for convenience but every day because he knew also that she loved him, making his pain all the worse, never able to send her away for her own good.

He drained his glass. She simply hadn't understood. Or had she, all these years harbouring his dark secret deep in her own heart? She'd repeated his oath verbatim, as he did each night, never forgetting, never wanting to forget his true destiny. Never once had he suspected.

He filled his glass. They needed time apart. Yet she'd been by his side for twenty-one years, knowing what she did, and he doubted he could breathe without her. He would miss her, when after so many years their destinies would take them along separate paths. But he'd done all that he could do. He was tired. He believed he had nothing left to give. So many years had gone by, and suddenly he was given hope.

His head pounded. The letter had come as a shock to him. Anita Juárez wasn't wrong. His heart was empty. That it beat at all was as much a source of great sorrow as it was the cruellest of miracles.

He seldom slept. To dream was to awaken a tempest of memories and remembering brought pangs of anger and remorse, hopelessness and regret, the shame of uselessness and guilt, of promises broken. The letter had changed all that. The old woman's guilt before her death was his redemption. His long-faded dream of killing the man was reborn, he was reborn. He smiled, studying the burgundy liquid. He had never let himself forget Enrique Mendoza, not once. As for Anita Juárez' prayers, her time would be wasted.

He remembered the one time he met the man. How he'd previously imagined a greasy resident of darkened alleyways, a rodent amongst men, a pimp and drug dealer, an unkempt nocturnal predator who cared nothing about life, a punk who'd spent his teen years in and out of jail, his twenties in and out of prison. He also remembered the tailor-made woollen suits that came later, the Italian shoes and cashmere coat, the deep tan, bright smile and tinted glasses. He remembered the chrome-plated .357 and Mendoza's promise never to forget, never to stop searching for the man who murdered his cousin.

As far as anyone was concerned, Mario Mendoza fled the country to escape twenty years to life. Only a very few knew that he died from a bullet shattering his left temporal bone, or that he'd been found a few days later following the Loma Prieta earthquake incinerated to a skeletal state in the charred ruins of a car completely gutted by the flames. The crime went unsolved, the investigation steadily losing momentum from weeks into months. No one cared about an apparent settling of accounts for whatever reason: betrayal, collusion. Somehow the man believed to be in the car

190

screwed up, known for playing both sides of the law to his advantage. The official report stated that the woman with him was simply in the wrong place at the wrong time, cheating on her husband, an unhappily married woman and the young mother of two girls and a boy.

That day he made a pact with the devil. That day he closed his eyes to a cruel and unloving God. That day he promised to one day kill, the day he shook hands with Enrique Mendoza in a lifeless place that stopped being his home.

That was then. Now Mendoza was a businessman, a crime boss who was virtually untouchable by the cops who either worked for him or were afraid of his far-reaching influence and sense of self-preservation. They would meet again soon.

He sank into his favourite high-back leather seat, his arms dangling over the sides. How would the Governor of California possibly meet with the wealthiest and most resilient crime boss in the Southwest…and how quickly? And what had he done to trigger Santa Anita's mood swing? She was the one leaving him, not the inverse. Not once since they met had he thought of leaving her, of sending her away. What would he do without her? And how many times had that thought crossed his mind over that past several months? She needed a change, which was fine, but why blame him when he was the injured party? ¡Ay! ¡Las mujeras!

That she'd remembered those words he'd spoken so long ago unnerved him. She had suspected all these years and said nothing. What was he expected to do, just walk into her office on the last day of the month and say "Anita, after working with me for twenty-one years, and in consideration of the fact that you might at last find somebody else more deserving, would you marry me? Oh, and by way, due to recent events previously believed by me to be improbable, I will now have to kill someone first."

He drained his glass of wine. Some secrets were best kept to oneself. Perhaps one day soon he would finally sleep in peace to dream and not awaken each night to wish he would never awaken again.

He fell asleep where he sat.

25
Thirty Years Ago

Maria and Fernando were by their son's side in the lounge at Mercy General Hospital. Jennie was waiting anxiously by the phone while John Canyon tolerated the excitement with his usual cool manner. Diego Hidalgo Arquero-Duval was born February 28th, fourteen days following his parents' solemn vows. He entered the world with calm and contentment, quietly and unafraid.

Two days later Scott Gibson was called upon to play his part, first with the Duvals then with the Gibsons, though the cooing didn't last long. The men had little or no interest and neither woman had any idea what a nanny would do under similar circumstances. Children were to be attended to. They were an act of necessity, a social commitment with which to continue the bloodline. How Francine would manage on her own in such a small apartment was beyond them.

Three months later Hidalgo completed his third year at Golden Gate first in his class and began his summer-long workload at the Estates. That his wife was a millionaire didn't matter. They'd decided before Diego's quiet arrival that they wouldn't argue about money. She was wealthy, he wasn't, though he did agree that a baby didn't belong in the backseat of a Mustang which was once again his alone to enjoy.

*

Scott Gibson achieved his LL.M and began his law career at Duval & Associates. He drove home that first day in a new BMW. On his way he paid for his drinks with his new expense account and drove the girl home the next morning on his way to his newly furnished office. He had big plans, dreams that were equal to or greater than Franklin Duval's expectations of him. No one at the firm got a free ride. You got things done, or you got out. Losing a case to the DA, though on occasion such failings did occur, was not acceptable. Neither was excessive financial penalties incurred by their clients. Their fees were exorbitant for a reason and being married to his daughter should not infer an easy existence, he was told. Was that understood?

Gibson did understand, thankful Duval hadn't asked about Francine or his supposed son whose invented name he'd scribbled at the edge of his notepad.

*

The year passed with amazing swiftness, Maria and Jennie finding any excuse to drop by and see Diego. Not that they needed an excuse. And when they weren't cuddling or cooing over the baby they were in the kitchen cooking Mexican while Fernando was teaching Diego Spanish.

At the end of May John Canyon invited them to his hacienda for a Mexican barbeque and, of course, the state's best wine. He knew very well that Fernando would commandeer the grill and that Maria would inspect every dish for the slightest American flaw in her native cuisine.

What they weren't expecting, however, were their co-workers who had arrived earlier, the dance floor constructed the evening before and the mariachi band. The day would be one of celebration, secrets and surprises. He just didn't know to what extent.

The week before Hidalgo graduated with honours from Golden Gate, Maria and Fernando proudly sitting with

Francine, Jennie and John Canyon in the front row to watch the young man humbly cross the stage of the auditorium to take hold of his future and to address the audience as valedictorian. Fernando saw most of the ceremony through a viewfinder, instructed by Maria not to miss a single moment. The same week, with no less pomp and circumstance, Maria and Fernando crossed a similar stage to receive their testaments to determination and hunger for learning as Hidalgo was holding the camera. They'd graduated high school with their twelfth grade. They also had succeeded beyond their wildest dreams.

When the dancing, eating and singing was over, the warm glow of the sun a faint hue in the West, John and Jennie invited their special guests inside for a glass of Special Estates Reserve. He wasn't much for taking centre stage, though he did have a few things to get off his chest. He couldn't be prouder of Maria and Fernando, what they had accomplished both for him, the Estates and for themselves was nothing short of amazing. He gave them each a thick envelope, telling them not to spend it all in one place. Maria, of course, was flustered, John waiting what he thought was a reasonable time before pleading with Fernando to pull her away, not expecting his key manager to also squeeze and kiss him, though neither one would realize the full weight of ten-thousand-dollar bundles until they arrived home later that night.

Then Hidalgo took the floor. He too had a surprise for them, his long awaited dream. This was the moment he'd worked so hard towards, more than his honours degree. He had spoken weeks earlier with John out of respect, not wanting anything to go wrong. He was sending his parents to Paris; they were leaving the following week for the entire month of June, all expenses paid. In that envelope were the flight coupons, hotel reservations, a car reservation and a gift certificate in his mother's name from one of San

Francisco's finest women's boutiques. He'd saved a little each week since his first pay envelope so long ago.

Maria was awestruck, furious with him, more so when he wouldn't wipe the smirk from his face. And Francine wasn't much better. At first she'd argued with Hidalgo that she had the right to play a part in his dream, when what she meant was that she should be allowed to contribute to the expense of such an extravagant trip. Hidalgo refused, kissing away her tears. This was his dream, not hers, not theirs to share. She had to understand. She had travelled to Pichilingue; she'd seen the humble beginnings. She had to understand. And, finally, she did. She had also come to understand that John Canyon was his benefactor insofar as his education was concerned. But that one day he would repay the full amount himself, without her help. He would not live his life indebted to another man.

Maria turned to Fernando for help in a blur of Spanish. The boy could not afford such foolishness, she insisted. And Fernando agreed, suggesting with a smirk of his own that she should return the gift certificate from the boutique. For what they had achieved, Hidalgo added, for everything they had given him, this was a very small gesture in return. He put up a hand, he wasn't finished. He had another surprise, this time for Francine.

Keeping his promise to Señor Canyon... John, he'd waited until graduating. They were going to Vegas. Francine was going to have her honeymoon, John's wedding gift to them, the reservations made by Jennie. They were leaving the next morning. Then John told him to sit down. He'd stolen enough of the glory. What made anyone think he would give a simple two weeks in a hotel room, he questioned?

He glanced at his watch nonchalantly. The Estates' corporate jet was fuelled and waiting for them at the airport. So why were they sitting around? Between Maria and

Jennie, the kid would be fine. Nothing would happen to his godchild, he assured them.

Hidalgo's mouth dropped open. He was speechless. Señor Canyon had done so much for them already. This generosity was too excessive. Francine pushed Hidalgo from her path, John Canyon bracing himself for another attack. She was crying, Maria was crying and Jennie was on the verge. Francine had never felt so ecstatic, not since her vows and Diego, but could she say something, could she share a surprise? She squeezed Hidalgo's hand, facing them, teasing them with silence.

"My beautiful husband," she began, "will have another mouth to feed, I think sometime in January."

John Canyon dropped into his Lazy Boy, shaking his head. He'd been upstaged. He could easily imagine what lay in store for him.

26

Francesca Maria Arquero-Duval was born on a brilliant mid-January day, though she wouldn't know that or care for years to come. Nor would she know that her brother Diego was six weeks from his second birthday. She had greater, more pressing concerns. She was demanding attention, reaching out to all those whom she deemed worthy and Maria was her favourite by far.

The ones she instinctively did not like were Claire and Arthur Gibson and, in particular, her supposed father who Francine hadn't allowed to touch her. Nor had he ever touched Diego. Nor were Franklin and Mrs. Duval received with much more enthusiasm on the girl's part three days into her life.

Since Francine's supposed marriage to Scott Gibson, Francine had gone to the Gibson home on four occasions, each time a Sunday afternoon save for the parents' first and only visit to the ocean view apartment for the dual purpose of curiosity and critiquing such a ludicrous choice. They visited with the Duvals on equal occasions, their mutual opinion of the apartment, albeit somewhat less caustic, was no less disparaging. In total, she was seeing Scott Gibson eight hours each year, eight too many for Hidalgo who was never far away. His one consolation was that Mrs. Gibson and Duval were stuck up bitches and the men had no interest, real or imagined, in children. Scott Gibson, on the other hand, had met Hidalgo. He understood in very clear terms not to "fuck up, amigo." And he didn't, content with escorts or the underage girls he often picked-up in bars or at the beach. Life was good. And, in law, his paid hours were all that mattered to his father-in-law.

Life was very good and in a few years he'd be rid of the bitch. He could wait her out, and he would. Let her believe she had the upper hand. If her father were ever to discover they were never married, that she'd married a Mexican, that his grandson was a half-breed, that the pure blue of Duval blood was diluted with Mexican red, he'd disown her on the spot. Why not a Black or an Indian? He on the other hand was already proving himself at the firm and living a charmed life. He had achieved his dream: Duval & Associates. Though, the firm, he realized, was stale, out-dated and at the threshold of obsolescence. That was not what he envisioned as his future at Duval, Gibson & Associates or, one day, Gibson's Associates. That he would be a senator one day was a given, given his father's influence, his academic standing that was a matter of record and the career already well on its way. And with the combined Gibson-Duval fortunes the acquisition of a comfortable seat in Sacramento wasn't impossible. He could be governor, and quite possibly would be. Elections had nothing to do with the popular vote; winning had everything to do with money, Gibson-Duval money.

Then unexpectedly, in the late spring of his fourth year with Duval & Associates, he was informed matter-of-factly that he would have to move once again to a larger apartment, this time with three bedrooms he would never use: two filled with dolls and plastic kitchen sets, one filled with toy trucks, building blocks and model planes, doors he would never open save for two possible occasions, mandatory invitations he wasn't pleased about extending.

Gabriella Martina Arquero-Duval was now a day old.

The bitch was pushing hard, but he was halfway. What

was another four years and eight months? Not that he was counting.

*

Neither Diego nor Francesca yet knew they should be proud of their father. They likely thought that the commotion was about them. But it wasn't. The evening was all about Hidalgo Felipe Arquero, Attorney at Law and their new sister.

Away from the women and his father, Hidalgo spoke privately with John Canyon. John understood both the irony and complexity of Hidalgo's dilemma. He was the husband of Franklin Duval's daughter, the father of Duval's grandchildren, yet he couldn't very well clerk in the same law office as Francine's supposed husband. But Duval wasn't the attorney for the Estates and Hidalgo began his year-long clerkship a week later.

When the party was over, in their bed, Hidalgo confessed the reason for his sombre mood. Francine patted his hand, telling him not to worry, things were under control. John neither wanted nor expected anything more than a brilliant legal career. Though John had expressed to her how much the Estates would miss him. Hidalgo was good for business, he told her privately: "I should never have brought the kid into the fold. Guess we don't appreciate a good thing till we don't have it anymore."

She didn't tell Hidalgo, John asked her not to. He felt badly enough about no longer working at the Estates. What she told him instead was that her investment advisor had recently sent her an updated review of her portfolio. She was worth five million. The man, she told Hidalgo, was doing his job. She also had a surprise, one she knew he wouldn't like, but everyone else would. So he would have to deal with it.

At Christmas they were flying to Vale. She'd rented a villa. She wanted to see snow. She wanted to feel it, scoop it in her hands and eat it. She'd spoken with John. They would fly in the corporate plane, everyone, and John had already cashed her cheque in payment for the fuel. He had objected vigorously at first, finally understanding her need for independence. It didn't matter how much, she answered Hidalgo, and she had also paid up front for the landing fees. So, if he wanted to spoil everyone's Christmas, he could stay home. However his presents and children would be in Vale.

He saw no purpose in arguing. He kissed her instead.

27
Twenty-five Years Ago

Francine had her special Christmas. She hadn't celebrated with her parents in five years. Mr. & Mrs. Duval had begun travelling from mid-December through to mid-January to Polynesia, leaving the Gibsons to host the New Year's Ball at the club. The Duvals, in turn, hosted the Midyear Dinner & Dance Evening which their daughter and son-in-law never attended.

Francine seldom thought of her parents. Maria was more of a mother than Mrs. Duval had ever been and Fernando couldn't be more like a father, a doting father who would bounce her on his knee and laugh with her, telling her endless stories about Hidalgo. He continued never speaking English with her. He didn't have to; her Spanish was fluent to the extent that, on occasion, and with a pout, she would now correct him much to Hidalgo's and Maria's unabashed amusement. Five-year-old Diego spoke English with his mother and Spanish with his father, occasionally choosing not to understand either when to his advantage.

She never thought of the Gibsons. Her bi-annual visits to their home were brief, functional, and immediately forgotten. By both parties, she had no doubt. She could live with the subterfuge four more years, not a day longer, often amazed by the parents' lack of interest in her. Her grandparents weren't like that, she once told Hidalgo, the day she heard the news.

Mrs. Duval's father had passed away in Spain, and his only daughter hadn't so much as thought of going to the funeral. His granddaughter, however, did. And Hidalgo went with her.

She knew both her grandmothers. She loved the old women deeply. And when they heard her story, when they heard that the handsome young man accompanying her was her real husband, they forgot their grief for a moment and chuckled. They thought Senator Gibson was an old fart. And his wife Claire was no better. They hadn't raised their son or their daughter to be that way. The fact they thought more of that pretentious club and being seen than they did of their daughter was horrible. The fact that neither one had come to the funeral was unforgivable, and would not be forgiven.

They'd decided between them, the two old women, that Hidalgo was very charming and humble. He was polite and very unpretentious. And they wanted to know more about him. They took him aside to drill him and enjoy a glass of sherry, while Francine spoke with her grandfather and too soon they were once again at the airport, Hidalgo pleased to have met her family who promised to visit with them soon in Vallejo to meet his parents.

That never happened. Within a week Hidalgo and Francine returned to Spain. Mrs. Duval's mother could not survive without her husband of sixty years. She passed away in her sleep after writing a letter to Francine the day before, a letter she was not to receive for a while.

Francine asked and pleaded with her father's parents to return home with them to Vallejo where they could be together for what time was left to them. The old folks declined. They were at home. They had dear friends in Spain; it's where they belonged, and where they would remain.

A few weeks following their first trip, alone in bed, sharing a moment of quiet between sporadic bouts of colic, Francine said out of curiosity: "Mi amor, you never told me what gift my grandmothers gave you that was such a deep, dark secret they wouldn't share with me. Can I know now?"

He knew the question would surface eventually. He'd never considered an answer because he knew that whatever he decided to say wouldn't come out the way he wanted. So he simply said: "One million dollars. They told me that gifts from the living were so much happier than gifts from the dead."

He paused, waiting for her to stop laughing.

"That's my nanas, Hidalgo. That's how I want to be when I'm old. I'm so glad you got to see them."

"I have repaid John with the money. He did not want to accept it at first." He chuckled. "Then I told him that neither did I want to accept it, but someone had to. I told him that my father would not respect me to know that I had taken his friendship for granted. With the rest I will open my law office. Now I will not have to work for someone else. I will make your grandmothers proud that you married me, mi corazón. My time has finally come to repay all these kindnesses."

Within a month of the old woman's passing an elegant gentleman knocked at their door. He hadn't called in advance of his visit; he simply arrived and asked for a few moments of their time. He'd travelled from Spain specifically to meet with them on behalf of his clients.

He was an estate attorney. He'd brought with him a letter recently written by Francine's grandmother, now deceased, and from her paternal grandmother. He also had a brief message for Hidalgo and Francine on her behalf.

They believed at the wedding, that her marriage to Scott Gibson was a terrible thing arranged by selfish and uncaring parents for their personal gain: a travesty in their eyes. Their granddaughter was much too lovely, much too bright to become a Mrs. Somebody who wasn't anybody. They had immediately redrafted their wills, all four had, entirely disgusted with their own children.

To that end the attorney continued, addressing Francine, the shared and individual physical assets of her maternal grandparents were recently assigned to friends and charities according to their express wishes. The entirety of their financial assets was also to be divided and would now be disbursed according to their express wishes. Such was the reason for his unannounced visit.

"Señora Arquero-Duval, I will require your signature as proof that you are in receipt of these twelve million dollars. This is your copy of the transfer stating that the documentation will remain with me until the transfer is satisfactorily concluded with your bank. And, Señor Arquero, your signature is required as well for these eight million."

A pin dropping would have shattered the quiet. The gentleman displayed no emotion. There was no joy in the transaction. Francine's tears were real. She'd lost two people she loved, so happy that Hidalgo had seen for himself that her family was more than her shallow mother and father.

When the gentleman took his leave, suggesting they meet the next morning to finalize the transfer with the bank as expeditiously as possible, Hidalgo gave her space to read the letters. When after a while she came to where he was sitting, his mind was either numbed or flooded by what had just taken place. He couldn't tell which. She was smiling, her face was wet. She had told her grandparents everything about the annulment, her trip to Pichilingue and Hidalgo. The letters were their way of saying that she had done the right thing. They were proud of her. To have done differently would have ruined Hidalgo's future. They knew their children. They were self-serving and mean-spirited individuals. They'd forgotten their upbringing, polluted by fame and fortune, and what was known by them of Senator Gibson and his wife was no less disturbing. When they'd first heard of the intended Gibson-Duval joining they were devastated, now they were overjoyed for Hidalgo and Francine.

What she did to circumvent tragedy demonstrated courage and inventiveness. She was indeed their granddaughter and they'd agreed amongst themselves before her grandfather's passing that whatever corruption had spoiled the previous generation was too well engrained to reverse. They were, in a word, disowned.

As for Scott Gibson, Francine said, the ruse would continue. Arthur Gibson would not tolerate being publicly ridiculed by the front page news of his son being married, the marriage annulled, and living the deception for so many years while his supposed wife and children belonged to another man. The fallout would be disastrous. He would allow nothing to stand in his son's way. Scott would be a full partner one day soon, and as such, one day, an equal partner in the club where deals were made and assurances given. The plan was that he would one day sit in the senate and being dismissed from Duval & Associates would ruin that hope, not to mention the fathers' finely crafted friendship.

Francine knew he golfed with both fathers and had begun shaking hands with senators and congressman, although at home his name was never mentioned. She couldn't imagine the ramifications of telling Hidalgo that Gibson had punched her in the face. They met four times yearly, setting the dates for those joint visits weeks in advance, and since the arrival of Gabriella Martina the children weren't involved, a fact that pleased Scott no end.

Francine abruptly laughed again, a sudden chortle

caught in her throat, a thought that she knew would please her nanas. Her parents would be furious at being excluded from the grandparents' fortune. Her idea, though, she had no doubt, would put distance between them and solve the Scott thing. Yes, she would call her mother, and Scott, and she would take pleasure from each and every gasp, shriek and hateful word.

*

Francine was right to assume that her already wealthy parents would react furiously with her, neither one happy for their daughter's windfall. Nor was Scott for that matter. Her father threatened legal action, which Hidalgo knew was not feasible. The will was legal and binding, drafted by a foreign law firm and the transfer was from a foreign bank beyond their influence, overseen by the same law firm so that any confusion might and would be avoided.

Mrs. Duval was beside herself. She could not understand at all how her daughter could be so heartless, so thoughtless. Francine responded that she believed not going to loving parents' funerals was pretty thoughtless, pretty heartless. The conversation ended abruptly without goodbyes either warm or cold and strangely, she thought, without any emotion other than one-sided rage. How she would have liked to be a fly on the wall, she told Hidalgo. Yet, she was calm, she told him. She felt infused with warmth, as though nana and grandpapa were holding her close in their arms.

Francine knew she wouldn't see her mother for a very long time, which was fine with her. She was beginning university towards a B.Ed.; she had three kids, a husband and parents who did love her. She wasn't in the least upset. What she didn't know, however, was that she would never see her parents again. Scott and his family ties were another matter. She would, she decided, see Arthur and Claire once each year through to the tenth year and together they would, beginning immediately, play the troubled couple.

Money, she explained to Scott, was the primary cause of marital unrest. He was a lawyer, he should know that. She had twenty-five million in the bank; he earned a paltry 150K. She would earn twenty-five times that much in interest alone each year. So, yes, her parents, and his, would believe a failing marriage. And if he played nice she might even agree to a trial separation in two years and move out with the kids.

Scott crashed the phone into its cradle and went to the wet bar. He would be in his forties before having anything near half that much. He poured two fingers of bourbon, swallowed the mouthful and poured two more. She couldn't possibly have come up with this plan herself. This was all the spic's doing.

The good thing: He was rid of her but for once each year. As for Duval, let him deal with his daughter if he didn't like what she was doing. She was insane.

*

The next morning the Spanish lawyer met with them at the bank, the bank manager understanding that not all twenty million would remain with his branch. But in one thing Francine stood firm. Two million of her inheritance would be added to Hidalgo's eight, they were partners, and she would also share equally in Maria's and Fernando's gifts.

The question was how to tell them. Of course they were always welcome at the Estates and they hadn't seen Jennie or John for a few weeks. So what better time?

In her office Maria did as they asked. She called the bank. She knew her deviously playful son. She knew something was in his head, but when the bank manager assured her that the million dollars was hers, she shrieked. John Canyon was first in her office, crashing through the door, expecting he didn't know what. Fernando followed, the two men exchanging confused glances. Even Fernando had trouble understanding Maria until she passed her husband the phone. Yes, the bank manager confirmed, his account was also a million dollars to the good.

John strode back into his office. Even his best wine couldn't get him through this debacle. He needed a very strong and very large tequila, and only when he felt sufficiently fortified against the worst possible news did he re-join the excitement and confusion.

What in the hell was he going to do without them? He wanted to know. He wanted answers. He'd lost one Arquero, he wasn't losing any more. A couple of million wasn't that much, he cautioned, not the way Maria frittered away money on extravagant clothes and Fernando wasn't any better with his expensive taste in wine. They were too young to retire, period. Besides, working kept Maria young and beautiful, that wouldn't take long to change what with fine restaurants and idle living. Beware the lazy woman, he warned Fernando. Busy women were the happiest women.

Jennie told him to shut up. No one was going anywhere except to the kitchen for dinner, she admonished.

Maria couldn't stop chattering in her vibrant tongue throughout the meal, Pichilingue never having faded from her memory. She would never forget her meagre beginnings, and now for her son to be so wealthy at such a young age. She kissed her cross. ¡Santa Maria!

"This is because of you, John. So many years ago you saw something in my Fernando that was good, as I did, as he saw something in your kind heart. It is because of you that we are here, blessed with this good fortune, with our daughter Francine, with you and Jennie as such good friends." She shook her head. "No, you are family to us. You know that you are. That these kind people have passed on to their time for peace is sad, I will pray for them tonight and light candles for each of them on Sunday. But you have done this for us. I know this is true. Believe me, we are going nowhere. You are stuck with us. Besides, how could we leave Jennie alone to deal with you?" She pushed her chair from the table, stood, and went to him, kissing his cheek, winking at Jennie. "And thank you for saying that I am beautiful."

He had nothing to say. He knew what she meant. A glib response would ruin the moment, and in his heart he knew they had done much more for him than he could ever repay. He wouldn't say that either. He didn't want to open the floodgates of his past, when she was alive, when she died, when he believed he would never smile again except for Jennie in his life. Instead he raised his glass in a toast to three beautiful women and everyone's good fortune, his included. He was the one with the most to be thankful for.
*

That same morning Franklin Duval was on the phone with his elderly father in Marbella. The conversation was concise. When he disconnected, had he not known the source of his anxiety attack, he might have believed he was experiencing severe cardiac arrest. He wasn't. His daughter, he was told without the slightest hesitation or discomposure in the old man's voice, was getting everything when the time came. Francine was the primary beneficiary noted in their wills, beyond a few baubles and trinkets to be disbursed amongst their closest friends. In short, she was getting all their money.

When Duval enquired as to the extent of the estate, the old man answered with obvious humour and satisfaction in his voice: substantially more than from your wife's disadvantaged relatives whom we've just lost...bless their souls.

Next he called his wife, to rant. If their daughter did not make immediate amends of her own accord and without inducement from either one of them, or Gibson and his wife for that matter, she was never again to set foot in his house.

She was no longer his daughter. She was forthwith disowned. What she'd contrived behind their backs, colluding against them with aged and senile parents, was despicable and reprehensible.

He slammed down the phone, pressed the extension for Gibson, ordering him to get his ass into his office.

"Good morning, sir."

"What the fuck is good about it? Sit down."

This wasn't good. Franklin Duval never lost his cool. His thousand-dollar suits were never creased and his hundred-dollar haircuts were never mussed. Conversely, what confronted Gibson could not have been more out of place. He'd scarcely finished his third cup of coffee and the old-fashioned sitting on Duval's glass-top desk was empty.

Gibson sat. He didn't know what to say or what to expect, his mind in turmoil, searching for the best immediate answer. Duval never made statements, he asked questions, he dug, he interrogated, most often with difficult, near impossible questions and woe betide him or her who put forth an incorrect response or, worse, dumbfounded silence.

Duval poured a second scotch from the bottle in his drawer. "Gibson, what the absolute fuck is wrong with that damned wife of yours?"

"Francine, sir...I don't understand. She's doing very well. We both are."

"Bullshit. The only thing she does well, from what I see, is squeeze your balls."

"I don't understand, sir. We're very happy together. More than we ever imagined."

"Is that right? The last time you were over you barely spoke to one another. So, once again, what the fuck is wrong with that little bitch? What's her mental state, and what is it you aren't telling me?"

Gibson inhaled a deep breath, exhaling a slow,

pressurized stream between pursed lips he was afraid to moisten. "I don't know, sir. I suppose we're still getting used to each other. We really weren't expecting the kids to come along as quickly as they did." He shrugged. "Things happen. We've had no real quality time together because of them and my career here at the firm. So when we are together we like to spend our time alone. We know we should spend more time with family, but it's not like the old days. We have so many demands. And now that she'll be attending university for a B.Ed., our time alone will become even more precious. Mr. Duval, sir, I haven't once felt as deeply about anyone as I do your Francine. That she agreed to marry me is the happiest of my dreams come true. And the kids, what can I say?"

"She wants to be a teacher, her? God help us." Duval coughed a laugh "You know what I think, Gibson?"

"No, sir, of course I don't."

"I think you're more full of shit than the only outhouse at the beach on the fourth of July. I haven't once in my life met a man single or married who can swear on his life that he ever wanted kids. Leave that for the Third World and the Mexicans. Here in the U S of A it's all about our good neighbours, keeping up with the Joneses, feigning piety at church when the good padre probably gets laid more than any of his righteous flock, and proving to the world that you don't shoot blanks. Shoot blanks and, likely as not, they'll think you're a queer. It's the way people think."

"Mr. Duval, I love those kids."

"Save that crap for your wife. You've taken on a whack of shit, boy: a wife who was brought up wanting for nothing, albeit by me, three spoiled kids and an ocean view condominium on your salary. Are you shitting me? You'd better not be thinking of letting your paid hours drop anytime soon. That's a whole lot of pressure for one man to bear. Personally, if I were you I'd already be gone, unless you're sticking around for the money."

"Sir, we have separate mandates. She takes care of our home, I pay the bills."

"Is that a fact? And who took care of your home and your three kids when she was in Spain sucking up to her grandparents? Or didn't you think the fact that she went off on her own to Europe was worth mentioning to me?"

Shit! "No sir. I didn't, because I believed you knew. I mean after all, she was going to visit Mrs. Duval's mother. And, quite frankly, with my workload, I..."

"She went to her grandfather's fucking funeral while I was here swimming with alligators up to my ass and Mrs. Duval was beside herself with grief."

Gibson was visibly stunned. "Sir, I promise, I didn't know. She didn't tell me until she got back. I believed she was going to see her grandparents for a simple visit. She hasn't had a real vacation in sometime." Shit! Shit! "And the kids, they stayed with a neighbour. She's a retired paediatric nurse, a saint if I ever met one. The children just love her."

An invisible sword was level with his neck. He could feel the cold steel. Duval leaned forward, Gibson for some reason focusing on the purple gums outlining Duval's costly white teeth.

"When a man talks to you, boy, you look into his eyes. Or were you screwing some co-ed the day they taught that lesson at law school. You're gone two weeks twice a year and you're telling me that isn't enough R&R for a woman who hasn't worked one fucking day in her life? Is that what you're telling me?"

"Yes sir. I am. Because when we travel she wants me to relax. It's all about me, sir. She handles the kids. I'm telling you, she's a fantastic mom. When we get home she's more tired than when we left and it's because of me. Sometimes, I don't know, I feel so sorry for her, like I'm not doing enough to help her."

"That shit won't get you where you want to be. Up and comers have to be seen. People have to know you're a responsible husband and family man. That means you're the man, she's the wife and the mother. That's your job, that's her job. That doesn't mean she washes dishes and diapers. It means she starts being seen with you in public, working the floor for you, getting you noticed. Get a frigging live-in and, for Christ's sake, get a real fucking house for once. It's not as though you can't afford a goddamn mansion." He paused. "Are you getting this, Gibson?"

Gibson slouched into his seat. "Sir, you mean the money."

"No. I mean the twenty million dollars she sucked out of Mrs. Duval's parents and her second trip to Spain to coerce and swindle my parents, the other trip you didn't see fit to tell me about. Care to explain when you were thinking of telling me about that one?"

"Sir, I can't. I just found out myself about the money. All I can say is that we'll be paying off the mortgage this week. The rest will be held in trust for the children and our retirement."

"Jointly," Duval persisted.

"Jointly, sir, yes, however withdrawals must be by mutual consent."

"Which simply means that you require her permission to benefit in any way from her recently acquired wealth, whereas she may do as she pleases and at any time without your consent. Is that about right?"

"Yes sir. After all, they were her grandparents and our children are the real beneficiaries. Anyway, according to the pre-nuptial, what is hers remains hers, and what is mine remains mine now and in the future. I'll catch up, sir. As for Mrs. Duval's mother, well, I didn't know what to do or say. I was between a rock and a hard place. I mean, Francine

214

went to Spain, but not you or Mrs. Duval. And the way Francine acted about the whole thing...well; I just thought I'd better keep my mouth shut, especially since you hadn't broached their unfortunate passing with me. I really am sorry, sir. Please tell Mrs. Duval I didn't mean any disrespect."

"I'll do that. As for your catching up, not while I'm alive. Not unless Arthur or your mother dies first, which I don't wish to happen anytime soon. But let me tell you what I do wish. I don't want that little bitch anywhere near this office or my home until I can see her without having a massive coronary or wanting to kill her. Is that understood? What she's done to me and her mother is unconscionable and won't be condoned or tolerated. In short, if I see her with you for any reason, anywhere, you're screwed. Regardless of my respect for, and my friendship with, your father, I'll kick your ass out of here on the spot. You'll spend your career in fucking night court with drunks and ten-dollar whores."

"Sir, she's your daughter."

"She was my daughter. Now she's your problem. Deal with her. I've had my time with her and obviously she went astray at some point. I mean what I say. I will not tolerate seeing her." Duval reclined, sighing, operating the controls of his newly marketed ergonomic executive seat. "Now, I have you penciled in for a two PM. Believe me, I'm not ready for any more of this Gibson-Duval horseshit today, so tread easy. What is it? And it better be good. I've wasted enough of my day with you."

Gibson would have killed for even the slightest sip of scotch. "Sir, I recently met a man who might be interested in our services. In fact, I can say with complete certainty that he is very interested. He's currently without legal representation and is very familiar with Duval & Associates' incomparable success in criminal law. He confided in me that he was once refused by us, apparently for reasons of insubstantial financial resources. However, as I understand his current personal situation, he is more than capable of honouring that particular prerequisite to any Duval-client contract."

"He told you he's a criminal. He admitted to a crime before engaging us?"

"Not quite that directly, sir. Our discussion was somewhat less than candid for obvious reasons. He's very definitely a criminal and really didn't have to elaborate on his need for counsel. I'm sure you will agree that he's very high profile. I also believe he would be a major acquisition…my acquisition, sir."

"And his name would be?"

"His name is Enrique Mendoza. He's your two o'clock."

28

Enrique Mendoza was slick, he was upwardly mobile. He had flair; anyone seeing him would possibly think he was an artist or a musician. Once he had moved from the barrios of Los Angeles to the mainstream streets of San Francisco. He was thirty-five and not afraid of anyone or anything. Or so the rumour went, although he never walked alone.

He dropped out from grade six to help support his single mother by running numbers for someone who was tougher and meaner than him in the day. He grew up fast. He was given no choice, the option was dying young. He was arrested a dozen times for careless B&Es, usually caught with more broken glass around his feet than anything of value in his hands, often returning to the street within a week because his mother needed him. Not because he had anything good going for him.

She couldn't live without him. She could never hold down a job because when she did work most of her salary went to feed her continued deep affection for cheap booze and the occasional dime of smack when someone drunk enough to forgive her shortcomings of mind and body would agree to barter low-grade powder for her body that had already degraded well beyond the point of no return. At twenty-nine she died naked in her soiled bed days before her son's sixteenth birthday, coated with sweat from the summer's heat, enshrouded in acrid grey-blue smoke and the melding stenches of urine and fecal matter. The man lying beside her was passed out, insensate, two empty quart bottles without labels wedged between them.

Later that morning, not long after sunrise, the man was discovered in an alley huddled against a dumpster. He was dead. He hadn't been beaten or shot, strangled or stabbed. He was just dead: another John Doe plucked from the city streets. No one cared about the why or the how. He was black, skeletal, dressed in loose-fitting pants strapped tightly at the waist and made wet by his own urine and a tattered singlet stained yellow with ancient sweat and spotted with many other colours not found in any rainbow. No one cared, the assumption being that he either died without his shoes or that some passer-by had seen an opportunity. He was found in the barrio. No one cared.

Mendoza returned to his mother in the two-room flat. He covered her with a sheet, kissed her without touching her, threw the bottles from the open window onto the street and phoned the cops. He sat on the floor in the outer hallway of the tenement smoking a cigarillo, inhaling the thick smoke to mask the stench of all who lived there, shuffling his feet or smacking the warped floor with his open palm to scare away the rats as he waited for the police.

They never came quickly. This was the barrio.

She was pronounced from a distance by someone who didn't care, someone in a white coat and thick rubber gloves pinching his nose. When his mother was taken away Mendoza gathered what little he owned and became a citizen of the street.

He ran numbers by day and pimped by night. By eighteen he had a dozen girls, all of them young, all of them seeing in him what they had never seen in their parents. He loved them, and they loved him. He was good to them, he treated them like ladies. He respected them and they would do nothing to disappoint him or to hurt him. By twenty he had expanded his interests. He was dealing with a selective clientele. Fagots in shiny Corvettes knew where to find him. So did the doctors in Beamers, lawyers and glamorous escorts who either wanted to show their own clients a better time or forget that they were merely high-priced facsimiles of Mendoza girls.

By twenty-four he was living well. He was the one driving a shiny Trans-Am, a .38 stuck into his belt with not so much as a traffic violation to his credit. He was good at what he did. He knew where he was going and how to get there. He'd graduated from deadhead homeless girls who willing screwed or blew pathetic johns for chump change, girls who wanted to hurt their loving parents, girls who soon became too damaged beyond repair for those loving parents to ever want them back

He saw the value in more sophisticated and desirable young women who could see a more long-term future with him, more costly escorts, a better class of girls: nubile university students eager to pay off student loans, young single mothers anxious for a better life for their children and young divorcées wanting to redefine their lives while making money and having a good time.

They were flocking to him in droves.

By twenty-eight he was incorporated, legitimate, living in the fresher air of Marina Del Rey. He had a lawyer and an accountant. He owned a string of massage parlours, many of them operated by those college girls who either needed the extra money or weren't as appealing to the male ego as they were four years earlier or not as smart as they once believed they were.

Still, he wanted more. He wanted friends, important friends. Above all he wanted prestige. He wanted a yacht and membership in a prestigious club where others of his kind were not allowed. He wanted to rub elbows with men like the ones who rented out his women, who frequented his parlours for upscale attention to their aches and pains derived from the stress of privileged living. He wanted respect and he found it sitting in a bar one late afternoon just weeks from his thirtieth birthday.

She wasn't searching for love in all the wrong places, and told him to get lost. She wasn't interested. He placed her at about forty, but she was hot. He chortled and walked away to sit in a corner and study her. She wasn't like his other ladies. Even the brightest ones were only truly appealing when they were naked. But this broad was different, she had class. She wasn't perturbed at all even though she knew he was watching her. He was attracted by her cool and confident demeanor, her husky voice that was at once seductive and disarming. So he went to her again with a proposition. She would teach him how to deserve respect, on her terms; she would make his dream a reality in exchange for fifteen-hundred in cash and upfront each week.

He had no interest in what she had hidden in her panties, he told her. He could get that anytime in any colour, shape or age he wanted. He wanted what he knew was in her head. She was an upscale broad and he didn't care why she was slumming in the barrio. Did they have a deal he asked her, unfolding fifteen bills?

She began that afternoon and went home with 1500 dollars in her purse. They met the next day for lunch.

She taught him how to sit straight, how to lounge when appropriate, not slouch. She taught him how to dine, not to eat as though wolfing a dollar-fifty hotdog at a ball game. She taught him how to drink, what to drink, in what glass and when. She taught him how to dress, what to wear and when. She taught him how to use his voice to intimidate with cool detachment or to beguile with ardent attentiveness. She taught him that he must first give respect before gaining respect.

She was a model who'd passed her prime. She was

exquisite to the eye, well-spoken, well-educated, exotic and alluring, simply no longer alluring enough to stand, sit or lie in front of a lens in European panties and a laced bra. She'd made a big mistake. She married a lieutenant in the Marine Corps, a man who couldn't live without her, a man who was on top of the world when she said yes, who then suddenly couldn't deal with other men seeing his wife undressed, her glamour shots pinned to their locker doors or by their spartan beds in otherwise austere barracks.

Soon after the beatings took over from arguing as her career entered into a steady decline, consistent with what in his mind were disgrace and humiliation, her make-up artist increasingly unable to conceal the abuse.

Mendoza wanted badly to seduce her each time he saw her, which was every weekday. He'd never been with such a glamorous woman. She wasn't like the others he could have simply by snapping his fingers or lighting a reefer. However she was with him for the money, always refusing to mix business with pleasure despite their age difference, though he never did discover how much older she was. More importantly, she knew the difference between intrinsic and façade and the barrio was still very much a part of him. He wanted a new look, she wanted a new beginning: an ideal match.

She worked with him for six months before leaving him, her graduation gift to him a .357 chrome-plated magnum. She told him over lunch their last day together that if he sincerely wanted the world to take him seriously he would have to lose the .38, a girl's gun. The magnum was a man's gun.

He thanked her, mastering his new elegance with ease. The weapon felt good in his hands, natural. His gift to her was a flight to an island beach resort, the least he could do, a one week reprieve from, and in appreciation of, her difficult work. She was worth every penny. She had made him into a gentleman who now boasted a personal barber and a haberdasher. Regrettably he commented with a smirk, he would not be joining her. She never saw him again.

When she returned home she listened to an emotionless message on her answering machine asking that she contact the base commander immediately. The officer arrived at her home within the hour. Her husband was dead, shot in the face at close range by a large calibre handgun. The police had no witnesses, no clues and no motive. He was simply dead, the victim of a random shooting. He was in the wrong place at the wrong time.

The following week she sold her home and moved away. She knew, and she was grateful. With the money she'd recently earned, and what was due from the military, she would live a good life.

By thirty-three Enrique Mendoza had expanded his operation north to San Francisco. He was the new boy in town and aggressive. He owned several cocktail lounges in L.A. and had financial interests in several more dedicated to work-weary gentlemen, men in search of what they once had, had once dreamed of having or could never hope to have. And his forty-foot Pachanga was docked where he could see her floating from the bay window of his twentieth floor Marina Del Rey condo.

He had what he called Business Managers for each operation and a General Manager for each group of operations in both cities. Mario Mendoza, a cousin, was brought in as a favour to Enrique's aunt, a promise made years earlier to a woman who wasn't much better than his mother, whose time on this earth had run out. Mario was Enrique's junior by a few years, released on good behaviour after serving twelve of a fifteen-year sentence for voluntary manslaughter with a firearm.

After two years of proving himself as Business Manager of the Bay area's newest strip bar, Enrique promoted him to

General Manager of that club and three others. They met once each week at a different club, usually on Mondays when new girls who demonstrated above average potential during private interviews were hired to dance at the clubs on a rotating basis so that even the most ardent and frequent customers were never inclined to go elsewhere for fresh diversion.

The cops in both cities knew of him. In fact each Christmas he would send the mayors, commissioners and chiefs of police invitations to the Christmas Galas at each of his clubs when lucky winners of the draw would be entertained in private salons without the usual hundred-dollar surcharge. None ever attended.

But the fast Pachanga was no longer good enough; he wanted the mega yacht of his dreams. He wanted to host onboard parties, he wanted beautiful women in tiny bikinis strewn across the decks for his pleasure and the pleasure of anyone who would see the value in knowing him, who could and would bring him value, which would never happen unless he made the first move.

Highly paid whores, dancers, addicted queers and doctors, although well-developed profit centres, were increasingly uninteresting to him. They would never elevate him to where he knew he belonged. He had people he trusted to run those operations for him. He wanted his name on buildings and he had the money to invest in San Francisco where land was less expensive than in the City of Angels.

He needed a go-between, new and aggressive legal counsel that would keep most of his legal money in his pockets and much of his less mainstream revenue hidden. He needed a law firm that was respected, beyond reproach, yet able to represent his girls and managers when certain difficulties, certain conflicts or misunderstandings would inevitably arise.

He needed a law firm that knew their way around the system, who would see him as a businessman, not a member in good standing of organized crime, and his cousin Mario knew just the man. He was a regular.

He was their age, give or take, and the son of a frigging senator. He was married to the boss' daughter and the boss was the best known lawyer in town. He had a stick up his ass most times, but needed a place where he could unwind. Apparently his wife was cold as ice and Mario had a good twenty hours of unedited audio-visual tape showing the man with a dozen different girls over the past few months alone. His generous tips and affinity for premium liquor made him a preferred client. The girls liked him. He knew most of their real names, often booking them a day in advance for personal attention in the club's Prestige Salons. A few, on occasion, had gone home with him. He'd even been invited to a few after-hours private parties, and he did like to party. One of the girls had spent the previous Christmas with him in Aspen after he'd won her in the draw. She went home two days later a grand richer.

Mario had no doubt that if he was as good as he said, then, they'd found the right guy.

29

Despite his newfound wealth, Hidalgo's new law office was unpretentious. He found an ideal storefront location with easy transportation for his future clientele. The sign etched onto his window simply stated: Law Office - Bufete - Se Habla Español.

He hired a contractor to reface the aging brick façade and a local artist to create a mural illustrating the legal process from the initial meeting with an attorney to sentencing. The final scene depicted the judge thrusting out an admonishing finger, the juvenile boy shrinking before him, a schoolbag strapped to his back, pressing his hands together in grateful prayer. He wanted to show his younger clients that not everyone went to jail.

Meanwhile he worked with the three women in his life to make the interior equally inviting for girls as for boys, for women as much as for men. He had a kitchen installed which brought chuckles from all three co-conspirators. There was a Pizza Boy right next door, his primary weakness since that first day with his father. He had a small lounge for his clients, not a waiting room, with a vending machine filled with free milk, juice, soft drinks and newly discovered meal replacement bars. The cost was the push of a button.

There were books and magazines for reading or taking if time didn't permit to finish what was being read. And he arranged for a trained nurse to be available for counselling on-site once each week for whatever reason.

One wall of his private office was lined from floor to ceiling with leather-bound books in good, bad and poor condition that he acquired from a used bookstore, lending an air of distinction and credibility, he told Francine. He didn't expect that he would ever read them. Another wall was wallpapered to appear real, which Maria thought was practical, and a third housed any and all books he'd read throughout his university and law school years as well as the most recently published books, papers and journals on jurisprudence that he did or would read.

He once believed that he would take years to repay John Canyon, which now wasn't the case due to the graciousness of Francine's grandmothers. He remembered how he had once felt embarrassed for his father, that John Canyon was helping them, though he understood very quickly and very succinctly from John that help was not synonymous with charity. And John wasn't a man to argue with.

He had so much to be thankful for, so much to repay. He once had dreams, now diluted because of God's grace, of becoming rich and famous, of treating his mother like a queen, of buying her silk dresses, European cars and sending her on exotic vacations. And he would, but now none of that would be the same. He hadn't earned his millions, he'd walked into them. That wasn't what Hidalgo Felipe Arquero was all about, he told his mother. How, now, would he make his parents proud?

When Jennie and Francine were busy with colours and textures, Maria sat and listened to her son. When he was done she smacked his cheek and told him to pay attention. She and his father had never stopped being proud of him. That's all she had to say. Then she kissed him; she kissed her cross and beamed. God had blessed her with two fine men, she added, and the oldest would soon be even prouder of the youngest.

Hidalgo had explained to Maria that he wanted to work with kids before their criminal careers began in earnest, before they either could not or were not allowed to turn back. He wanted to help kids with potential who were never given a chance. He wanted to work with kids in the barrios, high school kids and dropouts, young mothers stealing food or hooking to feed their babies and young men stealing to keep their young wives and children housed and warm for another week or a month. Pimps and dealers were another matter, and not welcome.

Money wasn't an issue. His clients would pay what they could afford, or not. With experience he would soon discover those who deserved and those who did not, those who wanted a free ride at his expense before returning to their preordained life which he could do nothing about.

At first some would take advantage of him, but he would learn and one day he would be the best attorney in San Francisco. Everyone one would know Hidalgo Arquero. And he was right. Everyone would know Hidalgo Arquero, within four years, days after the devastating Loma Prieta earthquake. He just didn't have any idea of exactly how abruptly, or for what reasons.

30
December 06th of this Year

The weather outside was a balmy 72°. Inside the conditions were less seasonal, somewhat chillier, what one might expect to experience while sitting by a frozen lake or strolling across the Arctic ice fields

Anita Juárez was seated at her desk when the governor walked through her door towards his own. He didn't say much. What could he say after so many years that would make sense to either of them? She was absolutely stunning, gorgeous, sexy and sensual, simply not his. She would never be his, not now.

That she hadn't come by the mansion that morning, he understood. She was a woman. Despite her privileged station, she was a woman, more easily swayed by deep emotion than a man. She was telling him in no uncertain terms to...well, she was telling him that he had waited too long, as though he had a choice. What was he expected to do? He was the governor. The press and the tabloids would have had a field day with her, with him. And she would have been disallowed by common sense from working with him in her current capacity, where he needed her, where he wanted her every day.

"Buenos días, Anita," he tried.

"Good morning, Boss," she replied in English, not bothering to notice him.

He was a smart man, educated and well-versed in tactical confrontation. He said nothing more. He went into his office and closed the door behind him. When he did that, whenever he did that, she knew not to disturb him.
*

The man was a complete idiot. He was a fool. Worse, she had spent her entire weekend telling her pillow how foolish, how stupid he was. So what did that say about her? She felt ridiculous.

At 9:00 AM promptly the flowers arrived: two dozen white roses, her favourite flower, and extravagant in the extreme. She would not even consider walking into that office. He could go to hell. The man was sophisticated. He was playing her, sucking up to what he believed was typical female weakness: the ability to forgive and forget. Screw him, El Cacique, The Boss... the biggest Bastard on Earth. She wouldn't give him the satisfaction.

She read the note.

The tiny green light on her desk blinked. She wanted to smash it. She wanted to smash him. He was arrogant, thoughtless and blind. Yet she knew none of that was true. She hadn't cried into her pillow because she had wasted her life waiting for the impossible. She was putting one and one together and didn't like what she was beginning to understand from the incoming reports, the most recent of which had come from New Orleans the night before.

She'd told the men reporting to her that she alone was to receive the confidential data, no one else, especially not him. He was not to be informed until the very last minute, until she had time to review the data.

Anyway, for the next twenty-five days he was still The Boss. She went in.

"Good morning, Governor. I trust you're feeling more rested."

"I am, Anita."

"Thank you for the flowers. They weren't necessary, nor was there any need to apologize."

"I treated you unkindly last week. My mood was dark, and I am afraid you bore the brunt of my misery. You always brighten my day, Anita." He smiled: a rare occurrence. "Were you that preoccupied that you have not called me in five days, leaving me messages through your assistants?"

"I have much to finalize in our last four weeks together to ensure a smooth transition."

He nodded. "And what of Drew Carling and the women, do we have news?"

"No sir. That information is currently being compiled. I am told that you will receive completed files by this Friday. As of this moment there is nothing to report."

He knew she was lying. "When they are delivered to you, bring them directly to me. All three are for my eyes only. No exceptions."

"I understand."

He knew she didn't want to be standing in front of him. She could have had any one of a hundred different men over the past twenty plus years. He'd ruined her life as well. Her fault as much as his and how could he now tell her how he loved the way she smelled, that he'd never seen her as lovely?

"Will you let me know sometime soon?"

"Sir…?"

She gave him a quizzical look. She was playing hardball. So would he. He waited. No one just turned and walked away from a governor.

"You mean your note."

He nodded. "Yes, I mean the note."

"No, Governor, I don't see the point. They are very nice people, from what I know of them. However I would not feel comfortable."

Governor, that wasn't good. "Because of the letter, I assume."

"No, Governor, because of you. You have chosen to leave office early. I must also begin to prepare for my new life and career. Not much time is left to me."

He reclined, studying her face, her coal-black eyes that she could stop from blinking at will, when she felt the need to dominate, intimidate or make a silent point. And she apparently felt the need.

"I told you that next year will be my best in a long time, I did not say that it will also be my worst. I fear that somehow I have managed to drive a wedge between us, and not just the letter. Please reconsider my request."

He didn't say invitation, or that his Christmas would be so much happier with her. She couldn't believe he'd said 'request'. The man was a complete fool.

"The mall will remain open after hours this evening for your convenience, the stores that will be of interest to you."

He understood. "Thank you." He watched her walk away. When she was at the door: "Anita, I don't think it's possible for any woman to be lovelier than you are today. Those few flowers on your desk lose their fragrance beside you. Please, if you change your mind, I will come for you and take you home without any talk of business. Our drivers, I believe, deserve the day with their families. I would like more to remember you by than this office."

Too little, too late, she knew. She walked out without answering, wondering what they would talk about.

31
Twenty-Three Years Ago

Hidalgo was entering into his third year of a successful practice and Francine had changed her course study from teaching to social studies with two years left before her graduation. She wanted to be part of what her husband was achieving.

Not one of his 350 case files had gone to prison and only a few had gone to jail to serve greatly reduced sentences. Most were fined, commuted to community service, some were ordered into foster homes while others were sent to boot camp to learn the meaning of 'yes sir, please and no thank you'.

None of those doing time reoffended and many returned to school. He was making a huge difference. In two years Hidalgo had earned close to twenty thousand and had spent ten times that amount on school books for his clients, payments to gynecologists and obstetricians who agreed to help the girls for half the usual fee, haircuts for court appearances, new jeans, shirts and sneakers.

More importantly, he couldn't keep up with the soups and sandwiches, homemade tortillas, cookies, cakes, knitted socks and sweaters from grateful mothers and emotionally indebted fathers.

Diego was seven, his sisters, Francesca and Gabriella, were five and three. Maria doted on each of them and

Fernando refused to speak English with them. He spent time with each one, each night, on the phone or by their beds telling them stories of Pichilingue and how their brave father was working secretly with the police to capture bad men and put them away. But that they should never let him know that they knew, or the secret would be broken and guarding the secret was all that kept their father safe from harm. Not even their mother knew, or their grandmother, especially not their grandmother.

Francine went to the Gibson home on two occasions, for the briefest visit possible, making herself clearly understood that the Duval family, or what remained of it, was not a topic of conversation. The point was moot. Franklin Duval learned what he had to know from Arthur Gibson and Mrs. Duval was kept informed by Claire, completing the circle, though neither had much to say. They hadn't seen their daughter in over twenty-four months.

Neither parent was surprised by news of the couple's pending separation. They had spoiled Francine carelessly throughout her childhood and now they were all paying the price. That Scott had to endure her moods and her peculiarities was shameful. That he might lose his children was scandalous, the four grandparents coercing him into taking decisive action, not understanding his belief that things would work out, that she just needed time and space.

Francine called Scott in late September of that year. She wouldn't be seeing him again, she'd decided. He was now fully responsible for sucking up to her father without her help. She would call him again in two years when he could tell the world and her father that she was filing for divorce. He had that long to get his name in lights between Duval and & Associates.
*

Scott Gibson was in his sixth year with the firm, relieved the news was out, that Francine had left him to find herself.

Franklin Duval understood. These things happened. He'd married the wrong girl and everyone was to blame, he included. She was best forgotten. Somehow she'd gone wrong and wasn't coming back to the real world anytime soon, if at all. He was better off without her. They all were. Loyalty to Duval & Associates came before family. Every man and woman at the firm understood that, the good ones. This was no time to start pissing away a career because of a spoiled child.

Gibson couldn't have been happier. His life over the previous couple of years since meeting Enrique Mendoza had been an easy upward climb with no regrets. In fact the only time he did lament the past was when the phone rang once each year. He hated her with vehement passion for what she'd done, for the way she'd trapped him, manipulated him, unable to think of her for a moment without seething.

He was now legal counsel for all Mendoza's holdings in L.A. and San Francisco, taking on occasional clients referred to him by Mendoza as well as accepting lucrative cases from those who knew of his success and required his expertise in keeping them out of jail, prison or financial ruin. Money was never an issue.

He no longer golfed with his father or hers. He golfed with Enrique Mendoza, frequently invited onboard his client's eighty-three-foot Morgan to enjoy the open sea and any one, two or more of L.A.'s and San Francisco's youngest and best dancers at those cities' finest men's clubs. He certainly wasn't looking back and he certainly wasn't thinking about her.

He was as much a part of Mendoza's operation as Mario and certain others who had gained preferential consideration for one reason or another, generally something done for the betterment of the Mendoza family and never openly discussed.

His annual income had surpassed others at the firm. He was earning 200K a year, spending more than he earned by keeping up appearances. Mendoza liked people around him. Gibson was good for his social networking skills, but Mendoza wasn't the pot of gold at the end of the rainbow. The girls he entertained for free. He understood and they understood what was expected of them and none objected to life onboard a luxury yacht or the purest coke in the Southwest if they wanted to keep their fifty K per year job. Thing is, they didn't have expenses. Gibson did.

Away from the clubs, away from the yacht, Mendoza seldom paid. His lawyer paid. What the hell? Why else was he paying an exorbitant retainer? But coke and reefers were expensive, as was premium booze and Gibson's apartment was well stocked with all three. He was in debt and neither Duval nor his father would want to hear why.

He sold his condo, moved into a one-bedroom unit on a lower floor in the same building and made a hundred-thousand in profit. The kids' furniture he threw in the dumpster. When his debts were cleared he had less than ten grand in the bank and his 401K was depleted. Yet he couldn't very well approach Duval for a raise claiming child or spousal support. His daughter had twenty-five million, and that was then. Now, who knew? Christ, he hated the bitch. At least there was no more pretence and old man Duval hadn't seemed in the least pissed with him for what she'd done.

Most nights he had at least one reefer, or two, and maybe a few drinks to calm down. On the nights when one or more of the girls from the clubs came over he usually had twice or three times that much, although he generally reserved the girls for Fridays and Saturdays after their acts. Going on thirty-two made it difficult to attract eighteen and nineteen-year-olds with fake IDs, whereas the girls from the clubs were that young and fun-loving. Who wouldn't play for fifty K a year at that age?

In two years all that would change. He would be a full partner at a quarter-million a year to start, better expenses and fewer explanations.

He'd given up shaking the hands his father shook. He'd decided a while earlier that he didn't need the spotlight, the FBI and Senate Enquiry bullshit. They'd find out about her, her kids, the spic, Mendoza and the clubs in less than a day. Then shit would hit the fan big time. He'd be out of a job and disowned, denied a family fortune well over one hundred million. Thanks, but no thanks.

His father's dream of father and son at the State Capitol would fade in time along with his rage. In the meantime he would do what was necessary to please Enrique and Mario. In point of fact he'd realized some months earlier that he had no other friends or acquaintances apart from a few names and faces he knew from the fathers' club, where he often entertained Mendoza on the Duval tab.

Bankers and builders liked Mendoza, so did the girls and his managers, not so much the well-heeled and those whose pockets were brimming with old money. In fact Mendoza only went to the club to snub them, to adjust his belt or jacket so that just enough polished chrome was visible.

He would survive. All things considered, his life wasn't all that bad. Good booze, top quality drugs and as many gorgeous and willing girls in his bed as he wanted, when he wanted. All he had to do was point.

He was good, at the law and with Mendoza. They understood each other. No one would touch him, literally. Not with Mendoza watching his back. He hadn't paid a parking ticket once since walking into Duval's office with him that fateful day.

32

A year later Hidalgo and Francine travelled to Spain, as they had each year following her maternal grandparents' deaths. Her other grandmother, Franklin Duval's mother, had passed in her sleep a month before she'd hoped to see her great-grandchildren perhaps for the last time.

She'd left a letter, one she'd written months earlier, telling Francine how proud she was that the young woman was forging her own career path, wanting to work alongside her Hidalgo. She loved them each dearly. The rest was for her eyes alone and Francine sat quietly in a corner by herself to read the many pages. When she finished she was smiling, the way her nana would have wanted. She found Hidalgo and her grandfather on the veranda, laughing.

Her grandpapa wasn't sad, he said. Heck, no. He was too old to be sad. He would see her each night in his dreams and every day in his mind, until he was laid to rest beside her. He had no reason to feel anything other than joy. She was at peace, waiting for him.

He asked Hidalgo if he believed an old man's words. Hidalgo did. He knew he would never let Francine be taken from him; never would he let her be stolen from his heart. For his heart would stop, he said. Never, he promised her grandfather, would he live his life without her. They were one.

The old man nodded and smiled. The two, he explained to Hidalgo, were not the same. One could never promise life, lest He be the one calling a child onto Him. Hidalgo nodded. One day, he knew, he would inevitably comfort his mother or his father. He would, he promised the old man, never forget his words.

But he did, one year later, months after the old man was taken by the hand one night in his sleep. Francine told Hidalgo that her grandmother had come for him because they were each too lonely to exist apart. She wasn't sad, she was happy for them.

During their final visit with her grandpapa the old man received a visitor, the same gentleman who had come to their home in Vallejo three years earlier. The old man knew that Hidalgo and Francine would not listen to him, not take him seriously. However they would listen to an officer of the Spanish court.

He and his wife had agreed before her passing that he should live in a retirement home. He was far too old to travel on his own, even if he wanted to. The point being, as Francine's grandmothers had once told Hidalgo, gifts from the living were so much happier than gifts from the dead. The gentleman would accompany them home to ensure they would encounter no difficulty with the deposit of thirty-four million dollars into their account.

His needs were few. A million would easily see him through what few years remained to him. It's what he and his wife wanted. They knew the money would be spent wisely, put to good use to help others. He had one condition. His son was not to know until one year later, if ever. Franklin Duval had no need or right to know.

A week later Maria and Fernando simply sat holding hands, staring at each other, staring at their smiling children. The bank manager had called them to confirm the deposit of ten million dollars in each of their accounts. That night Maria went to church to pray and light candles. Fernando went to meet with John Canyon. A very short while later Canyon Estates expanded by several acres and Fernando with Maria owned twenty percent of the vineyard.

One year later, when Francine called her father at the office after hours, leaving a message on his answering machine to tell him of his father's passing, and of his mother's. She and Hidalgo were worth fifty million dollars, which she kept to herself. The law office was in the midst of an expansion. The adjoining floor space was being renovated to make room for Francine's office, her own counselling service. Within a few short months she would be a state-certified social worker and the part-time nurse had agreed to work full time with them.

She didn't tell Franklin Duval that either.

In October Francine shrugged the monkey from her back. She called Scott Gibson on a Friday, four days before the Loma Prieta earthquake.

*

Scott Gibson didn't hear the message until Monday morning. He'd spent the weekend pacing, drinking and doing coke alone in his condo. His world was closing in. He was into Mendoza for much more than a year's salary and the crime boss' accountants were merciless in their calculations of daily interest. That he was Mendoza's attorney kept him alive, not exempt.

He'd tried cutting out the booze, the parties and the girls, the lifestyle too engrained to do without. Besides, Mendoza wouldn't let him and he really didn't want to. He was living beyond his means, but he was living, having a good time. He was family, though his Duval account covered only a fraction of what he was spending. Now, wherever he went he had two girls on his arms, two debts, every meal, toke, snort or drink multiplied by three. And Mario hadn't helped, often with two girls of his own, just as often claiming that he was a little light in the wallet, telling Gibson with his usual snide smirk to hide both their expenses in his billing hours, which Gibson couldn't do. He'd just as soon kick Duval in the balls as cheat the man.

Francine's call could not have come at a better time.

Monday afternoon he requested a meeting with Duval. He and Francine had decided on a divorce. Reconciliation was not an option.

"Sir, she hates me and...I have absolutely no idea why."

Duval snorted, his chin resting on interlaced fingers. "I can give you several million reasons and, if that's not enough, several million more. She can do whatever she wants, and she is. By the time she's my age she'll be one of wealthiest women in the state. You, Gibson, are a pauper in her eyes and most likely a hindrance. I've researched every possible legal loophole. The money's hers and you're SOL."

"But the poor kids..."

"Forget them. You're better off without them. Not that you should ever have had them in the first place. Start over. Forget her. Believe me; it's not all that hard. Save yourself the migraine"

Gibson dropped his head, pensive.

Duval's response to the theatrics was a curt "what?"

"Sir, I've been to where she lives. I wanted to see her, talk to her. I actually went to her house three times. The first time I saw them I didn't think anything of it. I thought he was a guy making a delivery, or a neighbour. He wasn't either. He was with her each time, helping with the kids and, sir, he never left. She's living with a frigging spic. I'm sorry, some Mexican guy."

"I wouldn't make that slip with Mendoza, not unless you want to breathe through your neck. And don't forget who some of our best clients are, so clean up the mouth. Who she bags isn't your business anymore. If she wants to be a Mexican's whore, let her be one." He coughed a laugh. "For all you know those kids might not even be yours."

"It's hard, knowing what she's doing with him. I still love her." He rubbed his face. "Sir, I have to know. Does this, I mean, will this affect my future with Duval & Associates?"

"What you mean to ask is whether Duval & Associates will become Duval, Gibson & Associates anytime soon."

"Yes sir. I mean, she's your daughter. And," he shrugged, sighing, "I don't know, I must have fucked up somehow."

Duval ignored him. He'd been in court too many times, prompted and rehearsed clients too many times. He recognized bullshit from any distance. Gibson was playing to the jury.

"I made Arthur a promise, and I keep my promises. I wasn't expecting it this soon, until a phone call from that little bitch of a daughter of mine put me in the right frame of mind. Good timing on your part, or on hers. The corporate name will change on the first of the year; we'll go ahead with your partnership and remuneration adjustment on the first of the coming month. I can't see any reason to wait on that. I'll have Contracts draft an addendum to your current contract." He flipped open his agenda. "I'm out of office tomorrow. Pencil me in for a brief five PM Wednesday. Mrs. Duval's presence will of course be required as co-signatory, a formality. Congratulations. You're my full partner, just not with voting shares at this point. Now update me on the Mendoza case."

"He's out on a five million dollar bond posted by Enrique. He can't go anywhere. The Feds confiscated everything he owns, his cars, the condo, his bank account, not to mention the yacht. If he gets off, which he won't, he'd have to start over with zero help from his cousin. He'll be lucky to wash dishes. Enrique's really pissed about the yacht. The thing was his pride and joy. I'm surprised he never tried to screw the fuel tank. The idiot was caught offshore which makes it federal. They got him on the forward deck with a couple of naked dancers from the clubs, all of them higher than a kite when the cops boarded. He's facing fifteen to twenty and ten million in fines." Gibson shook his head. "Even if he was able to disappear, Mendoza would find him and kill him."

Duval nodded, leaning back. "Just make sure he doesn't kill you. Do better. Get his cousin reduced to ten. We don't need Mendoza anymore pissed than he is."

"There's no compromise here, sir. He's got nothing to offer and he won't get much sympathy because of who he is and the fact he went running for his gun while he was buck ass naked, if you can believe that, and that he's already done twelve for voluntary manslaughter. He's doing the twenty. He just doesn't know that yet. His trial is slated to begin on the 30th. Essentially, sir, he's royally screwed. He won't be going home. His good years are over."

Mine, he thought, are just beginning.

33
Twenty-One Years Ago
October 17th, 12:00 PM

Gibson was ecstatic, celebrating the night before with a couple of dancers and coke. He was in. The ten-year sentence of bowing to her whims, of acting like a servile puppet to her and her spic was over. He couldn't believe it. He was actually in; she was out, out of his life all together. And in a few years the old man would be retired, senile or dead.

He kicked out the girls by eleven. Mario Mendoza was expected. He was staying in a fifty-nine dollar motel room with no booze and no girl. He was leprous, verboten. No one wanted to be seen anywhere near him.

That he and Gibson were attached for the next two weeks was a condition of bail imposed by the court and Gibson thought having him as far away as possible from Enrique was a good thing. He'd been to the Santa Rosa apartment once each day for a month, checking in, maintaining contact, and never staying long. He was there for appearance sake. Despite Mario's screw-up, Latino blood was thick and Gibson needed Enrique to believe that he was doing more for his cousin than he actually was doing. When, if fact, there was nothing more he could do.

Mario Mendoza spent what little time he had in the apartment drinking and toking on the Duval tab. It's not that

Gibson particularly liked the man, he didn't, telling Mario the day before that whether he went away for fifteen or twenty years would pretty much depend on whether or not the judge got laid the night before, the flip of a coin, and Gibson wanted him relaxed. The man had a very big gun strapped under his arm and a very small brain concealed somewhere under a greasy head of hair. He was a loose cannon with not much to lose and watching him get high was unquestionably preferable to making conversation with him.

"If I go back, man, I won't come out. My cousin, not everyone loves the guy. I'm a dead man. He knows that."

"There's no if, Mario. You are going back, for fifteen to twenty and right now I wouldn't bet against twenty. You can also forget time off for good behaviour. What the hell were you thinking going for the gun? You're lucky they didn't blow your head off, or your balls for that matter. And don't think a couple of naked cokehead broads floating in the ocean would have been difficult to explain."

"The bitches, they stayed naked until the marina." He drained his glass. "Climbed from the boat naked and went through the marina in towels with their tits and asses hanging out. Want to bet they didn't get laid in the cruisers somewhere? You know they did."

"I don't care either way. They got a slap on the wrist. You're the one doing time."

"So, what's the plan?"

"Drink as much as you can in two weeks. It'll have to last you. Once the trial starts, you'll be trading Italian wool for American denim."

"Because Enrique, he wants me gone, man."

Gibson shook his head. "No, he doesn't. He's big, but not that big. You're going away for being stupid. Do anything else stupid and he'll cut your throat. Adding fifteen million to the cost of a yacht wouldn't be a good thing. That, he wouldn't forgive, not even for a cousin."

"I can't go back, man."

"And you can't run. The good thing," Gibson lied, "by the time you get out this will all be forgotten. He'll have a new and bigger boat, more clubs, more buildings and he'll be ready to forgive you. Things will work out. The last time you went in as nobody, a punk. Now you're someone. You're a Mendoza. That means something. You're family. We'll make certain you get good care. Life won't be that bad, and no one's going to kill you."

He passed Mario Mendoza an envelope.

"What's that?"

Gibson chortled finishing his scotch. "Your marriage contract, duly registered. She's a whore, twenty-two, not that pretty, not too beat up with big tits and a tight ass. I passed on asking her to strip for more details. I'm assuming she's anatomically correct."

"I don't get it."

"Conjugal visits. You need a wife to get laid in prison the regular way. It's the best I could do. She owes a few favours, made a few mistakes. I convinced Enrique that giving her to you was better than putting her out of service for a few months with broken arms or a messed up face." He waited. Nothing. "You're welcome. It's the least I could do."

"You got a picture or something?"

"Her face won't matter much once you're inside. Like I said, she didn't strip."

"Send her to the motel tonight. And I'd better pull out with a clean dick. If my cousin's sending me something dirty to get at me, you tell me now, man."

"I'll do that. I'll send her. And he isn't. So you see; he's already halfway to forgiving you. Why else would he set you up with tail?"

"He's pissed with you too, man. If I were you, I'd be

making plans of my own. I've heard him, man. I've heard him say things. A quarter-mill, he don't forgive that so easy."

"I'm working on that. Besides, who knows more about his operation than me? I'm the one keeping him squeaky clean and respectable. That comes at a price."

"Sometimes it's not so good to know too much. Some people, they don't mix their drinks. Him, he doesn't mix acquaintances and money. I'm telling you, man, make a plan unless you want to work for free and be his bitch until one day you OD to make things right. He won't ever kill you, man. That don't mean you won't want to do it yourself. Then he'll go pay his respects to your wife and those three kids." He pushed himself from the sofa to fill his glass with more bourbon. "You want that, Enrique banging your wife and pimping your kids? These IOUs, man, they don't ever go away. They're passed on like fucking syphilis."

"Like I said, I'm working on it."

They had nothing much else to talk about, nothing more to prepare for the courtroom. Mendoza had no wife, no girlfriend, no children, nothing to lend him the appearance of a man who deserved a third chance. And the prostitute certainly wouldn't be a favourable witness. Worse, he'd displayed no regret at his pre-trial hearing. Though he hadn't said the words, given the chance he would have killed those five cops and likely as not the two girls. He had no need to pretend, to demean himself. He knew he had to go away, to put distance between him and his cousin. All he and Gibson could do was to finish their drinks.

The dial on Gibson's watch. read 2:00 PM. He told Mendoza to stay close, to stay in touch by phone twice more that day and to come by again the next day at the same time. That was the deal unless he was morbidly anxious to wear orange denim."

When one Mendoza was gone, he called the other.

"I've met a couple of times with the DA. Twenty, that's it, that's the deal, and the difference between what they get at auction for everything confiscated and ten million. I'm thinking you'll be six or seven out of pocket. Everything at these auctions goes for dirt cheap and the yacht doesn't count. You're the documented owner, and if you don't come across with it, Enrique, they'll do everything including planting smack in your back pocket. My advice, buy back your own boat." He forced a laugh. "Get a couple of your boys to sit beside any serious contenders."

"You have any idea how much that thing cost me, hombre?"

"You told me."

"Yeah, so much that it isn't paid for. You don't pay for those things; you use them then sell them for bigger ones. He should have grabbed the anchor and jumped overboard. His life would have been easier, Scottie. This I can never forgive. Twenty years, with interest, he'll owe me thirty million. How does a go-boy pay back that much money?"

"He's your cousin. You'll work it out. He's family."

"Family doesn't fuck you up the ass, amigo. They don't. He did a bad thing. He showed me disrespect. People have to know I can't take that shit."

"I don't think I want to hear this."

"I'm not saying anything. Besides, we've got attorney-client privilege. That's what I'm paying you for. He loses twenty years and I lose thirty million. Or he gets off, and all I lose is the yacht that I can buy back for a tenth of the price."

"He won't get off. It's not an option."

"Listen, amigo. Twenty years, you die a little each day. Or you die once, and it's over. The only promise I made was to you, so send the broad to his room a few times before the trial. Let him enjoy his wife until then."

"What do I tell him?"

"The truth, that family does what is best for family. Or tell him nothing. Now tell me what I want to hear about you, amigo. Are we good, you and I?"

"We've always been good. That's not changing. Duval's made me a full partner. So, yeah, things just got a whole lot better. Now I'm positioned to implement changes that are good for both of us."

"And the other matter?"

"A grand more each week, which should clean my slate in thirty months."

He counted the silence.

"More like five years, Scottie. The interest, it's not something I can forgive. You live an expensive life, my friend."

"Agreed, five years, and from now on the boat rides and the broads are a perk, in exchange for which I'll get Duval to shave ten percent from your retainer. Or it'll just be five years, Enrique. I'm sure a dozen other firms would take you on as a client. I can't do both. My life's expensive because my friends are," he laughed, feeling good, "amigo."

Mendoza sighed heavily into the phone. Ten percent was six-hundred thousand. "You see, amigo, there is always a way to find honour between gentlemen." Then he laughed quietly, without the slightest humour in his voice. "That is good. I am pleased that now I will not have to read the unfortunate news of your sudden passing in the morning papers. Because who then would keep me honest?"

When Mendoza disconnected Scott Gibson poured a tumbler half-full of scotch. Duval was the least of his worries. When the glass was empty he went shopping for a new car, something better suited to a full partner.

*

October 17th, 03:00 PM

Claire Gibson and Mrs. Duval had just finished a

shopping spree and a late afternoon lunch of smoked salmon and a glass of Chablis at a popular café-terrace. The day was warm, yet fresh. The sky was clear and the winds were light.

Claire drove home to Oakland to avoid rush-hour traffic, distraught by the women's conversation regarding the divorce, much more dismayed than her friend who showed no emotion whatsoever at her daughter's unconscionable behaviour. As she drove she tried to balance what was real to her and what she had believed was real since the beautiful wedding ten years earlier. She was beginning to believe that she didn't like herself very much. Francine was a lovely girl, whose grandparents loved her. She and Arthur, Franklin and Mrs. Duval were the ones at fault, forcing her into a marriage at such a young age so that one man could have a career and two others could maintain each other's enviable footing on the same top rung of the same social ladder. What did it matter that the young woman had found someone else, or that he was Mexican? Good for her that her mind hadn't been poisoned.

She made a mental note to phone Francine when the dust of ill-feelings settled. As she turned into the mansion's gated property, she could have no idea that her protected world would come crashing down in ninety-four minutes.
*

October 17th, 03:30 PM

Francine had just arrived home from Vallejo's private school where Diego's inherent charm often failed him when pitted against his no-nonsense teachers. Nor did he ever manage much sympathy from his parents. His sisters were another matter. Francesca and Gabriella adored their brother. He was so much older, he knew so much more about the world and he was the handsomest boy in the school. All the girls liked him, but they were his sisters. They had him all the time.

He never teased them and when they weren't well he would sit with them while he did his homework. Often, when they were unsuspecting, he would spend his allowance to buy them little necklaces or ribbons, other times at school he would leave the older kids to buy them lunch and sit with them. He was Diego Hidalgo Arquero-Duval, his father's son, and his mother was the most beautiful woman in the whole world.

They were allowed to play for one hour, and then they would study. Not even Gabriella was free from the woes of education, though she didn't mind as long as she could read her picture books beside her big brother.

Hidalgo was in court, again, much to the chagrin of the local DA's office that began to wonder why they even went to work. Hidalgo was quickly getting known. He didn't just get kids off, he followed up. Much of the work he did was proactive, preventative, and the judges were aware of his success rate. The general assumption was that an Arquero client had a better chance out of jail than in.
*

Mrs. Duval remained in San Francisco to meet and drive home with her husband. She was in complete agreement with Franklin Duval regarding Francine and what should be done post haste to circumvent any future irrational behaviour on her part. She had clearly proven herself unworthy of their previous considerations for her future well-being.

She was also in agreement regarding Scott Gibson's timely elevation to full partner, not merely a junior position, particularly since they had no son and Franklin was sixty-one, for which reason Franklin and Arthur had met at the club to enjoy a few late-day cognacs. Franklin wanted to make very certain that Arthur understood that his son's future was secure, made so by Franklin Duval of Duval & Associates, now Duval, Gibson & Associates. But, of course, what were friends for?

Both men stood when she walked in.

What Arthur Gibson didn't suspect was why Mrs. Duval had joined them. She wanted to join in the glory. She read Senator Gibson like a book, insisting earlier in the day that she be present when her husband told his friend and colleague that, with the promotion, Scott Gibson would also inherit a quarter-share in the firm at the time of Franklin's death. Mrs. Duval would retain the majority share and, upon her death, Scott Gibson would enjoy full control and ownership of the firm.

The paperwork was complete. Young Gibson was on his way to a very lucrative career.

Arthur Gibson was elated. Then he happened to glance at his watch, excusing himself, somewhat embarrassed. He promised to call Franklin in the morning, to arrange a dinner. Such unheard of munificence had to be celebrated.

When he was gone, the couple sneered in a way each understood. Anyone watching would have understood. The senator had left to call his son.

What they hadn't told him was that they dared not wait a day longer. They wanted to scold their daughter in the most scathing way for her blatant disregard for them. What they had done, with the stroke of a pen, was to replace Francine's name with Scott Gibson's. They had disowned their daughter that quickly.

That evening after dinner they would co-sign the revised will and have the document duly probated the following day.

*

October 17th, 04:46 PM

Franklin and Sandra Duval left their club, disregarding their staff, as was usual for them. Arthur Gibson caught up with them in the parking lot. He was buoyant, his cheeks flushed with excitement, telling them he couldn't wait to tell his wife and his son…unless, of course, they would prefer to make the announcement at a restaurant of their choosing later that evening. Dinner, of course, would be on him.

They didn't. They had previous commitments and thanked him.

Traffic from the centre of town to the Bay Bridge was unusually light, probably, Gibson thought, because of a warm-up practice for the World Series between the Oakland Athletics and the San Francisco Giants, not that he cared. He just wanted to get home to tell his wife the incredible news.

*

October 17th, 05:04 PM

Doing seventy-five Franklin Duval veered from the 80 onto the 880 toward Oakland, chuckling, certain, he told his wife, that he could see Gibson's face in the rear-view mirror. The man was beaming, talking to himself. Then Gibson disappeared. He was gone. His car was gone and Duval instinctively slammed his foot hard onto the brake pedal. The manoeuvre was pointless.

He screamed "holy fuck" at the sight of the concrete tsunami undulating towards him in slow motion. He was paralyzed, gripping the useless steering wheel, his elbows locked, his knees locked, his legs forcing him hard against the back of his seat, the brakes locked, the European import bouncing atop a heaving crest of concrete and asphalt, crashing them into a steel and concrete ceiling, concaving the car's roof. Then instantly they were plunged into a valley of twisted steel and carnage as though he was driving a boy's miniature toy, the Nimitz Freeway erupting around them, grinding, exploding, the upper deck crashing down to crush them. He never once looked to his wife. He died without saying he loved her, her maniacal screams in the few moments preceding her death completely obliterating any thought of him. They died within the ten to fifteen seconds the Loma Prieta earthquake took to eradicate sixty-three lives.

Not a word was shrieked or squealed in fear or in praise of the God they went to each Sunday, not a single regret was whimpered to a daughter they would never again see. Senator Arthur Gibson died with them, more likely than not without once thinking of his dear wife or the young man whom he had years earlier come to pretend to love as a son.

*

Hidalgo had returned from to his office not many minutes earlier, catapulted from his seat onto the floor by the sudden and violent shaking of the earth. The office sustained no heavy damage beyond empty bookshelves replaced by instant knolls of tomes rising up from his office floor, nor did he have any idea of what had just taken place until the nurse came running in from the street.

He called home at once, frustrated, having to redial a dozen or more times before getting through; relieved that Francine and the kids were unharmed. Francine had felt the intense edges of the shockwave, however their home was unaffected. She'd been explaining to the kids what had happened, not that she was quite certain what did happen. She phoned the Estates, relieved to hear that Jennie and John were fine. They too had felt the shockwave. Maria and Fernando, however, had left for the day several minutes earlier. She didn't know, she told him. She was certain they were safe. She'd left a message and would not stop calling them.

As she was speaking she turned on the television, gasping at the televised aerial view of the destruction. Hidalgo was not to come home, she insisted. She would keep calling Maria and Fernando to make certain they were unharmed and he was to stay where he was for the night. The city, the announcer was saying, would soon be devoured by chaos.

He agreed, just as the line went dead. Maria and Fernando, hearing the message upon arriving home, went directly to their children's home where they spent the night anxious about their son.

*

October 17th, 06:00 PM

Oakland was the worst hit community by far, including the city hall which would take six years to rebuild and cost 85 million. Claire Gibson's home was a shambles inside. Not a single picture frame remained on the walls and few dishes were left unbroken. Yet she was unhurt. She was sitting in her private parlour waiting, her eyes glued to the television that had crashed to the floor.

She had immediately sent her worried staff to their homes to see about their families. She had already called the club, by which time her husband and the Duvals had left an hour earlier. They always came home by the Bay Bridge. Yet somehow she knew, not this time.

She had tried calling her son Scott several times, leaving increasingly plaintive messages. She was frantic. She had no idea where he might be. Neither was she aware of Franklin's good news, Mrs. Duval hadn't told her at lunch.

*

In Santa Rosa to the north, Scott Gibson had both felt and ignored the tremor. Tremors were nothing new along the San Andreas Fault. They happened all the time. Until the trial, Mario Mendoza was his sole preoccupation and now he was certain there would be no trial. That's what Enrique was hinting at. He was going to have his cousin killed. How was he to keep a secret like that? Though, he would. More importantly, he was safe, granted a reprieve, and old man Duval would have to see the reasoning behind reducing the Mendoza retainer. Mendoza was fast becoming the firm's largest client. What wasn't earned by a yearly retainer could be made up by fictitious billing hours. Mendoza wouldn't be any the wiser, not with his expanding operation.

*

October 17th, 10:00 PM

Claire Gibson left her home and drove to the Duvals who hadn't answered any of her messages. The streets were dark, the hundreds of people milling around appearing like lost and ghoulish spectres. Dim light shone through several of the mansion's front windows, one of the few lighted homes on the otherwise black street. The mansion's front gate was closed. She fingered the code into her remote and drove through.

She knocked several times at the main door without a response, half wondering, half hoping that Francine would come to the door. She walked to the rear where the trees, the grass, the patio and pool were all blackened. No one was home. The staff, at least, had locked the house securely before leaving to attend to their own families.

Five hours had passed; thirty-two bodies discovered, she heard through her car's upscale quadrophonic sound system. She returned home to sit alone in her dimly lit parlour, the muted groan of the exterior generator eventually lulling her into a tearful sleep.

The next morning she woke, curled into the corner of the chesterfield. She was alone. The generator still working to transfer power to the radio: sixty-three bodies found. Her husband wasn't coming home.

34

Francine hadn't gone to her parents' home. They'd died a long time ago. Her true parents, the ones she loved, were with her: Maria and Fernando. She had no idea Franklin and Sandra Duval were dead until her phone rang mid-morning just as Maria and Fernando had left late for the Estates. Maria had wanted to make certain that her son was safe and she wasn't leaving Francine until she could make phone contact with San Francisco. Francine had kept the kids home from school for the same reason.

Franklin Duval's personal assistant was calling to advise her that Franklin and Sandra Duval had been discovered not fifty feet from Senator Gibson's Cadillac. Yet somehow her voice was controlled, as though she wasn't calling to empathize or to give her condolences. There was no grief in her voice, neither sorrow nor regret. She sounded pragmatic, almost stoic as though advising that Franklin and Sandra would be late arriving for dinner that evening.

"Francine," the woman said. "I'm terribly sorry. Everyone here at Duval & Associates is devastated by your and our loss."

Francine told Diego to take his sisters into another room. She was stunned; her mind was a complete blank. She didn't know what to say or what to feel. Her parents were dead, when, in her mind and in her heart, they were already dead. What was she to think? Her parents hadn't once entered into her worried thoughts over the past several hours. Now she had to feign a sudden emotion that wasn't real to her.

"Thank you, Virginia, for calling. This was the last thing I expected to hear." The confusion imprinted in her voice was authentic. She had to sit. "What you're telling me is…Oh, my God, I'll call my husband. He doesn't know."

That attempt wasn't.

"Which is precisely why I'm calling, Francine, to ask that you call him. We want him here as soon as possible." The woman's pause was professional, practiced and effective. "However, before you do, may I for a moment be very candid? Please understand that in law quite often matters arise that override our grief. I'm afraid that at times we aren't much better than morticians."

"You have my full attention, Virginia."

Virginia Meadows was a no-nonsense, mid-life pillar at Duval & Associates. Coyness wasn't in the least inherent to her.

"Because of your father's relationship with Senator Gibson I've been able to elicit certain efficiencies from the Emergency Response people. Your father, the day before yesterday, drafted documents which I know for certain were in his briefcase when he left yesterday to meet with your mother and the senator at the club. His car, and the senator's car are being taken to the state vehicle impound as soon as possible this morning. I should be in possession of your father's briefcase by noon. Two of our senior associates are at the impound lot as we speak, waiting."

"Now you're losing me. I'm not in the least interested in my father's cases, or what he might have in his briefcase."

"I know; you've had a falling out, which is unfortunate. But that's all in the past, isn't it? You will be interested in what I have to say, Francine. Believe me. Or should I call you Mrs. Arquero-Duval?" The pause was deafening. "First, let me tell you that my husband was very truthful with you. He never did tell me about his work with you or what he discovered, which doesn't mean I didn't do a little investigating of my own. We knew the wedding was a sham. My husband refused to attend with me; neither could I attend once seeing the disgust on his face. I told your father that he came down with a serious ailment and that I had to stay with him. We were devastated. We couldn't believe what you were doing. That's why we did a bit more investigating. I don't know how you pulled off that annulment, Francine, but good for you, which is precisely why you must and will be interested and why we need you in this office this afternoon with your husband. I understand he's an extraordinarily gifted attorney. We all look forward to meeting him. We need you here by noon, Francine, at the very latest so that we can brief you and Hidalgo."

"Hidalgo... Virginia, you've known all this time."

"Yes, for nine years. And how was your trip to Pichilingue? You must tell me sometime." Her smile came through the phone. "I suppose Diego has his father's good looks. And that Francesca and Gabriella are blessed with yours." Virginia Meadows chortled. "I must say, certainly an improvement over Ted, Betty and Margaret. You should be in Black Ops for the CIA, Francine, which is why we need you here no later than noon."

"What do you expect to find in the briefcase, Virginia?"

Virginia Meadows answered: "An addendum to Gibson's contract and your father's revised will in which he disowns you and transfers a twenty-five percent share of the firm to Gibson along with a full partnership. The thing is, Francine, your mother was to maintain her three-quarter share. Now that's she's also gone from us, the worst case scenario, Gibson stands to get the whole enchilada. And we can't let that happen. The man's a complete dickhead. Pardon the expression. He's made a lot of enemies here, particularly amongst the women. If he does gain control of the firm he'll be SOL and working here by himself. Absolutely no one, me included, would stay to work for Gibson & Associates. And that will happen. The end result: Duval & Associates would crumple faster than the Nimitz Freeway and we don't want that to happen. Many of us have too much of our lives and careers vested in this place."

She took a breath, waiting, fully appreciating Francine's dilemma.

"I'm not a lawyer, Virginia, and Hidalgo has his own practice."

"What's your point? We're talking about you coming to arrange your father's affairs. Fine, you're not a lawyer, probably a good decision on your part, but your husband is. And a very talented one according to a few judges I spoke with before calling you. Listen, Francine. Let me cut to the chase because your father really messed up my day by dying. If those supposed documents aren't yet signed, or if they never existed and can't be proven, you're the big mama. This is your firm in accordance with the existing will. So get your husband here because dickhead already knows your father's dead. He's here right now and I can't prevent him from getting into your father's office much longer. Can you believe the son of a bitch came here before going to his mother's? And I can tell you that what he's doing in his own office isn't anything good."

35

Francine dropped her children off at school before driving to the Vallejo ferry terminal. She kissed them and promised that mommy and daddy were alright, telling them that nana Maria would put them to bed at night and grandpapá would tell them each a story if they were good.

She hadn't been able to get through to Hidalgo's office to speak with him and didn't want to chance getting stuck on the Bay Bridge. From Fisherman's Wharf she took a taxi into the city-centre, Hidalgo's face a veritable canvas of amazement when she rushed through his door. He was alone. She gave him a quick summary of her conversation with Virginia Meadows and they left, arriving at the Duval offices thirty minutes later.

To say the least the reception committee was curious. What attorney in the Bay Area hadn't heard of Hidalgo Arquero, The Benefactor? And to suddenly become aware that he was the real husband of Franklin Duval's daughter was an earth shattering revelation to all.

Scott Gibson worked single-mindedly towards his own end in his closed office, unaware that in the boardroom his senior level colleagues and Virginia Meadows sat with Francine and Hidalgo who were in possession of the briefcase and the pertinent documents not yet signed by either Franklin or Sandra Duval.

Hidalgo read the documents meticulously, passing each page to Francine. When they were finished he stood and went to the crosscut paper shredder before a roomful of witnesses. The document had no legal validity, as though Franklin Duval had never meant to alter the original. Neither was the addendum to an original employment agreement valid, which was neither dated nor signed and quite possibly intended as a template for future consideration.

Certainly, Franklin Duval had not intended the initial drafts for any current use. All those present concurred.

Virginia Meadows had spent the morning well, passing duplicate copies of yet another document to Francine and Hidalgo. Francine Arquero-Duval was, as of the passing of her father and mother, the legal and sole owner, CEO and president of Duval & Associates. Hidalgo shrugged and smiled. She was indeed the big mama.

And Francine was prepared to assume her duties, though she paused for a moment to gather her thoughts. Addressing a class of her peers at school wasn't quite the same as speaking to a boardroom full of experienced trial lawyers. She knew what she had to say. She was certain since disconnecting the call with Virginia Meadows earlier that morning. When she was ready she stood, informing everyone present that what she was about to say was final. No further discussion would be required or solicited. She made direct eye contact with Hidalgo. She was firm in her resolve.

From then forward the firm would be known as Arquero-Duval & Associates. Hidalgo would assume the most senior position as sole owner and president. Mrs. Meadows, for her part, would assume, if she accepted, the position of CEO. Her husband, she added with a smirk, was a fantastic attorney; however she believed that he might need a little help being a good boss. She couldn't think of a better person to keep him in line than Virginia Meadows.

"Now," she went on, "I believe Mr. Arquero has an

appointment in his new office with his new CEO. If neither of you would mind, I would like to conduct that meeting as my first and last official duty here at Arquero-Duval." The two nodded their assent. "Then, Mrs. Meadows, would you please ask Mr. Scott Gibson to join us."

None had ever before applauded with such enthusiasm in the staid, if not archaic, surroundings.

*

Gibson walked into the heretofore sacrosanct office thirty minutes later, as requested. Virginia Meadows first wanted to discuss an important matter with Hidalgo in private, a matter in which he concurred entirely.

When Gibson walked through the door, his narrowed eyes and visibly contorted face betrayed him instantly. He hadn't knocked, his interpretation of confidence, his cool self-assurance escaping through every pore for all to see.

Francine was the first to speak. She was seated beside Mrs. Meadows to one side. Hidalgo had taken his place in Duval's once favoured throne. The two women had similar files in their laps, their faces devoid of expression. Hidalgo sat leaning somewhat forward, his forearms on the desktop, his fingers interlaced, studying Gibson's stance, his every movement. What he saw he didn't like. Gibson was in no way as cool and relaxed as he wanted to appear.

"Scott Gibson, it's been awhile. Please don't bother sitting. We won't take up much of your time. I'm not very good at this, so I'll get right to the point. Your services to this firm are terminated."

Gibson burst into a rude laugh. "Bullshit. I've got an unbreakable contract. Not only that, Francine. For your information your daddy made me a full partner before he died, with a quarter-share in the firm, once he's dead, the rest when your old lady's dead...straight from the horse's mouth. So yeah, good luck with that. This is my law firm."

Virginia Meadows reached between her seat and

Francine's for the briefcase. "As Mr. Duval's personal assistant I drew up those documents for Mr. Duval to co-sign with his wife, as well as preparing a copy for you. May I ask that we see your copy, Mr. Gibson?"

"Duval intended to give me copies of my revised contract and the partnership agreement this afternoon, which you are fully aware of. As for the shares, that's public knowledge. He told me, he told my father and probably my mother: two names that mean something in this town. We had a five PM. The papers are in this office somewhere, or in yours, signed and ready for my signature. If they're not, he took them with him yesterday, which I somehow doubt."

"They aren't in this office, or mine, and we found nothing in either his briefcase or his home. If indeed he left with them yesterday, Mr. Gibson, for Mrs. Duval to co-sign, he clearly had a change of heart."

"This is bullshit."

"This is Mr. Duval's briefcase, extracted from his car this morning. We examined the contents very carefully."

Francine cut in. "You'll be paid until the end of the year with a month's severance."

"I'll sue. My original contract continues in effect…"

"…which," Virginia Meadows continued, "is made null and void by the acquisition of Duval & Associates by Arquero-Duval & Associates."

Francine said: "You'll be accompanied to the door by Mrs. Meadows and a senior associate. Unless you would prefer that we call security. Leave your credit cards, car keys and business cards on your desk. You will also leave all your case files here with us."

"With one exception," Virginia Meadows continued. "Arquero-Duval will not be representing Mr. Enrique Mendoza. However, in light of his cousin's upcoming trial, we understand that you will require those particular documents for your arguments. Consider his account a supplement to your severance and Mr. Mendoza will be refunded what remains of his retainer for the current year which is approximately one million dollars." She stood. "I believe this meeting is concluded. Shall we?"

He glared at Francine. "You bitch."

She didn't flinch, neither did she mock him. She'd done what made her feel good, requited for what he'd done to her. Then, from nowhere, "Yeah, I remember that face, the day you punched me in the face."

At that Hidalgo eased away from his desk, standing without the slightest histrionic, asking Francine to accompany Mrs. Meadows. When the three were at the door, he said. "Gibson, I believe these women will require some time alone to examine your office and to make certain you won't have forgotten anything. Please stay behind. I need a few words with you."

*

When Gibson did go to his former office Francine wasn't there. In her place was a tall and sturdy senior colleague who'd been an all-star before developing an interest in the law.

Gibson emptied his pockets of the keys and his wallet of credit cards without a word of protest. He left with a briefcase brimming with Mendoza briefs and several boxes of law books carried to the street by the building's maintenance staff.

He was escorted out by Virginia Meadows with his eyes focused on the carpet, not daring to glance either to his right or to his left. The men, who wouldn't have missed the gauntlet, or his fall from grace, shared a common thought: they too would have enjoyed a few minutes alone with Gibson. The women shared a common thought as well, enjoying his humiliation: He didn't seem so sophisticated, smooth and bon vivant with his eyes turning black, his shirt crumpled where another man's fist had held him in place, and his own blood smeared across his face. In fact, they saw him exactly how they each knew he really was.

When he was gone everyone returned to their work.

Hidalgo hadn't expected any of this and he told Mrs. Meadows as much. He was available to her at any time, though for a little while the office was hers. He was up to his proverbial in court cases and he required some time to think things out. He wasn't about to abandon the troubled kids who needed him and any thoughts she might have as to what he should do would be appreciated. To say the least she was dumbfounded by his confidence in her.

Before leaving he asked her while standing in the main corridor, and in a somewhat higher pitch, "What would be wrong with some fresh paint, brighter carpeting, more modern furniture and a bit of music, Mrs. Meadows?"

She would have carte blanche with his office as well, but could she please remember that he was Latino and way under forty. Loud applause and cheers broke out again.

36

No one had to tell Scott Gibson he was screwed and, to make current matters worse, flying to Vegas would have cost less than the taxi to his condo in Santa Rosa. With his files strewn across the floor he called Mario Mendoza to make certain he hadn't done something stupid, like run. If anyone was to ask him, they were together between two and 4:00 PM.

He mindlessly filled a tumbler with scotch, thinking he wouldn't drink it all, but he did. Ready, he called a cab and went to his mother's home. He didn't want to; he had to because he was a loving son. When he arrived Claire Gibson was horrified by what she saw.

"Scott, are you drunk?" she asked. "And what happened to your face? Why haven't you answered my messages?"

"No mother, I'm not drunk. It's the medication. I'm sorry I took so long to get here. I've been trying since yesterday. They were only letting emergency vehicles through and the ferries were impossible." He touched his face. "I was with Mendoza; he's got a place in the Marina District...a wall collapsed. It's nothing."

Claire took a step backward, letting him in. "Are you alright? Are you injured?"

"I'm okay. I just wanted to make sure you and dad were okay. Where is he?"

She closed the doors behind her, leaning against the wrought iron lacework and glass. "Your father was killed yesterday, Scott, trying to make his way home. I'm told he died quickly. Franklin and Sandra were with him. I've already called Sacramento. Arrangements are being made."

Scott's eyes filled with tears. "Mom…" he whimpered, "no!"

She stiffened, taking a deep breath, pushing herself from the door. "That won't do any good at all, Scott. My lawyer is coming by to see me tomorrow morning. What with our staff, the club and other obligations, we shall have to put our grief on hold until a more appropriate time. These more pragmatic matters must come before all else. He'll do most of what must be done, though I suppose I will have a mountain of papers to sign." She went into the main parlour. She poured a sherry for herself, letting Scott see to his own scotch. "Poor Sandra and Franklin were also killed. I've tried calling Francine, but she mustn't be home. I couldn't bring myself to leave a message. I simply couldn't find the proper words. You must go to her, Scott. The poor girl must be beside herself. Despite her questionable actions, to lose both parents so tragically is beyond one's imagination." Claire sipped her sherry. "How those poor children will suffer through all this."

"I will go to see her mother. Otherwise I sincerely doubt she would talk to me or even answer my messages. She hasn't in the past. The terrible way she treated me aside, I suppose you're right. They are, after all, my children." He gulped a mouthful, wincing. "Mother, my car was completely demolished by the wall that collapsed. I suppose Enrique and I are lucky to be alive. Regrettably, I had no choice but to come to you by taxi."

"Then you will take my car. This is no time for petty differences to resurface. Those children are your responsibility and will need all the help you can give them. Who knows? Perhaps this horrible event will serve to reawaken Francine and reunite the two of you."

He downed his scotch. "I hope so, mother, and thank you. But what about you, what will you do? I can't believe that after all these years you'll be alone...without father."

"I don't see that my life will change to any great degree. Being a senator's wife prepares one for such adversities. You'll understand one day, how the wives of such men survive." She put down her glass. "Now you must go to care for your wife and children. A pending divorce doesn't negate your responsibility to them. I'm through the worst of it, although I imagine I will have certain matters to discuss with you after tomorrow."

"I'll go to them at once." He hesitated. He was embarrassed, stranded before his mother without options. "Mother...I was unable to find a bank that remains open, so many are closed. I'm afraid the taxi depleted the few hundred I had."

She thought nothing of the indiscreet request, reaching into her purse for several fifties. When he was gone Claire went about gathering and sorting her papers preparatory to her lawyer's visit. Scott Gibson drove home. He had to think. He had to find answers.

He was out of a job and in debt for over a quarter-million to a pseudo-sophisticated drug dealer and pimp. Ironically his single lifeline was Enrique Mendoza. Without the crime boss he was dead in the water. No credible firm would give the slightest consideration to a Duval cast-off, irrespective of his Gibson association. A dead senator was just that, with no favours to call in. And not everyone, in fact very few, would want Mendoza for a client. Most of the ivory tower types Scott Gibson was acquainted with wanted to sleep at night.

But how was he supposed to confess to his now only client-employer that he had no car, no job and no money? Or worse yet, that not in five, fifty or five hundred years could he repay the staggering debt? He filled the tumbler and sank into a sofa wondering what was worse, a gunshot to the head or a garrotte, treading water a few miles offshore before drowning or seeing the high beams of a stolen vehicle before his splintered body was flung a few hundred feet farther down the road. Or how he would feel to have Enrique Mendoza playing yo-yo with his balls for the rest of his life?

He had to believe that he still had time. The trial wasn't for another twelve days and Mendoza never asked about Duval or the firm. All he cared about was keeping his Mexican ass covered. And if he was intent on putting Mario down, that wouldn't happen until a few days before the thirtieth. By then his mother's attorney, who wasn't a Duval associate because she didn't believe in friends knowing such intimate details, would have settled the larger portion of the estate worth additional incalculable millions by way of insurance policies. His father couldn't have chosen a more propitious time to die. Things would work out.

He gulped what was left in his glass, wanting the sedative consequence to engulf him quickly. He needed to sleep. He was tired, drained by the day's events. He made a mental note to pass by his mother's home late the next day and couldn't help thinking of the obvious. With a friend like Mendoza, why would he have to take shit from anyone?
*

In Vallejo Maria was cooking for her family, scolding her son for acting like a hooligan, and Fernando for encouraging him, secretly smiling with Francine, proud of her son for settling a long overdue account. Arquero men always took care of their women, she told Francine.

As for Hidalgo, he wasn't ready to talk about his newly acquired position. He had much to work out. All that he knew, he promised his mother, was that he would not for a moment forget their promise to John and Jennie Canyon. The law firm of Arquero-Duval would be available to everyone, rich or poor. No one would ever be turned away for lack of money.

Oddly, or possibly in keeping with their inherent natures, what neither he nor Francine cared about nor thought about was the Duval estate. The head of that department at the former Duval & Associates had promised to speak with Francine before week's end. Mr. and Mrs. Duval, he told her privately, were meticulous in their personal affairs.

She answered by instructing him to put her parents' home and their fifty percent share in the club up for an immediate sale. To that end, due the partner's first right of refusal, he was to contact Mrs. Claire Gibson as quickly as possible and with all due respect.

She added however that, should Scott Gibson be in any way involved in the acquisition of those shares, the selling price would increase substantially. Otherwise she wanted the place gone in the shortest possible time at whatever price.

37

Claire Gibson's Thursday meeting with her attorney was brief and to the point. She was the sole beneficiary of her husband's estate. Her son was excluded without explanation. None was required.

Until her death she would receive his pension from Sacramento, the mansion would be transferred into her name, his portfolio worth some 100 million with fifty more from insurance on his life and Franklin's was now hers and she wanted his shares in the club sold immediately. She was to contact Franklin Duval's attorney within the shortest time frame.

By mid-afternoon her home, and the club with Francine's consent, were listed for private sale. Claire had decided to move closer to the seashore. She had also decided to reinvent herself. She was fifty-five and, despite the fact that he was dead, she was weary of being a senator's wife. She had determined over the previous twenty-four hours that she would become a different and possibly better person. She wasn't certain exactly how; she could only do her best.

Arthur Gibson's funeral would take place on the Sunday. She had already spoken with his office to request a private service for Arthur's dearest friends and his closest associates. His secretary would take care of the arrangements. Claire didn't feel as though she had the strength.

*

Francine's attorney was no less efficient. Her parents' home was on the market privately. And, she'd decided, all their belongings would be auctioned by month's end. There was nothing she could think of that she would want as a memento. Hidalgo suggested that she wait, that she might feel differently in a few days. She didn't think so. She walked away quietly after answering him with a telling glare that she'd learned from Maria. He chose not to pursue the matter.

Her parents' joint assets not including the firm or the club were valued at close to ninety million not including the fifty million she would soon receive from insurance benefits. The club and mansion together, the Arquero-Duval attorney told her, would likely bring another twenty million. He'd spoken with the Gibson attorney. She and Claire were of like minds regarding the club. Mrs. Gibson also sent her sincerest sympathies. She would like at some point to have lunch with Francine. What was past was past. She also hoped that her son was of some comfort to Francine the previous day. The attorney and Francine exchanged smirks before she instructed him to do what was necessary to conclude the transactions as he had explained them and to deposit half of everything into Hidalgo's personal portfolio.
*

Mendoza called Gibson early Thursday. Gibson, despite his crushing hangover, was infused with a deep sense of relief. All the bullshit with the Duval broad, all the pretence was over. He remembered years earlier sitting in on a Senate Disclosure meeting in which would-be Senator Gibson's entire financial portfolio, professional and home life were disclosed. His father had no idea that Scott Gibson was seated in the public gallery.

He didn't answer immediately because he couldn't. He couldn't clear his mind quickly enough to make sense to anyone but himself. So he lay there and listened to the message. Enrique wanted an up-date on his cousin's morale. He wanted to know that the young whore was being appreciated. Anyone else would be dead for what they'd done. Mario, he was getting laid. He should know that. "He should know, amigo, that family takes care of family. They don't go fuck each other up the ass when they're not looking." All this time he had Mario's back, and what did the "hijo dc la chingada" do to repay him?

The message went on. Gibson wanted to press END, afraid that Enrique might soon ask a question or say something that he would later question. The man was royally pissed, Gibson very content to be in his bed and not sitting anywhere near a crime boss that sounded pretty close to the edge.

Mendoza heard about the senator. "Very sorry, hombre, but, shit, it happens. And your wife's old man and mother… how can such tragedy happen to one man?" Mendoza could understand that Gibson was a little brain-fucked, that he needed time. "Just get back to me when your head is straight, amigo. ¿Comprendes? But don't wait long. We need to talk, amigo, about your future. What is this shit that I have read this morning about Arquero-Duval. Who the fuck is Arquero, amigo? Give my regards to my cousin. Between you and me, Scottie, I feel that I should see him one last time before he leaves us, to set things straight between cousins. I want him to know how I feel. I want to see for myself that he understands." A slight pause happened. "You should be with us, amigo, like a buffer between injured feelings, to remember the good times on the yacht. This, amigo, we should do one last time."

The answering machine clicked off.

Jesus Christ. Mario was a dead man beyond any reasonable doubt; the man would not make it to trial. All the same, he'd just been sentenced.

273

Gibson stretched out. Arquero wasn't a problem. He would be easy to explain. Duval & Associates, because of his wife who was now the CEO of her father's company, wanted a younger approach, a younger clientele that would make them look good, give them a more modern public image.

He, Gibson, was offered the position of president, primarily because of their marriage, but, as such, one hundred percent of his time would be spent at the office shifting paper from one side of his desk to the other, making room for his secretary's ass, pushing a pencil when he wasn't screwing her, and his favourite client would virtually never see him. The good days they shared would become a memory and he didn't want that. Nor did he believe that Enrique would either.

As for Arquero, he would be a name on a set of glass doors, a public image for the benefit of Duval & Associates despite the new name. Status quo, amigo, not a thing would change.

Gibson slid from his bed, his six-hundred-dollar suit strewn across the floor with his blood-stained shirt, his ruined tie and shoes. He pushed his boxers to the carpet and found his way to the shower. He should have tilted the brushed nickel toggle to the blue zone, to refresh and jolt himself. He chose the red, standing amidst stinging pellets and steam until he could no longer see through the fogged third-floor windows.

He fell back against the ceramic wall. He'd never seen a man die, he'd never wanted to, though he would very soon. Mendoza was indoctrinating him, lifting his paws from the floor like a master training his puppy. And that was the trade-off. He would become Mendoza's go-boy, his everything, his advisor, counsellor, pimp and yes man.

So how long was too long? He called Mario, told him to be over by noon and to come alone. His conjugal wife didn't quite fit in with the more urbane population of his building.

Mario Mendoza seemed not to have a care in the world. Either that or he was resigned to leaving prison on the wrong side of middle-age to live out his life in misery with a tin cup in emaciated hands in the hope of earning enough to pay for one more night in a flophouse.

Gibson was studying a man who would be dead within nine or ten days, dropped into the sea or shot in the head. If he had any input at all, any influence, if he had to see the man die he would convince Enrique to drown his cousin. He'd once heard that the affect was euphoric, calming. Mario would feel as though he had a chance to survive, more than he would with half his head missing. All because he wanted to lay a couple of brain-dead dancers in the middle of the ocean, broads barely out of their teens who would screw any customer for an extra few hundred after hours and would probably end up working street corners for Enrique or giving ten-dollar BJs on their own to make ends meet.

He refilled his glass. That was something else that would have to change. When had he started drinking so heavily, and doing drugs? Some of that would stop with Mario gone, or so he believed. Drinking was a convenience, something that facilitated banal conversation, something to get him through his hours each week with a man for whom he could do nothing. He couldn't help thinking of Mario as a buffoon. The man's sole preoccupation each day was a half-quart of scotch or tequila and a reefer, as though spending half of what remained of his life in prison was a natural thing.

Perhaps Enrique pushing his cousin into the sea would be a kindness. How could anyone survive a prison cell after so many years of avarice and hedonism?

Gibson was walking a thin line. He'd never had a reason

to lie to Mendoza. Everyone made excuses when owing a quarter-million. That was different. Excuses were expected, but he was suddenly catapulted to a new level because of Duval's death. He would call Mendoza that evening when his tone and easy manner would convey a confidence which was temporarily lacking. He would get rid of Mario at the motel and visit with his mother to help her through her grieving period, after which he would call Mendoza and put the man's worries to rest.

Much to his surprise Claire Gibson answered the door unlike a woman who had very recently lost her husband. She was refreshed, rejuvenated, and not dressed as one would expect. In the parlour, away from the ears of her staff, she poured a sherry and sat waiting, noticing that he was filling an old-fashioned with far more scotch than she considered appropriate for the occasion and the hour.

She was cordial, though not at all passive or meek as he believed she would be in view of her loss and subsequent confusion.

"Yes, the meeting went very well. I'm told that the estate should be settled within a week. Arthur's will was very clearly written in plain language with not the slightest ambiguity or possibility of misinterpretation."

"What does that mean, ambiguity, possibility of misinterpretation? He would never think to consider anyone outside of family. People of our social rank never bequeath to friends or colleagues." He chuckled. "Millionaires bequeathing to millionaires, what would be the point?"

"You're quite right; he didn't, for that very reason, particularly in the case of Franklin and Sandra whose own net worth wasn't much less or more than our own."

"May I see the will?"

"No, Scott, you may not, in accordance with Arthur's wishes. The document was intended for me alone."

His brow furrowed. "Mother, wills are generally meant

as familial documents. Anyone named in the will has the right to review the content."

Claire nodded, taking a moment to sip her sherry. "The club is being sold. Francine has agreed through her legal counsel that it's the best thing to do. Neither one of us has any interest in maintaining the place."

His twisted expression was real. "Mother, you're not serious. You can't let that happen. Why didn't you tell me? You know I would take control of the club without the slightest hesitation."

"Then speak with Francine. I'm surprised she hasn't told you. With the monies Franklin has most certainly allotted to you from his estate, unless your differences with his daughter gave him cause to reconsider, I imagine you could easily afford the twenty million...or the better part of it. I can't see that any bank would deny you credit for whatever amount you would require to finalize the purchase."

"Excuse me. You would expect me to pay. That club is my right."

"No, it is not. Arthur wasn't given that club on a silver platter. The name and reputation came with time and hard work in conjunction with Franklin's efforts. If you're determined to assume ownership of the place, speak with Francine. However I will expect a full ten million which, as I understand the market, is bargain basement pricing. Though I don't expect she'll be overly enthusiastic about joining you in the various aspects of its daily management given your unresolved issues. Otherwise she would have made you aware prior to our coincidental decision to sell. She must believe that you have no interest. And, really, why would you?"

"To continue my father's good work, his name, for the prestige that it brings the family."

"Scott, I am the family, and I've had quite enough prestige in my life. Like this house, it's really quite mundane, which is why I've placed it on the market as well. Once sold, I intend moving to the shore to live my dream for a change. I've had my fill of being a senator's wife. I'm actually eager to making new friends who will see me as Claire and not someone to ingratiate or as prestigious name on a guest list. Quite possibly, Scott, Arthur's passing is my rebirth."

"Mother, that's a horrible thing to say. He was your husband and my father. He was devoted to you."

"Oh, come now. Don't play the shocked child. Arthur Gibson bedded more internes, hookers and wives of other men than I had dreams of other men. However he was an important man and got to act out his fantasies with young bimbos while I stayed home managing this house, our affairs and you."

"This house as you call it is the home where I grew up."

"It's brick and mortar and uncomfortably huge, with rooms I haven't walked into in a year."

"At what price?" he asked. Fear was beginning to fester. Why was she talking about Duval's will?

"Best offer, give or take a few million, the furnishings and décor included. None of this will suit what I envision as my beachfront home. It's really quite dreary once one takes the time to see past the haughtiness of it all. Not that I'm in desperate need of the money. I could very well give the place away."

Claire saw what was coming.

"Transfer the deed to my name. With a few renovations this would be a perfect home for me."

"The asking price is eight million, somewhat beyond your current ability, I'm afraid."

He jerked involuntarily, the sudden surge of pressure in his veins, the heat behind his expressionless mask threatening to betray him with a dark crimson flush. "But you just said…"

"...that I could, not that I would."

"Then I'll buy the place...and I'll buy the club."

Claire, years earlier, had learned to read a person's eyes. Faces were most often too easily sculpted to one's own advantage by those seeking favouritism, and they were many. She had also become adept at conveying compassion, understanding and empathy through her own eyes while remaining completely indifferent.

"Then you'd better speak with Francine. If she didn't tell you yesterday about any possible inheritance from Franklin to one of his more profitable associates, she must have a reason. He quite possibly excluded you for reasons of your pending divorce. If so, you must be thankful that he didn't dismiss you from the firm out of consideration for his grandchildren's well-being, despite her new wealth which is considerable."

"She can go to hell for all I care. What I'm talking about is my inheritance from father, of which even a fraction will pay for this place and the club."

Claire sipped her sherry. She was calm, unruffled. She knew this moment would come. She'd known for thirty-five years.

"By misinterpretation, Scott, I meant to imply that I am the sole beneficiary named in Arthur's will."

"I don't believe you. He would never have done that. The man never once refused me. He was my mentor, he moulded me, trained me. He made me what I am. Why would he ignore me so blatantly now?"

"Arthur did what he did, sending you to the best schools, making certain you were at the top of your class, even though you weren't, introducing you to the best people and conspiring with Franklin to give you a wife and a career because he wanted another Gibson sitting in Sacramento if not in Washington. You were a pawn, as was Francine. Her father was no better. Franklin was equally eager. With his daughter married to a senator his law firm would have been incredibly well positioned. That's the kind of people we are."

"My father would never have disregarded me this way," Scott insisted, heaving himself from the chesterfield to refill his glass.

"No, he certainly would not. Your father was a good man, kind and thoughtful. He was handsome and strong. The last time I saw him was the night before I married Arthur Gibson. While Arthur was out doing what men do before their wedding, I was saying goodbye to a wonderful man I'd known for three months, a fleeting moment and a lifetime of memories. He was the man I should have married. You're his child, not Arthur's. The reason you're excluded from his will is that he discovered the truth some months later. You see, I was quite popular with the boys throughout my school years and after graduation. I was the attractive little rich girl that every boy wanted. I had no problem whatsoever attracting boys. I was, in a word, promiscuous. Though I never thought of myself as such, nor do I now. I was simply doing what every boy thought he had the right to do, and with as much pleasure. I was doing what I wanted to do, being equal in a hypocritical society. As for Arthur, he was injured mere days before the wedding. He broke his leg. He told me it happened while playing football when, in fact, he was no better than me. He probably broke it jumping out from some girl's window to escape a father or husband. He was never very athletic, particularly during the first several weeks of our marriage, the culmination of which was delayed out of necessity." Her lips curved into a thin smile. "His cast was rather cumbersome, not at all conducive to matters of the heart."

"I'm a bastard?"

"You're a lovechild. However by the time you were born Arthur had only been a complete husband for seven months. To his credit, in the public eye, he conceded that we had been together prior to the wedding, eager young lovers throwing caution and decency to the wind. I knew differently, as did he. He was protecting himself, ensuring his future. No one becomes a senator by marrying a harlot with a decidedly vivacious past." Claire, for a brief moment, was lost in time. "Quite frankly, Arthur was a huge disappoint in that area, in no way equal to his ego. The same ego which I suppose prevented him from ever accepting you in his heart of hearts as his son. If indeed he ever had a heart. He never did forgive me, which speaks plainly to his duplicitous nature. He could really be quite a loathsome bastard himself at times."

"He had good reason. You were sleeping around."

"I was completely enjoying my youth, as I plan to continue doing now that I'm free of him. And my memories of your father are by far my fondest thus far."

"And, I suppose, after your wedding, the perfect wife and mother."

"No. I succumbed to occasional indiscretions, which made Arthur tolerable."

"You cheated on him."

"I did with other men what he did with other women, just not as often and much more selectively."

"He never suspected?"

"He never said. He never asked and I never felt the need to confess my proclivity for change that was considerably less pronounced than his. As for your father, I'd like to think he's somewhere in the South Seas living in a hut on a beach, drinking rum and coconut juice. He was very much the dashing bohemian."

"So I'm left without a dime because you cheated on your husband with some sort of gypsy."

"Arthur wasn't my husband at the time. And, in case you weren't listening, I merely did what he was doing, what he continued doing throughout our marriage. In a word, Arthur was a whoremonger who, at the time our marriage, wasn't earning the kind of money you're making at Duval. Nor did we inherit money from our parents. By the time they were all dead we were quite independent." Her smirk was condescending. "To coin a phrase, Scott: millionaires bequeathing to millionaires, what would be the point? I expect no less of you. You might also consider the extent to which you disappointed him when you so abruptly ceased your aspirations for political office. He was quite upset with you. You spoiled his dream. And, in doing so, you also disappointed Franklin. Your situation today might well have turned out differently, if you had."

"Meaning that I'm not to expect any consideration from the loving mother I came here to console."

"You're thirty-five and a successful attorney, put through school by us. What more consideration do you require or wrongly believe that you merit? You should, at the very least, have your first million by now, apart from your wife's many inheritances. As for any imagined emotional support you believe I may need, my attorney consoled me quite adequately this morning. According to Arthur's gentlemen's agreement with Franklin you were to earn a partnership. I don't see how his death would change that. You should be speaking with Francine. She is, after all, the mother of your children. She's not the kind of girl to act punitively simply for the sake of spitefulness. Talk with her."

Gibson pushed away from the chesterfield once more, for the same reason.

"Before father's death, mother, I encountered a few difficulties. For reasons that are hard to explain, even harder to comprehend, I put myself in debt out of necessity so that I might help a friend in dire need. I was about to approach Franklin to discuss terms, who did, incidentally, promote

282

me to partner. So let's not talk about that little bitch as though she's so righteous. She has deliberately destroyed whatever proof existed of Duval's decision in order to ruin me. I was also entitled to considerably more remuneration, which she has also delighted in taking from me. Starting to get the picture, mother? Duval would have loaned me the money I require, with reasonable terms, but not her, not that bitch. And I'll be damned if I'll grovel at her feet. Now, because of her, my credit will be jeopardized, my reputation, everything because of her."

"What is the extent of your debt?"

"As we speak, a quarter-million with interest that will double the amount each year."

Claire's expression displayed instant and undisguised revulsion. "Double, so that in two years you will owe a million and, in three years twice that amount."

"You begin to see my dilemma."

"I begin to see why you want this house and the club, which can only mean that you're involved with something dirty and, given the fact that you're canvassing me so unashamedly, I must assume that you have no written contract with this friend stating terms of repayment. That's not Francine's problem, Scott. Blame your friend or yourself for poor judgment. If Arthur taught you anything, he taught you never to lend money…and never to lose it. Your friend is responsible to you for that money, no one else, which also tells me the reason you came here to console me without once asking how I am." She stood. "Arthur's funeral will be held Sunday afternoon. Should I expect to see you?"

"No. With what you've told me, I don't see the point."

"Sandra and Franklin will receive their final respects on Saturday as their preparations involved fewer formalities. I shall attend, of course. As I am certain Francine will. Despite whatever issues she might have had with her parents, I can't for a moment believe she would humiliate them in their final hour. And you, will you pay your final respects to a man who essentially made you his heir apparent?"

"No. He should have acted sooner, instead of waiting until she decided she wanted a divorce. He should have cemented plans for my future years ago, when I first joined the firm. He didn't. So how do you figure I owe him any respect?"

"Then enough said. Goodbye, Scott. You may continue with my car until yours is repaired or replaced. If in fact you own one."

He drained his glass and left. Claire put hers beside his and went about her day. She was still young, attractive, and would not wear black on Sunday or any other day while playing the despondent widow. She was reborn and her first gift to herself would be a new wardrobe. She was filthy rich with no intention of playing a secondary role to anyone ever again.

On his way home Gibson stopped at a realtor's office. He hated living in Santa Rosa, each day a reminder of how she'd used him. The condo was worth two hundred easily, with nothing owing save his debt to Mendoza that was increasing at close to twenty K per week. If he sold within a month he would still owe Mendoza 150K.

He poured several more drinks before dialling the number as though all was well with the world. Not phoning would set off alarms in Mendoza's head and that wouldn't be good. Calling would at least give him time to think.

Mario Mendoza was uppermost on Enrique's mind. He'd decided that Thursday of the following week would be a good time for cousins to make things right, to say goodbye, to come together one last time before the trial, to forget a dark future and remember the gaiety and good times now in the past. Mendoza, while waiting for the government to auction off his yacht, had leased another albeit smaller yet adequate forty-foot cruiser. He was anxious to once again breathe the salt air and feel the fine mist sprayed from the crest of waves self-destructing against the hull.

He'd also planned a going away party, Mendoza style. Mario was to leave his whore wherever she was. The girls coming to the party were top notch, the best. Everything he was bringing in would be the best, as always. Above all, Mario wasn't to know until the morning of in case something happened, a change of plans, whatever. Things happened, amigo.

Not a word was mentioned about the growing debt. They were men of honour. Each knew what was expected.

38

Gibson stayed awake through most of the night, cursing Arthur Gibson and his mother who was as much a tramp as Duval's daughter who'd promised to honour and obey him, all the while mocking him by screwing a Mexican. Going to her to beg for money was out of the question, especially in front of the Mexican. He would rather deal with Mendoza.

When he did sleep his rest was fitful, tossing and turning, waking often, his dreams usurped by vivid images. In six days Mendoza's cousin would be chum or without much of his head. What he had always found strange was how quiet a gunshot actually was, especially on the open water, still half disbelieving the reality that was encroaching on his life.

After Mario would come more parties, booze, drugs and dancers, the same two he hadn't seen in weeks or others just as young. There would always be others and at some point his luck or Enrique's patience would run out. The 200 K from the apartment wouldn't last long. Then what? His once convenient management of the truth had ballooned into full-blown intentional deceit. Mendoza would discover the fake marriage and the kids, not that he would care. What he would care about was the lie, and the inheritance of tens of millions that Gibson was excluded from when all he needed was a few hundred thousand to settle the account. He would care about his legal counsel not having the prestige of Duval & Associates, and he would care about the club: a posh, WASP sanctuary where he would never otherwise be allowed beyond the valet parking unless wearing a name tag on a bright red vest, black slacks with a red stripe down each leg and a bellman's cap. None of which would complement a chrome-plated .357. And what of the million-dollar rebate?

When Gibson dragged himself from his bed to the shower Friday morning, he had the basis of what he believed was a workable plan. His mother hadn't demonstrated the slightest compunction the day before, though she would, he was certain, were she given the proper set of circumstances to weigh on her conscience. If she was devoid of a mother's tenderness in her callous heart for him, perhaps her female's Achilles heel would serve to induce her towards compassion and what was right.

He had somehow managed to make himself entirely dependent on Mendoza. No respectable firm would touch him despite Mendoza's deep pockets and constant need of legal counsel. Nevertheless, on Mendoza's payroll he would never earn what he needed to support the lifestyle that was expected of him. For that he needed Duval money, Duval expenses and the club. If he were to live, work and play with Mendoza he would need a catalyst to jump start a new life and Mario was the one whose help he needed. They would help each other.

He drove to the motel to meet with an unsuspecting Mario, who knew never to leave his room, who didn't care that his lawyer sat watching the young whore crawl out of bed to stretch, shower, towel herself and dress. Neither did she care. She knew Gibson was the one who saved her from Enrique Mendoza's sense of fair play. Doing his cousin in a fifty-nine-dollar motel room or in a prison yard trailer didn't matter. Such was the price of forgiveness.

She asked Gibson if she could do anything special for him before she dressed. He declined and when the show was finished she left without saying goodbye. When she was gone the men went for breakfast, after which Gibson contacted the courthouse according to the court order to assure them his client was still in his custody. As soon as the brief conversation concluded they drove to Vallejo, to a home that belied the occupants' vast wealth.

Francine Duval was never intended to inherent those millions, and no way in hell did old man Duval ever intend for her to take over the firm. That money wasn't hers, he confided in Mario. She had no moral or legal right. Nor did his mother have the right to so unkindly turn him away penniless.

They observed the house from different distances and vantages until mid-afternoon when the school bus stopped in front of the house at 3:15. Francine went out twice, each time in her Lexus sedan, each time for an hour, each time parking inside her garage. When her kids got home she was at the door to greet them, the older boy walking behind. He would be the most difficult, Mario suggested. Gibson remained quiet, he didn't believe so.

What they needed to know was what time the bus passed by each morning. Not many mornings remained. When the red Mustang veered into the driveway at 5:45 they had no reason to stay longer. They drove to a liquor store where Gibson bought enough to get Mario through the weekend. They would see each other again on Monday. In the meantime they would each contact the court each morning and afternoon to guarantee Mendoza's precise whereabouts, which was the motel. He was not to leave. He was not to drink more than he needed to forget the trial and he was to send the broad home before Gibson arrived Monday morning, early.

Friday night Scott Gibson was too agitated to sleep, excited for the weekend to end. He had contacts at City Hall and higher-ups in Sacramento who were often guests of the club at Arthur's invitation. Not once throughout his entire life had he imagined devising such an incredible plan. By Thursday he would be a free man. Free of the insufferable bitch, free of Mario.

He called Enrique on his private line. He was elated, anxious for Thursday. They would be together like old times, the way they were before Mario fucked up. They would be on the ocean, the way it should be. He couldn't think of a better way for Mario to make amends than amongst friends who would forgive him. However, first and foremost, he was anxious to make things right with a briefcase filled with pristine hundred-dollar bills. Debt paid in full.

Enrique agreed. Family should not be broken apart by such a simple matter as a few dollars in arrears. The timing was good, amigo. Not once did he doubt that Scott was an honourable man. And to show his love and his devotion to family, he would send Navarra to him Saturday morning. She was nineteen, Colombian and intact, a recent gift to him that he had not yet opened. She would be a fine addition to the premier club once broken. However, until Thursday when he would take her back, she belonged to Scott Gibson.

39
December 10th of this Year

Anita Juárez sat in her office letting her mind wander to boundless limits where she no longer knew what to think. Or that she did know, and didn't want to believe or accept that what she knew in her heart was true. She wanted nothing more at the moment than to walk into his office and slap his face, to let her pent up energy travel from her every pulse through to her open palm to his face, to let him feel the complete impact of her complete collapse of self. She didn't feel disappointment, she felt betrayed, humiliated, that he would do such a thing to her. New Year's Eve was to be their goodbye. Now what would she do?

Three weeks remained in her mandate to serve him: for her an eternity.

For eight years they had done their Christmas shopping together in a closed mall after hours, the one day each year that the security detail joined them for dinner at the same table, the governor promising the highest level of secrecy regarding their one glass of wine, though after so many years it wasn't much of a secret. This year there was no restaurant because he'd decided he wasn't in the mood. Neither was she. This year she stayed home, wrapping her final gift to him, because he wasn't in the mood.

The white roses on her desk were the talk of the office. The steady flow of curious women had taken half a day to abate. The men came in en masse, flooding through her door, a united front, unwavering in their opinion that, at fifteen bucks a stem, some guy had struck pay dirt. Sadly, not one of them, they cried. The oldest and most senior aid taking her hand so that she had no choice but to stand, guiding her into a pirouette, the bunch of them producing the guttural sounds one would expect to hear from a patron at a fine restaurant about to demolish a delectably sweet dessert.

She corralled them, shooing them away, admonishing them to stop acting like children as she closed her door. At her desk, though, she missed them at once.

The fragrance emanating from the petals was as fresh as the beginning of the week, though she decided to take them home. They were a distraction. He was a distraction and she wondered for how long a time she would think of him each day before forgetting him entirely. She had to move on. She was young and beautiful, she knew that. What she needed was someone to tell her, and not from behind a desk when she was walking through a doorway.

The office would close in two weeks, pretty much for the rest of the year, when the staff would transition, mould themselves to accommodate a new governor. She would leave. She had only ever worked for him, never anyone else, and she didn't know how she would say goodbye. Would she shake his hand or hug him as she would a distant cousin, or squeeze him tightly with tears blinding her eyes? She didn't believe so. She would feel his kiss on her cheek, a birthday kiss, a Christmas kind of kiss and she would press her cheek to his as she would to a distant cousin. Then she would leave him. And she would hate him.

She didn't think she could be his friend, not for a while, not for a very long time. Her dreams of him had become nightmares since reading the letter, visions of the new governor reaching for his phone at 11:53 to speak the words that would put a man legally to death.

Each of the nights that El Cacique had reached for the phone, she had been with him. She had felt his unease, his torment and his burden of justice. But in her dreams she was not with him. He was alone, abandoned and waiting, hearing at the eleventh hour that justice would be carried out.

Friday, and she wanted to go home with her flowers. She wanted each Friday to come quickly until at last she could begin a new life. She reached for the files. She'd read each one the night before, in her bed, each one as complete as it was incredulous. She knew at that moment that no one would stop him from what he must do. He was El Cacique, not a man who would disavow a solemn oath.

The day before the two men came to her office to recap verbally. They were State Police detectives assigned to his office, experienced, streetwise and tight-lipped: Detectives Del Campo and de la Vega. The governor was unaware, each appointment timed so that The Boss wouldn't be troubled by the temptation to personally interrogate them as to their findings. Some things weren't done, not even by him. Governors did not question cops. That was the purpose of the State's Attorney's Office, most times.

De la Vega, the one assigned to Drew Carling and Deidre Commons was comfortable with what he'd written into his reports along with photographs and long-distance sound tracks. Speaking to an L.A. cop was virtually impossible cop to cop, he told Anita. No different than one woman wanting to speak with another woman while claiming she's not a woman. It just wasn't possible. Carling would have known immediately, not so with technology which allowed Carling's entire lunchtime conversation to be included in the file. The easiest part was obtaining his complete file from the LAPD. A piece of cake when state trumped local.

Ditto for Commons, though her history did take a while longer to compile. He was a cop, a big guy who looked like a cop. Some things never got better with time and he'd been a cop for thirty years. Women like Commons had nothing in common with guys like him, even if La Bonita had approved a thousand-dollar suit. A cop is a cop, he told Anita, in a towel or in a tailor-made suit. But what he saw, he liked. In his opinion, as per his files, Commons was good people. So was Carling, under the subterfuge that kept him alive. Something, he was certain, she would not like very much.

Darcy Wilson was another matter. Her investigator was Del Campo and he came to the Capitol with nothing good to report. In fact, he hated the thought of going into her office that day. It wasn't rocket science. The governor needed to know about a stripper for a reason, probably a good one. He didn't need to know, which didn't prevent him from wondering: the daughter of a friend, a niece, some other cop's informant on the run. Whatever she was, whoever wanted the update wouldn't be pleased. The kid had nothing going for her.

The photos said what had to be said. The rest of the file was superfluous. As for one on one, his being able to talk with her, Del Campo had to admit his surprise. Strippers and cops were usually oil and water unless in the back of a squad car or interacting as one professional to another. Anita knew the detective; he'd spent many days and nights protecting her home, sharing a coffee with her. When he told her that his conversation with Darcy Wilson was all business, no funny stuff, she believed him unconditionally, apologizing for assigning him. She had done so for that very reason.

Anita Juárez opened the CARLING file, skimming the pages of a report written as though from a friend or acquaintance per his instructions.

Deferred Prejudice

*

Drew Carling is now thirty-years-old, born November 14th, 1980 (approx.), adopted at the age of age nine (approx.). He has no siblings. He was raised in New York City, attended Columbia where he obtained a degree in Behavioural Psychology and entered the police academy at twenty-one. Tired of the Big Apple and slow advancement, at twenty-five he moved to the west coast for a fresh start and fresher air. His mother tongue is English, though he does speak a passable colloquial Spanish.

He's earned a dozen citations without a single stain on his record, hundreds of arrests with five reported shootings and three righteous kills. He first worked undercover with the Anti-drug squad. He was the new boy in town, unknown. He was a natural, making detective at twenty-seven. To-date he's had no run-ins with IA and his psychological state is excellent.

Both his parents are living, his mother a typical housewife, his father a retired Brooklyn cop working security at a local mall to keep himself busy.

He's unmarried with no kids, hetero with no female friends and keeps to himself. He's the quintessential loner. He has no friends, not even other undercover cops or the 'meet in a bar after work' kind of friends. He doesn't drink much, the occasional scotch, and he doesn't smoke. He goes to the gym every morning for an hour and has no apparent association with any political or social association. He doesn't attend church, he calls his parents once each week, has no debt and drives a current model Corvette.

He lives on the edge of the barrio most days, in a high-rise with barred windows and 24/7security. He never has visitors. On his days off he lives by the sea in a one-bedroom villa that has twenty years remaining on the mortgage.

He's best described as 5'10, Caucasian, reddish-blond

hair, clean-shaven, hazel-green eyes, dresses in black leather, tee-shirts, boots and guns. At the beach, he has no reason to be alone, the quintessential surfer type. On the streets, someone I wouldn't want my daughter to bring home. He needs to play the part, to appear real, and he does. He's pure attitude.

Observation: I wouldn't want to be the guy he has a reason not to like.

*

Anita slid the photographs from the file. She'd studied each one the previous night as she lay in bed playing the tapes repeatedly, intrigued by the sound of his voice. She slid the file to one side.

*

Deidre Commons is twenty-eight-years-old. She was born November 07th, 1982 (approx.), adopted at age seven (approx.). She has no siblings. She was raised in Chicago until the age of eighteen when both parents were deceased by virtue of a fatal car accident. The father was a newspaper magnate, the mother a socialite, by all accounts decent folk who left her very financially independent (very wealthy). She moved to Miami at age nineteen to work as a model, later moving to California where she currently resides in Sacramento while maintaining her home in Miami.

She studied Advertising and Business Management at Cal State. Her mother tongue is English. Her second language, Spanish, is equally fluent. She currently owns and operates Commons Communication as CEO and president. Her financial status is undisclosed. She is debt free and is not listed on any stock exchange. She owns her two condos as well as one very impressive yacht, Life's Compensation, with fractional use of a corporate jet which she uses most weekends between the cities. She is unmarried, has no kids and she lives alone.

She seems happy with her life.

She has no close friends, lovers or close associates. No apparent bad habits. No citations issued at any time. She stays to herself. She has a private table in Sacramento and in Miami where she normally dines alone.

She's best described as 5'8", Caucasian, reddish-blonde hair, clear complexion, hazel-green eyes, immaculate in every way, charming, very beautiful and a workaholic.

Observation: She's lonely. She needs a life or, better said, someone to share hers.

*

Anita inserted the tiny bud into her ear, feeling guilty that she could overhear the conversation between Deidre Commons and the maître d'. She was ordering wine, but more than that she was talking to the man as though she was truly interested in what he had to say. She was asking about his family as though she had known him for quite some time. Maybe she had. However long she stayed, when she left she called him by name when she said goodbye.

Her voice was the voice of a good person, a kind person. Perhaps one day soon, Anita thought, Deidre Commons would know the reason why.

The woman was undeniably beautiful. She walked straight. When she spoke with people she didn't lose her smile when she turned from them. Cameras never lied. De la Vega had successfully captured her essence. Deidre Commons was a good person. How could she not be?

WILSON, DARCY was neatly printed on the tab of the next folder.

*

Darcy Wilson is twenty-six. She was born October 31, 1984 according to her records at the hospital where she was found abandoned. She was adopted months later near or at the age of five.

She was raised in Detroit, her education ending abruptly with an incomplete grade nine, her scholastic standing was then within the lower twenty percentile, working nights to help her father who'd fallen on hard times once displaced by the auto firm where he'd worked for twenty plus years.

Her mother left when Darcy was fourteen. She never came home. At fifteen, Darcy dropped out, working several jobs at coffee shops and diners, doing what she could. At sixteen she left home because she had no home, which she discovered one evening after her second shift. Her father was gone.

That night she slept on the street, in her uniform. The next day she boarded the first of many buses to nowhere, working where she could, one step away from hooking, too many steps away from escorting. She did what she could. Then she heard of New Orleans, a city delivered from hell onto the precipice of a new existence. So why didn't she deserve deliverance from hell? She left the next day, arriving with less than a hundred dollars tucked into her cut-off jeans.

She was twenty, with no education and tons of smarts. The girl is smart. Given the chance her past would be just that, but she's trapped, struggling quietly to escape. She has no car. She resides in The Quarter, close to work where she waits tables and dances. She does not, however, do private salons, refusing to give her body away for a hundred an hour to expensed out-of-towners or local husbands who steal from the household money for sixty minutes of youth a few times each year. That said; she does very well her way, so far.

She has a bank account with close to a seventy-five K saved: confirmed. She's enrolled in a community college: confirmed. She wants to become a nurse. She wants to be a nurse because she doesn't believe she's smart enough to be a doctor. She's wrong about that. I've seen plenty of doctors she'd put to shame. She needs a chance; she needs to break free.

She stands 5'6"; she's petite with reddish-blonde hair, salon-tanned, hazel-green eyes, well-toned, trim and athletic. And she's young enough to close her eyes and her mind to the past. Once she gets the help she needs.

She knew I was a cop, which I admitted, though I strongly and quietly convinced her that I wasn't NOPD or a narc, not even close. When she asked why I was there I told her that I believed not for anything but good. And I know that I'm right. I told her not to do anything stupid, that I was certain things were going to get better for her pretty soon. Someone please tell me I'm right.

She asked me as I was about to leave the bar if I was there because I knew who she really was. I answered: I believe that's not wrong, that somebody very important, from very far away was concerned enough about her to have her found and followed. I hope I'm right.

Observation: Get this girl help PDQ!
*

The detective had scrawled the last line with his own pen and with a pressure that spoke of his emotion.

Anita Juárez was cold. She wanted to go home. She felt betrayed, gutted. She pressed the button on her desk that would alert him. Then she walked in.

"Governor today is the tenth. I have the files you requested."

He was depleted, too exhausted to play cat and mouse. Their time spent together since Monday was tense, neither one knowing what to say, what not to say.

"Put them on my desk, Anita. Thank you." He paused. "You've read them, no doubt."

"Yes. I have read them."

"I specifically told you not to."

"Then fire me."

He coughed a curt laugh, standing, walking to the bar concealed behind a fake armoire where he poured a glass of his finest Pinot Noir. "Would I cut off my right arm?"

"You already have."

She turned and walked out, closing the door gently. Not ten minutes later her private line chimed. He was calling. She held her breath, reaching for the receiver, saying nothing.

He ignored the silence. "Anita, Detective Drew Carling is on special assignment to me as of this moment. Send my personal jet with the same officers immediately to meet him at LAX, though, in case he's inclined to refuse my invitation, have the Attorney General issue a provisory warrant for his arrest which is to be enforced immediately should the officers detect a problem. I want him in Sacramento this evening. No one is to interfere, not the mayor, not the commissioner. I don't care what case he's working. He'll spend the night in luxury, or in a Sacramento jail. Please see to his comfort and have your chauffeur meet him at seven AM tomorrow for a meeting here. Inform security that he's expected. I'll expect my car at the same time. Enjoy your weekend, Anita. I will see you Monday"

He disconnected. She waited a brief moment before slamming the phone into the cradle, albeit with as much decorum as she could muster.

Enjoy your weekend, Anita. I will see you Monday. Like that would happen, Cacique, ¡idiota! How little he knew of her. He would do such a thing for a tough street cop, yet not for a young girl in such desperate trouble as Darcy Wilson. He was becoming more despicable each day. She made the necessary calls, requested her chauffeur and went home early for the first time in twenty-one years despising him.

*

By day's end Friday Drew Carling was onboard The Boss' private jet from LAX to SMF. Sipping Johnnie Walker Blue, he enjoyed. Giving over his two guns and stiletto to the state cops, he didn't like. Nor did he argue. His captain had read the warrant and hadn't given him much of a choice. Instead he refilled his glass and enjoyed the smooth ride in plush leather seats. He knew who wanted him. What he didn't know was why. Neither did Del Campo who instructed the pilot to remain in the flight deck once again while the passenger disembarked.

At Sacramento he was met by a limousine, the two state cops walking shoulder to shoulder with him. They didn't much care for undercover hotshots, though, knowing what they did, they gave him some latitude. More importantly they cared about La Bonita who was stepping from the car and the guy between them was scary.

The chauffeur remained inside, per her instructions. She had to see this man with her own eyes. She had to accept or deny what she believed was true. She was satisfied, albeit, she had to admit, unnerved by seeing him that close, thinking that, if not for Del Campo and de la Vega, the man would have frightened her.

The cops didn't like the idea of leaving her alone with Carling, which wasn't her intention. She introduced herself to Carling, shaking his hand, welcoming him to the city. He was to enjoy the governor's hospitality to the fullest, whatever he wanted. She bid him a pleasant night, telling him that she would arrive at the hotel at 7:00 AM the next morning and that he was invited to join the governor for breakfast.

Closing him into the limo, she turned to her cops with a wide smile, her thumb poking invisible holes into the air, asking if she could thumb a ride to her home... but first.

"Luis, Carlos, I must ask you both a favour. Do not feel the need or any obligation to accept if you feel uncomfortable with what I ask. This I ask for myself, not the governor."

Luis said jokingly. "Señora Juárez, we will gladly take

care of any man who has disrespected you or hurt your feelings. Tell us where to find him."

She thought for a moment, shaking her head. Not such a good idea. "Thank you, Luis. I may ask that favour of you very soon, if I don't kill him first. However, this favour I ask of you, although not illegal, may cause you to lose your jobs. And I, mine. So please do not answer me quickly."

Carlos and Luis exchanged curious glances. Her expression could not have been more solemn, her penetrating black eyes unblinking, surprising the men with a piercing whistle while raising an open palm to halt the pilot in her tracks.

"Señora, what could you possibly ask that would make us lose our jobs?" Carlos asked.

"Carlos, that young girl in New Orleans, I must speak with her...this evening. Please, think before you answer. I will understand. Believe me. I will. I realize the gravity of what I am asking of you and of Luis."

She left them to speak with the pilot, Carlos and Luis studying the woman's reaction to La Bonita, watching her climb the steps to re-enter the aircraft. Del Campo spoke quickly to de la Vega. Anita Juárez was stalling, giving them the time they needed. What La Bonita was asking was not a simple matter. If not kidnapping, they could certainly be charged with interstate theft of an aircraft. Taking part in what she was asking of them could and probably would jeopardize their shared retirement plans if not land them in jail and divorce court. They'd been cops for thirty years, partners, with five years left to go before heading to Oregon to open their dream hunting and fishing lodge. They gave the matter serious thought. The decision was a no-brainer.

Carlos spoke first. "Señora, I have brought Luis up to speed about the girl. Such a place is not for you. Tell us what you want and we will do the rest, without you."

She shook her head. "I must see this girl for myself. I

must speak with her, but I am a stranger to her and I believe she will feel more at ease with someone she knows…that is you Carlos. I believe she will trust you from what I read in your report. And, Luis, when we are done, The Boss has the best tequila onboard. What he does not know will not hurt him," she paused, "which, caballeros, is the problem."

"That The Boss does not know of this is very clear, señora."

"He does not. And he may not entirely agree with my actions should he find out."

"Will we help the girl?"

"I do not know. I hope so, which is why I must ask for your help."

Carlos said: "Vamos."

Luis snorted: "The best tequila, for this I would never again sleep with my wife's sister. "Sí, vamos."

Anita's mouth dropped open.

De la Vega's wife didn't have a sister.

40

Anita wasn't a prude. She saw nothing wrong with topless women wearing thongs at the beach, something she'd always thought would be fun with the right man. Nor was she blind to the artistic value of the nude form interpreted on canvas, in glamour photography or sculpted by gifted hands. This was different. She could never have imagined a cavernous room dotted with small, round stages with young women contorting their naked bodies into all manner of impossible poses. Or half-naked women navigating their way between tightly placed tables, managing trays filled with glasses and bottles. Or the young women completely naked and gyrating on stools in front of mesmerized men leering between their open legs, their buttocks inches from the men's faces, or leaning into them with their breasts practically touching the men's faces.

Luis passed the bouncer a fifty, not for the best seat, rather for a more secluded spot at the far corner. The man nodded and guided them. He knew they were cops. The broad with them he wasn't sure about. Cops were always coming to the cabaret for a free dance and beers, some of them making it as far as the private salons which Carlos had advised against. The rooms were not all that private, he warned.

He assured Anita that naked girls were always more interesting to men than someone else's private conversation. When they were seated:

"I assume that you have been to such cabarets before, Carlos, as a man of the world."

"No, señora, this is only my second time. My first was to obtain information on Darcy Wilson for you. This is all new to me. My initial shock has since worn off."

"And you, Luis, you have never been to such a place before. This is new to you also?"

"Like Carlos, señora, I am truly shocked by what I see. I could never have imagined such a thing."

She made a humph sound, scanning the cabaret. "I do not believe either one of you. I believe you are both terrible liars. And," she whispered, leaning into them, "I feel more than a little overdressed."

They let that one go.

Carlos signalled one of the girls to the table. She was smiling, acknowledging Anita with a flirtatious wink. She bent forward to take their order, nodding, glancing again at Anita. When she left he explained to La Bonita that it wasn't unusual for straight women to frequent such places in the company of sophisticated men. Doing so was an easy way to be naughty, to enjoy a dancer or two before going home to fantasize.

And how did he know this, she asked? He had a friend who worked vice, he replied. And did Luis have such an informative friend, she enquired, her eyebrows raised. Luis shrugged, apparently so. Though neither man could ever have imagined they'd be sitting in a strip bar in New Orleans with the to-die-for personal assistant to the Governor of California.

The four drinks arrived. Moments later Demure came to them carrying a stool that she placed closer to Anita than Luis, giving Anita all her attention. Anita was too self-involved, studying the girl's body, face and mannerisms. The cops were too self-involved watching La Bonita watch the girl as though speaking in a crowded bar with a half-naked girl was commonplace to her. No one would ever believe them, no one would ever know.

Her name was Demure and only when Carlos heard Darcy tell Anita that she was allowed to touch if she wanted to did the cop pat Darcy on her bare hip.

"Hey, it's you. Hi."

"Yeah, it's me, kid."

She noticed Luis. "He's another cop from far away, isn't he?"

"You got it."

She glanced back at Anita. "So…do I dance for your lady friend, or what? Is this like a threesome thing?"

"Not quite. This evening's been strange enough so far. This fine lady has come a very long way to see you, Darcy. Why? I don't know. I don't. But when she wants something, she gets it. She's a very important lady, and she's very nice. She is not here to harm you."

"Thank you, Carlos. You are kind to speak so well of me." She patted his hand. "Now may I ask you to please offer this young woman your jacket?"

"Señora, I'm sorry, I cannot." He tugged his jacket partway from his body.

Anita nodded, understanding his dilemma.

"Oh, that's okay; I'm used to being naked in here. Really, I'm good."

Anita didn't agree, not hesitating to unbutton and pull away her own bolero-style jacket, stand, and place it over Darcy's shoulders.

Luis and Carlos had never once imagined how La Bonita might look in a three-quarter black laced bra. Now they didn't have to imagine, her sheer black blouse serving to accentuate her appeal, in no way concealing a very desirable woman. And she didn't have a man in her life, they both thought.

"My name is Anita Juárez, Darcy."

"So, what am I supposed to do?"

"You are to sit and talk with me."

"That's not really allowed. I'm usually good for a few hundred every hour. The boss won't like me sitting here just talking."

"We don't care about your boss, Darcy. We care about you."

Anita reached into her purse, placing a crisp hundred on the table as Luis gave the girl his seat and dragged over another from a nearby table.

"Where are you from? Carlos just said that he was from far away."

"We come from California."

"You're the one who sent Carlos, aren't you? You're the one who knows who I am?"

"I don't know. Or, better said, perhaps I do know. I hope so. What I can tell you, whether I am right or wrong, which doesn't matter at all, is that you will become a nurse one day soon and if you truly wish to become a doctor, you will. I will make that happen for you. That, I promise you."

Darcy looked to Carlos. "She can do that, just like that?"

"Like I said, the lady's important. Listen to her."

Darcy reached for the club soda in front of her, drinking barely enough to moisten her lips. "Why? Why now? How long have you known about me? And what do I have to do?"

Anita was calm, not unaware of the attention she was attracting from the men seated at surrounding tables. "The first two answers are not for me to give. I'm sorry, I simply cannot. As for the third, we have known for a week. We had to be certain, and still we are not. Regarding your fourth question, I wish for you to leave with us, right now. You will not return to this place. I will go with you to your changing area if you wish."

Luis interjected quickly. "That's a negative, señora." He

wasn't joking, despite the black eyes.

Carlos said: "Go get your stuff. Don't worry about the paycheque. Just leave." He saw Darcy staring at the entrance. "Believe me, kid, he's not a problem. Neither is your boss."

She was confused, wanting Anita to say something more. Carlos and Luis were silent, stone-faced, Anita's simple nod jerking her to her feet.

Carlos stood, taking Anita's bolero, holding it out towards her, not quite certain when to let go as she stood and slid each of her arms into the designer sleeves. From behind her he mouthed a silent 'wow' to Luis whose grin betrayed them. At least some men appreciated her, she mused, feeling every bit as sexy as she was.

She thanked him for being a gentleman, and Luis. Then she sat scanning the room while drinking in their visible discomfort along her with her club soda. They were good men. She would miss them.

Darcy joined them inside of five minutes dressed in jeans, a tee-shirt and stilettos. She was nervous, excited. She asked where they were going, not certain she had asked before she went to change.

Anita leaned in closer to whisper. "We will go first to your apartment for your personal possessions, after which we will fly to California on a private jet. Tomorrow morning you will be pampered at a spa and in the afternoon we will go shopping, you and I. You must be properly attired as a beautiful young woman, Darcy, and well rested, before I present you to the Governor of California. He is the one who sent Carlos to find you. I am the one who shall take you to him."

Darcy slowly reached a low-pitched hysterical laugh, needing to grasp her stomach, stopping abruptly when she realized she was the only one. Anita simply tilted her head, her black eyes telling Darcy this wasn't a joke.

The man at the door thought to stop them, changing his mind when he saw the ten-millimetres and gold badges. He didn't give a shit about the badges. He just wanted to get home that night in one piece.

Outside Luis returned the hundred to Anita who asked him why they hadn't paid for their drinks. He told her it was Ladies' Night. Neither did they go to the apartment. Darcy paid in advance by the month and had nothing of value. Still she wasn't convinced she should believe them, not even when Carlos held open the door of the limousine. She'd been through so much in her life. Not even, when at the airport, weaving through rows of private planes and jets and stopping at one whose engines were purring, did she believe.

"Who's that, Anita? Is she waiting for us?"

"Yes, she is. Her name is Diane Quinn. She is our pilot, the governor's personal pilot when his flights do not involve state business."

"So I'm personal business."

"I believe so, yes."

"Anita, no way, she's so tiny. How can she fly that big thing?"

"She can, and she does. I have flown with her several times. She is also an accomplished markswoman. She is able to hit a quarter-sized target from fifty feet without taking the time to aim. Also, not many men would want to make her angry. She is very good in many other ways." Anita took her hand. "Come."

At the bottom of the steps leading to the companionway the pilot greeted each of them by name, shocking Darcy even more. The woman knew her name. Inside the cabin Darcy grabbed Anita's arm, squeezing. She was scared. Whatever was happening to her was beginning to seem real. An hour earlier she was tucking a fifty into her panties, giving the guy a final peek before tugging the silk side ties to her hips, now Anita was buckling her into a plush leather seat inside a corporate jet and Diane Quinn was serving her a light snack and a selection of beverages.

When everyone was served, Captain Quinn left them.

Moments later the lights dimmed and Darcy yelped. They were moving, taxing to the runway, Darcy's eyes glued to the porthole by her seat, the quiet purr of Rolls Royce engines increasing to a dull roar, becoming a high-pitched whir. She reached across for Anita's hand. She'd never flown, not once in her life. She was afraid of the mild vibration and the speed, of the coloured lights flashing past her along four thousand feet of runway, until nothing, total darkness, her body forced into the soft leather during a near vertical ascent at 3600 feet per minute, her heart racing.

In the flight deck Diane Quinn remembered her first flight, her own feeling of wonder and fear. She enjoyed the vast pale blue of daylight, the endless curvature of the earth, the dark of night and her closeness to the stars that was hers alone in her place, her time. This was her special place, her jet, at least until he found out that she'd stolen it. She sighed. She'd done the right thing and this was a special flight. So why not give Darcy something to remember?

"Miss Wilson, good evening, this is Captain Quinn. We are approaching the Texas-New Mexico border at an altitude of 32,000 feet. Our current speed is 440 knots. Our ETA is two hours, thirty minutes. I was wondering if you might consider joining me in the flight deck for a different view of the world. I'm certain the other passengers won't mind, for a little while."

The other passengers didn't. Anita nodded her approval, bringing a cautionary forefinger to her lips. Del Campo and de la Vega were each on their second glass of the governor's finest tequila and in the company of La Bonita. Life didn't get any better than that.

Yet, too soon, Darcy returned to her seat for the landing,

Diane Quinn's strict policy.

In Sacramento the pilot called Darcy by her first name, a rare lapse in her own sense of protocol, hugging her and wishing her good luck. Prior to departing for New Orleans Diane Quinn had told Anita that she believed helping a young girl escape a bad life was worth her job. Someone had once helped her in much the same way. It was payback time. She was in, for better or worse. And after her time with Darcy in the flight deck she was certain she'd made the right decision.

As for Darcy, she'd always suspected that one day she would be in the backseat of a police car, scared, afraid of what might happen to her. And she was afraid of what was happening to her. Why her? She was nobody, a stripper. Best of all, she'd been in the front seat of a private jet while the cops sat in the back…wow!

At the hotel Carlos and Luis said goodbye to Darcy in the lobby, assuring her that everything was fine. Her dancing days were over. She hugged them both. Hugging cops, she told them. Her life was changing.

They would wait for Anita, they told her. Flying The Boss' private jet and drinking his premier booze was one thing, letting anything happen to La Bonita would be much worse.

She didn't argue. She went with Darcy to the four-room, penthouse suite where she ordered a late-night dinner for one with the maître d's recommendation for a suitable wine. A half-bottle would suffice. She wanted Darcy to sleep, not pass out.

They walked through the suite together. Darcy had never seen anything so luxurious. She sat on the bed and bounced. She'd never slept in a bed as big or as soft. Tears began welling, threatening to trickle down her cheeks. She wanted to know when all this would end. Why her? She didn't even know who the governor was.

Anita assured her that what was happening wasn't the end, rather the beginning. She told the young woman that her wake-up call would come at eight, that her treatments at the spa and her appointment at the hair salon were booked. Anita would see her again at noon. They would do lunch and spend lots of money in the most exclusive boutiques.

When Darcy asked why once again, Anita skirted the real question. She answered, "Because I've never had a kid sister."

41
Twenty-One Years Ago

Gibson had always regarded his mother as a glamorous socialite. While other high-end mothers wore dresses to below their knees, Claire Gibson wore her hems well above her knees. While the other women wore camisoles and bras under silk blouses, Claire wore one or the other, or neither when her dresses were sufficiently décolleté.

Now he thought of her as a harlot.

Enrique Mendoza was never in the company of unattractive women. The dancers who worked his clubs were all catwalk quality. Even his hookers and call girls were glamorous, a step above. So Gibson had to assume that Navarra would be something special. His intercom buzzed near noon.

He had intended to spend the weekend perfecting his plan, making certain that nothing would go wrong, anxious for Monday morning when he would add the school bus schedule to the equation. But when he saw her coming through the door that he'd left ajar, his plan could suddenly wait. She wasn't anything typical. She could have been a junior college co-ed, more like a cheerleader than a soon-to-be dancer.

She was six-foot in heels, slim with straight chocolate brown hair to her waist, small breasts, a tight ass and dark caramel-coloured skin. Her eyes were innocent, her lips full, and her teeth bright white. But if Mendoza was giving her to him how innocent and intact could she be?

He was anxious to find out, deciding not to rush her. She would definitely be a top earner, from Gibson's perspective better put to use as an escort than a dancer.

She had two brothers, both young and new to the drug trade, each believing they could do a better job supplying Mendoza than the cartel they'd been drafted into. What they hadn't counted on was Mendoza's sense of honour. Within twenty-four hours of their first meeting they were found dead, victims of a rival cartel, the Bogotá newspapers reported. The head of the cartel, wishing to show his gratitude to Enrique Mendoza, sent him their sister to further punish her family.

She felt no grief for her brothers; she felt pain for her mother whom she would never see again. She also understood what would happen were she to have trouble adapting to her new life. She wasn't afraid, she was resigned. She didn't like the idea of men paying to touch her, though she knew she would adapt. She would survive.

He asked whether she knew why Enrique had sent her to him. She answered that she didn't and he took her into the bedroom. An hour later he left her whimpering atop the damp sheets and called the courthouse, confirming that Mario Mendoza had reported in as well. Then he went back to her.

By the time they went to dinner she'd stopped crying, realizing when they returned that tears would serve no purpose. By Sunday evening she was as comfortable with her nudity as she was dressed. Over the weekend Gibson had told her about the parties, the yacht, the cars, the clothes and how much she could earn in a single year if she were smart enough to be the best.

She would be, she promised, soon falling into a deep sleep. He lay beside her, studying her, fondling her. She was beautiful, flawless. He was her first. Mendoza had indeed been generous. If she were the best she could retire at forty, move away, get married and pretend she was never a whore. If not, he'd be the first of a few thousand. By thirty she'd look forty and by forty she'd be lucky not to be living on the streets and raped each night by homeless guys.

He fell asleep, not once thinking that his father was buried early that afternoon.

*

Monday morning when he left to meet Mario Mendoza he told her to stay in bed. He saw no need for them to know about each other. The Mendoza world was too small and eventually, very soon, she'd be servicing Enrique as well. Pillow talk wasn't always a good thing and the less one Mendoza learned about the other, the better.

Mario Mendoza owned what was on his back, transmuting into a hapless indigent more each day. That would have to change. The contented citizens of Vallejo were unaccustomed to seeing the less fortunate walking their streets or sitting in a car in front of their middle-class homes.

They arrived not far from the house in time to see the Mustang leave, the school bus stopped in front of the house at 8:30.

"So now that we know what do we do with her, man?"

"Not we, you...tomorrow, if that bus comes at 3:15 and again tomorrow at 8:15. That gives us seven hours."

"To do what?"

"You, you're going to let her know that she's been kidnapped, that you're going to visit the bank with her to help her make a withdrawal. I'm thinking five million should do. It's pocket change for her. Then you'll keep her occupied until my part is done which should be just before the school bus gets here at 3:15. As far as she's concerned, do whatever you want with her. Have a good time. It'll serve the bitch right. Think of her as my parting gift to you."

"What if she don't play nice?"

"She will, once you tell her that you'll drown her kids in the bathtub." He eyed Mendoza from head to toe, snickering. "She'll believe you, and when we're done I'll have enough to pay off your cousin, you'll have something for when you get out, and with what's left I'll be where I should have been if her old man hadn't died on me."

"You'd do that for me, man?"

"Yeah, it's the least I can do. Just no way could I get that sentenced reduced."

Mario studied the house. "She don't look like she'll go down easy." He grunted. "I never did a rich bitch before. Or a friend's wife."

"Which is why, when you're back from the bank, you'll sedate her. You've got her until 3:15. And she's not my wife, so have a good time."

The garage door went up, the two watching with wide grins as Francine reversed onto the street and drove off. They didn't follow. They spent a few hours drinking, eating lunch and going over every detail of what they would do. Mendoza was a clinical moron most times, but crime was his forte and he wasn't disguising his anticipation of enjoying his time with her. Then Gibson took him for a haircut, telling him to clean up his act by the next day. Gibson wanted him in a suit with a clean shirt and a tie. He didn't need zealous neighbours calling the cops to report someone who didn't belong.

When they were finished they made a call to the courthouse. Gibson drove Mendoza to his room to wait for the whore and went home to Navarra who was stretched out on the private balcony taking in the sun.

In Colombia, she told him, she'd always dreamed of living in a fine home and wearing fine clothes. That part of

315

her new life she was excited about, she wasn't so certain about being fondled, poked and prodded by men she didn't know. What, she asked, if she were to dance and do nothing else, be his woman and no one else's? The other girls had told her that very soon she wouldn't see the men staring at her, that she'd just do her job and go home like anyone else. She believed she could do that, take off her clothes, just not the other, standing to show him what she meant.

When they were finished he called his mother, asking to see her the next day. He had something to tell her that she must hear, though not on the phone, in person. When the polite conversation ended he went to the bar where he poured a generous scotch and tequila before joining Navarra on the balcony to share a joint.

42

Tuesday Hidalgo Arquero kissed his wife and daughters, shaking hands with Diego who believed himself too old to be kissing his father. He left home precisely at eight. He was happy; delighted that Francine had found nothing to fault with his plan regarding Arquero-Duval & Associates.

He'd spoken with Virginia Meadows the previous day, asking her to call a general meeting for Friday evening, making her privy to the details. Each of the senior associates would become senior partners, each of the junior associates, junior partners. They would share equally in the firm's fiscal success in exchange for which they would each contribute equal time to his storefront law office where they would work without pay in jeans and sweaters, not fancy suits or Italian-made shoes. The women included.

When she put down the phone Mrs. Meadows sat quietly in disbelief. He'd told her that her new position with the firm required that she drive a somewhat more prestigious vehicle. The owner of the European dealership would call on her later in the day to personally assist her with her choice.

Fifteen minutes later the bus arrived, Francine hugging and kissing her children, including Diego, telling them to be good, especially Diego, and to listen attentively to their teachers.

At twenty past the hour she heard the knock at her door, hesitating with the keys to her car in her hand.

"Good morning, señora," he said. "I am sorry to trouble you, I…"

Francine smiled. "Yo hablo Español, señor. Por favor," she prompted.

"Si, yo sé," he answered, crashing an open hand across her throat, pushing her backward into her foyer. "Spanish it is. My English, it is not so good."

Francine was sprawled on the floor, dazed, grasping her throat with one hand, pushing down the hem of her skirt with the other. "What is it that you want? If you need money you can have what is in my purse."

"I do not need what is in your purse." His eyes were fixed on her skirt. "I need much more than that."

"I am a mother. You cannot…"

"Lady, your kids, they will be home in seven hours. Before then you will call the bank. You will tell them to have ready five million dollars by one o'clock this afternoon. The place where you bank is very big. They will have such an amount. They open at ten. You will call the manager at nine with your instructions."

"Five million, I cannot. I do not have that kind of money."

"I know what you have Francine Arquero-Duval. Do not bullshit me. Refuse me and I will enjoy what else you have to offer until your kids come home to see you on the floor, stripped like a common puta, when I will drown each one of them in your bathtub for your husband to see floating when he arrives. Do as I tell you and you will have dinner with your family as usual, with nothing to explain to your proud husband unless you want to." Mendoza looked around. "Now, where do you keep your liquor?"
*

Scott Gibson arrived at his mother's at nine. She advised him before greeting him that he had one hour of her time. She was expecting a prospective buyer at ten.

"Mother, on Thursday I wasn't entirely honest with you. Truth be told, I had no intention of telling you the truth out of fear that I would distress you more than you were. It's true that I owe a quarter-million, and you were correct to presume that my debt is to someone very dangerous. Now, however, because of certain developments, I must be very candid. The man in question, mother, is Enrique Mendoza, the crime boss. I must also tell you that my apartment is on the market for a quick sale." Gibson produced the contract. "But it's not enough. He's started threatening me. He knows about Franklin and Sandra and he doesn't believe that father neglected me in his will. He wants five million, mother, and he's threatening to kill Francine and our children if he doesn't get the money by this afternoon."

"Isn't he your client, Scott?"

"He was, not since Francine fired me from the firm. Something else I couldn't tell you. I was too ashamed." He blew a stream of air from between his lips, pressing his palms to his face, rubbing hard. "Can you believe it? She fired her own husband."

"I remember the wedding so well. She was a lovely bride."

"I loved her so much."

"Yes, I'm sure you did, until you punched her in the face, until she annulled the marriage and married Hidalgo Arquero, the man of her dreams, to have his children, not yours. Imagine my surprise when I saw them at the funerals. They came to Franklin's out of respect. I must say she's done very well for herself. Mr. Arquero is very much the gentleman and her children are adorable, much better suited to their names than the ones you invented. She apologized to me for the ruse; she also explained why she felt the need. I must say, Scott, you are a very despicable and entirely odious man. Franklin, had he been your father, would have despised you thoroughly for what you have done. Your real

319

father would likely have pommelled you into the ground."

"She's as culpable as me. What I did, I did for father, Arthur if you prefer. As I told you on Thursday, she's the least of my worries. And her spawn, I haven't seen them for years. So the real truth is out, good. The fact remains that Mendoza lives at the bottom of the food chain. He's dangerous and he wants five million by this afternoon or he's going to kill her and the kids, then me after he rapes her. Not just once and not just him, he likes to party. He likes to watch." He strode to the bar. With his glass filled he turned to Claire. "He believes they're mine, that I'm married to her. The fact that I'm not won't save her or them, or me for that matter. Think you can live with that, mother?"

"Or quite possibly this is another vulgar fabrication. Your credibility is somewhat nonexistent. You must know that, Scott. When I saw Francine on Sunday she was quite well, very well."

Gibson went to the phone, bringing it to her. "Dial her number. Ask to speak with her."

Claire did. Francine answered. The man whose voice she heard next was rude, caustic, his snide laughter causing Claire's stomach to revolt. She waited a few moments, composing herself before dialling her bank manager's direct number.

Moments later Francine placed a call to her bank manager, leaving a message that he should call her immediately.

Within an hour Claire had her answer. The cash withdrawal would be available to her at 1:00 PM as she requested in thousand-dollar bills. Francine's call came at ten. Her money would be available an hour later. The manager apologized, telling her that, for some reason another branch he'd called to assist him with the urgent request was temporarily unable to meet the demand.

*

Gibson left his mother's mansion before ten. She didn't want him there. He was despicable to her, a contemptible blight on the Gibson name.

She met him at the bank. She had no desire to accompany him and when the transaction was concluded she asked that he never bother her again, steadfastly refusing the extra million he asked of her so that he might get his life in order. He was to conclude his business with Mendoza and return her car that evening without disturbing her.

She would not see him again for twenty-one years.

*

Mendoza spent the morning waiting, speaking once every hour with Gibson. He drove the Lexus to the bank, not Francine, assuring her that, if not that day, some other day he would come to drown her children if she believed that calling the police from the bank was a good idea. She came out after thirty nervous minutes with a briefcase containing fifty bundles.

From Francine's home Mendoza called Gibson, confirming the five million. Gibson said nothing about his briefcase. What he did say was that Mendoza had an hour to play.

Francine had never been as terrified in her life, pleading with him to leave, not to harm her children. He just laughed and told her to take off her clothes, very slowly. When she didn't, he punched her. When she refused a second time the impact from his fist crashed her to the floor. Her skirt was ripped from her with a single violent tug, jerking her into the air. He gave her a choice: the floor or the bed. She didn't answer. Instead she began screaming and kicking. Mendoza was on her instantly. One hand pressed painfully over her mouth and nose, the other tearing at her blouse, his knees forcing hers apart.

She was beating his arms, stopping when he drove his practiced fist into the side of her head. He tore at her bra, groping her, and she began with new strength to push him away as he grabbed at her panties. She refused to stop struggling, twisting, trying to hurt him, to throw him over, pulling at his hair until he punched her viciously several times in the stomach. She couldn't breathe; she was suffocating, blood from her nose seeping between his fingers. He was groping her, squeezing her breasts, rubbing a hand roughly between her legs. He was laughing. Then he was flat against her, crushing her, his free hand under her, groping.

Then she felt the searing pain, her body convulsing, moving with his. She closed her eyes, squeezing tears onto her face. There was nothing she could do. In her mind she cried out to Hidalgo. Her children must not see her like this. She tried one last time to twist herself free of him, for Hidalgo. Her husband must not think that she had let this happen. She couldn't move. His breath was putrid. She wanted to vomit.

He hadn't stopped laughing, pressing down harder on her face with every thrust, pushing harder inside her. She had no sense of time, five minutes or ten, or of where she was until she felt him stop. Her body was no longer jerking, rubbing cruelly against the floor. She could no longer feel his weight or the pressure against her face. The worst was over. Hidalgo would forgive her.

When Mendoza was finished he pulled away from her. He was breathing heavily, ordering her to stand as he cleaned himself with her skirt. When she refused he slammed his foot into her side, her body barely reacting.

Francine Elizabeth Arquero-Duval was dead at age twenty-nine.

43

Gibson arrived at three, paralyzed by the sight of Francine's naked body splayed facedown over the back of a sofa as though mounted in a perverse saddle. He stood, his mouth open wide, and stared.

"I didn't know where else to put her, man. It went bad. She started screaming right away. I just wanted to shut her up."

"Didn't I tell you to sedate her? Did you think she'd just lie down and let you in? Shit!"

"I guess I was anxious, and time was running out real fast. You told me that"

"I said you had an hour. What did you do to her face?"

"I had to smack her a bit, to shut her up. Shit, man, she must have choked while I was doing her. I thought she was just calming down, you know."

"I told you to fuck her, to teach her a lesson, not to frigging kill her." He stared at his watch, as though time might stand still for him. "Take her into the garage, put her in the trunk. I'll get her clothes."

Mendoza pulled Francine from the far side of a bare hip, dropping her onto the floor, taking her by her ankles. Gibson gathered the torn skirt and ripped panties, using them to wipe her blood from the hardwood floor. He didn't have time to think of anything smart.

In the garage Francine was crumpled in a heap amidst containers of windshield wash, a briefcase and clothes she had expected to take to the cleaners. Mendoza was holding her tattered blouse and bra in his hands. He tossed them on top of her; Gibson did the same, telling Mendoza to give him his gun, the holster and any spare clip he might have. Mendoza did. He was accustomed to playing the village idiot when confronted with superior intellect. Instructed to remain in the garage, he did.

Gibson ran into the kitchen. He was on a high; adrenalin was coursing through his veins. He began snickering at the thought of what he was doing, his mind racing. He didn't want to kill three kids, not necessarily, but Mendoza would if it meant not being executed himself.

He took three glasses from a cabinet, filled them with milk. He ran to the dining room, to the hutch searching for anything clear. He found tequila, not bothering to measure how much he added to the milk. He dropped the powder from two capsules into each glass, stirring with a forefinger. He'd barely finished when he heard the brakes of the school bus grinding to a halt.

He waited at the door. Francesca was the first to scurry in, followed by Gabriella and Diego. Gibson closed the door quickly behind them.

"Diego, hi there, buddy. My name is Detective Smith. Hi, girls. I'm here because your mom was in a little accident this afternoon. She's not hurt, not at all. Don't worry. She's fine. We simply had to take her to the hospital to be certain. Your father should be here in about twenty, thirty minutes to get you, to take you to your mom." He had no proof, no badge to flash. Instead he let them catch a glimpse of his gun. "In the meantime, Diego, your father Hidalgo instructed me to make sure you have a glass of milk to fill your stomachs before he arrives. You'll be going to a restaurant tonight because mom won't be cooking for a while. She'll need a bit of time to recover and you'll have to be good for her."

Gabriella started crying, Diego trying to comfort her, telling her the man was a police officer and that he wouldn't tell a lie. Mamá was safe and papá would soon be home with them. Ten minutes later the three were sound asleep. Two hours and fifteen minutes remaining before Hidalgo's world would implode.

Gibson had a lot of thinking to do. First, he would drive his mother's car into the garage. Then he would take a deep breath. Okay, so, Francine was dead. He'd get over that. Images of her nakedness were already usurping thoughts of seeing her dead. Of greater importance was disposing of her and the kids. Even a cop with the intellectual capacity of Mario Mendoza would link him with the disappearance.

Francine's five million would be tied-in with his mother's and he was undeniably and publicly tied-in with Enrique and Mario. He'd told his mother about Enrique's supposed threat and, for that, he'd be the first one interrogated. And he wouldn't appreciate being charged with first degree murder. California supported the death penalty and death row was never as full as other states with the possible exception of Texas.

He drained his glass of tequila and went into the garage with that and the three others, throwing them carelessly into the trunk. He went with Mendoza into the house, each of them taking a girl into the garage and stowing them into the backseat of Claire's car. When they were done they took Diego by the ankles and arms and pushed him in beside his sisters.

Gibson knew of a place at the north end of San Francisco Bay miles from Vallejo and at the end of a deserted road, a secret place for girls to experience their first love and for boys to be the first lover, later comparing notes with one another when the girls were gone. The car wouldn't be discovered for days by which time, he told Mendoza, the trial would be over and they would be wealthy men.

Mendoza didn't think past the obvious. He didn't have to, there was nothing linking him to the crime. He wanted his gun, Gibson refusing, reminding Mendoza that the court had confiscated his driver's permit, that if the cops stopped him for any reason, saw the gun and searched the trunk, that he'd be up shit creek. Mendoza agreed, and they left, agreeing where to meet and when. The real problem, however, was Gibson's to solve on his own, he told the other without saying that he already had.

They met an hour later, Gibson leading Mendoza to the exact spot. No one was there. Girls anxious for first love and boys eager to get laid were at home eating dinner with their parents who believed their children were pure and innocent.

They were perfectly concealed. No one would see. No one would know to call the police to report something suspicious. Still, he didn't have much time. Mendoza was seated in the Lexus, the window down, gazing at the sunset as though he hadn't just raped and killed a young woman, waiting for instructions. Gibson seemed to know what he was doing. He'd said he was going for a shovel and, where they were, she wouldn't be found for years, if ever.

Scott Gibson went to driver's side of the Lexus. He was smiling, Mendoza was smiling. Gibson scanned the area one last time before putting a bullet in his client's ear. Quickly, he opened the door, keeping the head from falling against the horn, rummaging through Mendoza's pockets, exchanging the man's wallet with his own. He removed Mendoza's ring, and his own, making the switch.

When he was done he took a moment to relax, to review. At the trunk he struggled with Francine's dead weight, letting her sprawl onto the ground, taking a moment to examine her, appreciate her, running his fingertips across the contours of her cool skin, his palms across her breasts

326

and between her legs, chortling at the fact that he should have had her before Arquero. Certainly before Mendoza, but then he did have Navarra. In fact, he couldn't now very well live without her.

He dragged Francine to the front, hauled her into the passenger seat, positioned her with her clothes at her feet, closed the door and put a bullet into the side of her head through the window.

Of the five plastic jerry cans he'd bought and filled with fuel while Mendoza believed he was buying a shovel, he emptied one into the trunk, two onto the backseat, one at her feet and the last over Mendoza. Life was good and getting better. He was a millionaire, and he was free. He threw the match and walked away.

From Claire's car he watched the inferno for as long as he dared. Scott Gibson and his supposed wife were dead, murdered by Enrique Mendoza. His cousin, Mario Mendoza, had somehow managed to flee the country. He would never be found and never serve his term.
*

At the apartment, Gibson told Navarra the truth. He had little choice in the matter. Earlier in the day a call came in from L.A., someone, a friend, wanted Mario to know that his cousin was intending to murder him while yachting on Thursday. Mario was gone, running for his life. The police were searching for him and questioning Enrique in Los Angeles.

He explained what Mario had done, why he was going to prison and why Enrique wanted him dead. He explained his own million dollar debt and the real way Enrique treated his girls. She would never just dance in the clubs. Soon she would become an escort for old men who could afford her body. Five or six years later when she was tired and less attractive because of their demands, she would work the streets for him, having sex in the backseats of cars or in dank motel rooms with men desperate for any woman.

Now that Mario was gone, if they went together to the boat on Thursday, he would be killed because he didn't have enough to reimburse the loan which was growing each day. She would begin stripping Thursday night. Then she would go home with one of his lieutenants, and someone else the next night. Mendoza always gave his new girls to his men to enjoy, like he would on the boat, just like she'd been sent to him. Gibson could not let that happen to her. Since first seeing her he'd felt a connection. He couldn't stand thinking of her with so many other men, or that she would see him killed.

He confessed that he was married, had been married. His divorce was granted a week earlier with a cash settlement of almost a million. His wife had never loved him; never really wanted his children and they were part of the deal. But giving all the money to Mendoza wouldn't save him. He would still owe tens of thousands and never be free. Neither would she or his children. He had to run. He had to leave with his three children, right away. He would take the kids to his sisters who lived up north where they would be safe from Mendoza's reach and his cruelty.

He opened a briefcase.

"Come with me, Navarra," he pleaded. "Like you said, I can be your only man. I'll be good to you. You won't have to work as a whore, letting men ruin your body. We can be happy together. He'll never find us. I promise you. You will have all the fine clothes you want and a beautiful home." He put a bundle into her hands. "For you, Navarra, fifty thousand dollars whether you come or not. Though if you do, this is just the beginning. We'll start over, get married and have children of our own."

"Where will we go?" she asked, believing him.

"There are ways to escape, to disappear, but we must leave soon. Once the police are finished with Mendoza, if they haven't already, he will come for us. He will. He'll regret that he sent you to me. He'll suspect you know something that you don't. Either way, he won't believe you. This way, Navarra, we can be happy," he paused, "and you will see your mother again. When we're settled she can come to live with us."

She looked at the stack of crisp bills. He'd never treated her badly and she believed what she was hearing about the man who had her brothers killed. She also knew that men wanted young and beautiful girls dancing naked in front of them, to fondle, poke and prod, and that one day she would grow old, unable to please any but the most pitiful. When she herself would be pitiful.

"Yes, I will go with you. Besides, you will need me to care for your children until they are safe." She nodded, vigorously. "Yes, I will go."

Gibson left her with instructions to pack her clothes while he went to the garage for the children, bringing one at a time to the apartment where he laid them on the bed with open capsules tucked into their cheeks. When he was packed he left with Navarra to buy her a new car, explaining that he wanted to begin proving himself to her. All he could hope for was that one day she would learn to love him and be his wife.

Two blocks from the dealership he left his mother's car running with the keys in the ignition and the windows down. Returning to the apartment he made a final check. All that remained were most of his clothes and a few inconsequential papers. Scott Gibson was dead.

By midnight of the twenty-fourth, seven days after the Loma Prieta quake, the couple drove into Salt Lake City with Gabriella, Francesca and Diego sleeping soundly under a blanket in the back of the luxury sedan.

Wednesday Navarra saw Wyoming and Nebraska where the kids slept in one bed while she lay with Gibson beginning to understand how gentle and kind a man he was. She felt good with him, she felt safe the way he promised she would. He wanted to protect his children, she thought, doing his best to conceal the emotion of leaving them behind until he could once again be with them. He was a good man. He was doing what was best for them. He'd told her a dozen time how he knew in his heart that his sisters would love each one as their very own.

Thursday they arrived in Chicago, on the outskirts, not far from his sister's home. Eighteen-hundred miles away Enrique Mendoza was standing in Gibson's Santa Rosa apartment.

44

Thursday night Hidalgo was at home, refusing to remain in his bed, despite the fact he was heavily sedated. With him were Maria, Jennie and John Canyon. All of them numb, all of them devastated, their hearts ripped out. They sat in the living room, Maria and Jennie on either side of him each holding his hands, staring at the patch of blood on the couch.

John went into the kitchen where he could hide his tears.

For two days they and a team of private detectives had searched for Francine and their children without pause and without success, until late in the day when they opened the door to a couple of Vallejo homicide detectives. What was left of Francine's car had just been discovered, the bodies of the occupants incinerated beyond recognition. They had found no sign of the three children.

Fernando went with them to the morgue, threatening Hidalgo with tears flooding his eyes not to disobey him, that he would strike Hidalgo to the floor rather than see his son tortured by what must be done. John Canyon stood ready with him. Hidalgo was going nowhere.

When Fernando returned, sitting by his son's side, unable to speak, he put Francine's emerald ring into Hidalgo's quivering hand.
*

Navarra was at the hotel waiting with Francesca and Diego. Scott Gibson was with Gabriella. He was taking her to his sister's. He had wanted to take all the kids with Navarra, so they could be together as family, but his sister was a devout catholic, he told her, and wouldn't approve of another woman so soon after the divorce. Navarra believed him.

The Chicago Medical Centre was crowded with patients and visitors. He took his little girl from one floor to another, looking for the best place, somewhere not overly crowded, somewhere not too deserted. She wouldn't wake until the next morning when she would require attention to clear her body of drugs and regain her strength. Gabriella Martina would remain lost for a very long time.

*

Friday Mendoza sat in a hotel restaurant reading the early edition. Francine Arquero-Duval's death covering the front page, murdered just days after her parents' funeral. Claire Gibson read the same headline, as did her bank manager and Hidalgo's bank manager. The police were suddenly very busy and very interested in Enrique Mendoza who, they were disappointed to confirm, had a perfect alibi: the L.A. cops.

The coroner had determined that the second body in the car was male, who Claire Gibson believed was her son based on what she'd been told about his uncertain future. All she agreed to do was to give them a photograph. She would not view the corpse. She'd been put through quite enough by him. His death, she told them, did not in any way forgive or negate his previous actions. He was where he should be.

She believed that her son was the dead man and that Mario Mendoza had seen fit to deceive Francine and her son into believing that ten million dollars would somehow ensure their well-being. Apparently such was not the case and the police had little reason to believe otherwise, the real question being: why was Francine with him in first place and why had Gibson been driving? The official assumption was that Mendoza had killed them immediately upon leaving the bank.

Friday afternoon Enrique Mendoza went to the Arquero home. He went alone to pay his respects and to give Hidalgo Arquero a message. He understood Fernando and John's reluctance to leave them alone.

"Señor Arquero, Hidalgo, believe me or not, overwhelming sadness grips my heart for what has happened to your wife and to your children. I have just now called on Señora Gibson to tell her what I believe, to tell her why I believe that what is thought to be true should remain so. I thought she would be afraid of me, the evil crime boss, so to speak. She was not. What she told me was that she wasn't interested in me, my cousin, or her son. She did, however, make me aware of her grief for your wife."

"You went to her for what reason, the money he owed you?"

"I went to tell her that the man in your wife's car was not Scott Gibson. He was my cousin, Mario Mendoza beyond any doubt which might one day return to haunt me. I tell you this because never would Mario Mendoza do such a thing to any woman. To first murder her for no reason, then to kill her twice in so horrible a way. When certain of my less trustworthy colleagues must atone for their actions, we do what must be done. This is a matter of honour for my family. Mario has done many things which are best not discussed, but I will tell you that not once has he killed anyone in such a way, especially a young woman as innocent and as lovely as your wife. This you must believe. The fire, señor, served one purpose, to conceal the truth. Also, Gibson was not catholic; he did not wear a cross."

"You are saying that Gibson is alive."

Mendoza opened his palm, showing them the disfigured chain and holy pendant. "This I took from the morgue with Mrs. Gibson's permission. This is my cousin's cross, and

Gibson's mistake. The ring, I threw into the street. Nothing else remained."

Fernando crossed himself. "You are certain of this."

"I am. And that Gibson did this terrible thing to disguise that fact. He owes me a great deal of money, money he could not repay in a natural lifetime. We have, señores, you will understand, a certain sense of right and wrong. It is our code of justice, if you will, a line that must not be crossed. Scott Gibson is alive somewhere, señores, and I will find him. If, on the other hand, the police succeed in finding him first, he will serve twenty, maybe twenty-five on death row possibly dying of natural causes before justice is served. My sentence will be much more in keeping with what he has done to your wife, Hidalgo, and what he may yet do to your children." He studied Hidalgo for a moment, Fernando and John. "For that reason, señores, may we agree that Scott Gibson is truly dead and that my cousin, in fact, is the murderer who has taken your children. To do otherwise will serve no purpose."

"And when you find him, if you find him, what then?" Hidalgo asked. "What would you do that would send him to hell?"

"I will kill him myself...once. He will die as Francine died, if I may call her by her name, without the benefit of a bullet to ease his passage into hell. My cousin, he was not, shall I say, destined to spend much of his life in prison. In fact I did not intend that he spend any time in prison, which was my decision to enforce, not Gibson's. That Gibson did for me what was intended for my cousin by my hand alone does not absolve my cousin of the shame he has brought on the Mendoza name. As for Gibson, he took from me what was rightfully mine, my cousin's life."

John said, "I don't see a problem with that, Señor Mendoza, none of us do. However we all know that the memories of most men are short and a man with ten million can dig a lot of holes to hide in."

"Not my memory, Señor Canyon. Francine will become a cold case inside of one year, forgotten, whereas Gibson will never be free of me. If I die, others will continue my search. This I promise you."

Fernando said, "If you find him first, before the police, we will do nothing to prevent you."

"Hidalgo said, "Señor Mendoza, I have never seen the cross which you now hold in your hand, not tonight, not ever. Find a place to bury it with the dignity its meaning deserves. Tomorrow, in my mailbox, you will find one million dollars. You have many friends in many places of interest to me right now, as do I. Let us use those friends to our advantage and let us agree that Scott Gibson died with my wife. Let the world think what they might as they search for your cousin and we search for the one which you and I together, Señor Mendoza, will kill. You will not kill him alone. We will do so together. Swear to me on your family's honour."

"I swear, amigo. Together we will send him to hell."

Mendoza took Hidalgo's hand firmly in his.

John interrupted. "Half that million is mine. Is that understood, chavo?"

Fernando was quick to add, "We will share this million equally, as Francine shared her love with us equally."

"Muchísimas gracias, John. Gracias, papá. I accept for Francine." He grasped each of their hands. "She shares her love still with us." He turned his attention to Mendoza. "When we find him, Señor Mendoza, I will strike the match, no one else. If you lack anything, anything at all to complete your search, you will call me. Spare no expense. My pockets are deep. And do not forget the contents of my mailbox."

"I have no need of your million, amigos. In fact I have received your cheque for one million from Arquero-Duval with a letter of explanation which I understand given the new administration. This million, however, I will accept so that you will be certain that we search for him together. The money will be used for no other purpose." He shook John Canyon's hand, and Fernando's, as though he were an insurance salesman or a real-estate agent leaving them. "I will light many candles this evening to guide Señora Francine's way into heaven and pray that she has found peace. When next we meet you will strike your match, Hidalgo, this I promise you. This horrific crime against innocence will never be forgiven. Buenas tardes."

He tipped his hat and left.

When Maria and Jennie joined them in the living room moments later, the women realized that somehow the men would never again be as they once were. Those men had left them and would not return for a very long time.

45

Sunday Gibson wanted time alone with Navarra in Detroit, anxious for the first half of their trip to end. He called his sister while Navarra was showering. His sister had always liked Francine and never agreed with the divorce. They weren't on the best of terms, but she loved little Francesca. She simply didn't want to see the woman who she believed broke up the marriage, not then. Maybe she would in a few months.

Gibson drove Francesca to the Children's Hospital wrapped in a blanket, telling a security guard that his daughter was already admitted, waiting for a bed, explaining that he had to visit the men's room. He never returned and Francesca Maria was mere days from a foster home. She would be made well, her little body drained of toxins over time. She would only see her mamá and her papá in her dreams until one day soon they would leave her forever.

That night, a capsule tucked into his cheek, his stomach filled with milk and bread, Diego slept alone as Gibson and Navarra went to dinner and an evening of dancing. She was sad for the children, yet she understood that their medication was their one salvation from such deep sorrow.
*

Monday and Tuesday they drove the remaining 800 miles to New York City where they stayed three nights. Wednesday, though, Gibson drove with Diego to another sister's home who was waiting for him. She'd told him on the phone that, once the boy was settled, Navarra would be welcomed into her home. She just needed time, like the other sisters. Families didn't change overnight. Again, Navarra understood.

His sister's home was The Allen where he left Diego in Emergency where he would spend the next week being detoxified and nourished. His father, his hero, no longer existed in his mind.

Gibson felt relieved, vindicated. He had escaped a certain death warrant and no one was the wiser. He had killed Mendoza, who would have been killed anyway, and Francine should have known to leave well enough alone. Had she kept her mouth shut, she wouldn't have died. What happened wasn't his fault. Mendoza wanted the taste of something different, something rich and white and she was it. Something he would never get in ten lifetimes. What happened was not his fault. She messed up by losing control. She went and got herself killed.

He'd promised Navarra a vacation, exotic hotel rooms and exquisite dining once they were alone. They hadn't thought about Mendoza in a week and Navarra was elated at the prospect of Fifth Avenue and Club 54.
*

Francine Arquero-Duval was laid to rest four days earlier. Everyone from the law firm attended, as did Francine's fellow students, her neighbours and friends. Seated by herself in the very last row was Claire Gibson, dressed in black, the sorrow she felt stained with shame. At the cemetery she remained in the background.

Hidalgo stood at the grave, Fernando on his one side, John Canyon on the other. Maria stood between Jennie and Virginia Meadows. When everyone was gone Hidalgo leaned against the headstone, staring blankly at the mahogany and brass casket lowered halfway into a precisely carved void. Inside laid his wife. In his heart she was dressed in her finest silk peignoir and slippers, her long blonde hair draped over her shoulders, her green eyes closed in peaceful slumber, though in his mind horrible spectres of her reality swirled in a black maelstrom of venomous hatred.

In the distance he saw the woman standing by a tree studying him as though she wanted to speak with him.

He dried his face with the palms of his hands and went to her, a woman he'd met briefly twice before, at her husband's and Duval funerals, the mother of Francine's killer. By the time he left her, Claire hadn't said a word. She was too afraid, too traumatized by what he suggested. What Hidalgo told her was too incredible to be true, yet she believed every word.

Hidalgo knew what he must do: deny his parents their right to comfort him. He needed to be alone, to understand what had happened to him and why. Fourteen years after coming from the dusty town of Pichilingue he was happily married with an enviable family and loving parents. He had good friends; he was successful and had never thought of himself as wealthy, simply fortunate. He'd spent his career trying to help those who could not help themselves or didn't know how, and Francine was soon to join him. Now she lay in the cold ground, sealed in a box beyond his touch, and his children were lost to him.

Fernando and John understood what Maria did not. The man needed to grieve in private. Sunday the movers had come to empty the house and put his worldly goods in storage. Monday he went to the offices of Arquero-Duval to apologize for delaying what he had come to tell them. However, despite his difficult time ahead, each of them had the right to hear of his or her promotion.

He asked Mrs. Meadows to arrange for his house to be sold immediately, at whatever price was reasonable to the buyer. He would never step foot inside the place again. He went from the office to a condo he'd leased by the month and from there he went to the storefront office where he gave the nurse an extra few weeks' vacation with pay and when she was gone he began getting drunk. Francine would forgive him. She always did when he would do something foolish.

By Friday he was drowning in misery and liquor, not once through the week answering calls from his mother. He was at a precipice, a juncture, leaning more forward than back, willing and wanting to plunge into the black abyss sitting on the desk in front of him. He'd lost count of how many bottles lay on the floor of his office.

The door opened so timidly that he scarcely noticed the nervous little Latina standing in the doorway until a loud thunderbolt shattered his stupor, her small frame backlit by a white flash of lightning.

46
December 11th, of this Year

The Boss' limousine arrived at the Capitol at 7:15. Anita Juárez was seated at her desk, dressed to kill, which, she mused, could not be more appropriate.

He was dressed in his usual black suit, this time with a bright white shirt, yellow silk tie and pocket hanky. He was elegant with French cuffs protruding half an inch, his titanium and hematite diamond links were her gift to him the previous Christmas, an impeccable complement to his black Cartier watch. They had exchanged their gifts at the office before she left to spend that Christmas with her mother and stepfather.

"Anita, I was not…"

"…expecting me, I know."

He nodded. "I am expecting…"

"…Señor Carling. I will advise you when he arrives."

"Gracias. Also, I believe Señor Carling would not object to breakfast…"

"…in your private study. I have advised Catering."

He hesitated; he knew when he was swimming in dark waters. "Anita, are you…"

"I am very well. The thought of my new position is preoccupying me. That is all."

"You should not be. You will do very well, a change long overdue. I am very proud of you."

Her phone chimed. A moment later: "Your guest has arrived."

He nodded, as he usually did, as though he were dreaming, when, in fact, his cognizance was instinctively razor-sharp. He closed the door to his office behind him. Carling would be at least another five minutes.

In spite of their casual talk, with her new career and his firm decision to live a quieter life, she somehow knew that last twenty-one years would dissolve over the next twenty-one days. How many times had she wondered who had saved whom, Santa Anita, a young girl saving a desperate man, or the young, angry man who had grown to become The Boss saving a scared young girl. She pressed a fingertip to the tiny cross at her neck. She remembered the day so vividly, as though reliving that first day of her new life.
*

"Señor, perdón, pero yo necesito trabajo. Yo busco empleo, señor, por favor."

Her voice was soft, timorous. She was very young and badly dressed. Her soaked sweater was littered with microscopic balls of lint, which her skirt didn't match and her flat shoes were moulded from rubber or badly crafted off-shore from cheap plastic. The toes were curled upward, the backs were scuffed and the stitching was loose. Her blue-black hair was swept across her face in wet strands, her single piece of jewellery a simple gold cross, her vinyl purse paper thin.

The instant loathing in his eyes stole her breath. She was afraid, though not as afraid as she was of her father, terrified of returning home to him without a job, the reason her father had taken her out of school in Mexico and brought her to the United States to work and do her part to support his family.

He bellowed at her to leave, to get out, to go away and leave him alone, waving his arms maniacally in the air, trying to stand, lurching forward, falling backward. She had seen the rage many times before, while she huddled into herself, crouched into a corner, waiting for the stinging blow, the kicks. She twirled, and was gone, pulling the door shut. What he didn't see was the grimace etching itself into her face. She knew that, for such a failure, her father would certainly beat her.

Outside, a hapless victim of the downpour, she winced at the dull thud of something exploding against the inside wall, the faint crackle of shattered glass. Her mind was filled with hectic images of so many bottles strewn across the floor, his desk littered with papers and folders, everything else so pristine and orderly. He had seemed so fearsome and dangerous yet, somehow, beneath the ugly mask, she had seen his sorrow and his agony.

She had no coat and the weather was worsening. She was shivering. Across the street was a coffee shop. She had no money for coffee to infuse her body with warmth but she would try, perhaps they would need a girl to wash dishes or clean the floor. Anything was better than cleaning hotel toilets or closing her eyes and her mind to foul men. She had little chance; she was soaked through, rainwater seeping through the perforated soles of her shoes.

Yet she was determined. She must try.

The shop was crowded with people seeking shelter from the tempest. Most were dressed in jeans and sweatshirts, mostly young, their hair dripping, making their coffees last or sharing them. They were in the barrio.

The manager saw her at once and snorted, pointing to the door. She ignored him, persisting. She went behind the counter to where he stood and started washing dishes to prove that she would be a good worker.

He told her to stop. She didn't. She continued washing until, gently, he pulled her away. All he could do was give her a cup of coffee and a sandwich for the little work she had done. That was all. He was sorry.

Tears squeezed from her eyes. She kissed his gruff hand for his kindness, and the cross that hung from her neck. She never knew how badly he felt at seeing her step into the darkness of the heavy rain. As long as he lived, he never told her.

She ran across the street, splashing rainwater to her knees. She'd passed the point of caring about her appearance, which would be much worse in an hour, once she walked into her father's home.

She tried the door, praying to God and Mary that the man would not kill her. It opened. She stepped in quickly, placed the sandwich and coffee on the floor, wincing at his expletives, closed the door and ran as fast as she could.

Climbing into her seat was an effort. She wanted with all her heart to drive somewhere far away, stopped by the imagery of what her father would do to her mother. She slumped into the broken seat, squeezing the wheel with her small hands, wanting to cry until her heart froze. She stopped breathing. He was coming after her, to kill her, sliding his body against the buildings so that he wouldn't fall. He was coming closer, his arms reaching out, stopping, his hands groping the rough walls, bending and grabbing his head, leaning against a brick façade, his face twisting into so many horrible masks. He was crying, sobbing. He was staring straight at her. People hurrying by were slowing to stare at him, but she could not hear what he was telling them.

He pushed himself from the wall, struggling not to crumple onto the sidewalk, swaying, coming towards her in a crooked line. She locked the door. Then his head crashed against her windshield, blood beginning to trickle from his nose, his face a distorted montage of expressions that at any other time might she might have thought comical.

His hands were pressed against the glass, thick rivulets

of water rushing between his fingers until he pushed away, pressing his hands together. He was talking to her. He was asking for her forgiveness. She didn't know what to do. He was young and strong and could easily hurt her. Or her father would for coming home without work, her clothes ruined by the rain.

She slid from her seat into the deluge, taking his arm, slamming the door, leading him to the wall, letting him bounce between her and the unforgiving brick until they reached his door where he fell through onto his hands and knees.

She waited at the door, watching, waiting to see what he would do. He coughed, "lo siento. Disculpéme," and struggled to his feet, crashing to the floor. When he tried again, she went to him. She helped him to the couch, laid him down and covered him with a blanket.

When his eyes closed she went about cleaning his office, stacking his files, sweeping the broken glass of the frame he'd smashed and the shards of a broken bottle, gathering the many other vodka bottles and stopping to check on him every few minutes. When she was finished she went to the washroom to comb her hair and to wash her face and hands. When she came out, thinking to leave, her hand at the handle of the door opened onto the street, he called to her. He said, "You're hired," and signalled her with a careless wave to where he lay. He gave her a collection of bills in lieu of a signed contract that was somewhat beyond his current capability. Then his head fell against the padded arm of the couch and he travelled to another place.

It was then that Anita cared for his damaged shoulder, she remembered, after he'd fallen asleep, not him. She remembered how she sat by his side, wondering about him, wondering what she should do. He'd given her a thousand dollars, enough for her father to pay the rent and her mother to buy a new dress. She remembered her father's violent smack later that night, not believing that any man would give his daughter so much money for doing nothing. She remembered telling him that would be the last time and with the five hundred that was left she spent what remained of the evening in stores, making the most of her money, treating herself to a hair salon, new make-up and a purse made of real leather.

The next morning was Saturday. She arrived at her new office early, ready to work. She'd wanted so badly for him to notice her new clothes, her purse, and that she was wearing nylons. He didn't, and she was afraid that he would want his money back. He didn't. He was a mess, his clothes were filthy and he smelled, his blood still diluted with alcohol, searching for his car keys. That's when he noticed her purse, her hand clamped tightly and protectively over the silver clasp.

He laughed at her, not in a bad way, asking her whether she spoke enough English to call a taxi, never once mentioning the money. She said that she could, when she could not. He didn't seem to care. He simply walked out and waited. She spent the day sorting his files by words she didn't understand.

Very late in the day he returned, expecting her not to be there. Yet she remembered so clearly his words as he came through the door, the ice cold surging through her body. He wasn't the same man. He apologized to her, begging her forgiveness. He was handsome and elegant. He asked her with a curious grin how much he had given her the night before. And she was afraid. Nothing was left of the money. Yet, when she told him, he simply smiled as though he was dreaming. She thought that very strange, because at the same time he was intent. The money wasn't her salary, he told her, merely a portion of her fee for having saved him from self-destruction. He gave her another thousand which, he told her, was her first week's pay until he could get the paperwork done.

Then he took her to dinner, the first of so many evenings, to a restaurant she could not have previously imagined in her lifetime. He treated her like a lady and listened to her every nervous word. And she listened to him, forcing back her tears. When he drove her home he kissed her hand and went into her modest home with her, ignoring her pleas, promising her that everything would be much better very soon.

He went to her father who was drinking tequila that he'd bought with her money. He told the man that he was never again to touch her, to harm her in any way, unless he wanted to find himself deported to Mexico, alone, and without his teeth. Very soon after, Anita moved out.

*

Anita pursed her lips. She really did want to cry. She had loved him from the very moment he came through the door that Saturday afternoon. He was so confident, dressed in his black suit and burgundy tie. So unlike the man she had left the night before sleeping on his office couch, twisted into his soiled clothes, his emerald pendant an iridescent anomaly between the edges of his tattered shirt: His gateway to the past, her impediment to the future.

He had more than changed her life. Because of him she had a Master's, a beautiful home and a job most would envy. She could write her own ticket, and she had done just that. She was so angry with him.

For twenty-one years she had been his shadow, his assistant and sounding board, never his friend, never his lover, which was the one gift she had ever wanted from him.

When he decided to run for office nine years earlier she was with him every step of the way, at conventions, lunches, town halls and dinners; the most senior partner of the most successful law firm in the Southwest winning by a landslide. And she was with him, raising his hand into the air. And what did he do? He hugged her.

She had met the president with him, most other governors and European leaders, dining but never dancing with him at all formal occasions. She was the lady on his arm, never in his home unless she had a briefcase full of documents for him to sign or a breakfast to cook because being in his mansion sharing a breakfast was more convenient than going to the office. She hated him for not being honest, for keeping the truth from her.

She took a deep breath, the guard escorting Drew Carling was knocking at her door. She had read his file a dozen times, studying his photographs, and had seen him once for as long as she needed to imprint his image in her mind. He had intrigued her and scared her at once, and she was pleased that he was between Carlos and Luis. His demeanour was cold and aloof, detached from the world around him. Yet she sensed that behind his silver glasses he was scanning the world as though through the lens of a camera. Now she wanted to see more of the man in her domain.

Drew Carling was not meeting with the governor; he was being recruited to do what The Boss could not, not until January, not until his term was over.

She stood to greet him, admitting to herself that she was nervous. He didn't look like a cop. He looked as though he might…He looked as though he didn't care, about anything.

47

Detective Carling came through the door with easy confidence, unimpressed, not in the least intimidated, once again deprived of his weapons. Only the State Police assigned to the Capitol were armed. No exceptions were permitted.

Seeing him that close once again, without his mirrored glasses, she was certain, though she really had nothing to say that wouldn't sound trite beyond the niceties of her position. She signalled the governor from her desk, asking Drew Carling to follow her. She knocked once and proceeded through without waiting. The governor stood, stepping from behind his desk as she swung open his door.

As the men stood facing each other she introduced one to the other. "Detective Carling, may I introduce the Governor of California, Hidalgo Arquero." She glanced from one man to the other. "Governor, Detective Carling of the LAPD."

She turned and left them.

"Governor Arquero, I have to tell you that I've never believed kidnapping could be such a luxurious event. Thank you for your hospitality."

"Detective Carling, please join me in my study. The seating is more comfortable and I have arranged for breakfast. I trust my personal assistant's choices will be agreeable to you."

"I can't imagine any woman as beautiful as she is doing

anything disagreeable. You must enjoy coming to work each day and hate going home each night." He glanced over his shoulder at the door. "I certainly would."

"Indeed, I do, for that very reason. She breathes life into the office, though as a man you realize that many of the most beautiful of nature's gifts are the most dangerous to the males of the species." Hidalgo forced a rare smile, guiding Drew Carling through another door with an extended open hand. "Were I to dine alone this morning, Detective, I believe I would first have my meal tested by others."

"Which isn't the reason you called me here, I presume."

"You do so correctly." The two men were seated, Hidalgo waiting for the waiter to arrange the first course of coffee, juice, fresh fruits, and leave them. "I have read a good deal about you, Detective Carling. Your service record is very impressive."

"What you mean is, you had me investigated... my compliments to the State Police."

"Everyone speaks highly of you. Your record, of course, speaks for itself."

Drew Carling reached for his coffee. He wasn't much for preamble. He didn't have any friends to banter with and his business associates weren't given to effusiveness. "Why am I here, Governor? The plane ride was very smooth, your scotch even smoother, but for what reason? And why out of the blue without any protocol? My captain's a little pissed, if you'll pardon the expression."

"Not the first person I've managed to piss off, Detective Carling, nor to the exclusion of a certain member of my staff. Expression pardoned." Hidalgo reached for his cup. "Do you believe in destiny, Detective Carling?"

"I believe that one day my luck will run out."

"I believe in destiny. I also believe in cruel fate. As for your luck, Detective, I believe you may soon change your mind. To that end, my term expires in twenty days. Until that moment you are on special assignment to me."

"I work undercover in L.A., Governor, not the kind of job you walk away from on a whim. Sorry. Find yourself another guy. Besides, what could you possibly want from me that the State Police couldn't do?"

Hidalgo sipped his coffee. "I want you to contact a man. I want you to arrange a meeting between us, soon. He won't expect your visit, but he will not refuse you. I assure you. If anything, he will make you welcome."

"And he would be...?"

"His name is Enrique Mendoza, you'll find...."

Carling put down his cup, raising his open palms, calling timeout. Camouflaging his shock was pointless. "Whoa. No way. That's not going to happen. Governor, thanks for the coffee. Unfortunately this conversation stops here. I know where to find Mendoza. Under his thousand-dollar suits he's dirty as soot. Just follow the trail. He's a dangerous man with more than a few LAPD boys in his pocket. But you probably know that, which is why this won't work. My luck will run out one day, part of the job, just not right now. What could you possibly want with him?"

"Mendoza is searching for somebody, a man. He's been searching for over twenty-years, as we once agreed, he and I. For so many of those years I despised myself for sleeping with the devil, as it were, for not seeking immediate justice. Yet, destiny prevailed. I am now in possession of information regarding the man's whereabouts: my destiny, Mendoza's, and his are irreversibly linked. What I require of you is simply to make Mendoza aware."

"If Mendoza's been on the hunt for twenty years the guy must be good at playing dead or very good at hiding. The next question is why."

"My law firm, Detective, from which I temporarily

stepped down eight years ago, has a policy of not representing the guilty, with the exception of redeemable youth. We devote our time to the innocent, whom we tirelessly investigate, with all due respect, more minutely than the police with our own very talented team of detectives. When we discover guilt, we abandon the case. We have the resources to be selective. We do so because our success rate would put too many criminals back on the street before their time. The answer to your question is, very simply, equitable justice."

"Governor, I thought it fair, since you obviously knew everything about me, that I should know everything about you. My time in the hotel wasn't all that restful. Mendoza, he wants his cousin Mario Mendoza. And you want him because he killed your wife and he's suspected of abducting your three kids. So are we on the same wave length here...sir?"

"Excellent detective work, Detective...partially. My wife's case went cold a very long time ago, as a matter of convenience to me and to Mendoza, as did the dossiers pertaining to my children. Hence the reason for my firm's strict policy." He pointed to the red phone. "Also the reason I have never once commuted an execution."

"Cold cases are bureaucratic in nature, not enough time, not enough men, yet I've never heard them referred to as convenient, unless by the perps."

Carling pierced a small wedge of fruit.

"In this case convenient for me, Enrique Mendoza and, because I knew this day would come, also for you. His cousin neither killed my wife nor stole my children from me. He couldn't. He was dead. He was the male victim in the car, killed by the one whom everyone supposed was the victim."

"And you know this how?"

"You know the answer. In your career, have you ever

seen a person killed twice, destroyed beyond recognition by the likes of Mario Mendoza?"

"I never knew him. I was barely out of diapers."

"You were nine, four months before your tenth birthday and out of diapers for many years."

"Sorry, I was born in November, the first."

"November 01st is when you were found in Emergency at The Allen in New York. You required several days of treatment to detoxify you, and to nourish you. You were born February 28 in the City of Vallejo, California. The man we have sought for so long is the cruellest of men, vile. He is the man who murdered your mother before kidnapping you and your two sisters."

Carling's hand was too slow to cover his cough. "That's insane. My mother's alive."

"Your adoptive mother is alive. Your biological mother was savagely murdered by a man whose name was then Scott Gibson. Your mother's name was Francine Elizabeth Arquero-Duval. Do more detailed investigating if you wish, or as you should. All you will find is the truth. Your name is Diego Hidalgo Arquero-Duval. I am your father. Your grandmother is Maria and your grandfather is Fernando. I hasten to add that they have no knowledge of this meeting, or of you, however much they pray each day for your safe return to them…and the return of your sisters."

"I don't believe any of this."

Hidalgo reached to the floor for an envelope he'd earlier placed against the table. Inside were photos.

"The younger woman is your mother, Francine. The older lady, still very beautiful, is your grandmother Maria. She told me at Francine's funeral that your mother's heart would always beat in mine and that I must be strong, but for a short time I was not. She told me that one day I would find you and your sisters and that she would not leave this life to fly with the angels until she could tell her Diego,

Francesca and Gabriella of their sweet mother. She believes that is her destiny. The man on whose lap you sit is Fernando, your grandfather who spoke only Spanish to you. Perhaps one day soon you will remember the bedtime stories he read to you by your bed of our modest home in Pichilingue, Mexico. Their hope of finding you has never diminished. You will meet them one day soon, when you begin to believe what you are hearing. This girl is Francesca Maria; this little one is Gabriella Martina. She adored you. You were a hero to each of them. These are copies of your birth certificate and theirs. Take your time to believe what I say, Diego, and you will excuse my use of your first name. I have waited many years for the privilege of speaking the name your mother gave to you. Nothing I have told you is fabrication."

"You're telling me I'm Mexican."

"You're American, with proud Mexican blood."

Diego brought up his hands. "I guess that accounts for the natural glow. No one could ever tell me. And, the girls, what happened to them?"

"Both are alive. Francesca is very well, Gabriella soon will be. Her life has not been good. I have immediate plans for her."

"Why now? And how after so many years do we just pop up if, in fact, we have? Three kids don't just go missing. Shit, there's Amber Alert, all sorts of ways to track missing kids."

"You know that such things happen every day and, so long ago, in three of the largest cities hundreds of miles apart. It happened. The world was much less organized in such matters."

"Except for you and Mendoza who you want me to contact, which means you found the guy."

"No, I did not, much to my regret. That person is now deceased, very recently. She made Gibson and my children

354

her life's work, for which I shall be eternally grateful to her. Her information, I can tell you, is verified and true."

"Who was she?"

"Someone I misunderstood, or someone who over time came to believe a horrible truth once told to her by me. She waited all these years in the belief that she was protecting me. These girls are your sisters, Diego. Scott Gibson murdered your mother and I have brought you here to ask a favour, that you find Mendoza and bring him to me, nothing more."

"So that you can find Gibson and kill him."

"To tell Mendoza that his cousin's killer will at long last sit on the scales of justice, nothing more."

"Governor, I can't do what you're asking. I'm a cop, although not to everyone. Mendoza's one of the bad guys and most people believe I'm just as dirty. A lot of people are trying to bring him down, I'm one of them. This could get a lot of good guys hurt. You couldn't have chosen a worse candidate. I'm out, sorry."

"I disagree. I believe you are a very appropriate choice, and Mendoza would agree. Does Mendoza know you, personally, by your face, by your name?"

"No, not personally, he's built too many layers around him. He knows my name. That's about it. He prefers the company of private club types...like you. That doesn't mean I can walk up to him and say 'hi, remember my dad?' It won't work, Governor."

"I propose that you meet him at the airport, onboard the jet, a restricted area. When you call him, your name is Diego Arquero-Duval. Believe me; he will not refuse to speak with you, or to meet with you onboard. Your papers will be in order by noon Monday, your credit cards, bank account, everything. You will once again be Diego Arquero-Duval, if you so wish. What you do with Drew Carling is your decision."

Drew speared another sliver of fruit. "Then what?"

"I was your age when your mother died, shot once in the head and incinerated; left in a field for days while my children were taken across the country by Gibson and a woman whose name was Navarra Carrera. I spent many days wallowing in self-pity. That woman sitting outside the door saved me. Were it not for her, well, the State of California might have a Democrat seated in this office instead of me. I want you to meet with Mendoza, to tell him what you know, that we shall once again meet in the coming weeks. Then you will travel alone to Florida, to Key West to find Gibson. And when you are ready I would like you to meet your family. Your adoptive mother and father, naturally, will not be excluded. Nor would I for a moment ask you to betray their belief in you or ask you to bring shame upon my parents."

"But you want him dead."

"His fate was decided many years ago. I realize a simple and cryptic letter to Mendoza would suffice on my part. I have chosen this way for my own greater satisfaction. Not once have I asked something of someone that I would not do myself. As for Ms. Carrera, she was killed a few weeks after Gibson's escape. Her body was found that November 15th in Virginia, murdered in an attempted carjacking according to police. I know better, as will Mendoza. She was a gift of respect to him from a cartel, who in turn he loaned to Gibson. Sordid, I grant you, and yet another reason for Mendoza's long-standing hatred."

"And when I find him?"

"Compile information which I am missing: home address, bank accounts and girlfriends, what he does and when."

"Do I have a choice in all of this?"

They stopped speaking as the waiter came with the second course and left.

"After what you have heard, do you want one?" Hidalgo glanced over to Diego's plate. "Please, we can talk as we eat."

"Eat? You must be joking, a drink maybe."

"Good, you will leave for L.A. Monday morning. In this state, at least, you will enjoy priority take-off and landing. My assistant will arrange for a driver. Tell Mendoza the time has come to strike the match."

"Some sort of code?" Drew asked.

"No, Diego. The very last words I spoke to him before we shook hands. I haven't seen him since. Yet not a day has gone by that I have not thought of him."

Hidalgo reached again to the floor, placing two small packages and an envelope near Drew's side of the table.

"More surprises, Governor?"

"That is fifty thousand dollars to cover your expenses over the next few weeks. Tell me when you require more. This is a sample of my DNA, to ease what must now be a troubled mind. My driver will take you to the lab when we have finished talking, a conversation I would like to continue at dinner if you are available. The envelope contains the receipt for a deposit of five million dollars into your account last evening. Consider it as your accrued weekly allowance over the many years gone by, the years of your youth stolen from both of us and your mother. Your sisters will receive the same, very soon."

Drew couldn't help chuckling despite his head beginning to ache. What he was hearing wasn't real. Five million, right. He didn't believe a word.

"Does this mean dinner's on me?"

*

The governor and detective spoke a couple of hours longer. Father and son would come later, one hoped. The other was waiting for proof which he would have by day's end.

When Hidalgo led his son to the door at the far end of

Anita's office, she wasn't there. She'd gone, posting a note on her phone to advise him that she would return later in the day to complete what she had begun. He wasn't hungry for lunch. He was too excited, yet disheartened. He wanted so badly to call his mother, to tell her that his children and hers were coming home, but he couldn't, not until they were home, not until they were truly his children and hers once again.

He returned to his office and closed the door, reaching for a book in his personal library that he hadn't opened in years. Jennie Canyon's signed copy of the Governor's Last Wish, the story of a young Mexican boy who migrated to the USA, who worked with his parents in a vineyard, who studied hard and survived unspeakable tragedy to one day become the first Spanish-speaking Governor of California. His wish, he'd told Jennie at his inauguration, was that he would never have to speak into the red phone at 11:53 on the eve of a desperate man's or woman's execution, desperate because they were seven minutes from joining their victims in heaven or hell.

Everyone believed the call came at midnight. It didn't. The plea for clemency came hours before. Only at seven minutes to the hour was the execution confirmed, though not once while in office had he commuted a sentence.

Hidalgo Arquero checked his watch: twelve noon. The time was different; however he would show no leniency, offer no reprieve from evil. Scott Gibson's execution would be carried out as planned, the date, time and place to be determined.

In the meantime he would send his best cops to escort Darcy Wilson from Louisiana to his office. Deidre Commons would, of necessity, wait another few days for the shock of her life. Santa Anita was another matter. Something was eating at her.

At four o'clock his private line chimed. The news was

358

as expected. He had at last found his son. At 4:30, when he was about to leave, the green light on his desk flashed, Anita's even voice asking for a moment of his time.

"Yes, of course, you should know better than to ask. But first call Del Campo and de la Vega. Fly them at once to New Orleans. Advise my pilot. I want Darcy Wilson in Sacramento this evening and please see to her comfort."

She asked, "And would you like to see her immediately, once she arrives?"

"At the earliest hour, once she is rested."

Anita disconnected.

48

A moment later he was telling her through the closed door to come in. Why had she started acting so uncharacteristically?

She stepped through, partway. "Governor Arquero, may I introduce Ms. Darcy Wilson to you?"

Hidalgo stood, his expression testing Anita's, neither one giving in to the other. The girl did not resemble in the slightest way what he'd seen in the photographs, save the colour of her hair. She was exquisite. Her was hair styled into what he recalled was an updo and her clothes were all designer, he knew, yet simple. She might easily have been a young career women from a well-to-do family, which she soon would be.

"Ms. Wilson, come in. My name is Hidalgo Arquero. Welcome, and thank you for joining me this afternoon. May I offer you a glass of wine, a juice or coffee?"

She knew what to say. "Thank you, Governor. Anita has told me that I should try your wine. So I would like a glass of red…if you have one open. Thank you."

"May I suggest a Cabernet-Sauvignon '85?"

"Yes, please. That would be delightful."

Anita was watching her, she was doing well.

"A fine choice, in fact '85 is my most favourite." He gestured to a sofa. "Please, Ms. Wilson, make yourself comfortable. And will you excuse Señora Juárez and me for a moment while we attend to the wine." He was smiling warmly. "Most of our staff has gone home and we must fend for ourselves, I'm afraid."

Darcy Wilson nodded graciously, again taught well, and Anita knew what to expect.

When he was alone with Anita:

"How exactly did you accomplish this, Anita?"

"I flew to New Orleans, sir."

"And you did so by yourself?"

"Yes, by myself."

"And how much must I repay you for the flights?"

"The flights were free, Governor."

"Ah, I see. You used your points, from all your shopping sprees, like the one this afternoon with Darcy. She looks delightful in her new ensemble."

"That is correct, sir. And, yes, we went shopping."

"Amazing, and at the last minute and you were able to arrange such a convenient schedule. Yes, truly amazing."

"The airline was very considerate."

"A considerate airline, you must have made use of those black eyes, Anita."

"I've noticed that they have an effect on some people, sir...not everyone."

"Indeed. Well, thank you." He paused to select the wine and uncork the bottle. "Perhaps, Anita, the next time you fly with this...considerate airline, you might thank the pilot for her commendable service to you and the attendants for taking such good care of you. I trust you travelled without much concern for your safety by virtue of their dual concern for you?"

"That is correct, sir."

"Ah, so rarely do we find people willing to go out of their way to help others." Hidalgo coughed a laugh. "I would thank them personally, but you know I don't fly commercial."

He knew. He'd probably known all along. Bastard! And

he was smirking, actually smirking, she thought.

She wasn't. She hated him.

Then he peered deep into her coal-black eyes. "Anita, I apologize."

"For what, Governor?"

"For whatever I've done to make you call me Governor and Sir."

She didn't know what to say. "I accept your apology."

God she was increasingly frustrating. "Thank you. Perhaps, if your evening allows, you will join Darcy and me for a glass of wine before dinner. I believe she may soon be in need of a friendly face and warm hands to comfort her in a way I cannot."

¡Cómo! What! "Perhaps you should speak with your daughter alone."

"You know?"

"I suspected."

"She's about to become very confused."

"I like her very much. I will be happy to sit with her, Governor."

"Thank you. First, however, please arrange for a private dinner somewhere intimate, quiet, for a party of four. And would you please advise my son when to expect the limo?"

"Of course Darcy will be with you. Should I also contact Deidre Commons, your oldest daughter?"

"No, Anita. Tonight I want to be alone with Darcy and Diego…and with you, if you will bless us with your beauty and your charm." He took the bottle in one hand, the three glasses by their stems in the other. "Perhaps later, when brother and sister will want time together to make sense of this unexpected revelation, you will allow me to escort you home for a quiet nightcap away from the security detail."

¡Ay! ¡Qué decía! She couldn't believe what she was hearing. What was he saying?

She was stumped. Sir! Governor! Cacique! What did he

want from her! "Sir, I believe the guards would talk."

"You mean about The Boss and La Bonita. Let them. I won't betray your honour by staying overly late." He chuckled. He never chuckled. "Or should I stay just late enough to make them curious. And now, Anita, we have left Darcy alone far too long."

*

"You are exceptionally lovely, Ms. Wilson."

"Thank you. It's because of Anita." She sipped her wine, which was nothing like the house wine at the club. "So you're the governor. Wow. You don't look like a governor." She sipped more wine. "You're the one who wanted to find me?"

"I am."

"You're very handsome, not old and stuffy like I imagined."

"Thank you. I don't believe I've heard that before from where you're sitting."

"Can you tell me why? I asked Carlos and Anita, but they haven't told me anything. All they say is that it's nothing bad. Do you know who I really am?"

"Yes, Ms. Wilson, I do."

She sipped her wine a third time, trying not to gulp, sipping again at seeing Anita coming to sit beside her. "I'm not going to like this very much, am I? This is really going to be bad."

"No, Gabriella. I believe you will like what I have to tell you, very much indeed."

Her head twisted towards Anita. "Is that my real name?"

Anita nodded, patting Darcy's knee.

Hidalgo continued. "You are Gabriella Martina Arquero-Duval…my youngest daughter."

She gulped the rest of her wine, letting Anita take the glass.

Hidalgo went to his desk before sitting beside them,

giving Darcy a photo album, explaining each photograph. Then he said, "This, Gabriella, is a sample of my DNA, so that you might be completely certain in your mind once the confusion has settled. And this, as I told your brother Diego this afternoon, is the allowance I was deprived of seeing you save or spend over so many years of your missed childhood." He gave her the envelope, reading the question in her eyes that she didn't want to ask. He answered, "Enough to buy and do whatever your heart desires."

She didn't hear him. She had a sister and a brother. She was crying, her sobs muffled by Anita's lap. Hidalgo stood and walked away.

Anita said, "You have a horrible way with women of late, Cacique. Perhaps we should have that drink tonight."

Hidalgo didn't believe at that moment that Canyon Estates produced enough wine each year to get him through the evening and into the night. He could but try and went to pour himself another glass.

He told Gabriella the truth, according to what he knew and what he believed, to the exclusion of the Florida Keys, Mendoza and the promise he'd made to Gabriella's mother years earlier. Telling her that Francine's killer was about to feel the merciless lash of justice was sufficient.

Before she left with Anita, Darcy asked: "What did I call you, you know, when...?"

"You called me papá. You were beginning to speak Spanish very well."

She took a moment, studying him. "I think Gabriella Martina will be too much of a lady for papá. I think I will prefer... father."

49

Darcy thought she was living a dream. She was treated like a queen at the spa that morning, as though she was actually someone important, and now to discover she was a governor's daughter she felt scared.

Her shopping spree throughout the afternoon with Anita was a fantasy. Walking in and out of boutiques she never would have afforded, and hopping in and out of the limo illegally parked most of the time without the driver showing the slightest concern about the ticket maids was fun. However ladies always changed for dinner, Anita told her, particularly when dining with the governor.

Anita accompanied her to the hotel. Darcy wanted help choosing her evening wardrobe. She also wanted to repay Anita for all her clothes and shoes. Anita refused, smiling, telling her that everything was a gift from her father, and what she was experiencing that day was only the beginning.

She was nervous about meeting her brother. Anita told her not to be. Diego was once her hero, he would be again. He was a nice man, a kind man. The black leather, boots and silver Ray Bans were all subterfuge, part of his job. Anyway, he would be the most surprised. He wasn't aware that his little sister was in Sacramento.

Anita sipped from a glass of Chardonnay while Darcy showered and dressed. When she heard the squeal, almost a scream, she bolted through the bedroom door. Darcy was standing by the bed wrapped in a towel. She was holding a copy of the deposit slip in her hands.

They cried together for a long while, though Anita didn't want to rob El Cacique of his special night. She and Darcy left the hotel well before he arrived in his limo to meet his son. They went to her home where the security detail addressed them each by name. The driver had called ahead to advise the man that La Bonita was en route with Ms. Wilson. The girl was dumbstruck at what she was seeing. She'd never seen such a fine home, telling her new friend in a daze that she couldn't imagine living in such a place. Anita answered matter-of-factly that she had no need to imagine, merely to choose where she wished to live.

They left for the restaurant at 7:45.

The restaurant was crowded, the private dining room set intimately for the four guests. Seated outside the curtained French doors were two fashionably dressed couples with 10mm Glocks tucked under their jackets or into their evening clutches.

The head waiter escorted the women through the doors to their table where Hidalgo and Drew stood to greet them dressed in blazers and open collars. Anita wore a simple slip dress, her shoulders covered with a silk shawl; she'd helped Darcy choose an elegant tube dress and matching linen coat. She glowed, a teenage princess feeling completely out of place and scared. She didn't have to be told her brother was a narc, despite the expensive blazer. What must he be thinking of her? If she knew he was a cop, he had to know she was a dancer.

Anita squeezed her hand. She could see the change in the governor clearly. Despite his vast fortune, the man's one dream in life had come true. He'd found his family.

The niceties were brief, Drew and Darcy taken aback by the hugs and kisses, half smiling, half blushing at Anita's comment that they would once again have to learn to be Latinos, cautioning Drew that simply shaking his sister's hand would not do at all.

Darcy was seated between her father and brother, Anita between Drew and a stranger. Or was she without warning the stranger? She believed so. For twenty-one years she had him to herself, from afar. Now she had no one, her thoughts suddenly pre-empted by the young woman facing her.

"Can I say something, everyone? Please?"

Hidalgo said, "Say whatever is on your mind, Gabriella."

"Listen, father…wow, is that weird." She paused, clasping her hands in her lap. "I know you're the governor, which is pretty cool, and that Anita is a very important lady. And I know Drew is a cop. I know what he does is pretty scary. I also know that you all have important things to talk about. I don't, not anything that I'm proud about." She shrugged. "I just thought you should know."

Drew put a hand over his sister's, pressing lightly. "Three weeks ago I killed a man up close and personal. It's not like in the movies. His feet left the ground and he landed several feet away with his eyes and mouth frozen wide open. I had to, I had no choice. I'm not proud about that. I simply did what I had to do to survive…to see my little sister. And, believe me; I'm just as nervous as you right now."

"I'm trying hard to remember you."

"The present is always more important, kid. If that guy had killed me instead, what good would my past do me? Besides, by the end of the evening you will have something to remember. So will I." He glanced toward Anita, and to his father, both faces wearing the same curious grimace. "Yeah, three since leaving the academy, all righteous and never officially recorded, the same way street cleaners don't report road kill."

Anita kissed her cross. "I'm sorry, Drew."

"You wouldn't be if you'd ever met or known them."

"I meant that I'm sorry for you, carrying such a terrible burden at such a young age."

"I feel no burden, Señora Juárez, none at all. Thank you, though, for saying what you did. Those men were beyond bad. They were vermin; removing three from the equation probably saved twenty or more."

"Will you stay a cop, Drew," his sister asked, "after all this?"

"Being a cop isn't a job for me, not something I can walk away from very quickly." He faced Hidalgo. "If I do, whenever that is, I will certainly have to forget I was ever Drew Carling. Who knows? First I'll have to get through this, like you, though I always did have a thing about opening a classy restaurant. I hear there's some good wine to be had around here."

The wine came, much to the relief of Hidalgo and Anita, neither of whom liked such talk of death.

They toasted Francine, Maria and Fernando. Throughout the sumptuous meal Hidalgo told his children very little about his life in Pichilingue. He preferred waiting for Francesca to complete his family, he told them. Instead he gave them each a copy of Jennie's latest book. He told them about John Canyon and Jennie, how Maria had first thought that John was ancient and so big, how for years since John was shameless in his transparent excuses to exhort invitations to her home to share in her famous Mexican cooking.

Then, with dessert and digestives, came: "So, what are we doing for Christmas? Is that when we'll meet our grandparents with Jennie and Mr. Canyon?"

Hidalgo was the centre of attention, except for Anita who sipped her cognac. Darcy leaned onto the table, looking directly into his eyes. She wanted to see the woman she once called nana, and her grandpapá. Drew sat with his legs crossed, swirling the amber liquid in his glass, watching his father, reading his eyes. The man hadn't contemplated the question.

"Yes."

"Will our sister be with us?"

"I don't have that answer just yet, Gabriella. I hope so."

Darcy turned to Anita. "You'll have to help me with all the gifts I have to buy, except for yours. Father can help me with yours."

"Gabriella…"

"Governor," Anita broke in, "I don't think you realize how the time has passed us by. And Drew, addressing me as Señora, and not Anita, makes me feel considerably older than my years. Unless you mean to imply that I am old. You must learn to pay attention to such details…unlike certain other men."

Drew nodded sheepishly. Somehow, he thought, the bullet was meant for his father.

"Thank you, Anita. I will. However, in defense of myself, I did mention to the governor this afternoon how beautiful you are. And thank you, Governor, for an evening I never knew to expect. Can I suggest, though, without appearing ungrateful, that Darcy and I return to the hotel on our own? That way you…and Anita… can have an earlier night. I imagine the two of you must be exhausted after all you've done for us. I know I am. And I'm sure my little sister here won't mind walking a few blocks with me."

His grin was mischievous, undeterred by Anita's raised eyebrows and wide-open black eyes. Standing, he went to his sister, proffering his hand. He shook hands with his father and kissed Anita's cheek, hugging her, waiting for her nod of approval before stepping aside so that his sister could kiss and hug both of them.

Drew swept up the evening's tab tucked into a leather folder. He'd checked his bank balance. The evening was his treat, the least he could do after all that had happened, he insisted. He would call the office Monday morning.

Hidalgo asked who would be calling. His son answered, "At least until January, Drew Carling."

Darcy hesitated. "Father, what Drew said about the present, that it's more important than the past," she glanced at Drew and Anita, "well, I thought you should know that I am Gabriella Martina. I'm not Darcy anymore."

He tilted his head ever so slightly, acknowledging her huge decision, wishing he were alone.

She hugged him again. Then she and her brother walked out, Drew pausing to acknowledge the four cops who were trying not to be cops. A good enough reason for Diego Hidalgo Arquero-Duval to remain missing another few weeks.

Behind the closed door The Boss and La Bonita prepared to leave, each one attempting to conceal their uncertainty.

50

The driver called ahead.

Most times Governor Arquero drove with the privacy shield down, unless in the company of other dignitaries, discussing state business with various advisors or the one time Fernando's birthday wish was to chauffeur the Governor of California for his first official visit to the Canyon Estates. The real driver didn't mind. He got to drive a vintage Mustang in pristine condition.

Usually the governor would talk with the drivers, asking their opinions, asking what they heard in their day-to-day lives, being that their neighbours and friends knew what they did for a living. Not so the evening of December 11th. He dismissed the driver, knowing full-well the closest unmarked car would arrive within minutes of his call to escort him to the mansion.

When La Bonita and The Boss passed through the wrought iron gate, the state cop on duty that night had his hand on the doorknob, swinging the door open, not certain whether he should wish them a pleasant evening or pleasant goodnight. He said neither.

Inside Anita removed her shawl, suggesting that Cacique attend to the bar while she retouched her make-up. She returned to see him sitting on her sofa studying the artwork on her walls.

"I was admiring your paintings and thinking how far we have come together."

"The evening was lovely. Thank you for inviting me, for letting me share your family with you. Gabriella is an enchanting girl. Her past will soon be behind her and Drew reminds me of a younger Hidalgo Arquero, once I was able to get past his appearance. Francine named her son well. She would be proud of both of them."

"In one way, I feel as though they were never taken from me, Anita. While in another I lament that I will never recapture those lost years. Thank you for being with me, and for helping me through the evening. What would I do without you?"

"Time will soon tell, Cacique."

"We are going through a difficult time, you and me."

"Separation is always difficult."

"Sí, comprendo. Así es."

"Your decision is made? You will live out your life picking grapes when you know in your heart where you truly belong, what you really must do? You continue to believe that you will put such selfishness before the hope and the trust of so many others who believe in you."

"My parents made a good living making wine, and still do. They refuse to retire."

"Sí, claro, because they are proud people, proud of their son who conquered so much grief to one day become the governor of this state. Or do you forget the stories you told me of your first years without your father as he broke his back in silence for you and your mother. What will they think of you now?"

"And where do you believe it is that I truly belong?"

"You should once again take control of Arquero-Duval, with Virginia Meadows. You do not belong in a hammock. Or were we all so wrong to hold you in such high regard?"

"So finally I discover why your dark mood has permeated the entire office these past weeks, because I want to enjoy the fruits of my labour, to live my life quietly for once."

"Partly, yes, because you have not yet finished the work you must do. And, more importantly, to realize you never trusted me enough to tell me the real truth after all these years."

"I have never lied to you."

"You are a lawyer. You know very well that the absence of a lie does not constitute the truth."

"Spoken like a true ADA, although the hour is somewhat late for riddles, Anita."

"Not once have you told me that you know who really killed Francine. This I had to discover from a letter written by a woman before she died. Her son committed that horrible crime against Francine and you, and now you know where he lives."

"I do."

"And you plan now to kill him."

"No one confesses in advance to a murder, Anita. And were I contemplating such a thing, you certainly would not be privy to what I intend."

"No one has to confess. You cannot do this thing, Cacique. You will humiliate your family and disgrace your friends, John and Jennie. And why have you given your son the use of your private jet for an entire week? You have known him less than one day and you will do this to him. That you want him to contact the dark man described in the letter and to find Francine's killer is immoral. I would say despicable, but admitting that I dislike you to that extent at this moment is difficult. What I do know is that implicating your son in this way makes me ashamed of you."

Hidalgo's face virtually concaved. She could not have wounded him more deeply. He reached under his collar, taking a moment to collect himself.

"She was young and very beautiful, gay and alive. Her bright eyes always shone with curiosity and hope... no longer. My father and John Canyon prevented me from seeing her one last time. They threatened to restrain me physically, and for a long while I was filled with contempt towards them, as well as towards my mother and Jennie for depriving me of my right to say goodbye. To this day I ask God to forgive my cruel thoughts. Then I met you. You saved me. You taught me that I was wrong, not them. As usual you were right, Santa Anita. But what you do not know, what I did not tell you in the restaurant that night, was that much of what was originally written into the police file was obliterated, completely erased. Someone who understood my need, a good friend, knew of a clerk in Records who was willing to help. I did not want my children to one day hear the truth, once they were found. I did not want to be the lawyer whose wife was first killed, and I believe raped in our own home, and then incinerated in her vehicle. I did not want my parents to endure their neighbours' side glances, rumours and innuendo. Some might argue the improper use of my wealth and, in law, they would possibly be right. But I did what, in my mind, was decent. That fact that she was incinerated was important to her family, no one else. And certain others agreed."

He gave her no space to speak. "Believe me when I say that not once have they regretted their collusion, each one out of the kindness in their hearts and for no other reason or motive. Each one believed I was doing what was right. As I do to this day. The clerk wanted nothing in return, which I was unwilling to accept. Her son was in trouble with the law, serious trouble for such a young man. He is now a junior partner and prominent lawyer with Arquero-Duval. Her daughter also remained in school, who first thought her life was to follow her brother into the streets of San Francisco. She went on to become a very expert pilot. In fact you know her, Anita. She flew you to New Orleans to bring my daughter home, I presume with the help of your favourite state cops. Their mother still works where she has for years."

"I make no apologies. I never lied to you. But this, if you wish to know, is what really happened that day. She was murdered by Scott Gibson, not Mario Mendoza. That was a fabrication designed by myself and Enrique Mendoza who is the dark man, as you call him. She was shot once in the head, which is what you know. What you did not know is that she was soon after incinerated beyond any possible recognition. Her beautiful body was completely charred to the point of cremation and left in an open field. She was naked when she was killed. The investigative team found proof of her clothing at her feet. That is the reason you found me so drunk in my office that day."

Hidalgo cupped his pendant, the emerald ring in his hand. "This is all that remained of her. And, yes, I have known who for all these years. The woman who wrote the letter was indeed his mother. Her delay these many years was her way, rightly or wrongly, to protect me from the consequence of what I must and will do." He inhaled deeply, standing. "I deeply regret that I have shamed you, that you see fit to despise me. That, I must confess, I did not see in your eyes this week or this evening. Yet, however difficult, I can live with your shame more than I can the guilt of knowing that I have willingly disavowed my wife after so many years of missing her, thinking of her every night. As for my son, I never intended his complicity. I merely want him to see and understand the abominable animal he is about to hunt, the one who murdered his mother twice. I have sworn him to secrecy. Neither girl will ever know the details."

Anita's hands were trembling. The usual warm glow of her youthful face faded to a colourless pallor. "Cacique...."

"Yes, I am Cacique, or Governor, or Sir. How many

nights have my dreams of my lovely Francine been interrupted with thoughts of how I would like to hear you say my name once, even whisper my name?" He put his snifter onto the coffee table. "I suppose as many nights as I hated myself for betraying her with my thoughts of you." He chuckled, or thought to. He just wanted out. "So, yes, I will live out my life picking grapes and, I hope, being a good father to my children. I have much to compensate for."

She thought she would die. She could hear her heartbeats resounding in her ears, as though from all four corners of the room. Her entire body was cold, hearing his words, the horror of Francine's reality fused with the disbelief of his confession which she hadn't expected.

"I…"

"No, Anita, this is not a time for impromptu words. I will expect your resignation by e-mail on Monday. I do not see that I will be able to face you again for any longer a time than I need to walk through your door, which, of course, shall remain guarded until year's end. Such words as we have spoken this evening cannot be undone. I trust that you understand what I must do, more so than before. I do thank you for everything, especially for what you have done to bring my daughter to me. I do, however, have a Christmas gift for you, a parting gift. If I may, I will have the office deliver it here to your home. You have been a good friend. Not to do so would make me feel worse than I do. I trust I have chosen well, that I will not add to your disappointment. Buenas tardes, Anita…y Gracias… por todo."

Facing away, hearing the door close behind her, Anita Juárez burst into an uncharacteristic flood of tears, punching a down-filled cushion, wanting to scream, wanting to punch herself.

"Hidalgo," she whimpered, her brave façade gone.

51

Sunday Anita spent the day in bed. She didn't work out, eat breakfast or shower. She didn't eat lunch and struggled through a meagre and ill-prepared supper. She looked terrible and felt worse. She hated herself for what she'd been thinking, never fully understanding what Hidalgo had lived through or the devastation she interrupted that first Friday. Only now did she understand that his metamorphosis that first Saturday was truly miraculous.

She hugged her pillow. He was gone, just like that. He had walked out so matter-of-factly, as though stepping from the podium in the press room. Worse: She hadn't found the words to stop him.

*

The night before Drew and Gabriella walked arm in arm to the hotel several blocks away. Neither wanted the evening to end, enjoying a nightcap in the bar. Sunday they spent the entire day together, trying to remember each other, grasping at the faintest glimmer of their past. They were together for breakfast, lunch and dinner.

Late at night they went to their separate rooms, each one in a state of reverie and confusion.

*

Meanwhile Hidalgo spent the day bathing in self-loathing. He was practically confessing to the woman that he had loved her all these years. Yet if he was to spend eternity in hell for what he was about to do, he had no right to expect that she would endure those dark fires by his side.

He went to the office where he secluded himself with instructions that he was not to be disturbed. He appointed a temporary assistant and penned a letter to the staff explaining Anita's unexpected need to resign forthwith. She hadn't said a damn word to stop him after he'd bared his soul.

He called Maria. He wanted to celebrate Christmas the American way on the twenty-fifth. He had his reasons, he told her. He also wanted to celebrate their traditions on the sixth of January, El Día de los Reyes, but he needed her to decorate the American way for the twenty-fifth. He would explain why once he arrived early for hot toddies and a turkey dinner, for a turkey dinner he repeated, nothing Mexican. He also wanted her to invite Jennie and John Canyon, if they were not yet otherwise committed.

When they disconnected, Maria went off in a dither to Fernando. Governor or not, children did not instruct their parents. They hadn't celebrated in such a way since Francine's first Christmas with them. When Fernando called the Capitol he was told "the governor is unavailable." When he dialled his son's private line, he was transferred to the message centre.

¡Qué diablos! All he could do was to phone his partner at such short notice and apologize for his son's sudden and apparent lack of social skills. When the air settled, when he thought her mood safe, he went to his wife and asked her when the last time was that her son had done anything without a very good reason.

They would not speak with Hidalgo until the morning of December 25th when their son would arrive with his arms filled and others bearing gifts.
*

Monday his son arrived at the Capitol as Drew Carling, still not very pleased at having to surrender his weapons, seeing no need to explain the eight-inch stiletto attached to his forearm.

The governor's new assistant was taken aback at seeing the unsmiling man dressed in black leather not quite walking through her office, not quite sauntering directly to the governor's door on his own. She didn't like him. He scared her, yet she hurried after him. Her job was to ensure the governor's privacy. She was seconds late.

"I don't believe she likes you. It could be the ponytail and the facial hair. So is this once again the undercover costume du jour?"

"Yeah, I have that effect on people. And this, it's all I've got hanging in the closet. That way I never have to worry about what to wear. What's the smile for?"

"Your mother, when she first saw me, she despised me. Or she pretended to. I was a Mexican in black leather and boots. I had a ponytail like yours and wore dark aviators, obviously destined to become a drug dealer or hired killer. I didn't want to be like the other boys. I wanted to stand out. Finally, she broke down. She couldn't resist me. The rest is history. How's your sister?"

"She's curious, happy, talkative, anxious, all of the above. My ears can probably do with a few days' rest. She'll be phoning Anita this afternoon. She wants Anita's help finding the right condo. I think they have a synergy thing going on." He paused. "What?"

"Anita has decided to leave government work early, so that she might properly prepare for her new career."

"So the evening didn't go as planned for you guys. The two of you were as nervous as high school kids sneaking behind the bleachers. I've seen more relaxed people when drug deals go bad. So you took her home and you pissed her off."

"I will accept that interpretation in order to circumvent further conversation on the matter. In the meantime, how are Drew and Diego?"

"I'm good. The father thing will have to wait a while longer, but Diego will be meeting Mendoza, not Drew. Is everything done?"

Hidalgo passed his son a thick envelope. "Meet Diego Hidalgo Arquero-Duval, at your convenience. There is no spending limit on your cards. You've been driving since the age of eighteen with a spotless record. Your address is a condo by the sea, owned by Arquero-Duval & Partners. Unfortunately you will not enjoy the penthouse view. The place is a perk for the partners in lieu of paid hours for pro bono work."

"Was she ever there with you?"

Hidalgo paused. "One was, in my heart and in my mind, the other…well, the timing was never quite right."

"And now that she's pissed with you, not much chance. You told her about Mendoza, didn't you?"

"I told her everything, to the extent I felt comfortable, which did little to warm the interior of her home. But enough of what is behind us; my pilot is waiting for you. Do your best to stay out of trouble."

"I should say the same of you. Gabriella's on a cloud. She thinks of Anita as a real friend, her one friend right now. You may want to take some pre-emptive action, like taking the lady to dinner, kissing and making up before someone trespasses your turf. Women like that don't come around very often. Spend too much time licking your wounds and she'll be gone. In case you're still not aware, that woman wasn't expecting you to leave last night." He pointed to the red phone and snickered. "Perhaps you should call yourself and commute the sentence."

"I'll take your concern under advisement." Hidalgo stood, circling his desk to face his son, embracing him. "Return safely to me and your sisters."

"Yeah, like I said. I might say the same of you.

Mendoza's easy. You're the one who has to watch your back. You might want to think about flowers and chocolates. A bit of grovelling goes a long way."

"Diego, allow me a final word before you go…officially."

"I'm good at this. Don't worry. I'll see you in a week, latest."

"That's not my point. You're no longer an L.A. cop. You are officially on special assignment as Drew Carling to the Governor of California. As such, do whatever you must to stay healthy. You have full immunity issued from this office. Do you understand? "

Drew shook his father's hand and left.

*

Captain Diane Quinn was in the companionway completing the mandatory pre-flight check of her Citation X; she glanced over her shoulder to see the black Corvette, thinking nothing of it. Just another jock in a black phallic symbol with windows so heavily tinted that their inadequacies wouldn't show through. Governor Arquero's guests always arrived by limo. She returned to her work.

"Step aside, munchkin, and go tell your daddy I'm ready to roll."

She twirled, in a nanosecond taking him all in, gasping, her breath stolen. She jerked backward from shock before nimbly regaining her composure and her stance. She was ready, a maelstrom whirling in her mind. He wasn't four feet from her, standing with his arms relaxed over his head, his hands against the top of the open doorway. He wasn't smiling. He wasn't anything. She saw all of him, and she saw nothing, trained to focus on his chest, to wait for the slightest gesture. But all she could see were the Berettas under his arms and the dagger strapped to his forearm. A leather jacket was flung over one shoulder, his grim face covered with thick stubble, his ponytail longer than hers would be on her time off and she could see herself in the glare of his glasses. She couldn't disguise her fear. She was very frightened. The guy was trouble. She was in trouble.

She thought her lungs would collapse. "I need to see your ID, right now."

"I'm Drew Carling. I'm expected." He brought down his arms, squeezing past her. "So where's the pilot? I was told he'd be waiting. Let's get him here, pronto, munchkin."

"I am here. I'm Captain Quinn, the pilot."

He chuckled. How could anyone laugh without changing their expression, she wondered?

"Sorry, I thought you were the onboard waitress. So I'm guessing you sit on a phone book or something, you know, to see over the dashboard."

Her body relaxed slightly.

"No, I sit in a highchair, and it's not a dashboard."

She thought: You're a complete macho asshole. Her heartbeat was beginning to settle. He was taller than her by about a foot. He was intimidating. He wasn't smiling. Everyone smiled when they came onboard. He looked dangerous in a roguish, devil-may-care kind of way, but what was with the arsenal, the black tee-shirt, the leather pants and boots? Then she saw the Corvette, instructing him to take his seat.

He thought: Nice package. Your breasts could be bigger, but your pants certainly do justice to what must be a Class-A butt. With five million I could marry a girl like you. We're going to get along just fine.

Diane Quinn was petite, 4'11" and trim. Her uniform, designed for her, was form-fitting red slacks, red leather pumps, a white silk blouse and red silk scarf tied loosely. Her aviator glasses were trimmed in red, her hair was a deep brunette styled into a French braid and the ruby earrings set in sterling silver, he guessed, weren't imitation.

Drew squeezed past her again and into the co-pilot's

seat. He didn't ask, he just did, wondering why all the most beautiful girls were beyond his budget. He had to get out more. There had to be more to his life beyond drug dealers or sitting in the sand on weekends watching other guys get lucky. Maybe he would do that restaurant thing. Maybe Drew Carling was pushing his luck.

"This is a restricted area. Your seat is in the cabin, sir."

What Diane knew was that he was a VIP. She didn't like him. She didn't like the way he looked or the way he was overtly inspecting her. He made her nervous. He just sat there saying nothing, eying her without making eye contact. He was undressing her. She knew he was undressing her. He was completely full of himself. She knew the type.

"Sir, your car is illegally parked. You might want to move it before take-off."

"It's not my car. It's a rental with the governor's insignia on the dash. I don't like limos, they draw too much attention."

And you don't, she thought? Creep.

"Sir, this is a restricted area. I can't have you sitting in the co-pilot's seat."

"I'm afraid of flying. I need to be with someone. I'm staying. Get used to it. Think of me as a sky marshal. And by the way, Captain, you have a very cute tush."

She didn't hear that. She shook her head. She did hear that.

"Sir, that comment will be reported to the governor, officially, as well as in the flight log."

"No need. I'm sure he's already very aware. Besides, it already is official. You have a cute tush. And no panty lines. I like that, a complete look."

She left him to close the companionway and the door to the flight deck, in her mind slamming both. She contacted the tower, furious when he put on a headset to eavesdrop. He wasn't nervous at all, taking everything in without uttering a word as she taxied to the runway, positioned and waited fifth in line. When permission for take-off was granted he watched the instrument panels, her hands and the muscles in her thighs working under her slacks. He couldn't see her feet.

And no, when he finally did speak at altitude, she would not let him touch the controls no matter how charming he thought he was. If he did, he'd be greeted by FBI agents in L.A. And no, he didn't have to know where she was staying. Why was he even asking, and what was with the ponytail and the scruffy face? What was he, some sort of super spy, some sort of macho avenger? How would Governor Arquero even know such a jerk? What she did give him, per the governor's instructions, was her cell number. He was to have a meeting onboard the plane the next day or Wednesday and she was to find something else to do. She wasn't to remain anywhere near the hangar or the plane. When his meeting was over she was to fly him to Miami. That was the moment she realized he was the one she'd flown from L.A. with de la Vega and Del Campo.

After his initial failed attempt at conversation, he hadn't spoken another word for the remainder of the short flight. He just liked being with her, certain she was doing her best to impress him with her competence as a pilot. She felt right. In L.A., when he offered to share a cab, she refused, closing herself into the flight deck once he stepped out.

Monday evening Drew called a number from downtown that he knew would eventually lead to Enrique Mendoza. He simply gave the number to his disposable cell and said: The time has come for me to strike the match.
*

Earlier, Gabriella called her father's office to thank him for everything. She was put through.

He wanted to lie to her, unable to. He didn't want to lose her twice. Gabriella stood her ground, not the least bit

concerned about confronting her father. Just because he was the governor and couldn't recognize that the woman was to die for, didn't mean that he could keep her from having a friend. That night, after a day of shopping for the perfect gift, she called Anita. They spoke for as long as it took for Gabriella to hear a smile. Men could be such fools, even rich, good-looking ones.
*

At one PM the operator at Commons Communications disconnected the crank call. At 1:02 she disconnected the same call a second time. At 1:25 a State Police detective arrived to speak directly with Deidre Commons. The Governor of California had called twice. What was the problem? Get her to the lobby, now.

The governor's limousine would arrive at her home address at 8:00 PM sharp, he told Ms. Commons. The governor was inviting her to dinner, unless she cared to refuse. She didn't. Oh, and by the way, you might want to have a talk with Blondie over there.
*

The limo arrived at the entrance to the exclusive condo complex precisely on time. The doorman called her apartment. Deidre Commons exited the elevator five minutes later.

She was dressed for business in a winter-white linen suit, red silk blouse and white satin sandals. Her reddish-blonde hair was a veritable explosion of thick curls. Her hazel-green eyes were bright and searching, set in a flawlessly smooth face.

The driver proffered his hand, which she accepted, helping Deidre into the backseat. Once on route he heard the tapping of her fingers on the smoky-grey bullet-proof shield. He lowered the partition. He didn't know what the meeting was about or why Governor Arquero had called her out of the blue. They would be arriving at the restaurant within ten or twelve minutes, he suggested, when she could ask him directly. She raised the screen. Limo drivers were always so damned taciturn.

The restaurant was out of the way, quiet, intimate for those with lovers, peaceful for those who had a lifetime to discuss. Deidre Commons wasn't accustomed to cops. She didn't dislike them, she simply didn't know how to act around them, especially the man and woman who met the limo and escorted her to the most private corner before taking their own nearby seats within arm's reach of the second team, close enough to protect, not close enough to overhear.

The governor stood.

"Good evening, Ms. Commons. Thank you for agreeing to join me this evening. I trust the venue is satisfactory."

"Governor Arquero, thank you. I have to say I was very surprised. I hope I won't have to wait long before you tell me why."

"Not very long at all, perhaps long enough to enjoy an aperitif and a bit of preamble." He forced a smile that a few days earlier had been real. "I assure you that my intentions are honourable. You need not worry on that level."

"I'm relieved to hear that, otherwise I would wonder why you're staring at me."

"Excuse me. I'm staring because sitting here with you now is reminiscent of my time once spent in such places with another woman who was as lovely as you."

He signalled the waiter, deciding on a Fumé Blanc with Deidre's approval. By the time the sommelier returned to fill their stemmed glasses, the unseasonably pleasant weather, her love of the sea and his love of fine wines were established.

"May I call you Deidre, Ms. Commons?"

"Yes, of course, though I have to tell you my curiosity is mounting. Usually my dinner meetings aren't this impromptu."

"I do apologize for the inconvenience, though until very recently I had no idea that we would meet. That you accepted my invitation so readily alleviated an unquestionable degree of malaise on my part. I appreciate how full your agenda must be."

"So right now I'm thinking if you weren't the governor, I'd be looking for a cop."

He almost managed to chuckle. "They're seated to your immediate right, and to your left, four of them, here to protect you as much as to protect me. You are completely safe, Deidre, even from me. They are the best, and I do understand how this must appear somewhat unusual."

She turned her head ever so slightly, seeing team two. "So I have my own security team. Why?"

"Simply put, I've waited for this evening a very long time."

"You're losing me, Governor. You had no idea, but you've waited a very long time and you were worried that I wouldn't accept. Why?"

"May I tell you a story, Deidre? I believe that is the best way to tell you why we are together this evening."

"Please tell me something."

"Thirty years ago a young couple who were very much in love married. They had a son whose name was Diego. Two years later they had a girl, whose name was Francesca and, two years after that, a little girl they called Gabriella. Their life together was idyllic, until one day when his wife was murdered and the three children were stolen, taken from him."

Deidre sipped her wine. "Not exactly what I was expecting. Thanks, Governor."

"After a week lost in grief, the father did everything he could to find them, though at the time the world was a different place, not as small as it appears today. Nor was he alone in his search. Finally, however, and very recently, they were found. Diego was taken at age nine to New York, where he was raised by decent people and grew to become a decorated police detective. He now lives in L.A. Little Gabriella wasn't as fortunate. First raised in Chicago from the age of five she soon left of her own accord at a tender age to survive as best she could in New Orleans. She has recently come to Sacramento where she will soon live as comfortably as her older sister. Her sister, and Diego's, was raised in Detroit by well-to-do parents who loved her, I'm told. She was seven when adopted. Unlike her sister, she has done well for herself. She is well-educated and resides here in Sacramento. She also owns an enviable condo and magnificent yacht in Miami and is the president and CEO of Commons Communications."

Deidre Commons was breathing heavily. She placed her glass on the table, not trusting her hand that was beginning to tremble.

"Governor Arquero, you're implying that I'm Francesca, that I have a brother and sister?"

He shook his head. "I'm not implying, Francesca. I am telling you that, yes, you have a family. They are well. They know about you and they are very anxious to meet you. I might add that they are financially secure. They want to reunite with their sister, nothing more."

"And my real father, what happened to him? Do you know him? Were you friends? Is he alive?"

"Yes, he's very much alive, as are Maria and Fernando, your grandparents who don't yet know of your proximity to them. They live in Vallejo and I wish to very soon reunite them with you, your sister and your brother. They have never stopped praying for your safe return. Each Sunday my mother, Maria, lights candles and prays for you, for Francesca Maria Arquero-Duval."

The air was heavy, oppressive. The dull sound of quiet

chatter in the restaurant abated abruptly. Her head began to ache.

Deidre reached for her glass, draining the wine, catching her breath. "I'm your daughter? That's what you're saying?"

"Yes. And now that you know, perhaps we should order."

Hidalgo ordered for her.

"How can you be certain?"

"Your brother passed a DNA test; your sister didn't see the need. The resemblance was obvious." He passed Deidre a small box. "My DNA, I wouldn't expect the CEO of Commons Communications to merely accept the word of a governor." His smile was thin. "These, Francesca, are photographs of your family. Your brother and sister have similar, not identical; my hope being that next weekend the three of you might join me at my residence and, the week after, join your family for Christmas in Vallejo. Gabriella has begun her shopping."

"Governor, if you haven't noticed, my glass is empty and, for this occasion, much too small." Hidalgo filled her glass and stood, pulling a chair from a nearby table to sit closer to his daughter, explaining each photograph in detail.

"There is one last piece of business, Francesca, before we dine. I have given to Diego and Gabriella five million dollars each, deposited into their accounts. In your case I chose to benefit others by sharing that same amount. Half was deposited into your personal account this afternoon. A receipt for the other half, donated to the children's wing of University Hospital in your name, is in this envelope along with a receipt for your portion. I understand that University Hospital is your primary area of philanthropic interest."

She reached into the envelope, verifying the details. "Not many secrets anymore."

"No, unfortunately not." He paused. "May I know why

you're laughing?"

"I'm laughing because I never believed all that goodie-goodie political hype about the wonderful Republican Governor Arquero, or how he worked in his early years for free, not charging his clients a dime, sending many of them to school, taking over a major law firm and turning high-priced hobnob lawyers into a bunch of pro bono do-gooders. And all this time I was talking about my father. What do I tell everyone after tonight? I'm not laughing; I just don't want to start crying. And what the hell am I supposed to call you."

"Your mother was Francine Duval. The law firm was her father's. What I did, I did for her and my mother before and after Francine was taken from me. You may call me whatever you wish. Your brother's having the same difficulty. For the moment he seems content with Governor, which he may want to reconsider by the thirty-first. Gabriella seems set on father. Hidalgo is also good. I would however appreciate your discretion until the first of the year."

Deidre was studying the photos. "I can't believe this myself. So how would anyone else? As for names, let me think about that. In the meantime, to help me get through this, I will be visiting a lab first thing tomorrow. But if all this works out, what happens next?"

"One step at a time, meeting Diego and Gabriella, meeting your grandparents, I would hope at Christmas."

"And if it doesn't, just to be clear, expect a cheque to cover my share from my lawyers…just to be clear, and with sincere gratitude for the charitable donation. Sorry, I voted Democrat. I didn't know."

"We're even; I always thought Commons Communications was a little overpriced."

She chortled. "Touché."

The first course arrived. Father and daughter closed the

restaurant. He accompanied her to her home, gave her his private number and continued on to the mansion wanting desperately to clear his head, wanting to sleep for a week.
*

In Los Angeles Drew Carling answered his phone.

"It has been a long time, amigo."

"Yes, a very long time."

"Since when exactly? My memory fails me."

"Twenty-one years, October. You came to see…"

"I went nowhere to see you, gringo."

"That's right. You went to see a man who lost his family. I am the first of three he lost. He wants you to know the time for striking the match is now."

"I know. I was expecting this call. I am pleased to know that such an important man has not lost his honour. I am glad to know that his heart may now begin to repair."

"We have to meet. Those are my instructions."

Drew told Mendoza when and where. Then he went to bed, smiling. He still had a chance. She had to fly him to Florida and back. He would surprise her. He would lose the leather and the glasses. He had to dilute the bad boy as much as possible if he wanted any chance at all of marrying her.

52

Deidre Commons was well-known at and by the University Hospital for her philanthropy; the children's wing was the best in the state in large part because of her. No one at Commons Communications ever waited long for a consult or treatment. She arrived at 8:00 AM Tuesday, by nine she was Francesca Maria without a shadow of a doubt. She just couldn't believe that she was and, as though that wasn't enough to think about, the Chief Administrator hadn't stopped thanking her for the anonymous donation made in her name. The manager of her bank also called.

When she phoned her father, she was transferred to the message centre. When she called his office she was told the governor was unavailable, which left her more than a little perplexed. She instructed her secretary to reschedule all her appointments until the first of the year. She needed time off and flew to Miami to figure things out.
*

While her sister was in the air, Gabriella stepped from her taxi and stood in front of a very big man, trying to explain that she wanted to see Anita. No, she didn't have an appointment, she answered. So what? Could he at least call her? He did, and he let her in.
*

At LAX Diane Quinn was at the hangar most of the morning and early afternoon preparing a light snack and bar service for her passenger and his guest. An hour remained before she would disembark the plane to relax in the pilots' lounge for however long they required to conclude their private discussion.

Drew Carling arrived thirty minutes early, but she didn't know that. Seeing the man standing in the companionway from her place on the tarmac she ordered him tersely from her plane. When he turned:

"I'm sorry. I didn't recognize you. Wow. I'm impressed."

"Impressed enough to marry me and have my children?"

"Not even close." She began climbing the stairs. "So, if you're not a sinister drug dealer or a car thief, is this the real you? You look like a cop."

"That's not good."

"Why not, got too much history with them?"

"Something like that, but I still want you to have my children."

He was dressed in a dark blue suit, Mediterranean blue shirt and midnight blue tie. His shoes were blue Italian leather. He was clean-shaven and she had to admit, not bad.

"So where are the Halloween costume and the ponytail? Get tired of looking like an ugly girl?"

"You're pretty mouthy for a government employee, munchkin. Anyone ever spank that little bum of yours?"

"I work for Arquero-Duval and Hidalgo Arquero personally, not the governor. And, while we're at it, don't call me that again and keep your eyes off my ass."

"Do I really come off as a cop? I was thinking more like an astute businessman."

"No, you're a cop. And probably not a very good one or you wouldn't."

"When I'm done here, how long to Miami?"

"Six hours."

He removed his jacket. The twin Berettas under his arms were chrome-plated and shiny.

"Don't you dare do anything stupid to ruin my plane."

"I'll try, but no promises. Anyway, listen, just in case I don't come out of this alive," he wasn't smiling, "perhaps just one kiss to make my dying worthwhile."

"You're serious."

"About the kiss, yes."

"I'm not kissing a cop."

He was half paying attention. "I've decided we'll depart for Miami tomorrow, early. I don't want my girlfriend flying tired. Anyway, we would arrive too late to enjoy ourselves if we fly out this afternoon." He slipped the holsters from his shoulders, scanning the cabin for a convenient place to conceal the weapons. "So where should we have dinner?"

"I'm eating in my hotel room…"

"Excellent choice, what time?"

His expression hadn't changed from no expression. She had no idea how to read him or what to think.

"You're very annoying."

"How old are you?"

"Thirty-two," and she couldn't believe she'd just told him that. "What?"

"Thirty-two, so I've come into your life just in time. You know, being that you're much closer to forty than twenty."

That hurt.

"I can't believe you said that, you self-centred, narcissistic…"

The black SUV was pulling into the parking area, slowing to a stop.

"You're leaving, right now."

He was dead serious. She was wrong about his face having no expression; she saw what little there was vanish. The transformation was instant. She peeked out from a porthole at the three men standing facing the plane.

394

"Who are they?"

"The guy in the middle is a very dangerous man. He's waiting for you to leave, so let's not keep him waiting. At the bottom of the steps you turn right. You don't even blink at them." Drew slipped into his suit jacket. "Go."

She reached for her purse, wrapped her arm around his neck and kissed him. Then she kissed him again.

"Raspberry, I like that. And thirty-two is perfect."

"Don't you dare do anything to get me in shit with Governor Arquero."

"And dinner…"

"Maybe, if you're still alive. So I won't hold my breath."

She did as he instructed. She descended step by step, slowly, turning right and walking away.

*

Mendoza climbed the steps alone. They didn't shake hands.

"So, you are Diego Arquero."

"I am."

"Welcome home."

"Thanks."

"How do you feel to, without warning, discover you are the son of a popular governor?"

"Better than not knowing, I suppose. The downside is discovering that my mother was murdered, and how."

"By Gibson, the best kept secret for so many years."

"You were expecting me?"

"I was expecting your father."

"He's understandably otherwise occupied."

Mendoza produced a letter. "Written by Gibson's mother, and cryptic to say the least, intended to advise me that I should be ready, nothing more. I hope your information is more complete."

Drew said. "Please, sit. May I offer you a tequila, scotch, anything?"

"Tequila, straight. Gracias." He noticed the spread. "Thank the young lady for me when she returns. Regrettably, I have already eaten."

They raised their glasses.

Drew unfolded the letter without further preamble.

*

Sir,

I have waited many long years to write this letter to you, which I do prior to my unlamented departure from this world with the fullest understanding of the consequences that will ensue.

I remember your visit to my home clearly, as I do your measured words and the coolness of your hatred. As I do speaking with another young man at his young wife's grave, then desperate to understand his tragic loss, desperate for answers to questions he now possesses after so many years. His hatred was seething and passionate, dangerous to himself and to all he holds dear. Yours was not, which is why I pen this letter, so that you might intercede to save a good man from ill-intent however justified he might be.

His children are found, yet he is a gentleman of honour who will not likely recant on his promise to seek and carry out this deserved retribution.

You and he chose different paths, crossed once by virtue of a cruelty impossible to recreate in my mind after all these years. Your paths must now cross once more. He chose a path of decency and justice; you chose a darker, unlit road. He is not prepared for what he feels he must do. His heart is pure. Whereas you, I believe, have prepared for this day since first we met with a heart less forgiving. You must do in his place what must finally be done with my blessing. Not to do so would be a grievous sin against the natural order of your respective destinies.

He knows what you do not and you possess what he does not, one half incomplete without the other.

Best regards, with deep regret,

*

"What does your father know that I do not?"

"His precise whereabouts, his name, pretty well everything."

"And your father wishes to wait until he steps down."

"That's right. He won't divulge the information because in his letter Claire Gibson sends the same message. He knows that you can do what he cannot. Yet he's determined. That said, he cannot be allowed to strike the match, whatever that means. He stands to lose a great deal."

Mendoza raised an empty glass. Drew stood and went for the bottle.

"You know how your young mother died, Diego. That she was…"

"Nothing was left of the car."

"That is what he means by striking the match. We are agreed, your father and I. Gibson's life is now over. Simply put, his end will not be one of celestial greetings with the loving touch of loved ones by his bedside to send him on his way. As I once told Señor Arquero, Gibson will not have the benefit of a bullet." Mendoza showed his appreciation of the aged tequila. "This I will do for your mother, Diego, not my cousin who died prematurely before I was able to save him from the shame he placed upon his family and mine."

"You're saying that Gibson saved you the trouble."

"He did. After all these years I can forgive my cousin. Latino blood is thick, not Gibson." He savoured the tequila. "Tell your father that what I will do, I will do for your mother, as I once told him. What I need to know is when. Let him believe what he will. I will not deny Claire Gibson's final wish. Your father's heart will remain pure. Nevertheless, he will strike the match as he must."

"I will call you when the arrangements are made."

Mendoza stood. "I anxiously await seeing your father. Tell him so." He snorted. "I voted for him twice."

"I'll be sure to tell him."

Neither man thought to shake hands.

"Be certain that is all you tell him. Let him believe what he wishes to believe. A man must have dreams." He stopped at the companionway. "Diego, a young woman went with Gibson. Her name was Navarra Carrera. Is she still with him?"

"He murdered her a few weeks after he ran."

Mendoza inhaled a deep breath. His expression remained calm. "Your father must be proud to have such a fine police officer for a son."

There was no point. "It's the suit."

"Sí, claro. Vaya con dios, Detective."

*

When Mendoza was gone, Drew dialled a private number that wasn't answered. He left a cryptic message. Then he called Diane's cell. She answered. Only one other person besides Virginia Meadows and Hidalgo Arquero had her number.

"I just wanted to let you know that your children's father wasn't killed, if that's important to you."

She pressed END without saying a word.

*

By the end of the day Gabriella and Anita had bought a new car that would be delivered in a few days and had visited a few possible seaside condominiums. Anita had never cooked dinner in her kitchen with other women just for the fun of it. She never had a girlfriend and she couldn't believe that Gabriella had never tasted Mexican, or that the young girl's unexpected gift to her was a diamond encrusted Lady Rolex.

"Anita, I don't want to ever wake up, because when I do, like this morning, I can't believe any of this."

"That this has happened to you gladdens my heart. You have family now, a good family. One day soon you will meet a wonderful man and…"

"…and have to tell him I was I stripper."

"Yes, you must, when the time is right. At which time you will remember what your brother Drew has told you. And if your man cannot find understanding in his heart, he is not a man." She admired her new timepiece. "Thank you, Gabriella. You are being a great comfort to me."

"I sort of think it's the other way around." Gabriella sipped her Chardonnay. "We're girlfriends, right?"

"Yes."

"So, girlfriend, he brought you home, then what?"

"The governor's life is complicated. Saturday evening I discovered how complicated."

"Have you ever told him?"

"You mean, that I love him…no. I would always come second in his heart."

"You've never had a lover?"

"No, I have never taken a lover. Your father always came first. I believed there was always hope and didn't want to disappoint him. It was a different time. Then, slowly, I stopped believing. His heart is too filled with love for another."

"My mother."

"Yes, for Francine. He wears her ring against his heart to this day."

Gabriella began giggling. "Hey, do you want to hear something really crazy?"

"Yes. I believe that would be very good."

"We're both virgins. Honestly, Anita, not once. I swear. That makes us pretty rare these days. And aren't rare things more valuable?"

"I see a big difference, Gabriella, between a young and beautiful woman yet untouched and a spinster."

"Don't ever think that way. The other girls at the club, they would do six or seven different guys a week at three or four bills a pop, depending, sort of like a menu. They earn more money in a week dancing and hooking than anyone else does in a month, non-taxable. But they're the spinsters, not you. When I saw you at the club I thought you were gorgeous, a little kinky, but really gorgeous. So what are we going to do about it? You want him, and he wants you. Even Drew says so. I think you should take back your job and punch him for being stupid. Then you should tell him to marry you. His heart is very big, Anita. There's lots of room inside for you, my mom, and the rest of us. I know."

"When you are fired by the governor, you remain fired. It is not a good thing."

"So you're okay with this. You're going to stay single until you find some old guy no one else wants, the wrong guy and never be happy."

Anita smiled. "My heart will tell me who is right."

"Your heart already has. You're just not listening, but if you're good with it so am I."

That evening they fell asleep in Anita's bed, Anita finally putting a pillow over Gabriella's face to stop her from talking.

*

"Thank you, Drew. Dinner was fabulous. I've never been out with a guy wearing guns and a dagger, a guy I know nothing about after four courses. Something I don't think I'll tell my mother anytime soon."

"You know where I live, room 1812. You know that you're beginning to like me, and that you're already thinking about having my children."

"Okay, so we've established what your dreams are all about tonight. Just keep them clean. I don't need anyone undressing me when I'm not there." She swiped her card through the lock mechanism. "Thank you again, Drew.

Departure's at 6:00 AM, arrival should be 2:00 PM local. I'll see you at the airport."

"Six o'clock, in the morning. You're serious."

"Yes, I am."

He didn't move. "Then the thought occurs to me..."

"Not a chance."

"You women are all alike. You have dinner with a to-die-for guy, like me, and right away you think we expect something. I was going to say that since you've already kissed me because you thought I was going to die, is it fair not to kiss me now that I'm alive?"

Diane let her purse slide to the crook of her elbow. She cupped his face in her hands and pressed her lips to his until he began thinking that she was sucking the air from his lungs.

When she closed the door behind her, he whispered. "I know you're watching me. And today's only Tuesday. Goodnight, munchkin."

He was definitely onto something.

From behind door, standing in the dark, Diane Quinn wondered who and what Drew Carling really was. She put her fingertips to her lips.

53

Wednesday Diane went for breakfast early, Drew didn't. He was giving her space. By the time he arrived the flight plan was logged and she was conducting a final check of the wheels, landing gears and engines. She was good to go.

When she heard the corvette arrive, the door open and close, she didn't turn. She knew what to expect: boots, black leather pants, black leather jacket, black tee-shirt, big guns and a dagger strapped to his arm. The man was so damned conceited. He thought he was so cool. She was determined. She wouldn't give him the time of day.

"Good morning, Captain Quinn, did you sleep well?"

"Yes, I did, thank you. And thank you for a lovely evening."

She continued writing into her log, ignoring him.

"Your company was delightful. I felt special being with you. I know it's a little late, I should have done this last night, but the evening was a little last minute."

Her first thought was, what now? Her second, when she turned, was holy shit!

"Is this a joke?"

"It's a single perfect rose, like you. I thought I was being romantic."

"I don't want romance, not with you, not ever, and I'm very aware that I'm single. Thanks for rubbing it in. I was talking about the beach boy thing. Do you clean old ladies' pools for extra cash when you're not killing drug dealers, or what?"

He was dressed in a white micro-fibre tee-shirt, white deck pants and white canvas shoes. A white nylon jacket was pinned between the floppy handles of his nylon sports bag. She was staring. His hazel-green eyes could not be greener, or the tan colour of his skin more perfect, or his white teeth whiter. He was, she thought, disturbingly perfect.

"Are we set for take-off?" he enquired.

"Yes, we're set."

"Well, then, I'll take my seat. Thank you, Captain."

"Sure. And...thank you for the rose."

He was beautiful, and obnoxious. No one dressed like that to sit six hours in a cockpit. He was coming on to her, playing games, and so obvious.

But when she followed, sealing them into the plane, he was seated in the cabin reading a newspaper.

She refused. He was so arrogant. That said; he was the passenger, the governor's guest. "May I serve you a coffee or a juice before take-off?" Perhaps with a little cyanide mixed in.

"Thank you, I'm fine with my paper. Would you call me, though, say, thirty minutes before landing?"

"Yes. Is that all? Can I do anything else for you?" Like smack your head.

"No, just arrive on time. Thank you. That's a good girl."

She swirled, disappearing into the flight deck, closing the door a little harder and little louder than she'd wanted. If she could have choked him through the peephole she would have. He was smiling like a senseless idiot. Then he waved at her.

Over the intercom she instructed him to buckle himself in. Some Clear Air Turbulence was expected, she explained. However the Citation X was very capable of sustaining itself, she assured him. She saw no need to divert from the original flight plan.

Over the intercom she heard, "Thank you, Captain. I have every confidence in your ability. I think I'll just nap for a while. My evening was very exhausting."

Several minutes later at altitude, Diane heard, "Captain, if you have a moment later, would you marry me? It's my understanding that captains can do that."

"Who in their right mind would marry you?"

She heard: "The most beautiful girl in the world, the most charming and interesting, the one whose lips are coated with honey, the one whose smile stops my heart…that girl."

"No," she answered.

She shut off her intercom and giggled.

"Okay, just asking. We are going to Miami, though, and I didn't want, you know, to cheat on my wife. Carry on, Captain. You're doing very well so far. I'll be putting in a good report on you to the governor."

Diane choked on the air, straining her arms. Thirty minutes later she heard his voice again.

"Captain, the thought occurs to me that you, being a single, hmm, more mature woman, that you might never have been to South Beach. Given your age I understand you might be a little reticent, but would you join me for lunch this afternoon at the beach. And don't worry," he hastened to add, "I know the ideal swimwear store for women of your, hmm, body type."

"You're eating by yourself, Mr. Carling, unless you find a little blonde bimbo in a sandbox to play with."

"I prefer brunettes, pretty brunettes, Captain. Did you know my wife is a brunette?"

"What!"

His eardrums practically shattered.

"Yeah, my wife, I'm going to marry her on Valentine's Day. She's a pilot, a little prissy, yes, I admit, and a little stuck up, but workable."

"Workable! I wouldn't marry you if…"

"Captain, no, no, I wasn't talking about you. You really should get over yourself. It's not very becoming. And, by the way, I'm sensing a little vibration in the cabin. Can you maybe work on that?" He paused, shuffling in his seat, making certain she heard. "I was talking about a beautiful girl whose voice is soft, whose eyes are liquid chocolate when she laughs so hard that she cries, whose sweet breath would awaken an entire sleeping forest, the girl I spent last evening with, the girl who fell asleep in my arms if only in my dreams…that girl."

"Congratulations, and please send her my sympathies."

Thirty minutes later: "Captain…"

"Yes, sir."

"This mile-high thing I'm reading about, can you explain that to me, you know, in layman terms so to speak. Is that like frequent flyer points? Does this airline offer Mile-high Points, Captain? And, if so, can I apply?"

"Mr. Carling, if I join you for lunch at South Beach, will you promise to just shut up for the remainder of the trip?"

"Yes."

"Okay, but no mile-high, not now on auto-pilot, not tonight, not ever. Is that understood?"

No reply came, not for ten minutes. He understood. Yet, she was waiting, he knew she was waiting.

"Captain," she heard, not surprised.

"What now, Mr. Carling? Are you cancelling lunch at the beach so soon?"

"No, I'm not, but this auto-pilot thing…really?"

On schedule the jet touched down at 2:00 PM local time with barely a hiccup. She was good.

She thought that at some point he would knock on steel-reinforced door leading to the flight deck. He didn't, and when she opened the door he was on the phone, speaking like a man who should be wearing black leather, guns and a ponytail.

She busied herself, trying not to listen. When he was finished, she sat with him.

"Drew, we're just doing lunch. No games."

"I scared you, the way I was talking just now."

"Sort of, yeah."

"Good. Scaring people like you keeps me alive. You can't marry a dead guy."

"I'm not marrying you."

"Can you keep a secret?"

"Yes, I fly the governor, I'm cleared."

"This, what you see, this is me. The leather, the guns, that guy yesterday and the day before, that's business."

"But you're a cop, right? You're working for the governor."

"Yes, on both counts. And while we're on the subject, after lunch you're on your own until Friday or Saturday. Enjoy yourself. Just remember you're getting married. Unfortunately for me, I won't get to see any of this," he eyed her from head to toe, "on the beach, I mean. So my loss is everyone else's gain."

"I have orders from the governor to be available to you." She stopped herself, seeing the instant glint in his eyes. "Don't even think of saying something stupid." She lounged into her seat. "So, where are you staying? I should know, just in case. I can't afford to lose my job because you've gone and done something stupid."

"Somewhere en route to Key West, I'll call you when I'm leaving. Until then enjoy Miami."

"Yeah, right, by myself. You're an idiot."

"So what you're saying is that you want to come with me. You're thinking, I don't know, get him on the beach, get a little tequila into him, seduce him with feminine charm and trick him into marrying you."

"Yeah, right. I simply meant that doing lunch in Miami would get you into Key West pretty late. Besides, if I go with you, other people, you know, other guys might not misinterpret your pretty outfit. You look so sweet and innocent, especially with your fashionable new coif."

His smile evaporated. "Diane, really, it's not a good time."

Her smile evaporated. "Not that I wouldn't have liked to see Key West, however I think I'll eat lunch alone today. You've got a long ride ahead of you and flying this thing for five hours isn't the most relaxing job in the world. I'll be ready when you call. Bye."

He stood. "I'll see you Friday, Saturday latest. Thanks for the smooth ride."

He walked out.

Diane went on with her work, noting details on her manifest, mumbling. She would have liked dong lunch on South Beach. She'd never worn her newest bikini because it was too tiny to wear anywhere at home. The last thing she needed was her photograph on the front page of some rag embarrassing the governor. And Carling, whoever and whatever he was, he was just another dumb jerk.

"But I'm a good-looking dumb jerk, right?"

She shrieked, and swirled. "What do you want? Forget a gun somewhere?"

"Well, first I want lunch with a beautiful brunette in Key West or somewhere en route, then I want to lay with her on the beach to learn more about her, and to see her in her new tiny bikini. But, Mrs. Carling, I am not, not under any circumstances, sleeping with you until you propose. I don't care how small your bikini is."

She searched everywhere for something to throw. Her lips were pursed; she wanted to scream how she hated his arrogance, how she hated his, his conceited smirk. God! He was so full of himself. There was no way she was going to let him win his childish game.

She sank into a seat, her arms crossed, her legs crossed. "It's very small…tiny in fact, which doesn't matter because you certainly won't see me in it."

He leaned against the companionway, inhaling deeply, exhaling with a measured slowness. "You want to kiss me again, don't you, Mrs. Carling?"

54

He agreed to her one condition: separate rooms and no adjoining doors. She was going with him because of her job description, for no other reason. She was following the governor's orders and he was not to get in her way when other men asked her out to dinner. And they would.

He understood. He rented a Mustang convertible and asked her what she'd brought to wear for their trip. It wasn't their trip, she told him. But when she had no choice but to tell him, they went shopping. No one wore slacks and sweaters in the Florida Keys. Besides he wanted the world see his gorgeous wife.

She refused to let him pay and, in one afternoon, the three new evening and three new day outfits had blown her entire vacation budget for the coming year. Now she really did hate him.

They ate an early dinner in Key Largo, on a deck overlooking the ocean. The setting was romantic. She felt like a woman, a beautiful woman. She was ravishing, unaccustomed to the effusive attention from waiters and other couples seated nearby, couples holding hands while her hands were in her lap throughout most of the meal.

They arrived late and in the dark to Key West. Diane was tired, lulled into a semi-sleep by soft music in the car and the muted roar of the ocean. He kissed her goodnight, on the cheek, like a sister, waited until her door was locked and went to his room an adjacent door away. He would invent some excuse by morning.

When he was settled in, he changed his clothes and left the hotel grounds. He wouldn't return until dawn.

*

At 7:45 Thursday the sun was lazily climbing over the infinity edge of the horizon. Diane stretched, half asleep, returning the ardour of his warm lips pressed against hers.

"Good morning, darling."

"Hmmm, good morning...What!"

"Good morning. I've decided since, you know, last night, that I should call you darling."

She was naked, half-naked. She was in her panties and bra. That was naked! She yanked the sheet to her shoulders, pushing him away.

"No, Drew, this did not happen. This did not happen!" Shit! Double shit! No!

He was wrapped in a towel. He was dripping wet, his hair was wet. He was leaning over her, smiling, reaching to touch her.

"You...were hot." He sank onto the edge of the bed. "I mean really, really, super-hot."

"Oh, God."

"Yeah, I know. But if there was one I'd be in that bed with you right now. I was talking about my dreams," he confessed. He stood straight, whipping away his towel. "Come on, time for an early morning swim before all the kids start pissing in the pool."

"So..."

"So nothing, you missed out, again. Or I did."

"So we didn't."

"Well, I did take a little peek before you woke up. I sort of thought that I'm going to see you in your bikini anyway, right. So what's the difference? And, really," he blew a silent stream of air through pursed lips, "a killer ass."

He was exhausting. She couldn't keep up, which didn't mean he was going to win. She said, "You're right. I do have a killer ass, and I hope you enjoyed your cheap thrill because this is all you're getting of it."

She tossed aside the sheet, marched her to suitcase, marched to the bathroom ignoring the drawn out whistle, shut the door and showered, leaving him by the bed with his mouth curved into a silly grin. When she came out she was covered in a one-piece and a silk sarong, turning anticipation into disappointment, his grin into a pout. She marched to the adjoining door that he'd left open, slammed it closed, and locked it from her side while giving him that 'don't do it again' glare.

Then she walked out and left him trailing behind, knowing very well that he was smirking like an idiot.

She did fifty laps, he did sixty, and when she refused to dip into the early morning calmness of the warm ocean waters with him, he carried her to those warm waters even though she refused to speak with him. He was the most aggravating man she'd ever met.

By noon he knew almost everything about her. How her brother had gotten into trouble with the law and how Hidalgo Arquero had convinced the judge to reconsider his verdict. How at twelve she was skipping classes, wanting to be cool like her brother, how Mr. Arquero long before he was governor had driven her around town showing her the bad side. How he'd taken her on his own time to museums, to a beach resort and to a fine restaurant to show her what could be if she worked hard. How he phoned her every week night to make certain she was doing her homework.

She told Drew how Hidalgo Arquero had attended her high school graduation, put her through university when her mother was having trouble making ends meet and how he was seated in the first row with her mother the day she received her Bachelor of Science. She was waiting for Drew to say something silly, chauvinistic or snide. He didn't. He just sat and listened to how Hidalgo Arquero had sent her to aviator school, the one thing she couldn't stop thinking about, dreaming about since her first time in a plane with him when she was fourteen, her nose stuck to the porthole. Then, one day, out of the blue, she got a call for an interview from Pacific Air. Once again his doing, though she'd proven herself and got the job flying Asian routes until a few years later when he called her with the proposition that she fly his personal jet. The decision was a no-brainer. He was like a father to her and, once each year, he took her to that same restaurant.

"He sounds like quite a guy."

"He's the best."

"What happened to your brother, something good?"

"He's a junior partner at Arquero-Duval."

"You think a lot of him, the governor."

"He's like a father to me. I love the man. If it weren't for him I'd be doing drugs and hooking to stay happy. So, yeah, I think a lot of him. You got something smart to say?"

He didn't, and by dinner he knew everything about her brother and a woman named Virginia Meadows who took him under her wing.

By midnight, under the moon, on a blanket laid out over cooling sand, she knew what he wanted her to know. He grew up in New York where his parents still lived. He got a degree in Behavioral Psychology, got bored and moved to L.A. where he worked undercover with some not so nice people. The leather, the guns and the dagger, they weren't a Halloween costume. They were his sole protection. He had no friends, he couldn't afford friends. Friends could get him killed.

When she asked about him and the governor, he told her the truth. He'd just met the man and was in Miami on special assignment. So far, he liked the guy.

And the man on the plane, she asked? He answered: an evil man who was about to do something good for once in his life.

Diane knew not to ask more. She fell asleep huddled into his arms, despite wanting more time with him. She woke the next morning lying beside crumpled clothes, half relieved, half disappointed that she was in bed alone.

55

Friday morning she called his room. He didn't pick up. She went to the restaurant. He wasn't there either and she was angry. Until a waiter turned her by her shoulders and pointed to the table he'd set in the sand for the man who'd been waiting at least an hour.

He saw her coming, she knew he did. God, she wanted to smack him. He was infuriating. He wasn't standing. He wasn't acknowledging her, just sitting with his legs stretched out into the sand and gazing towards the horizon.

"I take it I'm supposed to join you here, since you haven't had time to pick-up anyone else."

"I thought that since we're getting married we should start being a little more romantic."

"You mean like pulling out my chair."

He stood. "Is that a yes? You'll marry me?"

"Yes, Drew, I will marry you," she paused, patting his cheek, "like everything else, in your dreams."

"Darling," he grinned at the way she rolled her eyes. If she didn't know something was happening, he did. "You have a couple of choices: spend the day by yourself, or come with me and play the part of a devoted wife. Your choice, but I'm dead serious, Diane. If you can't play a convincing wife, you stay here. This is work, not play."

"Is this for the governor?"

"It is, until late afternoon when I finish on my own what I have to do and you get to do more shopping and make other girls jealous by how beautiful you are. Just don't cheat on your husband."

He was dead serious, and charming. Who was this guy who'd come from nowhere to confuse her? She was half-thinking that she could marry a guy like that, if it weren't for the guns, the knives and the arrogance.

She put down her cup. "I'm in."

They ate breakfast as he explained in the vaguest terms what she had to do. When they were finished they drove into town where he bought her a ring, sliding it onto her finger without any emotion or the Drew Carling glibness she had expected.

At the marina he took her shoes in one hand, her hand in the other. She had four things to do: remain quiet, be beautiful, be sophisticated, and say nothing. She was, for the next hour, Mrs. Drew Carling.

They circled the courtyard marina along three main docks, dissecting the basin slip by slip until they reached the one yacht whose slip number he knew. The man's name was Dan Adams, captain of the Burnt Out, the fifty-footer Mr. and Mrs. Drew Carling wanted to reserve for a full week of offshore fishing during the first week of January.

Adams had barely docked his fishing yacht and secured his lines at the end of a half-day fishing trip before Mr. Carling asked permission to board for a tour of the amenities and to negotiate a week-long contract for him, his wife, and four friends. They shook hands and boarded; Mrs. Carling remained on the dock. Her husband hadn't told her, but he didn't want her anywhere near such an inhumane creature as Adams.

Adams was fifty-six, his once flowing blond hair now thinned and streaked with grey. His once athletic form had transmuted into that of a man who had succumbed to the good life, his midriff expanded by several inches, his chest sunken by the same measure, giving him the appearance of a man who hadn't felt the strain of physical labour once in his life. His face and arms were dark from years in the sun, his eyes and his face streaked with fine red lines, Drew knew, from years of drinking to forget. Those years, he also knew, were over.

Drew Carling smiled and shook hands before disembarking. New Year's Eve was out of the question, as was the first of the year. They settled on the third to the eighth and Carling gave Adams five thousand in hundreds as a non-refundable deposit. Drew Carling walked away with a simple receipt, wiping his hands on his shirt. Adams had already disappeared into the lower cabin.

At the end of the dock Drew swirled Diane into his arms gently and without warning, kissing her just as gently and releasing her with as little warning, holding her hand as they strode to the car. She was breathless, barely able to maintain his pace, searching for something to say.

At the car:

"Thank you. I could have done this alone, but you being there made me much more convincing."

"But that wasn't a thank-you kiss."

"Yes, it was. Thank you for being sweet and innocent and pure. Thank you for giving me balance." He turned over the engine, peering through the windshield. "I've killed three men, because I had to. Him, back there on the boat, I almost killed because I wanted to. So, yes, thank you."

"What?"

"You're cleared, remember?"

"So why didn't you kill him, because I was with you?"

Drew drove off, not looking at her. "No, I didn't kill him because I'm going to marry you on Valentine's Day. Something really good has recently happened to me, including you, Mrs. Carling, and killing that slime would have ruined my chances with you."

"I'm not marrying you, Drew. I'm not even dating you and I'm certainly not sleeping with you. Cloak and dagger isn't my thing. All I want is my job, not some secret agent guy who comes home to say 'what's for dinner, and, by the way, honey, I killed someone today'."

"Good."

"Good?"

"Yeah, good, because if you're not sleeping with me you're certainly not sleeping with anyone else. I mean, why would you? It's not like you're that hard up. And by the way, honey, the three guys I killed were trying very hard to kill me. Not like in the movies, I mean with ten millimetres and sawed-off shotguns. So what are you so pissed about, that I'm alive? Just remember that I'm one of the good guys."

Her tiny frame sank into her seat. She had nothing to say and Miami was 168 miles away. Screw him. Her head ached. She might have held his hand, but he drove with this right hand, the left hanging over the door. She might have kissed him, but he hadn't looked at her once. She spent three hours thinking of something to say, but she knew nothing would come out right. All she knew was that she wasn't in any condition to fly.

*

At the hotel in Miami, on Ocean Drive, he halted the valet parking attendant with an open hand and his badge.

"Is this what it's like being married? Christ, I hope not." He paused, uncertain. "You'll never know what happened today, Diane, because I don't talk in my sleep. Those other guys, the ones you're fixed on, they wanted me seriously dead. I did them first because I'm good and because I had to stay alive for you." He reached over to open her door. "On the brighter side, you're on your own tonight. But if you don't propose to me by the time we land in Sacramento, I'll be leaving for L.A. and you won't see me again. I mean that, munchkin. So don't wait too long and don't drink too much because you seem a little upset. So let's say that we'll depart tomorrow at whatever time you feel is right. Leave a message for me at the desk when you decide. Have a good evening."

"Is Drew your real name?"

"Given to me by the only parents I ever knew."

"Can I ask where you're going?"

"No."

She stepped from the car. "Thank you."

"You're welcome...for what?"

"For not being killed. I'll be ready for departure at your convenience any time after 7:00 AM. Goodnight"

She walked away, thinking he would wait, or call out to her to wait, or invite her to dinner, or something. He didn't. All she heard was the groan of a performance engine.

56

Friday Night Drew Carling went into foreign territory, the marina where his sister docked her boat, part of him hoping he wouldn't see her.

He had no clue. He didn't know what he would say or how she would react; he simply stood by the portside and called out "Francesca Maria." Moments later a stunning woman stepped onto the afterdeck dressed in white slacks and a nautical sweater. Francesca stood paralyzed, her eyes flooding as he came towards her open arms. They hugged for long moments, brother and sister crying for having recently recalled precious past moments lost to them for so long and now slowly recovered moment by moment.

When the tears dried she gave her brother the royal tour, suggesting an early evening cruise. She could prepare a dinner at anchor and they could talk. Drew was tempted, asking instead whether they could dine out being that he was leaving Miami early the next day. Deidre agreed.

Ocean Drive was teeming with young and old, freaks and the fashionable, half-dressed and bikini-clad women, stylish and garish men. Deidre hadn't changed and Drew couldn't. Either way, they caught the eyes of most passers-by as they strolled through one sidewalk restaurant to another searching for Mexican which they thought was appropriate, testing their new names, though neither was certain they could abandon the only pasts they knew.

He was handsome, she was gorgeous, 5'10 and 5'8,

respectively, and elegant together. They walked arm in arm, leaning into each other, sometimes stopping to laugh, sometimes stopping to wipe away a single threatening tear.

They were happy because Hidalgo had brought them together after so many years, sad because they couldn't yet say that they loved each other. Diego couldn't remember ever once being a hero to his sisters, and Francesca couldn't remember that he ever once was. That was the saddest part for both, not remembering what their papá had known, that he'd remembered and had suffered throughout all those years without them. They felt good holding hands, squeezing often to dissipate the emotion of the evening. It felt right.

Neither was very hungry once the meal was served, the wine was more important, serving to wet dry throats as much as to whet the desire and need to know more, each one anxious to meet their little sister. Then he saw her sauntering towards them, swaying her hips from side to side, her short pleated skirt swaying in concert, her bare legs tanned and smooth, perfection personified, heads turning from both sides of the café to pay homage to natural beauty. She was a dream, an angel. She was his dream, his angel. Her smile though wasn't right; her pursed lips, her brown, piercing eyes warning of danger. He'd seen the look before, a split second before pulling the trigger.

She wanted to kill him.

Francesca began, "What is it, Diego? What's wrong? You look as though you're about to…"

He went to stand, falling back, his thin smile vanishing.

Diane stopped abruptly at the table, her skirt swirling against her thighs, sneering, which he thought wasn't so good, which he knew was not good at all.

"Diego, really. So what happened to Drew, my devoted fiancé?" She eyed Deidre, curling her upper lip into a snarl, then to Drew. "Isn't this the most amazing coincidence?

420

Here I am, alone, all dressed up in my new designer outfit that you wanted me to buy, with nowhere to go. And here you are, here, with this… whatever she is, just two months before our wedding. And you're holding hands. Isn't that so sweet? And, oh my, look at those teary eyes. You've been crying, sweetheart."

"Diane it isn't like that, this lady is…"

"I know who she is. She's your secret contact, OO-shithead."

She pivoted from the hip, reaching across the table behind her, pouring that carafe of ice water over his head in one fluid motion as she reached for the full carafe on his table, adding that two litres to the deluge as Deidre sat amazed, bewildered and amused with her hands clamped over her mouth and her eyes wide open.

"Enjoy your one-night stand, h-o-n-e-y. I hope she's worth it." She struggled with her ring, dropping the band into his wineglass and sauntering away to loud applause.

Drew jumped to his feet amidst a collection of miniature ice sculptures pelting the sidewalk at his feet, his hair dripping, everything dripping, calling after her.

"I hope you don't think this means you're not going to marry me, munchkin," he shouted over the clamour. "You love me, Diane! Admit it! Jealous women are always women in love. And you do love me! I know you do. And by the way, h-o-n-e-y, this beautiful woman is my sister. I love you."

She was gone.

He sat, after bowing to the audience, the thunderous applause subsiding. Out of necessity he showed his badge before removing his jacket. The guns were part of him, a second skin, though even his sister raised an eyebrow at the stiletto strapped to his forearm.

"What was that all about?"

"She's the governor's personal pilot and a little

eccentric. She loves me, but she's had some trouble adjusting to me. What can I say?"

"What you should say is 'thanks, sis, I've had a great time catching up, but I love that girl'. What are you doing sitting here, dripping, when you should be running after her?"

"I'll see her tomorrow when I'm dry and her thermostat's turned down a bit. Really, we've just been flirting for a few days, nothing serious."

Deidre reached for his glass, examining the ring. "A few days, really? This isn't a dime store bauble."

"Don't ask, Francesca. It's a need to know situation. I got caught up in the moment when I needed realism. She's not the bauble type."

"Yeah, well, your realism is now by herself in South Beach and pretty hot in case you didn't notice under the barrage of ice. Good luck with that." Deidre signalled for the bill. "By the way, brother, I don't believe a word of what you just said and I sure as hell wouldn't fly with her tomorrow. If I were you, I'd take a bus or fly to Sacramento with me."

*

Drew and Deidre finished their wine, ending their evening onboard Deidre's Life's Compensation. They had decided not to try recapturing their lost years in one night, not to force emotions that would come to them naturally over time. Warm embraces and kisses weren't inherent to either of them, a common barrier they instinctively lowered before she watched him disappear into a starlit night amongst shining white hulls, masts and rigging.

They would see each other in a couple of days. She was flying out late the next day, a little nervous about meeting Gabriella on Sunday at the mansion, very nervous about meeting Maria and Fernando at Christmas.

Drew wasn't. He was worried about Diane, worried that

he was a jerk. He rarely dated because his dates rarely lasted. Besides, he justified, women were too possessive to understand his work for which reason he never explained his work, telling most that he worked Burglary. Diane was no exception.

He declined Deidre's offer to hitch a ride, wanting to give her space, wanting Diane to share his space for the short time they had left. He decided they would fly home early Sunday. They would spend Saturday doing whatever she wanted and Saturday evening she could pick the restaurant, whatever she wanted, wherever she wanted to wear her new outfits. She was obviously upset about that. Sunday they would fly home, they would shake hands, he would thank her for everything and they would forget each other in a week. She would do her pilot thing and he needed to get his head around five million before sliding back into the slime of L.A.'s real nightlife.

At the hotel he thought to call her room to apologize, to invite her for a nightcap. Although if she wasn't stomping around her room, pissed with him, she'd be sleeping and she needed her sleep... unless they weren't flying out until Sunday. Until he read the note she'd left for him at the desk. Departure time was 6:00 AM, Saturday. He snorted, folding the terse note on the way to his room.

She was royally pissed.

57
December 18th, of this Year

Saturday Drew woke blurry-eyed at four, figuring thirty
minutes to shower and shave, thirty to get to the airport and
sixty to grovel before take-off. He left his room at 4:30 with
his guns and stiletto tucked into his sports bag. It was a
beginning, the least he figured he could do.

At the desk he asked for a taxi, thinking he would call
her room and invite her to ride with him. She was gone.

He arrived at the airport at 4:55, halted by security at the
Private Departures gate five minutes later, told that Captain
Quinn had departed the previous evening at 10:00 PM. He
checked his watch. She was probably at home in her bed.
*

Diane Quinn arrived home at two AM local time,
exhausted. She knew what she had to say, what she had to
write. She'd been stoic since leaving Miami. He wasn't
worth dying for and he certainly wasn't worth ruining her
reputation or losing the respect of the governor.

Sleeping was out of the question. She showered and
dressed in her fleecy bathrobe to write her letter. At seven
she called Governor Arquero's office and was put through.
She only used his private number when flights were
involved, even though, technically, such was the case. And,
as usual, he made time for her, inviting her to join him for
breakfast in his private study.

She arrived at the Capitol promptly at eight.

"Good morning, Governor."

"Diane we don't see other often enough." He stepped back to appreciate her. "You are absolutely delightful, possibly a new ensemble from Miami?"

"Yes, sir, not what I usually wear on a Saturday morning, nevertheless appropriate for what I have to say."

"Your tone tells me the hour might not be too early for a light mimosa." Hidalgo went to the bar for a bottle of Dom Pérignon, extricating the cork and adding a small amount to the glasses half-filled with orange juice. "Your mother and brother are well? This isn't about them?"

She sipped from her glass. "No, sir, this is about me. I'm resigning from your service."

Hidalgo's expression remained pleasant, unperturbed. "Then, as we enjoy our breakfast, you must tell me why in detail. Money, vacation time and hours aren't issues; these are simple adjustments between close friends. You know that, so what reasons have developed so abruptly and so early on a Saturday morning?"

"First, sir, let me say that I have always tried to make you and my mother proud of me. I can't ever repay..."

Hidalgo put up a hand. "No more talk of the past or talk of pride that never ceases on my part. Tell me instead what has made you so dejected."

Diane took a deep breath and sipped her drink. "I let you down. I flew Detective Carling to Miami, as you instructed. And I accompanied him to Key West. When he was finished with the man on the boat we returned to Miami and last night I flew home."

"Which is what a pilot does, ¿no es verdad?"

"Yes sir. The thing is; I flew home alone without Detective Carling. I left him a note advising him of an early departure today, by which time I was in Sacramento."

"You left him stranded, on purpose? You did so

425

intentionally?"

"Yes sir, I did. I don't like him very much. He was flirting with me a little, innocently, telling me I was going to marry him on Valentine's Day and that I was going to have his children. Nothing happened, and I suppose I did enjoy the attention. Working for you can be a little time-consuming, a little hard a girl's love life."

Hidalgo was himself just learning to smile, although his eyes were bright and happy. He was relieved. "So he did nothing but flirt with an entirely lovely young woman, and you left him."

"Yes."

"Is he still alive? You left him with no other injury beyond his damaged pride?"

"He was when I last saw him. He left me in Miami yesterday afternoon. He said he had something to do. I thought it was police business. I bought six new outfits, sir, because I went unprepared. I thought I was going to spend time at the beach while I waited for him. And I would have been content to stay in Miami, until he asked me to go with him to Key West. So I thought if we were going to spend a few days together that I would at least wear something different each day, something nice."

"So this is a girl thing. You bought new outfits and he completely and rudely disregarded your feelings."

"No, because I really don't like him. He's so into himself. I mean, who wears a knife on his arm? I mean, really. And how many guns does a guy need? The thing is, sir, yesterday, after he left me, I changed and went to dinner."

"In one of your new outfits, I imagine, looking very lovely as you always do."

She shrugged. "Anyway, I saw him at a restaurant with some woman he'd picked-up for a one-night stand. They were acting like children, crying and holding hands, like

426

he'd never been with a woman before. He was pathetic."

"Was he gentleman enough to introduce you to this woman, Diane?"

"I don't believe so. And why would he? The man's an absolute liar. Anyway, I didn't stay very long. I can't believe he was so shallow, watching me buy all my new outfits, helping me pick them out and then lying to me so he could spend the night with an overpriced escort. I mean, really. How desperate is that? He even told me he's never been to Miami." She went to sip her mimosa from an empty glass. Hidalgo corrected the situation and sat back. "Sir, I poured two really big carafes of ice water over his head and left him sitting with her looking a little ridiculous, which he deserved." She took a deep breath. "When I calmed down I flew home to write my letter. I was fine to fly, sir. I would never endanger the plane."

Hidalgo burst into a raucous laughter, slowing by degree.

"I'm sorry, Diane. You provoked certain images in my head. And, yes, he did deserve such decisive action on your part. So you really don't like him, nor should you under such unforgivable circumstances. But tell me about this woman. Was she attractive? Can you describe her?"

"Sir, this is my letter of resignation, and with it a cheque to cover his return flight."

Hidalgo accepted the envelope, tearing the letter and cheque into small pieces. "Your resignation is denied and Drew Carling can return on his own, insufficient punishment for how he's mistreated you. He will also reimburse you entirely for the cost of your new wardrobe immediately upon his return."

"Sir, he did offer to pay. I didn't let him, not that I believed that he would or that I needed him to."

"A fact which speaks well of you and does not absolve him: a wrong he will make right. Now please, Diane, tell me what you remember about his companion."

"Why are you even interested? It's creepy, paying to be with a woman."

"Please, humour me. Not that you haven't already."

Diane put aside her glass, lacing her hands in her lap.

"She wasn't very tall, skinny, green eyes if they were real and reddish-blonde hair that might be real. She was wearing too much make-up and perfume and expensive clothes. Nautical, if you like that sort of thing. Her jewellery looked expensive, diamonds, if they were real, when sapphires would have been a better choice. Maybe she got dressed too quickly."

He chortled. "And you say that you didn't stay very long?"

"It's not a girl thing, sir. I went for training with the State Police after you were elected. Remember? Besides, even though I might have liked company for dinner, she was definitely more his type. I hope when he woke up he still had his wallet."

She sat quietly, watching him think, watching him organize his thoughts.

Long moments later: "He did nothing to offend you, to hurt you in any way?"

"No, sir, he did not."

"And you despise him thoroughly. I can see that you do. He's a scoundrel."

"Sir, he's a jerk, but I suppose he's a good cop, just a little over the top with that greasy, leather, bad-boy thing. Anyway, I don't want anything bad to happen to him. I just don't want to see him again. I can't deal with liars and cheats."

"He will be appropriately punished, Diane. I assure you. However may I first tell you a few things about him, in strict confidence, as a senior employee of Arquero-Duval and personal aid to the governor? You must tell no one,

Diane. I mean no one." She nodded. "Drew Carling, contrary to the way he's treated you, is a fine young man. I assure you that he's not a liar and he's not a cheat, although possibly somewhat over the top as you say. The weapons, the leather, the hairstyle, they are requisite tools of his profession, a profession I hope he will one day soon decide to terminate. The woman you saw him with last night is his sister, the first time they have seen each other in twenty-one years. I must assume that's why they were crying, Diane. Her real name is Francesca Maria and tomorrow she will meet Gabriella Martina, their younger sister for the first time in as many years. Gabriella recently, as you might know, flew into our hearts from New Orleans by way of some very courageous people who took upon their shoulders the decision to bring her home on my behalf, people whose names I shall never discover. Were I to discover their names I would convey my warmest gratitude. As for Drew, his real name, Diane, is…"

Her chest was heaving, her face drawn, tears beginning to drip into her lap. "…Diego. But, sir, he told me Drew Carling was his real name. I asked him."

"And he told you the truth. He is also Diego Hidalgo Arquero-Duval. He's my son, Diane, recently brought home to me along with his sisters after a forced absence of many years. I remember telling you a little of their story over a few of our enjoyable dinners together."

She blanched, shaking her head in disbelief. Her mouth was instantly dry, her face and palms wet. "What did I do?"

"I suppose what any woman would have done after being misled in such an inexcusable fashion. He should have told you, at least in part." His mouth curved into a smile. "However, in his weak defence, I must say that I was also once as arrogant. I wanted to be different from other boys. I wore a ponytail and black leather before he was born and his mother, before she came to love me, she also believed that I was despicable and arrogant by trying to impress her with my bright red Mustang. So I suppose I must accept much of the blame for the way he appears and acts towards a lovely young woman. I might also tell you that, remembering Francesca as a very young girl, you probably made her laugh incorrigibly by dampening her brother's spirit."

"He rented a Mustang."

"Like father, like son."

"I ruined his evening, and his sister's."

"You ruined nothing at all."

"Sir, I can be in Miami in eight hours."

"No. You cannot and you will not. I would not endanger you that way. What I need is for you to join me at dinner this evening and I won't accept an excuse. The usual place, if I may suggest, and my car will arrive at your home at 6:30. Please wear one of your new Miami outfits. I would like to see for myself what Drew Carling sacrificed by his careless lack of attention to you. Drew Carling, Diane, whether he remains Drew or rediscovers Diego will be his choice. Is that understood, young lady?"

"I understand. Thank you, sir. And I'm so happy for you, for your family. We can do dinner another time, Hidalgo. You should be with them. And your daughter, she was really beautiful and elegant. I'm so embarrassed. What I said I…"

"Six-thirty, Diane, and dressed to kill. I will accept nothing less from a woman who epitomizes such beauty and charm." He smirked. "I'll reserve our usual corner." He stood. "However I believe breakfast would be anti-climactic at this point, young lady. Now give me a hug, wipe your eyes, and leave me to anticipate our evening. I will also speak with Virginia Meadows to see what we can do about improving your remuneration and your social life. We can't have you entertaining further thoughts of a better life elsewhere."

He put a finger to his lips and she knew not to talk.

*

When Diane was gone Hidalgo called his son to ask where he was and how he was doing, whether he had survived the ice storm and sudden downpour from the night before that the weather station hadn't predicted.

Drew didn't see the humour. He was at the Miami airport, standing by, desperately hopeful for a cancellation or a no-show one week before Christmas, surrounded by chaos. Apparently Captain Quinn had misunderstood her own instructions, which wasn't her fault. If anything the misunderstanding was his. She shouldn't be reprimanded.

Hidalgo agreed. He told Drew that his First-Class ticket was waiting for him at Client Services and that he wanted to have dinner with his son in Sacramento that evening, alone. His driver would arrive at the hotel in time for a 7:00 PM reservation at El Hogar. They had much to talk about and he was to come dressed appropriately for dinner in an exclusive restaurant, not an all-out street war with drug dealers.

Before they disconnected Hidalgo told his son that the next day which was meant for family was not meant to exclude certain significant others who were not yet family. Drew didn't understand and Hidalgo didn't feel the need to explain further.

When they disconnected Hidalgo called in his new assistant. He required a reservation for two at El Hogar, the usual table, and a dozen carnations were to be delivered anonymously that afternoon to Ms. Diane Quinn. When he was finished he called Virginia Meadows and invited himself to a peaceful dinner.

He couldn't and wouldn't go to his parents' for what was now a rare home-cooked meal. Knowing what they would think of him for keeping such a wonderful secret from them for so long was difficult enough. Christmas, he believed, would be the best and the second worst day of his life. Yet, what choice did he have?

58

Saturday Gabriella moved in to her new condo with Anita Juárez to help her. By five o'clock all the deliveries were made and either placed or put away. Gabriella Martina was home, with nothing in the fridge, so they ordered pizza and talked until Anita left at nine. That night in particular she didn't want to stay. She couldn't.

The Thursday before, Gabriella woke propping herself onto an elbow waiting for Anita to stir so she could begin where she'd left off the night before. She had so many questions. She'd decided against living at the ocean, favouring the second condo they'd visited, the one with the two bedrooms and big kitchen so that Anita could visit whenever she wanted and maybe Francesca would come also and they could all be girlfriends. The one Anita had assured her she would soon come to appreciate the most. The rest of the week was spent shopping, or speaking with her father on the phone when Anita wasn't nearby.

She asked Anita how her father could afford the five million dollars; Anita responded that he could very easily. And that the money was rightfully hers as his daughter. He was one of the wealthiest men in the state, one of the most generous and kind.

Not to mention one of the most handsome, gallant, and one of the loneliest, Gabriella added into a silent room.

Through the day and night and into Friday she was happier with each passing moment, being with her new friend. She hadn't thought of New Orleans once. And Saturday was no different. A bottle of twenty-year Paulliac accompanied the all-dressed perfectly until Anita left, and left Gabriella with a lot to contemplate.

For Francesca she'd bought a collection of silk scarves, not knowing what colour to choose, and for Diego a gold money clip. Anita had cautioned her that, because she was now well-to-do, she should not be excessive in her gifts. Her brother and sister did not require expensive gifts to once again love her. They would, very soon, without any encouragement. For her father she bought something very special, on her own, something that Anita couldn't help her with.

Anita felt strange driving the 60 miles to her home, alone for the first time in several days and not being chauffeured in a limo. She felt even worse walking through her front door, knowing that he knew, knowing that he wouldn't leave his post even were she to insist. He was under direct orders from the governor. He was there to protect her until the thirty-first at midnight. She chortled, when she might invite him in for a drink.

To the officer she was La Bonita. She always would be. He knew; they all knew that something had happened. He greeted her with a sincere smile and opened her door, pausing a moment to wish her a pleasant weekend and to tell her that he'd placed a package from the governor on her sofa table. He smiled again and closed the door.

The envelope was bright green with a single red bow in one corner. She dropped it onto the table, shrugged off her coat and went to her bar where she poured a generous cognac. She went for the package, dropped it onto the sofa beside her and stared at her Christmas present from the governor, not Cacique, not Hidalgo, the governor. She fought through her first glass not to open it. He'd already ruined her week, her month, her new career and her life.

What more could he take from her?

With her second snifter filled halfway she peeled away the bow. There was no letter. Instead she found a card wishing her great success in her new life and career. He would miss her deeply; she had always been a good friend in the most difficult times. He would, as always, think of her with fondness.

She tore the card in half, and in half again, throwing the pieces into the air. ¡Idiota!

Inside the envelope was another smaller envelope, thicker than the first. Inside that were travel and flight coupons for a one-week Caribbean cruise for two leaving Miami on the 24th, returning on the 03rd of January. The flights were First-Class seats departing one day before and returning one day after. She shredded the coupons and itinerary into tiny pieces and filled the air with confetti. ¡Ay! ¡Qué cobarde! ¡Estupido! Who did he believe she would take with her?

She sank into the soft cushions wondering why she wasn't crying. She wanted to. She wanted to throw something, at him. She wanted to scream at him and kick him. She wanted to tell him to his face for once that he was an idiot and a coward. Yet she couldn't, because he wasn't either of those things. Nor was he with her. Nor would he ever be.

She held the envelope to the lamp, her mind exhausted. One smaller envelope remained.

She sipped her cognac, placed the snifter on the table and opened the last gift, coughing a hoarse laugh. In her lap was a cheque for ten million dollars. She giggled. A ring, at most, would have cost him a few thousand.

She glanced at her new Lady Rolex. That was a gift from the heart, not a shameless pay-off.

She tore the cheque into a hundred little pieces and dropped them into the envelope. She didn't need or want his money. She slid onto the floor, gathered up each little shard of paper and dropped them into the envelope. She replaced the bow, went to the door, and asked the officer to make certain that the envelope was returned to sender.

Then she gulped her cognac, coughed, curled into a cushion on the sofa and stayed awake all night.
*

In her condo, tucked into her new bed, Gabriella wasn't sleeping either. She was too excited about her brother, her sister and Anita. Just for a few moments, every so often, she didn't like her father very much. She needed somebody she could talk with, not realizing exactly how close she was now living to her grandparents' home in Vallejo. Anita hadn't told her.
*

In Sacramento Hidalgo Arquero went to the Meadows' home for a late dinner. They were expecting him at eight. He arrived in his Mustang, a rare treat, the security detail trailing behind. By the time dessert was served Diane Quinn was up by ten grand a year, an increased uniform allowance and an extra week of paid vacation.

In just thirteen days security would be a thing of the past. He could come and go as he pleased, go to restaurants like normal people, be with his friends and family like normal people without a couple of big, black SUVs parked at the curb.

There was no talk of his future. Virginia was aware of his decision to spend his life in a leisure mode as much as he was aware of her disappointment and outspoken disapproval of that decision. She had reminded him of his first day at the office when he'd told her and the others that he wasn't about to abandon the troubled kids who needed him. That was all she had to say at the time. As far as she was concerned discussions were at an impasse and in no way resolved. She wasn't finished with him. He was the

436

essence of Arquero-Duval, no one else.

The storefront law office hadn't changed throughout his years in office, save for a few coats of paint and more modern equipment. Nor had the kids changed, they were still coming in hoping for something better. And what gave him the right to leave all that behind, much to his discredit? No, she wasn't finished with him.

However the evening wasn't for that, for that very reason. Heated debate was for the office, the evening was for homemade lasagna, good wine, good friends and well-kept secrets.

He'd carried his burden of guilt for so many years, feeling responsible for what happened. Now his guilt was in not telling his mother and father, Jennie or John the joyous news. Nor did he tell Virginia or her husband. He left them earlier than usual with warm praise for a delightful evening and an extra serving of lasagna wrapped in foil that he was not to put in the microwave, she reminded him.

He drove a circuitous route to the mansion with the top down to breathe the cool night air, certain that at least he'd done one thing right, that she would never again have a care or worry in her life.

*

Earlier in the day Diane went to the hairdresser and had her make-up done at the spa: her tradition when dining with Hidalgo. She'd done the same since the first time she and Mr. Arquero had gone to dinner in a fine restaurant, the first time she'd worn a pretty dress. Now he was Hidalgo, when they were alone or when she didn't think she was resigning. She'd felt like such a fool, but he never once made her feel that way.

All that afternoon she remembered the few times he'd spoken guardedly about his wife and his children, each time his expression stoic, his eyes sad. She'd felt so much sadness for him. She didn't know much about Gabriella,

437

Francesca or Diego, but he had told her a few stories about how Diego was his sisters' protector in all ways. How he wouldn't let the other boys at school tease them the way they did the other girls and how he bought them little gifts for no reason with his allowance. Now he had them back.

Drew had taken her to dinner and had eased her into the sea, ignoring her threats to drown him. My God! The way she'd spoken to Francesca. She would write him a letter, and another to Francesca, and ask Hidalgo to deliver them for her. Then she would go home and die of humiliation. How many terrible things had she said about him and his sister in front of his father?

The limo arrived at 6:30. Working for the governor required excellence. The chauffeur proffered his hand and she accepted his help. They knew each other by name, nothing much more, however decorum was always required.

At the restaurant, she knew to accept his hand once again, allowing him to escort her to the door where the owner of the restaurant took charge of her, escorting her to his most intimate corner table, one held ready for the convenience of the governor until 5:00 PM each day.

She was nervous. She'd acted like such a schoolgirl before boarding his 30 million dollar jet to fly home and pout. She was the jerk, not him.

She'd waited until the very last minute to put on her dress, not wanting to crease the silk, walking around her home in heels, panties and bra, a delicate diamond necklace and diamond studs. The dress cost 500 and she'd really wanted him to see her it. She was so tired of guys seeing her in her uniform. The silk was teal blue, décolleté enough to show a hint of her bra and short enough to show that her legs were flawless and tanned.

The minute or so she waited at the restaurant was an eternity spent staring into her moist palms, then:

"Waiter!" he called. "Yes you, could you please remove

438

all the ice water from this table and all the tables nearby. This gorgeous woman has a fetish for embarrassing her handsome and always charming dates."

The waiter obliged, grinning, and twenty dollars richer.

"Thank you, my good man."

"You! What are you doing here?"

"My guess, we were set up."

She cupped her flushed cheeks. "Drew, I'm so sorry."

"You know what's so cool, that a little thing like you can fly a big jet home across the country when most girls can't give directions to a cab to cross the city. That's really cool. And I'm the one's who's sorry, munchkin. I should have told you."

"Drew I know who you are, your poor sister. I am so absolutely ashamed."

"First off, she's far from poor, like light years, and she spent the rest of the night giggling at my expense. You also sparked memories between us. So thank you for that." He opened his suit jacket and pushed up his right sleeve. "See, nothing except a silk lining, like me. Now, may I join you...without an umbrella?"

She nodded. "It was funny, a little."

"Yes, a little, and I deserved every ounce."

"But I am going to scold Hidalgo when I see him."

"Ah, now he's Hidalgo, not Mr. Arquero or the governor?"

"I thought you were a VIP. I always call him Hidalgo when we're alone."

"I forgot. He's like a father to you."

"You should know. I'm so happy for all of you."

Drew ordered cocktails and the wine to accompany the meal.

"I was serious, you know."

"About what?"

"About us, you and me, about us getting married. I knew

the very first moment I scared you on the plane."

"You want to marry a munchkin. How nice for you."

"Yeah, I do. I'm quitting the force. I want a place like this and I do want a munchkin, you. And before you think I'm blind or stupid, you're stunning in blue silk and I love your hair cascading around your shoulders. And that little bit of embroidery on your bra peeking out isn't bad either." He raised his glass, touching his against hers. "Is everything else blue?"

"Yes they are, and very small...very small."

He inhaled an exaggerated breath, reaching into his pocket. "When I spoke with my father I didn't believe he wanted me to join him for an intimate candlelight dinner and soft music when a few hits at his mansion would do. So I took a chance." He opened the velvet box. Inside was a glittering titanium band. "I threw the other under my sister's boat last night, once I dried off. This one is yours, a friendship ring in case you won't marry me, which you will because I know how much you love me. Even Deidre says so." He took the ring from the box. "The inscription reads: To a beautiful munchkin from a total jerk. That's me. So you have to accept it. No one else I know can really wear it."

She took the ring, studying the inscription. "The date's wrong."

"Backdated to Thursday, the day you realized how much you love me."

"The day you broke into my room and checked me out under my sheets, the day you dropped me into the ocean."

"I eased you into the ocean, because I knew you wanted to feel my body against yours. I'm a cop, remember. I read faces. I also listened to your sweet voice on the beach until you fell asleep in my arms. Or don't you remember?"

"Maybe I was bored."

"Or enchanted, falling in love with me."

"God! Get over yourself."

She sipped her wine, her full attention on the ring. He sipped his, his full attention on her.

"Confession?"

"What now?"

"I didn't check you out. I wanted to, but I didn't. The first time I saw your bare little tush was when you wanted me to, when you took your time strutting to the bathroom and, oh yeah, bending over your suitcase. How obvious was that? I mean, really. Anyway, thanks for stopping my heart, if not my other moving parts."

Her eyes were chocolate saucers. "You're a complete pig, and how exactly did I get undressed in the first place?"

He shrugged. "I can't say. I'm pretty sure I laid you on the bed, unzipped you and left...after I kissed you. You did the rest, I guess."

He was reaching for her hand. Diane was at a precipice.

"I don't believe you." She watched him take her hand as though in slow motion, letting him slide the ring onto her finger. "Okay, so now we're friends, until you tell me you have three sisters. Friends, understood?"

He nodded. "Before and after we're married. The rest can wait a while now that I know I was right."

She blew out a sigh, rolling her eyes. "About what now, not that I think I want to know?"

"About your tush, how cute it is."

Even Diane had to giggle at that.

Dinner was served and throughout the sumptuous meal Diane let herself like the guy. She called him Drew because he was, though somehow she believed that would change very soon. She was forgetting who and what he was, thinking as he spoke in soft, fluctuating tones what he could be. Now that they had so much more to talk about, more to be honest about, more to enjoy without fear of disappointment or rejection, she was actually having a good time.

With dessert cleared away, their cognac snifters forgotten with barely a sip remaining, the difficult part came for Diane. How would the evening end, what would she do with him? What did he want to do with her? She wasn't going to sleep with him and Hidalgo wouldn't tolerate him being less than a gentleman. That was her protection. Still, he had that silly grin on his face and he was standing. Why was he standing without saying a word?

"Diane, thank you. It's been a very long day."

You absolute bastard, she thought. Why not just tell me to go home or get lost? Nice evening, but now I have to go get laid. She let him pull out her chair. "Thank you for another lovely evening."

He took her arm, leading her to the door. At the curb he chuckled, she didn't, at seeing the single official limo waiting for them.

She said, "That's mine."

He said, "No, that's ours."

What! She said, "No, it's mine, and now I really will scold Hidalgo for...."

"Scold him for what? The man's intuitive. He knows what women want." He filled his lungs with the fresh night air. "You can kiss me before we leave, if you want. I'm okay with it."

"You're okay with it?' She smacked his face. "In your dreams, remember?"

"My dreams of you would make you blush. And just so we're clear, I am not paying a cent for this dress until I see it on the floor with your flawless and naked body poised on a pedestal of blue silk or any of the other colours that grabbed you during your whirlwind spree."

"Get real. I'm out three grand for a couple dinners, one day at the beach and another at a marina and you think you're going to see me naked."

He nodded, checking his watch. "Yes, I do. Listen, Diane, I had a great time, you're a great girl. The thing is, the truth, I have a meeting I can't break."

She exhaled without inhaling. "Well good for you. Take a bus. That car's mine. You don't have your little guns, so I assume you're not leaving me to kill anyone. So have fun with her, Drew. And, by the way, you are a total jerk."

She twirled towards the limo, struggling to tug the ring from her finger, not expecting her feet to leave the ground.

"She's my oldest sister, munchkin…Deidre." With one hand he pressed their bodies tightly together. With his free hand he gently pressed their heads together, their lips into a warm kiss that she hated to want. When their lips parted, their noses touching, her breath was warm and sweet. "Oh, I forgot, you've already met her."

"Deidre's coming here for tomorrow, to meet Gabriella. I forgot."

"Yes, and we have to meet her in thirty minutes." He waited. "I said, we have to meet her, you know, at the airport…the place where you work." He chortled. "Did you really think I was leaving you?"

"No way, uh-uh, she's not expecting me. Now get your hand off my ass and put me down. People are staring."

"Let them. They're jealous that it's my hand on your ass and not theirs. And what's the big deal? Deidre wasn't expecting you last night either, yet things worked out." He squeezed her. "We're practically engaged."

"This is going too fast, Drew. I'm not family. Put me down!"

"Don't tell my father that. He has a different opinion on the subject that took me a while to understand. Now I do."

"Good, now put me down. I'm going home."

"No, you're not." He swept her into his arms, carrying her to the limo. He touched her feet gently to the sidewalk and opened the door. "Ms. Quinn…"

443

She straightened her dress. She needed something to do with her hands. "No. Drew, I practically called her a slut."

"She's one of you. She's on your side. That's the way you women are. She told me to run after you last night. She at least deserves a thank-you."

She wanted to smack his sheepish grin. Instead she gave in, twirling the ring on her finger. She knew she would hate herself in the morning, despite which she kissed him, whispering as she eased past him into the plush upholstery. "Don't you dare do anything to make me go for ice water, jerk."

59

At the airport Drew was forgotten, relegated to the lowly status of porter, and the initial apprehension Diane felt melted away in moments as the two women sauntered arm in arm through Arrivals to the limousine. By which time Deidre understood: her brother was an idiot.

In the rear he sat facing them, mute, listening to endless chatter on the way to Deidre's condo. Suddenly he was a cop sitting with a wealthy businesswoman and a female pilot who flew corporate jets at 500 mph. All he did was put bad guys in jail and nobody cared.

At her home Deidre told her brother to toss her luggage into a corner. She went for wine and glasses and wanted Diane to tell her and Drew everything she could about their father. She curled onto a sofa with Diane; Drew found his own place on a leather ottoman. They wanted to know about Maria and Fernando. Had she ever flown them? She had, many times, and still did. They were special people, she told them, unpretentious, and Maria continued to light candles for each of them every Sunday. They should expect a very emotional Christmas. They had no idea, she told them.

Had she ever been to the mansion? Yes, she had. Had she ever been to their grandparents' home? No, she hadn't. Did he have friends? Only a few that she knew, very close friends. Was he seeing anyone? No, he wasn't. He was always alone, except…"

"Except what?" Deidre asked

Diane thought for a moment. She wasn't talking about the governor. She was talking about her boss, Mr. Hidalgo Arquero, their father, not the Governor of California. She wasn't breaking any confidentiality rules.

There was one woman, she believed, everyone at Arquero-Duval and the Capitol had believed until…. Well, unfortunately, he'd waited too long.

Diane stood to leave at one AM, not feeling the least bit tired, wishing them a wonderful time with their father and Gabriella later that day, asking Deidre if she would mind calling a cab. She understood that brother and sister wanted more time together. Drew stood with her, ready to leave, disregarding her protests that she was capable of finding her way home across the city… if she could fly across the country. He didn't think so. He was escorting her home, no argument.

Instead Deidre tossed him the keys to her car telling him to be there at 11:00 AM, with Diane, not to bother coming without her, telling Diane that she'd be wearing slacks and a sweater, nothing fancy. Diane stood looking from one to the other, shaking her head, uttering excuses, repeating herself, pleading, frustrated that they weren't listening to her.

Deidre wiggled her way from the sofa and walked them to the door. The matter was settled. The two women hugged and pressed their cheeks together. She hugged her brother, ushered them out and closed the door, excited. She was going to have another sister.

The ride to Diane's Sacramento condo was quiet, each in their private world. Drew, though, shared his world with Diane in his arms, in his bed and in his life. He was certain they could work. He could leave the gutter and be the guy for her that he was on the weekends, whenever he had a weekend. He could be Diego for her.

Diane's agitated world was filled with images of

Hidalgo's quizzical expression as she would walk through the door of his home with Super Spy in just a few hours, images of what he would think, of what she had done that she didn't do. She imagined Drew serving the patrons of his dream restaurant with a dagger on his arm and guns strapped to his chest. That was a dream. That would never happen. She was Miss Professional Pilot and he was an undercover cop. How would that work? It wouldn't. It couldn't.

He was expecting a high-rise structure of glass and steel, elegant and sophisticated, surprised when he slowed to a stop in front of a three-story gated condo.

"I don't suppose you have a guest room."

"Drew, don't come by for me this morning. None of this will work. We've had fun, but you work in a dirty world, a world that scares me. I don't need to think of someone I like getting killed while I'm flying his father, his grandparents or anyone else. Hidalgo's too important to me."

"So, you don't have a guest room?"

"Why would I?"

"That's good, I like that. I've been avoiding asking if you have a boyfriend. I sort of assumed you didn't because of the way you've been coming on to me and you don't strike me as a cheater."

"Don't be an idiot, and I don't date. No one wants a woman who does what I do for someone like your father. Besides your father's personal staff are all single. The jobs are too demanding. Once they get serious they get transferred, no exceptions. He puts family first. So why would I possibly want a guy like you in my life? I don't."

"Yes, you do. So get over yourself. Listen, I've taken thousands of kilos off the streets and I've saved hundreds of kids from doing drugs. And here's something you don't know, Ms. Quinn. Several times each month I work with inner city kids to set them straight. And, yeah, I wear my guns and my knives to show them who's going to put them in prison, or possibly kill them if they go wrong. You're focusing on three pieces of shit. I'm a good guy, Diane. So I will be here at 10:30. Then we're going to Deidre's and my father's. You're going to meet Gabriella who's a real doll and I'm going to tell them all that I love you because I do. Do you have a problem with that, Ms. Quinn?" He intended no humour in his voice. He waited what seemed like a thousand and one heartbeats. "I believe I asked you a question, Ms. Quinn. Do you?"

She was on the verge of tears. The air was still, the quiet before the storm, to the point where he didn't know whether he was hearing his heart or Diane's. Apparently she did have a problem. He reached over to open her door, ready to fight another day, though not telling her that he wasn't giving up.

He was waiting.

She clamped a small hand over his wrist. "You can sleep on the couch, if you want, because it's late and if I look like shit in the morning it's because of you. I hope you're happy. And yes, if it makes your day, I'm beginning to like you even though you love yourself enough for both of us. That doesn't mean you're going to see anything very small and blue, or anything else."

He was good with that. As for Diane, she'd never before let herself be swept up between a man and steering wheel.

60

As much as Drew argued the need to make up the couch when she had a cozy and warm king-size, he slept on the couch. In the morning Diane sat in her living room with her coffee, watching him sleep like a baby without a care in the world, wondering how he could with all that he must have in his mind and in his past.

As he woke, one eye at a time, she admonished him that no one, absolutely no one, was to know that he'd spent the night. He agreed with a smirk, and she didn't believe him. She didn't think she ever would when he was like that. And no! She insisted, they could not shower together to save water. In fact he was going to shower in his hotel room where, hello, all his clothes were. Instead she made him breakfast and let him kiss her what she thought was at least a hundred times.

After breakfast he gave his word as a, he didn't know, a governor's son, that he wouldn't intrude on her privacy while she showered and dressed. And he didn't, which didn't mean he wasn't curious about the girl he was going to marry, listening, imagining, being a nuisance and calling out to her as he waited.

Her condo was quaint. She would have to move, he told her. Not a spoon was out of place in her working kitchen. Every utensil gleamed. He strolled around her bedroom as she showered, waiting to hear the water stop. He sat on her bed, which she'd made up with military precision, a teddy bear squeezed between matching shams. He meandered his way through the living room while she dressed behind the door he'd closed quietly. Nothing was cheap, everything chosen to blend, not be a focal point. In her little study not a pencil was out of place, one wall lined with books, a second dotted with photos of, he guessed, her mother and brother. With them were photos of Hidalgo at her graduations, sitting at a dinner table with her, and of Hidalgo standing with her in the companionway of the Citation X holding hands. Another was taken of her, Hidalgo, her mother and, he guessed, her brother, all standing in the reception area of Arquero-Duval. They had history. He was happy for her, sad for his sisters, for what Gibson had stolen from them. They had no such photographs or fond memories.

A third wall amazed him: a collection of framed certificates and awards. She was an honour student, first in her class, not just a pilot, but a captain, a certified aircraft mechanic, recognized for her volunteer work and, no way. He stared into the last two certificates, switching from one to the other. She was a prize-winning markswoman and a 3rd Dan. Crap. He had a psychology degree and had gone to bed how many nights with something cut, scraped or otherwise requiring attention. Lie with dogs, he thought.

Diane came out with her hair swept into a loose updo; he was sitting on the sofa. Her fifties-styled high-rise linen slacks were flared, a deep yellow and cinched at the waist with a dark green leather belt. A pale green, loose-fitting silk blouse with billowy sleeves completed the fashion statement in concert with yellow satin sandals and the diamond studs she'd worn the day before. She was, he thought, to die for.

At the hotel she waited in the lobby lounge expecting, she didn't know what. Until he walked from the elevator towards her in a black tailor-made suit, red open-collar silk shirt, black Italian loafers and a bright smile.

Okay, she mused. She might have been wrong. Maybe he had a chance. Not to mention she hadn't slept a wink thinking about the arrogant, self-infatuated, egotistical and patently annoying man approaching her with two small shopping bags dangling from one hand.

*

On the way to Deidre's he broached what hadn't been said previously. Neither he nor Deidre had spoken about Gabriella, not between themselves or with Diane, not wanting to spoil Deidre's anticipation of seeing her.

Diane recognized the difference in his voice, leaning into him, her mind a kaleidoscope of emotions and memories. He wasn't speaking matter-of-factly like a macho cop; he was telling her about his little sister. Gabriella hadn't lived a very good life, not her fault. She was a good kid with lots of hope. What he had to know was that Diane didn't have a problem with that because if she did...

She cut him off, recoiling, thanking him for thinking so little of her, reminding him of what she had told him on the beach that past Thursday about her life and her brother's before Hidalgo turned them around. She could have just as easily become a dancer, or worse, her brother a pimp or a drug dealer. So what was his problem? She liked Deidre very much and she would like Gabriella. He should be more concerned about what she thought of him, which wasn't very much at the moment.

At that he took the high road. He nodded his agreement and kept his mouth shut.

Moments later Deidre joined them, Diane thinking that 'nothing fancy' must mean fantastic. She and Deidre definitely shopped on different streets and she, too, had little shopping bags dangling from her hands.

Deidre was driving; Diego was sitting in the back. She didn't see any point in calling her brother by his adopted name. When she asked Diane what was wrong, and heard, she called her brother an idiot which he believed was entirely reasonable. From that point on they ignored him.

Turning into the governor's driveway, stopping at the gate to identify themselves to the security detail, Deidre began crying. Her sister was standing on the front steps of the elegant mansion, holding her father's hand. Diane patted her arm, reassuring her. Then she began crying, Drew wisely maintained his silence and low profile, stepping out to open Deidre's door as Hidalgo opened Diane's wearing an expression she'd never seen. He was beaming.

He took her hand, helping her out, putting an arm around her shoulder and offering his pocket hanky as they watched the two sisters kissing each other's wet face and hugging while their brother patiently waited his turn.

"Thank you, Diane, for joining us today. You have made my day complete."

"Thank you, Hidalgo. You've made my day a complete mess, not to mention my head. And don't think you're not in trouble with me, because you are." She wrapped an arm around his waist, pulling herself closer. "Thank you, Hidalgo. He's a real piece of work, but I think he's salvageable."

He took her hand. "Come, let's go inside. And may I say you are a vision of youthful beauty, undeniably enchanting. We're lucky men, he and I, to know you. However, should he at any time become a foolish one, you must let me know without delay and we'll have him arrested by reason of mental deficiency. We will never again let him see the light of day."

Inside, Gabriella went to Diane as though she were also a sister lost. She, too, wanted to know another side of her father and the three women huddled together on a luxurious daybed in the family room that had never before been used. Drew joined his father in the wine cellar. They spoke briefly of Diane, Hidalgo accepting his son's word when Drew replied to his last question in the negative.

"What does Diane know?"

"She knows that I wanted to kill him, which didn't do much to make her like me. She agreed to go with me as a diversion, which she did very well. He was paying more attention to her than me. He's expecting six of us in January, according to plan. Truth is; he's looking forward to three of her for a week."

"He'll soon have other concerns."

"He's lived the good life."

"And Diane is unaware of his future?"

"She is."

Hidalgo inspected two bottles. "And of the boat, Diego, what is the documentation which Claire Gibson was so reluctant to reveal in her letter?"

He didn't hesitate. "Burnt Out, the same boat he's had for twenty years. Sorry, Governor."

"Ironic. A name which I must assume he once chose to celebrate his vile destruction of pure innocence, not once giving credence to its eventual and true significance."

"I could have killed him easily, Governor, without so much as a blink. While I spoke with him I truly regretted bringing Diane with me, irrespective of immunity. I think if she hadn't been with me, he'd be dead now."

"Or did you regret having brought such a lovely young woman to within arm's reach of pure evil?"

"She remained on the dock, beyond anyone's reach but mine." Drew uncorked one bottle, his father the other. "By the way, I'm going to marry her in February, the 14th. Also, it'll take time; however I'm leaning towards Diego. It's who I am, who I should be. The hard part will be telling the good folks I know as my parents. Just thought you should know."

"The Carlings will always be part of your home, as they should be, and always welcome in mine. When you're ready

I would like you to invite them here on my behalf, to meet your sisters and Diane. I have no doubt they will enjoy the flight, although we shall have to wait to discover whether Captain Quinn has placed you on her No-Fly list. She's very particular, and seems somewhat unhappy with you at the moment. Why would that be?"

"It's a female thing. She misconstrued something I said."

"And what of Francesca's mild dissatisfaction with you, the same misunderstanding shared by the female bond?"

"You see my dilemma."

"As well as I do your inexperience with women. As for your wedding plans, I will consider them confirmed once I hear the announcement from a very special young lady…a very special young lady, Diego. ¿Comprendes lo que digo?"

Drew chuckled. "Do I have a choice? Between you, her, Deidre who's already taken sides, and now probably Gabriella, what options do I have? I think I'd rather tell Mendoza that I'm an undercover narc on his home turf."

"And what news do you have of Mendoza?"

"I should have kept the tail and the beard. It took me a full year to be convincing, then he takes me for a cop the moment he saw me, which isn't good. He got his own letter from the old girl, albeit somewhat less informative than yours. He's set to go. He's waiting for your word. The strange thing is; he doesn't want you involved. The Gibson woman seemed to believe he could do a better job. And, Governor, she made an excellent point."

"However we don't always get what we want. Do we?"

"Francine was your wife, but she was my mother, our mother. So let's have this conversation another time. Mendoza doesn't lose sleep at night, neither do I for what I do. You're a governor and a lawyer. You sit at a desk, or at tables in fancy restaurants. Pulling that trigger the right way is two things: instinctive and professional. You're neither.

You're not conditioned. Pardon the lecture, but amateurs generally don't kill very well. Believe me; you don't want your successor speaking into that red phone that I saw on your desk and talking about you, saying 'clemency denied, proceed with the execution'. I've seen a couple. It's not pretty."

"Thank you, Diego. However this crime of retribution has been twenty-one years in the making and, as agreed those many years ago with Señor Mendoza, we will participate actively and equally in its implementation. In the meantime, I would like you to return to Key West tomorrow. I want to be aware of his every move. You'll fly commercially, unfortunately. I believe my lovely pilot is due for some time off. I also believe she has too much on her mind at the moment to safely transport he who is, in fact, the source of her dilemma. Please return to us by Saturday to spend Christmas with your family. My office will make the travel arrangements."

"That might put a crunch in my wedding plans, Governor. You know, out of sight out of mind."

"Or, in this case, absence may make the heart grow fonder. The young lady has enough to think about without your further influence or distraction. Give her some space, Diego. And now we should return to the ladies. We have been sufficiently remiss in our attention towards them."

In the family room Deidre, Gabriella and Diane stopped talking in a way that would send out warnings to any man.
*

Previously:

Months and years would pass before the sisters would regain those lost years. Of greater importance was learning more about their father and the woman he let get away. Gabriella told her sister everything she knew about Anita Juárez: How she deeply loved their father, how they had been together for so many years, how their father was in denial, afraid to betray their mother, how she'd spent so much time with Anita that past week, how Anita had gone to New Orleans to find her and how her father was making such a huge mistake.

Diane agreed. She'd flown Anita many times. And, yes, everyone knew the governor was in denial, which wasn't to say that Anita was blameless. She wasn't. She was just as guilty of doing nothing. Even Maria and Fernando believed that Hidalgo should move on and not live his life in the shadows of the past.

Gabriella said, "You know our grandparents?"

"Yes, I do. Maria and Fernando have often invited me to join them for dinner when I've flown them somewhere." She glanced over her shoulder, knowing he wasn't near. "Hidalgo really shouldn't know that. It's sort of a secret. I can't imagine the hurt they'll feel when they discover you've been so close to them since Hidalgo found you, or the joy."

Diane lowered her head, staring into her ring.

"What?" Gabriella asked Diane. "What are you thinking?"

"I'm not thinking. This is not my business. Hidalgo has this all planned out. I'm not going to ruin his Christmas."

Deidre said, "Ruin it how? How does hooking him up with a woman spoil his Christmas?"

"It would, believe me. And I can't do that."

"Well I certainly can." Deidre countered. "Tell me how."

She was outnumbered, pinned between determined sisters. "I might know someone who can help us. She knows your grandparents very well."

"Who is she? Does Anita know her?" Gabriella asked.

"Anita knows everyone. What I can say is that she's someone who has missed you very much."

"Who is she, Diane? Tell us." Gabriella persisted.

"Please let me think this out." No one spoke. "Ladies, I didn't mean now. I meant tonight, at home, when I've got some space. God, I think you two are much worse than your brother."

Gabriella answered, "Does that mean you're beginning to love us too? He told me."

"Your brother's delusional, Gabriella. I don't think he's very stable, so don't believe a word he says." She feigned exasperation, letting the faint hint of a smile give her away. "Okay, what did he say?"

"When I asked who you were, he said you're the girl he's going to marry on Valentine's Day."

Deidre shrieked, "Say what!"

"No one's getting married. I just met the guy." She turned to Deidre. "Tell her, the ice water, coming home alone. Tell her."

Deidre ignored the attempt. "So do you love our brother? Because if you do that would pretty much make you family and entirely change the dynamics of your quandary."

"Your brother's a work in progress, one I wasn't expecting. Frankly, I like the two of you much more than I like him." She showed off her new ring. "But my quandary, Deidre, could change the dynamics between me and Hidalgo, which I won't let happen. So let me think about this."

"For how long, Diane?" Gabriella wanted to know.

"And we've got your back," Deidre added, "our big brother included. So don't worry about something that won't happen."

Deidre and Gabriella moved in closer.

"I'm going to regret this, I know. But give me until…"

61

Diane sat in awe, watching the Governor of California prepare a full Mexican dinner, giving each of the four specific instructions. She was dumbstruck watching him serve in an apron.

She was expecting a lot of tears when the evening came to an end, which didn't happen. Hidalgo insisted that Gabriella stay over. He didn't want her driving home alone at such a late hour. Deidre, who was not yet decided whether the world should know her as Francesca Maria, drove her brother to his hotel with Diane sitting in the front with her.

From his crunched position behind them, Drew suggested a nightcap, telling his sister that he could then drive Diane home later. Deidre declined, she had an early morning. And Diane answered without acknowledging him that she was tired. She hadn't slept well the night before. However she was certain he could find someone that he could drink pretty by closing time.

He whined that he was already with a two pretty women.

Deidre said, "He's whining. That is so pathetic."

"He is pathetic," Diane agreed.

"He does love you, though. He must have told us fifty or a hundred times at dinner, at least fifty."

"I don't know. I stopped listening. He's trying to convince himself. Like I told you and Gabriella, he's delusional. I can't imagine how he ever got to carry a gun."

"He's not hard on the eyes though."

"I've seen much better."

"So, we're good? We're going?"

"Yes, we're going."

Deidre peered into the rear-view mirror. "You heard the lady, lover boy. Looks like you're drinking alone." She leaned into the mirror, making direct eye contact. "And you'd better be drinking alone. Don't get all pouty and go do something stupid. Do you hear me?"

"I'll be gone for an entire week. Give a guy a break, one drink, ladies."

"Kiss the girl, and get out of my car."

He sighed, deeply, and loudly, pulling himself forward between the bucket seats. Deidre proffered her cheek. He kissed her first. Diane didn't bother, not giving an inch. He pushed back, opened his door and stepped out. He opened her door, reached in, undid her seatbelt and carried her out.

She was squirming, ordering him to put her down, pressed hard against him, her arms locked in, nose to nose, his hands firmly attached to what he knew was a very exquisite ass.

He didn't say a word. She couldn't. What she wanted was her arms around his neck as Deidre counted the seconds on her watch, leaning sideways for a better view. When he finished kissing her he let her feet touch the ground, holding her to steady her. When she caught her breath he helped her into the car, buckled her belt, said goodnight, and went inside.

Deidre could only say, "Wow!"

Diane could barely say, "Yeah, wow."

62

Monday Diego departed for Miami at noon with a new monogrammed money clip from his kid sister and a titanium pen set from Deidre. He also left with the keys to her yacht, keys she hesitatingly relinquished once he'd answered a few difficult seamanship questions, made him promise not to go through any of the drawers in her stateroom, and her father guaranteed the full value of the boat. His return flight was scheduled for Friday. His week was mapped out in his head.

Dan Adams wasn't the problem, Diane was. He thought size four, petite, and imagined a 32-B although he couldn't be sure. Monday evening, arriving at the marina, he called Deidre for help. He was far beyond his comfort zone. She didn't answer.

*

Gabriella woke early to cook breakfast for her father, constantly wiping tears from her eyes, showing him every few minutes the silver bracelet Drew had given her and the ruby earrings from Deidre. She loved them both, and she loved Diane. She hadn't awakened yet, she told him. She was still dreaming.

She made him promise to visit her new condo that week for dinner, before Christmas. And he did. She didn't say anything about Anita. She knew better.

At home she wanted all day to call Diane, forcing herself not to, until the soft chimes startled her and she

bolted for the phone.
*

Deidre was at the office by seven. Disappointed she couldn't tell anyone that her beautiful silk scarf was from her sister and the silver bracelet was from her big brother. How strange was that? And strangely, she didn't feel strange at all. Gabriella was a sweetheart and Diane was every guy's dream girl. As for Drew, he had a lot to learn about women and if he messed up he'd have a lot to explain. If he damaged her boat, she'd just kill him.

She didn't leave her office throughout most of the day until her secretary told her that Ms. Diane Quinn was calling.
*

Anita Juárez woke late. She didn't feel anger, she felt emptiness. She didn't hate the man; she was disappointed in him, which was worse. She dressed and went shopping. She had the perfect Christmas gift in mind for Gabriella and, although she didn't know them, she wouldn't exclude Deidre or Drew. She would simply ask Gabriella to deliver the gifts and say they were from someone who was happy for them. She bought nothing more for Hidalgo. She couldn't. Wondering what to do with what she had bought him was difficult enough.

Monday night she fell asleep after leaving Gabriella a message. Gabriella wasn't home.
*

In his office at the Capitol, Governor Hidalgo Arquero sat pensively staring at the two envelopes.

He'd spent most of night in his bedroom talking with Francine, telling her how their family was finally reunited, how lovely their daughters were and how well they had turned out. They were nice girls, good girls, and Diego was once again becoming their big brother. He was a good man, and would remain good. Nothing would happen to change that, he promised her.

He told her about Claire Gibson's letter and Miami. The vile creature who had taken her life so cruelly, tortured her and robbed her of her family, had two weeks remaining before he, Hidalgo, would strike the match that would engulf Scott Gibson in the dark fires of hell.

The first envelope was unsealed. Inside were ragged shards of paper. She was telling him goodbye, not to bother thinking of her as a friend. And he realized he'd stopped breathing.

The second envelope was sealed, from the offices of a law firm he knew, representatives of Claire Gibson's estate. Inside was a polite, perfunctory letter of explanation which he read several times not believing his eyes. With the letter was a cashier's cheque.

He, Hidalgo Arquero, was to disburse the 300 million dollars equally amongst his son, Diego Hidalgo, and his daughters, Francesca Maria and Gabriella Martina. Mrs. Claire Gibson's final spoken wish, the letter explained, was that they forgive her and seek to follow their father's path with their newfound wealth.

He folded the cheque, slipping it into his shirt pocket, remembering her letter three weeks earlier

*

Diane woke early, agitated. She had always wanted a sister to do girl things with, and now, without any warning she had a matching set. So what would happen with them if their brother went and did something stupid like getting himself killed? Why was he returning to Miami so soon? Why wasn't she flying him? Why did he need Deidre's yacht and why did he kiss her as though he really did love her? And why did he tell everyone they were getting married? They weren't.

She paced her condo in circles throughout the entire morning, composing the right words in her mind, fine

462

tuning her script to where she had no script at all. She didn't know what to say, or where to begin. What had she gotten herself into? And Hidalgo was a completely separate issue. She would probably never work again. She reached for the phone, dialled, asked the receptionist to connect her and prayed for the right words.

*

Gabriella and Deidre arrived at Diane's apartment while the late afternoon sun was still illuminating her living room with a warm, golden glow. They came in together, as planned, without knowing what to expect. They didn't recognize the older woman standing to greet them, yet they knew somehow to run to her, taken aback by Jennie Canyon's explosion of tears. Neither had she known, Diane hadn't told her over the phone what she should expect. She'd merely told Jennie that their meeting was requisite, regarding Hidalgo and without his knowledge. Yet Jennie knew her goddaughters immediately.

Diane wanted to leave them alone. She wasn't family. The three thought otherwise. They ordered in Chinese and spoke until midnight when Jennie went home, anxious to speak with her aging father early the next morning. At eighty-five John Canyon continued to put in a full workday.

Gabriella went home with her sister.

Diane went to bed, and sat staring at her phone. She hated herself, and kicked at the duvet. She punched her pillow, refusing to give in. She shrieked a high-pitched groan, and reached for the receiver.

"Yeah, what?"

"Yeah, what?" she repeated, disgusted. "That's how you answer a phone? Yeah, what? Are you that much of a misfit?"

"Who is this"?

"I'm your wife, jerk. Remember me, the one with the ice water?"

"I'm a drug dealer, remember?" Silence. "Can't sleep without me?"

"I thought I was calling Deidre."

He focused on the luminous dots of his watch. "At twelve-thirty? Some pilot you are. Ever heard of time zones?"

"Oh, shit. I'm sorry."

"No you're not. So what's up, munchkin? Checking to see if I'm alone?"

"No, I'm not, because I don't care. So, are you?"

"I am now. Good thing is I have her panties to remind me of her, how she felt when I held her in my arms and kissed her soft lips."

"I don't have to hear that, jerk."

"They're yours, munchkin. I took them from your bedroom when you were in the shower."

"You never stop, do you? I should have made you wait outside. What else did you take?"

"Your heart, I hope. That's why you're calling. You're worried. You don't believe I can pilot a little sixty-footer. Piece of cake. I crewed on yachts during my summer breaks for extra cash when I was a kid."

"You're going to Key West, to the marina?"

"I'm quitting the force so that I won't have to lie to you about what I do. Now go to sleep and dream of me. And, by the way, when I get home, I'm staying over."

"That's your dream, jerk."

She disconnected, jumping from her bed to rummage through her panty drawer. She snorted a giggle, crawling under the duvet to fall asleep purring.

63
December 21st of this Year

Tuesday morning Deidre monitored her messages. She returned her brother's call, telling him what he needed to know. Gabriella joined them on SPEAKER and they spoke for thirty minutes about the night before, Jennie and Diane.

Whatever he was doing, Deidre threatened, he wasn't to do anything reckless. He had someone important waiting for him who wasn't with them at the moment. Gabriella, however, was less oblique. Diane was falling in love with him, so don't go and get shot or killed or they would never forgive him.

He promised, asking what they were keeping from him. He knew they were looking at each other, uncertain. So what was up?

Nothing was up, Deidre promised. She would call him that evening.

She was a better manager of the truth than her sister, yet somehow he didn't believe her.
*

Gabriella called Anita, describing every moment with her sister and Drew until Deidre patted her shoulder. Perhaps Anita didn't want to hear every detail of what she'd been excluded from.

She promised to come by Anita's for dinner early on Christmas Eve for a Girls' Day. She missed her new friend and would see her soon. She had a big surprise.

Deidre, though, wasn't certain that was true. In spite of which she didn't burst her sister's bubble.

*

Jennie didn't phone her father. She went to him, joining him for breakfast. She asked him simply to trust her, which he did emphatically. She asked him to call Maria and Fernando to ask them not to come to the vineyard that day, to take the rest of the week off. She would explain why after the call.

Fernando had only missed work once for a brief time in the thirty-five years since bringing his family to the United States, Maria a brief time longer to assuage her grief. John Canyon, though, had a compelling way. He was still, at his age, a formidable man to stand against. What Maria wanted to know was: Were they coming for Christmas?

When he hung up he faced his daughter, waiting, puzzled by the welling tears and the eager expression normally reserved for the day she would ask him to edit her latest manuscript.

"Dad, they're home."

"Speak sense, girl. Who is home?"

"The children are, Diego, Francesca and Gabriella. Hidalgo found them, a little while ago. It's a long story, and a little insensitive on Hidalgo's part, though I believe he had a good reason for not telling anyone." She chortled. "What's new? He thought he was doing the right thing and he probably was."

The old man's face drained of its ruddy colour, his lips began quivering, his eyes turned instantly red and he began weeping. She went to him, wrapping her arms around strong, convulsing shoulders.

"He's kept them from Maria and Fernando. That's not the Hidalgo I know."

"Yes, he is. I can't imagine how he feels, guarding such a secret. That's why I couldn't tell you before you called.

Maria and Fernando can't come to work today. They're going to receive unexpected visitors this afternoon, including you and me. Diego won't be with us, which is just as well because the girls are plotting, which is quite another story."

John was wiping his eyes. He hadn't wept as much since the funeral, since the day he and Fernando had threatened to restrain Hidalgo with physical force.

"Plotting what, Jennie?"

"The downfall of the overly proud Governor of California, if all goes well."

*

Maria was miffed. She didn't know what was going on. She was particularly upset with her son. She hadn't seen him in a month, speaking with him a few brief moments since he'd begun spending most of his time with his successor to transition the government.

She was anxious to have Hidalgo to herself without all the fanfare, despite the hundreds of newspaper articles, magazine articles and photographs threatening to burst apart the spine of her scrapbook.

She didn't look a day over fifty. Fernando kept her young and beautiful, and quite often annoyed by his foolish antics. They were well-travelled, spoiled by their son's constant attention. Fernando was proud of her, that he was her husband. Often he would tell her that no one wanted to ogle old women on the beach, yet the rage he felt at seeing the lustful glances of other young men would one day stop his heart from beating before he had a chance to grow old with her.

Jennie called at noon asking whether she might drop by about three with her father. They had decided to finish work early. Hidalgo had ordered a case of special wine for them, wine he wanted them to enjoy at Christmas. She hung up, pleased with her lie, whereas Maria went around her pristine house with a duster, muttering. She could just as easily have brought the wine home herself from the vineyard, if they hadn't been told to stay home.

At one o'clock Diane called to wish them Feliz Navidad. She was fluent, something else Jerk didn't know about her. She wanted to pass by with a Christmas present for them and they weren't to call Hidalgo, or tell him if he called that she was coming. Could she pass by a little after three? She wouldn't stay long.

Maria insisted that she stay for dinner. Jennie and John would also join them at their table and for the next hour she muttered to herself in the kitchen. Something was wrong. Fernando didn't think so. What could be wrong? Either way, he knew to tread lightly.

"What could it be, Fernando?" she wanted to know. "John, he must have known this morning about the wine. And Jennie, she sounded excited. Her voice did not sound right to me."

"¡Ay! Querida, she wants only to bring us wine."

"No, it is more than that. Each year little Dianna she gives us a gift for Christmas, but at her plane or Hidalgo brings her gifts to our home. Never has she come here. Why is that? Why have we never thought to invite the young woman to our home?"

"I do not know."

"And now she comes with gifts, when ours for her are not yet wrapped. ¡Qué rabia! No hay tiempo."

"Calm yourself, querida. We have time."

"You do not understand what is happening here, marido."

"First we are told to stay home. We are told that Jennie will bring us wine, that John will come with her. Why does Dianna suddenly call to say she is bringing us gifts at the same hour? How does she know that we are even home?"

He shrugged, smirking "These questions, querida, they

are complex. I am a simple man. I have no answers for you."

"I will call our son."

"No, you will not. You have given your word. We do not know what Diane is thinking."

She told him to go away. She had to plan a dinner. A breath later she signalled him closer and kissed him, telling him once again to go away. She knew something was wrong.

*

At three Fernando opened the door to John and Jennie. As they did each morning at work, they hugged, kissed and shook hands. Each knew that life was too short and filled with too much uncertainty to take loved-ones for granted.

John had never changed. He stood as tall in his boots as ever before and had never forsaken his blue jeans, denim shirt and felt cowboy hat. His hair was pure white, his teeth perfect and white against his weathered skin, though Jennie was nothing like the Southwest girl portrayed on the inside jacket of her novels. She was wearing a silk dress under a cashmere coat, a wide-brimmed hat and gloves. She'd been to the hairdresser and was every bit a fashion statement.

John was John with a single bottle of his finest vintage, not a full case, which he knew didn't go unnoticed.

Maria had her hair in a tight bun; flour dotted her nose and cheeks. She was visibly flustered at seeing Jennie's outfit and John was wearing a blazer, not his usual bomber jacket. Jennie, of course, didn't know anything about Dianna coming shortly after. However she did suggest that perhaps Maria should take a few moments for herself, to have a bath and possibly change into something more comfortable.

Maria accused her, pointing the same finger at John and Fernando. Hidalgo was up to something. They were conspiring with him and Dianna was certainly involved.

None of the three pleaded guilty. They did however tell her to go upstairs, Fernando not quite knowing why. Nor did he argue when John suggested he might want to change into something a little less casual than jeans and a sweatshirt to meet the pretty Ms. Quinn.

Fernando gave him a look as though to say, "Look who's talking," letting himself be guided to the bottom of the stairway.

They had time. Nothing would happen until Jennie answered her phone.

*

Maria came down refreshed, wearing her favourite skirt and silk blouse, nylons and shoes strapped at her ankles. Her hair was lustrous and left to do its own thing. Fernando followed behind, wearing a thick cable sweater and cords, asking who had phoned.

Diane had, asking whether or not she was too early.

Why would she do such a thing Maria wanted to know?

No one knew.

A moment later the doorbell chimed. Jennie opened the door to Diane who stepped in quickly. Her hands were empty. She knew John and Jennie. She'd flown them many times. She couldn't stay long, she insisted. She came by to drop off special Christmas gifts for Maria and Fernando that were outside. She couldn't stay. But first, because she couldn't wrap them, Maria and Fernando had to sit and promise to keep their eyes closed.

They promised. But none trusted Maria. Jennie removed her scarf and covered her friend's eyes.

The door opened and closed. She and Fernando heard shuffling of feet, coats being removed and whispering. They heard stifled sobs and Maria became agitated, telling them she didn't like what was happening, asking Fernando what was going on. Fernando didn't know, though he thought it wise to at least threaten to open his eyes if he wasn't told

470

something soon.

At that, prompted by Deidre, Gabriella said, "Merry Christmas, nana and grandpapá. It's us, Francesca and Gabriella. We're home."

The room went silent.

"It's true, nana," Deidre said. "We've come home."

Fernando was first to open his eyes. Maria was afraid she'd heard a horrible lie. What she was hearing wasn't possible. It couldn't be. She would open her eyes and not see them, which she could not bear.

"Maria!" Fernando cried, leaping from beside his wife, "our girls, they are home. It is true."

Maria nervously tugged the scarf away from her face. She saw Francesca first, Gabriella second. She wanted to run to them, unable to move. She was convulsing, trying hard to catch her breath, John's strong arms pulling her close to comfort her, releasing her and easing to one side as the girls came to sit by their grandmother.

Tears and choked words were the common language. Only John Canyon had a clear mind as he stood and went to the door. Stepping outside, the door closed behind him, his voice bellowed with youthful projection.

"Ms. Quinn, you're expected inside, right now, unless you prefer being carried in over an old man's shoulder, which is very fine with me."

"This is family time, Mr. Canyon. I don't belong here."

"The hell you don't. You just get your pretty little self inside. You let us be the ones who decide who is and who isn't family. Git." He stood with his legs together, his arms crossed. He wasn't smiling, yet he wasn't unsmiling. "I'm not so old that I can't put a pretty young thing over my knee, girl."

Her shoulders slumped. She didn't think he was joking. She obeyed, stopping to hug him, passing through the doorway, feeling foolish, walking into Fernando's open arms.

Once inside, John blocked the door, crossing his arms.

When the tears abated, wet noses and blurred eyes the order of the day, Maria asked how. Her girls pointed to Diane.

"Dianna, muchísimas gracias. ¿Pero, cómo, pequeña?"

Maria always called her little one.

"Maria, Hidalgo did this, not me. He hasn't told you because he wanted to surprise you at Christmas. Diego will also be with you. He's a police detective now working for the governor on a special assignment. In short, I've done a lot to ruin his Christmas so I need you to help me or I'm going to be very unemployed very quickly."

Deidre broke in. "That's not a problem. I'll buy a jet and you can fly me somewhere. Nana, the thing is; father's got some issues. He can't let go of the past, he doesn't believe that our mother will forgive him if he does. He's very close to losing someone very close to him, someone whom we believe he loves."

Maria turned to Diane. "Dianna, are we speaking of our Anita?"

She nodded. "Yes, we are. Apparently Diego isn't the only jerk in town. That's between us, by the way."

Maria's brow furrowed. Deidre patted her knee. "It's a long story, nana. A lot's happened over the last couple of weeks and father needs a little help. He can't know that we've come here, not until Christmas. We have a plan. We do, not Diego. We don't trust him. He's too much into this hombre a hombre thing." She glanced at Diane. "He's also something else we have to take care of."

Maria hugged her girls together, not ignoring Diane, kissing her face a dozen times.

*

After dinner Diane thanked John for being strict with her. She would have hated not being part of the evening. He put his arm around her and let her talk, each wanting to give Fernando and Maria time with their daughters.

He asked what she really knew of Hidalgo Arquero, and Diego Hidalgo Arquero-Duval. Very little, it seemed, and John began a true story of a boy from Pichilingue, the little rich girl he loved above all else and their first child.

She listened, enthralled, not saying a word. When John finished his story, he said, "Your mother helped Hidalgo when he most needed a special kind of help. Enough said. Without which I wouldn't be sitting here this evening with a pretty little girl talking things over. Nothing happens without a reason, Diane. You think about that."

He kissed her forehead and stood to join the others.

*

Maria refused to let the girls go to their homes. She was adamant. She had plenty of room for all three of them.

John, though, managed to escape, pleading the need to take his medicine which Maria knew was a lie. He was simply being John. God, she told him, had once brought them together for a reason. He had a purpose. And He'd kept them together for a reason just as important: that coming Christmas.

He let Jennie take care of the appropriate response. He was a man more concerned with a good yield than salvation or higher powers. Nevertheless he was a good man, Maria knew. He was put on this earth to be a good man, she told him.

64

The twin 1100 diesels pushed Deidre's sleek cream-coloured 30-tonne Sundancer through four and five-foot swells easily, cruising just under the red zone, more than once the black Miami-Dade PD helicopter whirring past to check him out. He hated copter cops. In fact, he didn't have much use for uniforms in general. They got in the way. They were always trying to play detective, to save the day instead of doing their job, calling in the crime du jour and stepping out of the way.

He departed Miami at seven, an early sun barely defining the horizon. He passed through the breakwater of the Key West marina six hours and three beers later.

The dock master assigned him a slip after asking a few questions. He knew the yacht; he knew Deidre Commons and needed to see some ID. Satisfied, he sent a few of his crew to assist Drew Carling in docking between other sixty-footers. After which he went to his office and called Deidre for confirmation.

He was four docks behind the Burnt Out. The slip was vacant. Gibson was out, but with the shorter days he likely wouldn't be much longer and Key West wasn't a big place, which didn't give him a lot of time to find out about Dan Adams: who he was, where he lived and with whom.

The DMV was out, so were the Florida cops. Asking for help to investigate someone who was going to go missing very soon wasn't a smart idea. His first source was the phone book; his second was City Hall and Public Records with perhaps some Drew Carling charisma for good measure or a few 100-dollar bills. City clerks didn't care who went missing or why. They cared about people using their names, giving them attention and having a bit more cash for Christmas.

By five o'clock he knew that Dan Adams lived in a well-maintained bungalow on a street lined with high-end SUVs and Harleys. He had a double garage, a security system and his front and backyards were free of family clutter like bikes, a barbeque, a patio set, a fake fountain or a pool for his or the grandkids. He saw no garden, no garden hose, ladder or tool shed. For all intents and purposes, Scott Gibson lived alone, preferring to have others maintain his private world that would soon blow apart.

From a distance he watched as the Burnt Out reversed into its slip. He watched as the passengers disembarked, as the dock crew ran over with a trolley to carry away a fish that was big enough to feed ten families for a week.

Adams spent an hour hosing the afterdeck and transom of his boat before washing away a layer of dried salt spray from the hull, foredeck, windshield and Bimini. When he was done he went to the parking lot, stopping to talk with fellow boaters along the way, climbing into a Land Rover and driving away with Drew several car lengths behind.

Trailing wasn't required, Drew arriving at the house in time to see the garage door begin to close, in time to capture an otherwise empty interior on video. He passed by at seven, eight, nine and ten, seeing the blue screen of a flat screen hung on the wall. At eleven the lights were out, and Deidre hadn't called. Not that he blamed her. She had her little sister back. They were probably out doing female stuff.
*

Wednesday morning Dan Adams arrived at the marina at eight. His clients arrived thirty minutes later and by nine they were underway. By five PM Drew had discovered that Dan Adams was forty-nine, not fifty-six, the most recent census form showing that he lived alone. No children. He'd come to Key West twenty years earlier, almost to the month, January noted on his first property tax invoice. He'd paid cash for his home. A month later he paid cash for a fifty-foot fishing boat. A week after that he incorporated himself and was open for business with current annual receivables in excess of half a million. He had no debt, no credit cards and his last vehicle was paid for in cash. He had a perfect driving record with no demerits. No shit, Drew thought. The man must have driven twenty years on cruise-control. He had no landline; his cell phone was his link with the world, paid for each month in advance and in cash.

At the end of the dock he watched the Burnt Out end another day. He watched Adams go through his end-of-the-day ritual and followed him home. At minutes before eleven Drew passed by in time to see the television and the lights extinguished, wondering whether he should or shouldn't. He did, returning to Deidre's prized Life's Compensation with two bags of Scott Gibson's garbage which, he discovered at the Refuse Area of the marina, was collected once every other week.

He apologized to his sister in absentia for what he was about to do. He took a pair of tight-fitting rubber gloves from under the sink in her galley and a satin bed sheet from her linen closet, spreading it across the afterdeck before emptying the bags.

First he separated the five whisky and two forty-ounce scotch bottles along with two red wine bottles that he thought had to have cost fifty or sixty bucks a pop. Probably the reason Gibson crashed early each night. He separated the cans from plastic jars and microwaveable junk breakfasts from microwaveable junk dinners. There were no coffee grounds or teabags, no milk cartons, no pieces of fatty meat, potato peels or fruit rinds. Just one extra-large pizza box with the bill attached, dated the previous Thursday for double fries, double Cokes, double dessert cones, double knives, forks and plates. Gibson had called in the order at 9:45 PM, his forty-eighth order of the year.

Inside the box were wine corks, several hardened crusts with clearly different bite marks, and several used condoms.

He didn't care what shampoo Gibson used, how often he brushed his teeth or blew his nose. He knew enough. He knew what they would both be doing Thursday night.

After disposing of Gibson's garbage along with Deidre's sheet, he strolled along the docks wondering what was going on in Sacramento with his sisters, with Diane, wondering what was going on with him. Boarding Life's Compensation he called his father. They spoke for a while and when he disconnected he poured two fingers of his sister's Johnnie Walker Blue into an old-fashioned and lay on her bed to watch the weather station.

His phone buzzed the very moment he was reaching for a refill.

65

Wednesday morning Fernando and Maria stayed home, Maria cooking breakfast for her daughters and Diane, weeping as Fernando fritted about taking video clips and filling an eight-GB memory card as quickly as he could. Men worked, that's what they did, just not for a few more days.

He and Maria the night before, while Diane and Deidre slept peacefully, remained in the quiet of their living room with Gabriella who needed them to know something important about her. They listened intently to why and how her life had evolved, that she had told her father and Anita everything and that she had been ashamed, until Diego had convinced her that she wasn't a bad girl. That she had survived and that's what counted most. She needed to know that nana and grandpapá understood that she'd never done anything worse than dance for strangers. And she needed to be the one to tell them, because she was the one who knew the right words.

Maria put her to bed, tucking her in as she once had, lying beside her and humming a Mexican lullaby until her little Gabriella was soundly asleep, the way she once was in a kinder world.

In her bedroom, alone with her husband, she knelt by her bed and prayed before crying herself to sleep in his arms. Fernando didn't cry, sharing his false strength with her as best he could. He knew Diego had told his sister the truth, once again protecting her.

Yet the world appeared better when Maria woke much later than usual. She could smell the richness of brewed coffee and heard the girls talking quietly in the kitchen. She asked Fernando to give her a few minutes alone with them. He slipped under the covers.

The four of them were already in trouble with Hidalgo, she explained, as were Fernando, Jennie and John. All of them equally complicit, so what did they have to lose? She was also certain that Diego would choose sides wisely. Better to be favoured by seven than by one standing alone. He should not be excluded from their victory or their defeat. He would feel badly.

She wanted to spend the rest of the week with them, shopping for Christmas gifts she hadn't expected to place under the tree. Dianne must also come with them and Gabriella was to call Anita right away and invite her to dinner. Maria knew the ideal place.

At first Anita did her best to decline, at last succumbing to a young woman's pleas, agreeing to meet Gabriella for a quiet dinner and to exchange their gifts a little earlier than planned.

Diane also did her best to resist, utterly defeated. She did have some time off, she admitted, insisting that she would have to leave them at once when and if the governor called her cell. She went home to change, as did the sisters, and met them for lunch. She was being drawn in, as excited as she was afraid of what was happening to her.

By dinnertime they'd finished the first round of Christmas shopping, the trunk of Maria's Mercedes barely able to accommodate their secret purchases, and the four were seated at their table in the private lounge reserved for VIPs as Anita arrived precisely on time, incapable of disguising her shock.

*

Later that night in bed, feeling strangely alone and lonesome, Diane fought with her phone, thinking she'd won the battle when she slammed the receiver into its cradle. Somehow, she didn't know how, it ended up back in her hands, her fingers disobediently punching in the eleven digits.

*

He didn't have Caller ID. Not having it kept him alert, never knowing who or what to expect.

"Yeah, what?" he answered, his voice conveying a much worse and believable thought.

"God, you are so incredibly rude."

"You're the one calling me. You got a name? Or does this conversation end now?"

"Tell me you're joking, that you're not really like this. Please tell me something good."

"Okay. Well, I like your soft, firm ass in my hands for one thing. It seems like a good fit. I like the way you press your breasts against me. I like the way you breathe life into me from between your warm, moist lips, and that little tip of your tongue…searching."

"What!" She beat her mattress with the receiver. "I never did that! Listen, jerk, there is absolutely no way I believe those wonderful girls are your sisters. No way."

"Oh, it's you. Sorry. I was expecting another call. Not flying anywhere tonight?"

"You bastard, I'm hanging up."

"No you're not. You called to say how much you love me. So just tell me. Get it over with. You'll feel much better." She didn't. "Actually, I was expecting you to call last night. Out on the town?"

"No, I was with your grandparents, jerk…and your sisters."

That he was not expecting. "They went without the

governor? You went with them?"

"Yes, and I got stuck telling you, which I almost didn't. So listen up. You're going to keep your mouth shut about this. Understood? Maria's got something in her head and she doesn't want you getting in the way. And, by the way, she sends her love. She said to tell you that she will not stop praying for your safe return until she finally sees you, touches you, and kisses you. The entire evening was pretty emotional. John and Jennie were there also. So don't screw up and not a single word about this to your father. Please try not to be a jerk for once and Deidre wants to know if you've wrecked her boat yet."

"The boat's fine. So am I."

"Wonderful. Tell someone who cares."

He shrugged when the call disconnected. He refilled his glass and stretched out to continue watching the weather.

When his phone buzzed again, Drew Carling answered the way she expected.

"I didn't mean what I said. It was nerves. The last few days have been a little over the top for me."

He waited. "And…"

"And I suppose I'm starting to like you, a little."

"Well now we're getting somewhere, munchkin. Oh, and while we're on the subject, I like sleeping on the left side. Goodnight, darling."

He pressed END.

Drew sipped his scotch, beaming. She didn't like him a little, she loved him a lot.

Diane punched one pillow and choked the other.

66

Thursday morning Dan Adams arrived at the marina at eight. His clients arrived thirty minutes later. They were underway at nine. Deidre's Life's Compensation pulled away from her slip at 9:05 provisioned for the day.

*

Anita Juárez woke very confused, her mind troubled by doubt and apprehension. She'd convinced herself to get on with her life, to forget him, to live the rest of her life without him. Then she walked into a restaurant the night before, to hear from Maria what Hidalgo hadn't told her about his life, about what the papers hadn't reported, about the son she lost as well as a daughter the day Hidalgo buried his young wife. She listened as tears streamed from Gabriella's and Deidre's eyes and Diane sat holding their hands. Her training had taught her to think beyond her emotions.

Anita wanted to cry, yet she couldn't. She was depleted, drained by the disappointment she felt in herself as much as in him. Leaving the restaurant, she was noncommittal. She just didn't know. But she did know; she knew something she dared not tell Maria or the girls, that the Governor of California, her son and their father, was on the eve of committing a murder.

Thursday she'd barely had time to pour her first cup of coffee before her phone rang. Diane Quinn was calling; she was a block away and was wondering whether they might have breakfast together. They each knew something the other one didn't, Diane suggested. So why not have a little girl time?

Diane didn't waste time. Neither her timing nor the reason she'd come to Anita's home were appropriate to social niceties

"Anita, you have a serious thing for the governor. The entire world knows that you do. And he's no better at disguising his feelings than you are which is so sad after all these years. So here's what I think. Out of the blue, his children show up. How is that? You found Gabriella, he found the other two. Then Drew, or Diego, or whoever the hell he is, ends up in Florida on special assignment, an L.A. drug cop in Key West for the Governor of California, unofficially. He went looking for a man. The guy's name is Dan Adams. He's really creepy. The question is: why Drew, and why now, when any other cop could do the same work? Why did Hidalgo pull Drew from L.A. to do a simple job? And why is Drew in Key West as we speak. He wanted to kill the guy, Anita, and I'm pretty sure he would have if I hadn't been with him." Diane put up her hand. "That's another long story, for another time. Really, Anita, I've never before seen such hatred in anyone's eyes. He scared me. What I think, for what it matters, is that Adams killed Francine and Hidalgo wants to keep tabs on him until he steps down next week. You found out and you don't want to be around when it hits the fan. And I don't blame you. The question is: why now, after all these years? And another thing that doesn't make sense. Before we went to Miami and Key West I flew Drew to LAX where he met with some Mexican, a real slick guy in a fancy suit with a couple of thugs planted beside him like bookends. But when Drew came to the airport first he drove his car into the hangar where the guy wouldn't see it. He didn't want the guy to see the car or the licence plate that the guy could trace to Drew

Carling and not Diego Arquero. Not only that, Drew was clean-shaven, wearing a suit and tie, when a day earlier he looked like some sort of super dude in black leather, a beard and a ponytail. Anita, I think Hidalgo is going to kill Dan Adams. And I think you've known since all this began, since we went with Del Campo and de la Vega to bring Gabriella home. That's why you left the governor's office, and that's why you didn't say yes to Maria last night."

Diane took a deep breath. She didn't know what else to say. Anita stood to refill their cups, wanting time. She wasn't expecting this. She'd never expected the governor's pilot to be involved, intuitive or aware.

"You are correct, Diane, to assume how I feel about Hidalgo, or did once. I no longer do. I cannot love a man who intends to murder another, a man who has lived his life by what is right, who has saved so many worth saving and has never shown leniency to those who are not. You are also correct about Adams. His name is Scott Gibson. He is the one who murdered Francine. The other man, the one who came to the airport, he is Enrique Mendoza and Drew had every reason to conceal his vehicle from this man. He is very dangerous indeed, Diane; particularly to Drew were Mendoza ever to discover that Diego Arquero is the same man. For that, not even Hidalgo could protect him."

Anita sipped her coffee.

Diane set her cup into the intricate saucer, shaking. "The crime boss guy," she asked, "that Mendoza?"

Her voice was quivering.

"Yes, the one whose operation Detective Drew Carling has for a very long time tried to destroy. Because I have left the governor's office does not mean I have left my contacts or my close friends. He is a very brave man, Diane. He lives a very dangerous life, and I am certain he has not told his father or his little sister every detail, if any. We can only imagine the secret life he leads. We must be proud of him.

Gabriella has also told me how deeply you feel about Drew, and you must not worry. Hidalgo wants only that his son sees the one who killed his mother so horribly, nothing more. The girls will never discover what is about to take place and Drew will not become involved more than to maintain contact with Gibson until the hour of his death is determined."

"What does Mendoza have to do with any of this, Anita? How does Hidalgo even know such a terrible man? He's the frigging governor. I've never so much as heard him swear. Shit, now you're telling me he's involved with Enrique Mendoza."

"Days before Francine was buried Hidalgo was heavily sedated, at his father's request, so that Hidalgo would not do something that would haunt him throughout his entire life. He was delirious with grief. He was also an extremely wealthy young man with many influential contacts who respected him and, because of those friendships, much of what happened, Diane, was never reported. Files were destroyed or never created. Much of the evidence was ignored, conveniently lost forever, or never found according to the wishes of Hidalgo Arquero and Enrique Mendoza who together made a pact to one day find and kill Scott Gibson for what he did."

Diane clamped a hand over her mouth. "Anita, my mother, that's how Hidalgo knew of me and my brother."

"No, that is not true. That I swear to you."

"But, you know of me and my brother."

"I know you are an excellent pilot and very good with a gun. Your brother is a stranger to me." She saw the doubt. "That is the truth, Diane."

"That doesn't explain Mendoza. We're they friends? Did they know each other?"

"They were never friends, nor have they spoken a single word since. Gibson also killed Mendoza's cousin, the man who was in the car with Francine. That is the link, the common bond. He also murdered Mendoza's young girlfriend. Neither man has ever forgotten, Diane; neither man will ever forgive. Scott Gibson is a dead man. Nothing you and I together can do will change that."

"My God, Anita, they're really going to kill Gibson. This is real?"

"Yes, with the blessing of Gibson's mother. This is how Hidalgo knew to find the children, how he was able to at last find Gibson."

Anita told her in detail about Claire Gibson's letter.

"She knew about Mendoza all these years, she knew that her son was alive, what he'd done?"

"A secret she kept to protect Hidalgo. She meant well. I believe, in her heart, she was a good woman. I also believe that she welcomed her death so that she might at last ease her pain and her grief."

"What about our pain, Maria's pain and the girls' lost lives? They could have come home years ago. I can't believe this. We can't let him, Anita. Shit, he'll be sent to prison."

"No, he will not see prison. He will go to hell for what he will do, in his heart if not his soul. People like Mendoza kill more easily than you take flight from a runway on a beautiful day. Hidalgo is not that way. This revenge will destroy him. Yet what I do know, what I believe, is that he must do what he feels is right, as I must."

"Which is what, let Hidalgo kill someone? Do you think I'm really going to let Drew or his father kill someone? Bullshit. It's time for you to stop feeling sorry for yourself. We've got a common dilemma, you and I. You love one man and I'm beginning to think that I love another, each of them preparing to kill the same man for the same reason. So what do we do about this? The governor steps down in eight days, and I am not going to let anything happen to him, or to his son."

"These are powerful men, Diane. How do we prevent a tsunami by splashing our hands in the ocean?"

"You tell me, La Bonita. Before you left him no one ever went face to face with you unscathed. Now you're backing down. You don't think he's worth saving, like the many he's saved from a shit life… like me?"

She waited, feeling her every pulse point throbbing, but she was ready. One thing Captain Diane Quinn was accustomed to was turbulence.

Anita stood. "You are correct; I am La Bonita, someone who is not accustomed to discussing such important matters in her morning robe. Please stay, Diane, while I go to my room to change. I am afraid I have not been myself lately. Thank you for seeing what I have not."

Diane remained seated. She nodded once.

From the staircase came, "Diane, in the dining room you will find an unopened bottle of cognac, a gift from Hidalgo. Perhaps we have tasted sufficient cream in our coffees."
*

Diane poured an ounce into her coffee and while Anita dressed she poured another for both of them. She had a plan. She also had a headache. Not from the cognac, rather from Drew, Hidalgo, from the whole damned family she was getting trapped into.

Anita didn't hurry. By the time she came into her kitchen she was the essence of La Bonita. She was elegant, she was back. Nothing more had to be said.

She did have a plan; Diane had another, one she hoped she wouldn't need to implement. She knew now that she was going to do it anyway, one day soon. So what did a few days or a few weeks matter? But she wanted Diego Arquero to make love to her because he did love her, not because she went to bed with him for reasons of her own ulterior motive. But she would. The worst case scenario was that he would never trust her, never speak to her again and return to being Drew Carling: a man who thought more about killing and staying alive than loving and being loved.

She called Gabriella to cancel, disappointing her, as yet uncertain about Friday. She would do her best to make time for last-minute shopping, but she couldn't promise.

She knew in her heart that Drew would never let his father murder another man, not even a piece of shit like Gibson. Hidalgo was too pure of heart. He was a decent man. Conversely, Drew was too brave, hardened and apathetic, conditioned to being someone he really wasn't. He was a nice guy and Diane was afraid she would never see his other side, the real Diego Arquero-Duval when he wasn't playacting at being a jerk.

Anita was right. Hidalgo would live out his life in hell, alone. He would live his life in silent shame for what he would do. She had also seen Drew's clear eyes turn dark that day on the dock; certain he would have killed the man had she not been with him. He'd told her. Killing Gibson would be an easy matter. He had no intention of letting Hidalgo kill Gibson. Instead he was preparing to kill the man who murdered his mother, with or without Mendoza. That's why he was in Key West. She was certain. Then what? He would transition from jerk to murderer, from a nice guy who wanted to open a restaurant to a rogue cop who would never leave his infested streets. He would never know her; he would never know the softness of her skin, the saltiness of her tears, her weaknesses or her strengths.

She would not let that happen. He was a jerk. He was, she knew that, yet he was fast becoming her jerk. As for Hidalgo, the governor was wrong. She did have a debt to repay. And she would, in full, one way or the other, preferably the other, which was Anita's
*

Drew was adrift in the open sea, with sufficient beer,

sandwiches and SPF to last the day. He was one-point-five miles off the starboard side of Adam's Burnt Out, watching his prey through Deidre's high-performance scope as though Gibson was standing in front of him. When Gibson returned to the marina, Drew went with him. He was rejuvenated, he felt like a new man. He'd spent half the day diving into the ocean, frolicking like a teenager, feeling human, the other half spying on Gibson, wondering why he couldn't feel that way all the time, with her.

At the gas dock the crew emptied the head and filled the water and the fuel. When they were done Drew purged the fumes from the bilge and gave the lead crew his credit card. Three thousand dollars later he thought he didn't have to worry about loving a munchkin pilot who was playing hardball, he was having a heart attack right there at the helm. The most his Corvette in L.A. ever drank was forty, fifty bucks tops, and he still had to get back to Miami. He wasn't used to being affluent and, unfortunately, his day wasn't over when all he wanted was to hear her voice, annoy her as much as he safely could, drink his sister's Johnnie Walker Blue, and go to sleep.

He hadn't slept so well in, he didn't know how long.

67

At seven Drew was parked diagonally across from Adam's suburban home. At 7:30 a rosé-coloured Porsche turned into his driveway, honked once, and drove into the garage. He barely had enough time to see the girl or Gibson in the dim light before the garage door inched its way closed.

Diego called L.A. Twenty minutes later he knew the woman with Gibson was Donna Simpson. She was twenty-eight with four priors to her credit: three for soliciting, another for fraud. She had no convictions, no family and no current address. The dozen photos sent to him from L.A. showed a blonde, brunette, a redhead, ginger, auburn and black. She was a whore, Gibson's weekly pay-per-use one-nighter that did her job well, Drew thought. The little he'd seen of her as she stepped from her Porsche was all European, top notch and expensive, which accounted for the expensive wine labels if not the pizza.

She left at 1:30 AM, Friday, Christmas Eve. Gibson's lights remained on for as long as he took to secure his home. Then nothing but blackness amidst the flickering greens, reds, yellows and blues of a nicer world, a children's world...until they would grow to become adults who might, or might not, know right from wrong.

Satisfied that he'd established a routine, one he would verify once again the following week, he drove to his temporary Shangri-La, his escape, to where he could dream of a life that might be better, a life with her. He wasn't tired, yet he felt as though he could sleep for a week. He was lost, he was discovering more than ever before.

*

By mid-afternoon Thursday Sargent Carlos Del Campo came to Anita's home with the information she'd requested. He didn't ask for a reason because he knew he wouldn't hear the truth. In any event, he would do anything for La Bonita. That said; he knew she wasn't planning anything good. He pointed an admonishing finger directly at her, and at Diane, warning them that what they were thinking was not only potentially dangerous, but way out of their league. They had no business at all even contemplating using the information he'd given them.

When he left, they waited, peering from the window as he spoke awhile with her security detail. When he drove off the women left to go shopping. They went to an electronics store and bought a new cell phone they planned to use once.

When they returned they stood staring at the phone. They didn't know. They hugged each other tightly, pressing their cheeks together. They were afraid. Anita couldn't remember ever being as nervous, while Diane was just hoping he would answer, that she wouldn't have to call Drew instead.

They'd decided that Diane should call. And what was the point in wasting time, putting off the inevitable. She let Anita go, missing her comfort, dialling, taking Anita's hand before pressing SEND.

He wasn't picking up.

"Señor, Mendoza, hola y muy buenos días. Me llamo Diane Quinn. I am calling you on behalf of Señor Diego Arquero-Duval, without his knowledge, the man you met at the airport. I am the woman who disembarked the plane. Please call me back. I really need to talk with you. Please, sir."

She gave the number, dropping the phone onto the table.

By ten PM Mendoza hadn't called. Diane went home, not entirely disappointed. She hadn't really expected him to return her call. Why would he? She wanted desperately to crawl into bed and hide, anything to avoid phoning Drew and telling him they were going to sleep together.

*

At two AM Drew Carling's phone shook him.

"Make it good, hombre. You got ten seconds." He wanted to believe, but he couldn't be certain. "You got a name or what, before this ends right now?"

"Munchkin," she blurted. "My name is Munchkin."

"Hey, it's you. I see you still haven't worked out the time zone thing. I was wondering when you'd call. Sorry for the street talk. I've had rough day. Is this what it's going to be like when we're married, you waking me up all the time for a little...you know?"

"Don't be a complete ass. Are you alright? Are you safe?"

"Why wouldn't I be? I'm here taking a few days off, a little R&R. Of course I'm alright. How else can I come home to marry you? "

"Okay, listen, I'm not stupid. Do you understand that? Is this line safe?"

He chuckled. "I think you mean is the line secure. Yes. We are secure, Agent 00-Cute. What's up? Something gone bad at home, everyone okay?"

"Shit, what are we, in a frigging spy movie, 'something gone wrong at home'? You idiot, nothing's gone wrong at home. Can't you for once say what you mean?"

"Yeah, I can say what I mean. I already have, often. In fact, I'm losing track. You're just not listening. You can't stop being a prissy little...the most beautiful woman in the world long enough to listen to me for once and believe what I'm telling you. You're too hung up on stereotypes, this bad boy thing. Listen, when I'm off-duty, I hang out at the beach, alone, always alone; I listen to the classics on an out-dated Walkman and I drink lemonade. That's not the question, you are."

"Have you spoken with your father?"

"There you go, changing the subject. No. I will tomorrow. And I'll keep my mouth shut. Is that why you're calling? You think I'm that low?"

"Yes, I do."

"Why don't you say what you mean for once, Diane?"

"Okay, I will. Tomorrow's Christmas Eve."

"Wow, you really cut to the chase."

Her sigh was exaggerated, and he knew. "You didn't let me finish."

"It's Christmas Eve, so what? Deck the halls. It's not a big thing in my life. I get to see whores, pimps and dealers dressed in green and red. Good for me. The dust they snort is still white. That's my Christmas snow. Kids OD at Christmas, Diane, just like any other time. And I do have to say that right now I'm pretty brain-dead tired. So if you just called to update me on statutory holidays…"

Diane took another deep breath. This could blow up in her face. She was taking a chance, possibly for no reason. She couldn't be certain after what she'd done earlier in the day.

"That's not why I called. I called to tell you that I'm in bed, on the right side. I've just taken a steaming oil bath, my skin is soft and silky smooth, my toenails and fingers are painted deep maroon and my lips are the same colour," she lied. "They're soft, moist and I'm going to bed alone with an almost bare ass that's fantastic. I'm wearing mauve tap pants and a matching camisole. Get the picture? I couldn't be sexier if I were naked. And tomorrow, if you're interested, I'm going to wear my new cinnamon lounge shorts and matching silk robe until midnight." She paused. That part she wasn't fabricating. "After that don't bother,

I'll just know you really are a total shit. More importantly, you won't know."

"Okay, you've got my attention. I won't know what?"

"How beautiful I am standing naked on a silk pedestal. How I feel to the touch lying naked between satin sheets. And bring me back my panties, jerk. Do you have any idea at all how much I paid for those?"

"I do now, yes. You're going to be expensive to take care of." He sipped what was left in his glass. "So what's for breakfast?"

"That depends on how good you really are without your guns and dagger. My mom's not expecting me for dinner until later in the day. You've been doing a lot of talking, jerk. So, yes, I want you to put up or shut up. Show me how much you're beginning to love me or just get lost."

"I'm not beginning to love you, munchkin. I began loving you the first moment I saw you. I'm going to quit my job because of you. We're getting married in fourteen weeks. What more proof do you want?"

She wanted to hang up. She wanted never to have called. She knew he would one day very soon discover why she was playing him.

"Perhaps I need to know how much I'm beginning to love you. I also know why you are where you are, so don't do anything stupid to ruin my Christmas."

"You know what I think? I think that I didn't scare you that first day. I think you crashed backward because you knew, right then, right there, that I was your dream fulfilled, the guy you've been waiting for all your life. I think you've wanted me from that very instant. What I don't think, what I know is true, is that you already love me more than you're capable of saying. Otherwise I wouldn't be showing up tomorrow night before midnight because I'm not into one-nighters no matter how gorgeous she is in her clothes or naked. Tell me I'm wrong." He waited. "Still with me…hello, anyone home?"

"Maybe were both wrong. Ever think of that. And, really, I don't know where I am."

She disconnected, pulled the duvet over her head and cried herself to sleep because she did love him. She did want him, but she had just ruined what might have been.

68
Christmas Eve morning of this Year

Drew woke late, surprised that he'd slept at all. He didn't care about Adams. The marina was virtually deserted. No one cared about the catch of the day. Mommies and daddies would be doing last-minute shopping for expensive, sale-priced gifts they still couldn't afford that would keep their children loving them until the next expensive occasion. Men would be shopping for the perfect gift for their girlfriends, wives, or both, searching for last-minute, bargain basement deals that would allow their love to flourish another year. His shopping was done. What he needed was to dive into the sea.

Maybe we're both wrong. What the hell did that mean?
*

At eight Pacific Time, half of Diane's face was buried into her pillow, her mind hurtling at the speed of confusion from one thought to another. She hadn't been to bed with a man in years and the one or two she had known hadn't lived up to expectations.

First-year college girls had more experience with men, which was fine with her, had been fine with her. She didn't mind being alone. Working for a man like Hidalgo Arquero raised the bar impossibly high. Until super cop showed up to completely undo her status quo, lower the bar and screw with her head. Jerk.

She shrieked, the phone's unfamiliar shrill tone by her pillow jolting her into real time. She pressed SEND.

"Good morning, Ms. Quinn. Or should I say Captain Quinn? I trust I am not disturbing your early morning."

"No, sir, you're not. Thank you, for returning my call."

"It was impossible for me not to given the subject matter, however first I had to know who you are. And now I do. So why are we talking, Ms. Quinn? What is your concern about Diego?"

"That he's going to kill the man you're after. I know what Diego's planning. He won't let his father get involved. He's going to do it."

"Yes, I understood that from our meeting. What I find strange, though, Ms. Quinn, is that nowhere in this country is there a police officer by that name. Why do you suppose that is?"

"I don't know, sir. I'm more concerned about his becoming a murderer and going to prison, if he isn't one already."

"I would hope not. I would not like to think he's cheated me of what is mine to share with his father. Where is he now?"

"I don't know."

"I'm sure you don't. That being the case, what is your interest in this personal matter?"

"I don't want to marry a killer, and I don't want to work for one. This would ruin both their lives."

"I have great respect for your employer. I look forward to telling him in person how pleased I am that he has recently found his family. As for Diego, I'm certain he's no less a man of his word."

"I can't let this happen. I know about the letter, Señor Mendoza, from the mother of the man you're going to murder."

He snorted. "A poor choice of words, Ms. Quinn. We regard the matter differently. Our memories are vivid, your employer's and mine. Yours is not. You were ten or eleven at the time, interested in dolls, with no idea of three unnecessary deaths. Those were murders, committed to escape a debt. What we intend to do isn't murder, it is a sentence we could not be certain at the time would be carried out if left to the courts."

"In two weeks, I know that also. That's why I called, to ask a favour."

"You want me to exclude father and son, at the cost of my reputation."

"Yes, I do. These are good men; they don't have the connections you do."

Mendoza chuckled. "Tell me how I would do that, exactly. I have no idea where the man is hiding. Also, I made a promise to your future father-in-law. We are not discussing a simple matter of breaking a woman's promise to meet for lunch. This is family honour, his and mine. To deny him his right, that would ruin his life. And I have to tell you, Ms. Quinn, as a man. If you interfere in this matter your marriage plans will probably change very quickly."

"Señor Mendoza, I do know where he is, but I called you instead of the police because I do understand this male macho thing. I don't care that he's going to be killed. I believe he should be for what he did. I care about what will happen after. I don't want to lose either of them, but I'm willing to if it means saving them."

"Where is he, Ms. Quinn."

Diane swung her legs over the bed, wishing Anita was with her to hold her hand.

"You're a man of your word, Señor Mendoza. I know you are. Promise me they won't be involved. Promise me that and I'll tell you."

"You have my word, Ms. Quinn. Neither man will be

498

involved beyond what has been agreed between me and the father. I reserve that privilege. There is a big difference between holding a gun and pulling the trigger. I intend to pull the trigger personally, figuratively speaking. I also received a letter from the same woman, in which she wrote of concerns similar to yours. I have decided to respect her final wish. It was good of you to call me. It speaks well of you. Diego will not be allowed to interfere and you may happily become his bride. Nor will his father be haunted by what is unnatural to him. I would think quite the contrary. I would also hope that his nightmares are at an end and I assure you that no one is going to prison. So you see, Ms. Quinn, you need not have worried. Whatever he plans after the thirty-first, you will continue to be employed by a decent and honourable man."

"Thank you, sir."

"As for our subject's location, I have no need to know. I will be told when the time is right, when he steps down. You have no need to live your life keeping such a secret from your husband. For your sake Ms. Quinn, we have not had this conversation today. Good day."

*

She had expected foul language and derogatory remarks. She had just spoken with the Southwest's most important crime boss who, instead, was almost charming. She was stunned. Not until she dropped the phone onto her bed did she realize she was trembling.

When she was dressed she sat in her kitchen letting her coffee get cold, so deep in thought that she wasn't thinking at all. She called Anita to recount her conversation with Mendoza. When they disconnected she called Gabriella who was with her sister and Maria, inviting the three women to lunch. Someone had to do something before it was too late.

She called her service provider, cancelled her contract

and destroyed the phone. She thought of Drew boarding his flight. He'd be landing at five or six local time expecting to spend the night with her, to make love with her, wake with her and say something obligatory like he really did love her. Now she didn't have to. She'd spoken with Mendoza. Things had happened too quickly and she hadn't expected Anita to have such influence with the State Police. Now her deception wasn't required. She wouldn't have to lie to him. She could take her time, be certain how much she loved him.

She chortled. She was certain, but was he? She wanted flowers, soft words, dining and dancing. She wanted to be courted, to tell her few friends, her mother and her brother that she had a serious a man in her life, that she was getting married. The last thing she wanted was to regret having sex with the man before he ran back to L.A. to forget about her.

"Ten seconds. Don't waste my time."

"That's why I'm calling, so that I don't waste your time."

"Hey, it's my wife."

"Yeah, about that, about you and me…and tonight," she gulped, "I can't. I'm sorry."

"Well you're the one with half the love-making essentials. But we still are getting married, right?" He waited. "Diane, you haven't said a word in over a minute and I'm getting the evil eye here from the gate lady. Listen, I get it. We haven't had much quality time together. You're scared. You're afraid that I'm not the perfect guy that you think I am. Well, you're wrong. I am…perfect for you."

"I didn't mean to lead you on."

"I can't say I wasn't anxious to see you naked, to caress you, to kiss you and prepare a mean crêpe Suzette with a few hot toddies for breakfast. So what will you be doing and wearing tonight?"

"Wrapping gifts in a fleecy bathrobe."

"Do you have one to wrap for me?"

"Yes."

"Listen, I have to go. Call me sometime, when you're ready. We can have dinner or go to a movie. Just don't wait too long. I think I'll make a good restaurateur, however I do know how good a cop I am. Merry Christmas, Diane."

He disconnected, smirking at the unimpressed gate agent as she ushered him through before closing the door to the Jetway.

Diane sat in a daze, wondering what the hell had just happened. He wasn't at all upset with her. He didn't sound disappointed about not sleeping with her, anxious to see her or afraid of losing her. He didn't call her darling or munchkin or ask about his gift. He just pressed END, and that was the end. He was gone.

She had expected that he would at least ask to come over for his gift, to ask her out on a date, something. Instead she got a dial-tone.

She'd lied to him again, to save face, or to have something to say. Her gifts were wrapped, strewn around her three-foot high plastic Christmas tree dotted with miniature pink and white lights. She reached for his and tore away the wrapping. As though she could afford 400 dollars for a sweater, she mumbled. As though anything she could buy for him would make him less of a jerk or just an outright bastard.

She pushed the sweater into a shopping bag and left to meet the ladies for lunch, not certain whether she would tell them how much of a thoughtless idiot their brother and grandson truly was.

69

Near the end of the day Hidalgo Arquero was in his office. The government was closed. He thought to phone her, to explain. That all he wanted was for her to have a good life, to have whatever she desired. He hadn't intended the ten million as anything other than good for her.

He didn't call. He called his parents' home and spoke with his father. He would see them the next morning at ten. He had a very big surprise for them that would only be delivered later in the day because of unforeseen circumstances. Fernando listened, sworn to secrecy, knowing the inverse was true. Hidalgo was the one in for a very big surprise.

Then he called Diego, leaving a message that he would like to have dinner with his son. There was also a change of plans.
*

When he was through Arrivals Drew checked his cell. He spoke briefly with his sister and returned his father's call to explain that he had a date. However he would co-ordinate with Deidre and they would see each other the next morning.
*

Deidre had called her father after lunch. She was so sorry. However something unexpected had come up at Commons Communications and she couldn't see that she could join him to meet her grandparents before late Christmas

502

morning. Also, Gabriella wanted to stay with her. They would come together, but they would call first so that he could get Maria and Fernando ready for the big surprise. Could he please call Diego and let him know?

Then she called Diego and left her own message. He was to meet her for dinner that night and he wasn't to make feeble excuses or screw up. He was to call her at once upon landing, which he did.

*

At lunch the women spoke about Diego, Maria asking endless questions, Gabriella and Deidre telling her what they knew. Diane was more reticent. They spoke about Hidalgo, his big surprise, none of them feeling guilty, and when they were finished they left with a purpose after Diane called Anita. She needed someone to talk with. Could she come over, she pleaded?

*

Anita was expecting a tearful, love-struck young woman, taken aback by the entourage on her doorstep, her security detail not looking directly at her when she opened the door, more towards the sky. They hadn't given her the usual heads-up.

Once inside, Maria was very succinct. Her son was a handsome, intelligent man. He was successful, kind and generous, which didn't mean he knew everything, or was capable of everything. He had flaws. He was a man, sometimes blind and inconsiderate, which did not excuse Anita from her indifference. She was as much to blame as he was.

Anita would come to her home with them that very afternoon, she insisted. She would spend the night; she would spend Christmas with them and with Hidalgo. She would tell Hidalgo what he had to hear. Whatever that might be, he would hear the words from her.

Anita stood her ground. She could not and would not

beg a man to love her, to marry her.

She was missing the point, Maria scolded her. Hidalgo would be the one to beg, on his knees, in front of his family. Or, Anita could stay home. She could let him live his life deprived of beauty, love and friendship if that's what she really wanted. Because, she knew, it was not what her son wanted.

Anita looked to Diane who wasn't any help, then to Gabriella who stood with her arms crossed, waiting. Deidre was no better, asking what was taking her so long when she'd already made up her mind. The whole thing was a no-brainer. Wasn't it? Not waiting for an answer she asked Gabriella where the bedroom was and she went to the stairs followed by Maria, Diane and her younger sister leaving Anita with her mouth agape and her arms waving in protest.

An hour later Anita was sitting in Maria's home with Fernando and Gabriella, her gifts placed under the tree.

Diane went home; Deidre went with Maria to finish their last-minute Christmas shopping together.
*

Diane crawled into bed fully dressed and cried. Christmas Eve and she was alone. She was depressed, despondent, heartbroken, angry and disappointed. She felt like shit. He was shit, and she wanted to call him to tell him that he was. Despite which she was happy for Anita.
*

When they were done with their shopping, pleased with their choices, Maria went home and Deidre drove to the airport to meet her brother.

They hugged, kissing cheeks, as yet a foreign concept to them, neither one quite ready to tell the other how good their growing love for each other felt. They were getting used to each other.

At dinner the first order of business were the photos Diego had promised to take of Life's Compensation to prove that he hadn't destroyed her yacht. She was satisfied. He had even replaced her bottle of Johnnie Walker Blue. He had a great vacation, he told her, which he would continue the coming week when he would return the yacht to Miami in its original condition, he vowed.

The second order of business left him with very little to say and after dinner she went with him to his hotel to wait in the lobby while he changed into a suit and tie. She was taking him to meet Maria and Fernando.

*

Walking through the doorway, behind his sister, Diego stood speechless. The woman standing beside his kid sister was weeping, her lips quivering. He had no clue what to say. He hadn't practiced, believing the words would come easily to him.

"Maria, the governor told me you like yellow roses. I hope he wasn't wrong."

He'd never been squeezed so hard, kissed so many times in so few seconds.

She was beautiful, he thought, and so young, nothing like a grandmother should look. He put an arm around her, pulling her close.

"Fernando, I was told that you enjoy the occasional taste of fine tequila. I hope I chose well. My informant wasn't very specific." He glanced at Deidre.

"Gracias, hijo." Fernando pursed his lips, nodding his approval. "Sí, claro. Ven aquí, hijo."

Fernando opened his arms to his grandson for the first time in over twenty-one years, tears flooding from his eyes. He could speak no words, all his love and emotion conveyed through his tight embrace.

"It's good to see you once again, Señora Juárez, albeit somewhat surprised."

"Remember, Diego, my name is Anita. And I am no less surprised. I'm pleased to see that you returned safely from your vacation. Were the waters of South Florida very dangerous?"

He was squeezed between Maria and Fernando who weren't letting go.

"No, Anita. They were not. My days were very relaxing. I would say my vacation was a great success. I've come home feeling like a new man."

She smiled. "And with a clear mind, I hope."

She knew. "Yes, with a very clear mind."

Deidre suggested that Maria and Fernando give Diego some space. He wasn't going anywhere, not for a while.

Maria sat him between his sisters as Fernando hurried for his camera. When Anita stood to move, not to impose on a family portrait, Maria stood and forced her gently to sit, scolding her once more.

Diego had been in enough sting operations to realize that his father was in up to his knees, walking into a trap, a very lovely and elegant trap. He gave Anita a curious smile, which she acknowledged with one of her own.

At ten Deidre stepped away to place a call regarding the urgent matter at her firm. She left at 10:30 with her sister and brother after countless hugs and kisses from which Anita was not exempted. Maria had made very clear that she would either have a lovely new daughter by the next day or give away her stubborn son to anyone who wanted a thoughtless man.

Anita had nothing to add. She wondered why she'd even brought anything to sleep in because there was no way she was going to sleep. She was nervous and frightened. She wanted to run, yet she wouldn't. In twelve hours she would either know how much he loved her or how much one woman could be inexplicably humiliated. And for that she would be the bigger man, if he could not be.
*

Drew was getting used to sitting in the back, listening to

faceless women chattering around him as though he was cramped into the trunk or being dragged behind the car on a leash.

He had no real experience with women beyond prostitutes and drug addicts. Women like his sisters, like Anita, were pleasant aberrations to him, anomalies. He knew a few hard-ass, self-centred female detectives, but these women were different. They were classy. Diane was classy.

He messed up, big time. He should have…Should have didn't matter, he knew. What he knew was that he would take care of Gibson and go back to cleaning the streets of Los Angeles by mid-January. At least now he had had two families. He had called his parents to explain, promising to see them very soon, to invite them to Sacramento to meet the governor when he was no longer a governor, little Gabriella and Deidre.

The Carlings had wept throughout the long conversation, though he misunderstood and they told him so. They were not crying because he was now lost to them. They were crying because he'd been found.

His sisters' voices faded. He was in another world, remembering. When he suddenly realized, before he could say a word, Deidre turned in her seat and told him to keep his mouth shut, not to say a word. She would be back in a half-hour. The time had come for him to man-up and grow a pair.

*

Diane buzzed her in. She was expecting Deidre, not quite certain what her new friend's dilemma was. Or how many more dilemmas she would have in her own life.

"You look like crap."

"Thanks, I feel like crap."

"Listen, I don't have a lot of time. So get those clothes off, right now."

"Pardon me."

"You don't deserve to be pardoned. You've been very stupid." Deidre took her by the hand, pulling her into the bathroom where she stooped to pour a bath, standing straight, facing Diane to begin unbuttoning the young woman's blouse. "You get undressed and into that bath right now or I'll call in the troops who'll help me strip you naked and bathe you like the little girl you're acting like. Five minutes, before I come in and I'd better see you wet and soapy."

Deidre left her. She went into Diane's bedroom to rummage through her closet. She laid out midnight blue, full-length lounge pants and a matching full-length silk robe. Then she went to the drawer her brother had previously raided, carefully selecting dark blue backless panties and a matching three-quarter bra.

She called out to Diane, asking if she was in the tub. She was. Diane called out asking if, by chance, Deidre was a lesbian. Because if so... No, she wasn't a lesbian. She just hadn't met a man whom she could love more than she did Commons Communications. Start scrubbing!

When she was satisfied that the ensemble would do the job, she went into the bathroom. She sat on the edge of the bath, dunked Diane backward into the water, yanked her up and began shampooing her hair.

Each time Diane went to speak she was told to be quiet. She had nothing to say that Deidre wanted to hear. When she was done she reached for a towel, helped Diane from the bath and sat her at the vanity to begin blow-drying and styling her hair. When she was satisfied with that portion of her work, completing the look with the barrette, she led Diane into the bedroom and told her to dress in what was laid out.

Deidre went into the living room and dimmed the lights, tuning into an FM station known for playing late-night romantic love songs. She went into the bedroom where Diane was about to sit on the edge of her bed, ordering her not to. She didn't want the silk ensemble ruined with creases. She wanted perfection. And Diane was perfection.

She pulled the young woman into the living room and told her to remain standing. She would be back, she wouldn't be long, and they could get royally drunk together.

Diane asked, half-smiling, whether Deidre was certain she wasn't a lesbian. She definitely was not, Deidre replicd, at least not yet.

She left, closing the door behind her.

In Deidre's car Gabriella and Drew were talking quietly. Until the driver's door opened and Drew somehow knew to shut up, something he believed had to do with the finger pointing at him an inch from his face.

"You, listen up. Nana and I went shopping this afternoon, for this, for which we want a cheque tomorrow morning. You screw this up and I don't want you for a brother, neither does Gabriella. You got that? And, by the way, I've just seen the love of your life naked and if you don't marry her, I will." She gave him the velvet box. "Go. Get out of my car."

The sisters climbed from the car with him. Deidre's voice is what a confused Diane heard next, buzzing her in, wondering what the hell to expect.

Inside, by the elevator, Deidre warned her brother. "Don't mess this up, Diego. I like that girl. You get on your knees and you tell her what she needs to hear without being a smartass. I swear, if you come down before tomorrow…I don't know what. Go."

They shoved him into the elevator. On the third floor he stepped out, afraid, uncertain, on unfamiliar ground. He walked slowly to her door, waiting or hesitating, kneeling before he knocked once.

When the door opened Diane gasped.

"Diane Marigold Quinn, would you please make me the happiest man in the entire world by marrying me this coming February 14th ...or whenever is good for you. I'll wait as long as you want me to." He held the open velvet box in cupped hands. "I love you and I adore you. I have since the first moment I saw you. You are beautiful and gorgeous and stunning. I want the world to know that you're mine, that I'm yours. This is me, Diane, not that other guy. That was someone else. He's gone. He's not coming back."

Diane grimaced and shook her head, rolling her eyes in her head. He looked so pathetic.

"You are an idiot, aren't you? I liked that other guy, or most of him. And what are you doing on the floor? Stand up. Get in here and give me my ring. And you'd better not have lied about the crêpes, because I love crêpes almost as much as I love you, jerk."

70
Christmas Morning of this Year

Diane woke to the aromas of coffee and maple syrup served over strawberry-filled crêpes sprinkled with a light dusting of icing sugar, which she thought was wafting through from her kitchen.

She was wrong. He was standing by the right side of her bed with a tray, coughing lightly to waken her.

He didn't look quite the same standing at attention in her robe, though definitely as though he belonged to her. God, she thought, he was hers. There was no going back.

"Wow!"

"You haven't tasted them yet."

"I know. I mean…wow!"

He set the tray across her lap. "I knew you'd come across eventually."

She smacked him. "So we're engaged? We're getting married, Diego?"

"We can elope this afternoon if we can find a justice."

"Yeah, right, like that's going to happen. You're being a jerk again."

"February 14th, as planned, just tell me what time to arrive. This is more of a girl thing."

She smacked him again, ignoring him. She was starving.
*

Diego insisted that they had time; Diane insisted they didn't and sent him alone to his hotel to change. Making fantastic love was one thing; she wasn't ready to see him gawking at her in the shower.

When he was gone she called Deidre. She wanted Diego's sisters to hear the news first, and she wanted them to be her bride's maids. Diego's Christmas surprise she kept to herself.

When they were finished talking she drove to Deidre's home, the three continuing the excited, disjointed chatter throughout the short drive to the hotel where Diego stood waiting, looking like a conquering hero, boxes and bags of all colours, shapes and sizes strewn about his feet.

Gabriella hugged him, squeezing tears from her eyes. Deidre punched him and pinched his arm, to keep him balanced. Diane kissed him as his sisters stood waiting, watching, waiting for one of them to pass out. She was his Christmas gift, Diane told them, beaming, patting his cheek. She'd returned his other gift to the store the day before when she thought he was an idiot. Now that she was fairly certain that he wasn't. She had no time. The stores were closed.

When they arrived, Maria and Fernando were outside the front door with John Canyon, Jennie and Anita. Christmas wasn't the issue. Diane's ring was, at least for the women as the men hurried to empty Deidre's car of the gifts. Not much time was left. Minutes remained before Hidalgo was expected and Diego had yet to park Deidre's car out of sight.

By the time he returned Maria had shooed them all into her home. She stood alone on her stoop, waiting first for her grandson, pushing him through the doorway. Alone she waited for her son, her heart skipping a beat at the groan of his red Mustang and seeing the two black SUVs behind him.

She was firm in her resolve to see him happy, putting a

hand to his chest to stop him.

"Hidalgo," she said quietly, putting the little velvet box in his hand, "with all that has recently happened to you and to us, you must now do what is right."

"Mamá, what is this?"

"It is what is right. Put down your gifts and go inside to what you deserve and to what you must do."

He went to open the box, Maria's hand clamping over his. She stepped aside pushing him through the door open doorway.

The camera flashed. Hidalgo Arquero's expression of shock and amazement was frozen in time by his father at three frames per second. He was indeed frozen. His saw his children. His girls standing with John and Jennie, Diane with her arms wrapped tightly around his son, Anita sitting with Fernando between them, holding each other's hands.

Fernando said, "You are late, hijo, in so many unfortunate ways. What do you propose to do this very instant so that this special day will not be ruined by what you falsely believe? You stand alone this day to tell this young and precious woman what is in your heart. No one here stands with you. You are alone amongst family. The time has come to say what we all know."

He eased from the sofa to stand by his wife's side.

Hidalgo did stand alone. The silence was deafening. All he could feel and hear was heated blood coursing past his pounding temples. He opened the tiny box slowly, intently. The ring glittered.

Anita was a vision, sitting alone, wringing her hands gently in her lap; her head tilted slightly downward, her eyes peering upward into his, unblinking, her face devoid of expression. How often had he dreamt of this moment? How often had he dreamt of her? She was an angel.

He looked at his mother, her hands pressed against her heart, and to each of his children. They were waiting, expectantly. Then to Diane. She was smiling. He could see the love in her eyes, the sparkle emanating from the hand she was discreetly waving. He looked at John who responded with a curt nod and to Jennie whose nod was more compassionate than her father's.

He looked again to Anita, and went to her. He sat by her side and took her warm hands in his.

"Anita Juárez, I have not once seen you as beautiful or as disruptive to my thoughts as you are this very moment. It appears to me that you have many good friends surrounding you, whereas I do not, as well as a more loving and compassionate family, which I do not at this moment. I see in their eyes how they love you. I see in their eyes how wrong I have been for so long. Yet I have seen this very moment in my mind for so many years, to see my children, to see you sitting by my side, your hands in mine."

"We were wrong together, Hidalgo. We were afraid."

"We were wrong apart, and wrong to be apart because I was the one who was afraid."

She put a hand to his cheek. "I love you, Hidalgo, if that helps you. I have spoken these words many nights to myself, words that are true. I do love you."

"I suffered for many years for what happened to Francine and to my children after you saved me from my self-destruction, Santa Anita. You were the one who drew me from the dark abyss of my misery, no one else. You saw me at my worst, yet you did not see the worst of my pain, the pain of not keeping my promise, a promise which kept my pain alive. How could I have shared such profound grief with you? I could not, until now, because of my families, natural and adopted, who now bear witness to my shame, a family that has conspired so overtly against me to guide me towards the woman I love so deeply." He took the ring from the box. "Anita Juárez, please be my wife, please repair my damaged heart with your love and make my family whole once again."

She took her hand from his cheek, seeing him through a misty curtain. She was barely breathing, the warmth from the kitchen and the aroma of roasted turkey filling the room. The Christmas tree flickered with the bright colours of lights and bulbs under the silver and gold of tinsel and the soft white of angel hair. She looked at each of them standing so near to her, her new family and her new friends. She wanted never to forget what she was seeing, what she was at last living. This wasn't a dream.

"Hidalgo, yes I will marry you...Cacique."

He slid the ring onto her finger and she kissed him the way she'd always dreamt that she would, tears streaming from her eyes.

Hidalgo was instantly forgotten. Anita was the centre of attraction.

Fernando, John Canyon and Diego stole outside with Hidalgo, beyond Maria's reach. Fernando had a fine bottle of tequila to share; a gift recently delivered and didn't believe the hour was too early.

Inside, Maria took Diane by the hand and led her to the festive tree. She pointed to a box wrapped in green and purple foil, tied with a satin bow. She didn't really believe the day before that Diane had truly wanted to return Diego's gift to the store.

71

Monday morning, December 27th, Hidalgo and Anita woke together in her bed, the initial awkwardness of seeing each other as lovers after to many years transformed into eager anticipation of tender touches and words. They saw no purpose in beginning their life together in a mansion that was neither his home nor his as the Governor of California as of midnight Friday.

Nor would he now retire to live out his life in a hammock or squeezing grapes, he told his overwhelmed fiancée over a romantic breakfast. He had decided as he watched her sleep that he would return to the law in the New Year, to take over as head of Arquero-Duval & Partners alongside Virginia Meadows. As proof, not that Anita didn't believe him, he phoned Virginia with the news. Adding that, after so many years, he would need all the help she could give him. Neither woman heard the other giggle. Neither one saw the other's elated expression.

In the meantime he would devote the entire week to Anita. His job was done. He was the governor in name alone. He had nothing left to sign or debate. Most of the transition work was achieved and what little remained to do could be handled by senior staff. He did however, on the Tuesday, swagger through the Capitol and into his office holding Anita's hand, causing the building to come alive with gossip, the door to Anita's old office constantly opening and closing. Amongst the first were Carlos Del

Campo and Luis de la Vega, her favourite cops and co-conspirators.

As cops they needed proof, they needed to see the evidence for themselves, each of them calling through to the governor's office that it was about time he took care of business before someone else did. He retorted by asking what the penalty was for hijacking a private jet with two and then three attractive women onboard.

Hidalgo, once Anita was finished with them, asked for a moment in private with the senior cops. He did, in fact, have one last piece of business to discuss with them, off the record. If not quite ethical, what he was asking of them was not illegal in any way. If they agreed, for he could trust no one else to manage the task, their retirements would be much more comfortable, off the record. They agreed, though not for the money, they had good pensions coming their way, more for the experience of luxury neither one had ever considered.

Throughout the week Anita made no mention of Scott Gibson. She knew that whatever Hidalgo would do, he would do nothing to injure her love for him. Of that, she was now certain.

On the Friday when Diane and Diego arrived from Los Angeles to bring in the New Year at Anita's home with family and old friends once again assembled, Diane readily agreed to join Jennie and her father for dinner at the Estates on Sunday, frowning when Diego asked for a rain cheque with effusive apologies.

He stepped aside with his father to speak briefly before midnight struck. All was set, he told Hidalgo. He had called Mendoza the night before and had made the arrangements. Mendoza would fly into Miami on the coming Tuesday. He would depart late Wednesday after their meeting.

Hidalgo was pleased. He walked away without saying another word and five minutes later he was no longer the

Governor of California. He stepped into the night air to make one call that was a matter of convention and a second that was imperative. He felt younger, happier without the weight of the world on his shoulders and earlier he'd dismissed the security detail so that they might spend New Year's with their families. As with others of his personal staff, he gave them each a cash bonus for having served him well.

The first call was to his successor, to wish him well, apologizing for his absence at the State Ball. His second was to Mendoza who answered on the third chime.
*

The previous Monday morning Diane woke in a dreamy state, an arm flung across the empty left side of her bed. He was in the kitchen cooking her breakfast, ignoring her pleas to join her in bed. She padded into the kitchen wearing his shirt, pouting, hating him, or pretending that she did.

He wasn't fooled.

"Are you always going to ignore me after we're married?"

"I'm not ignoring you. I'm preparing a feast for you."

"You're leaving me, aren't you? You're going to Miami again."

"No, I'm not leaving you, though I am going to Miami and you know why. The good news is my flight's leaving only after you have breakfast and I have you, Captain Quinn. The governor believes I shouldn't be left alone and you'd better be packing the tiniest bikinis you own." A devilish smirk crossed his face. "Or none at all."

She leapt onto him. "You're serious."

"I'm serious. We're flying to Miami, driving to Key West and spending the week on Life's Compensation compliments of your crazy sister-in-law. Or whatever she is to you right now. Friday we fly to L.A. I wrote my letter of resignation last night while you were snoring. I'm a cop for five more days, munchkin, like I promised."

She punched him. "I don't snore."

*

They arrived in Miami too late to drive to Key West, throughout the flight Diego asking to try the controls, Diane refusing, Diego still curious about the Auto-pilot function and the Mile-high thing. Diane ignored him.

Tuesday they drove to the boat, Diane sucking in her breath as they approached the slip and heard what Life's Compensation might have cost.

They spent the day three miles offshore, within scope range of the Burnt Out, Diane surprised by how quickly she adapted to jumping into the turquoise depths naked. However on deck, she was adamant, and much to his dismay, she would wear her thong.

At five o'clock both yachts were floating at dock.

While Diane showered and changed, Diego went for a walk. He went to the Burnt Out where Gibson was rinsing away a day's worth of salt spray from the fibreglass decks and stainless steel bright work.

He went right to Adams who remembered him. Drew Carling was anxious for the week to be over, to reunite with friends he hadn't seen in such a long time, to spend the coming week on the ocean with them, deep sea fishing.

Adams asked about his wife. She'd never been on a boat, Carling replied. She was a little nervous, although very excited. She'd bought a drawer full of new bikinis, more like a pile of strings. At that Adams smiled, telling Drew that his female passengers almost never fished, preferring instead to soak up the sun on the forward deck. He chuckled. There were no rules. What happened on the Burnt Out, stayed on the Burnt Out.

Somehow Diego wasn't surprised by that and made a mental note to check the lower cabin of the Burnt Out at some point for recording equipment as well as the radar and

GPS antennae for hidden lenses before killing the man.

He would be set to go any time after 9:00 AM. Midnight dips in the sea were also possible, for a modest fee adjustment, which Drew Carling thought was an excellent idea. He suggested Thursday night which would give the women a few days to get used to the idea of being a little raunchy. And, hey, why wouldn't Adams bring his wife or girlfriend along. The more the merrier.

At that the men laughed. They didn't shake hands. Drew simply walked away waving his in the air, Adams went back to cleaning his boat.

When Diego returned to Life's Compensation Diane was sitting on the afterdeck wrapped in a towel, telling him she wasn't very hungry. A few minutes later he joined her wrapped in his own. Neither was he hungry.

Wednesday they left the dock at 9:10. She was amazed that he could handle such a large boat with such ease, and she wanted to try. He said no, not unless he could fly the Citation. She smacked him, reclining with her feet on the console, threatening to wear jeans and a sweatshirt unless he changed his mind. Past the breakwater, half a mile out to sea, he did change his mind and he reclined with his feet on the console, tugging at her strings. Diane stood at the helm, giggling. He was so pathetic, she told him.

She slowed to idle speed, and from idle into neutral, letting the boat sink its five feet of draft into the sea. She cut the engines and dropped the anchor as though she was doing something exciting, asking him how she'd done. He shrugged. She'd just turned a key and pushed a toggle switch forward, proof that she could do practically anything, he admitted. She smacked him again.

He retaliated, pulling her strings, coaxing her onto his lap. Life was good, really good, so much better than the dark streets of L.A.

They swam in the sea and bathed in the sun, Diego

520

insistent that her skin remain flawless, that only he could properly apply lotion to her body, all her body, at least once each hour, until Diane realized that wearing her thong was pointless. Her tan lines were fast disappearing.

They frolicked in the sea, leaping from the transom, diving from the bow, Diego scoping Gibson whenever Diane wasn't on deck. The man hadn't once deviated from the previous week's schedule, latitude or longitude, and Thursday was no different. Until Thursday night when after an early dinner Diego left Diane alone for a few hours.

Donna Simpson arrived on time, dressed to kill in a short skirt with legs to her neck, a push-up bra and an open jean jacket, making Diego a little curious. He thought about two-hundred an hour. Ten grand a year, minimum, and probably more, that she would soon have to find elsewhere. He had no reason to either know or care when she left. What he did know was that Dan Adams would be expected at his slip by the dock master near five o'clock each day without creating a reason for the man to call Adams over the public VHF.

There was no way Gibson would invite his hooker to what he believed or hoped would be a midnight dip in the ocean. And although he doubted that she would, he didn't want Donna Simpson showing up at the marina any time after asking questions about her regular source of tax-free income. He had a three-day window before she might become concerned. Zero time once he arrived on the coming Monday with Mendoza and his goons before Gibson would realize not to expect a party of three men ready to fish and three women ready to soak half-naked in the sun and a half-day at best before the dock master might become involved by asking other boaters to maintain a vigilance.

Diane waited for him and went to bed, leaving him to sit on the afterdeck alone, sipping the Johnnie Walker Blue he'd replaced. She never drank within twenty-four hours of flight time. He was set. He would tell his father that Wednesday, the fifth, was the ideal day and that he and Mendoza should fly in on the Tuesday, January 04th.

He called the airline and booked the first flight out Sunday from Sacramento. After which he called Mendoza, giving him the details, suggesting where they should meet in Key West. They agreed on the timing, Mendoza thanking him for not bringing dishonour on his father.

Friday they left the marina at seven, departing MIA at 8:30 to arrive at LAX at noon local time. Diane remained at the airport while Drew Carling went alone to end a promising career.

No tears were shed, no sorrowful goodbyes uttered. Few cops knew of Detective Drew Carling or of his commendations and those who did didn't like him much. They didn't like his attitude, his 'get out my way' demeanour.

He took a taxi to his apartment where he cancelled his lease and packed what clothes he hadn't taken with him earlier. He had no memories to take with him; he wasn't a collector, and whatever important documents he had were in safekeeping at the bank that he would deal with whenever he returned to put his seaside escape up for sale and drive his Corvette to wherever Diane wanted to live.

They departed LAX at six.

He wasn't sad. He had what he wanted out of life. He had Diane, he'd found his family, he was saving his father from a life of haunting nightmares and soon he would begin planning his restaurant while Diane planned their wedding. He just didn't want to speak and Diane understood, giving him space while he sat stretched out in the co-pilot's seat from Los Angeles to Sacramento.

He couldn't believe that his girl flew around the country like most people travelled along city blocks on a bus, getting off, getting on, albeit with a little more paperwork. Diane couldn't believe he'd just given up being a cop. She was floating on air. They arrived home at 8:30 local time

He didn't want to go, he told her. He was going for her and sat on their bed watching her dress in a simple black, short and décolleté cocktail dress, her hair twisted into a tight French braid, her ears and neck adorned with the rubies and diamonds he'd bought her for Christmas. She snapped her fingers twice. She wasn't joking; she wanted the panties he was twirling on his finger.

They arrived at Anita's home at ten-thirty. Diane went to Anita's side of the room after being pirouetted by John Canyon, praised by her boss and not believing Fernando's assurance that, if he were not already captured by one of loveliest women in California, he would fight with his grandson for her hand.

On his side of the room, with the men, Diego wondered how much John and Fernando knew. They had been with Hidalgo the day they threatened him out of love, the day Mendoza came to his home. They'd seen him with Mendoza that day so many years in their past. They must know.

At midnight the men hurried with happy faces to the other side of the room. The best part of the evening had come, particularly for John. Hidalgo made a toast to their success in the coming year, John, to the beauty of each woman in the room, Fernando to the children brought home to him, and Diego to his father.

He began: "My intention was to share this with you at Christmas, Governor, though for many reasons I didn't. Above all, I didn't want to usurp Anita's special moment or Diane's. This evening I am no longer a cop. More importantly, I am no longer Drew Carling. I am Diego Hidalgo Arquero-Duval, as I should be. And you, Governor, now that you are officially unemployed, and with your permission, will be Hidalgo to me."

He put the rim of his fluted glass to Hidalgo's. No words were spoken.

72
12:05 AM New Year's Day of this Year

Hidalgo stepped outside alone, wondering at all that had happened in the space of one month. With his last official duty behind him, his respects paid to his successor, he dialled.

"Feliz año nuevo, Señor Mendoza."

"Happy New Year to you as well, Señor Arquero. I welcome your voice and may I congratulate you. You have waited a very long time for this evening in many ways, I suspect. As I have. The beginning of a new year, a new life, and might I also wish you a long and happy life together with the fortunate young lady who has agreed to be your bride."

"Thank you."

"And now to a matter that has weighed heavily on both our hearts for such a long time. I spoke with your son yesterday. His intention is to deceive you."

"I am aware of his concern, though his intentions are honourable. However, he will be disappointed to learn that I have made alternate plans which preclude his participation in our affair."

"Then we are of a one mind."

"We are. I will leave here Sunday, arriving in Miami late in the day. I will drive to the final destination the next morning."

"For my part, I could not harness my eagerness. My celebration of El Año Nuevo can wait until I have proper cause to celebrate. I am in Miami as we speak. The headlights you see so early in the morning will likely be mine. I would also suggest that you leave your car in the town, at which time you will call me. We will travel to our host's location by taxi to avoid the curiosity of security cameras. Wear clothes you no longer wish as part of your wardrobe after we meet. You must also wear a hat. Touch nothing once you leave the taxi and until you are boarded. We will have new gloves for you. My men will precede us, playing the part of the others he is expecting."

"I am not very talented in matters of the sea."

"My men are, chosen for that reason."

"Then I will say goodnight to you."

"Until Monday, and Señor," Mendoza's chuckle wasn't meant to be humorous, "do not forget your match."

73

Sunday morning Diego woke early thinking to make breakfast for her, when Diane was in the kitchen making his. He was leaving her for two days, and she knew why. He believed he was going to save his father's humanity and rid the planet of human waste. Whereas she believed in Enrique Mendoza, regretting that she had ruined her phone, wishing she could speak with him one last time to remind him of his promise to her.

She was glad Diego was no longer a cop. She wanted to see him in elegant suits greeting customers at his restaurant, The Governor's Table. She wanted him home every night making love with her, being an idiot for her. Not coming home at all hours, never certain that he would.

She'd decided that she would play dumb, whatever happened, whatever Mendoza did to keep Diego from doing something really stupid. She would pretend not to know. And why would he think that she did? She wouldn't lie to him; she simply wouldn't tell him the truth. The only person she could rely on for support was Anita, who wasn't any better off. In this matter they were sisters. She decided she would call Anita and suggest lunch, as Diego was smothering her face and shoulders with 'goodbye' and 'I love you so much' kisses.

He promised to call each night and he left her as though going to the store for milk. They would need months if not years together, she knew, to erase his past.

He hadn't been gone ten minutes when her phone chimed. She'd spent the past week on the boat, in the air, in bed, making love, watching him, undecided whether he was a dear, a darling, a honey or a list of a dozen other of her synonyms for idiot and jerk. She settled on sweetheart, now that she had determined that he had one.

"Sweetheart, I've told you a hundred times today how much I love you."

"Thank you…Diane. The thought warms my heart. However perhaps we should keep your sentiments between us and not share them with my son or with my darling Anita."

She giggled. "Hidalgo, I'm so sorry. I thought your silly son was calling."

"And so he should, many times each day, never allowing himself to take you for granted."

"He won't be home until Tuesday."

"A lifetime for young lovers to be apart, however he is in good hands. I assure you."

"I don't understand."

"You will soon. I lament the short notice, Diane; however I do require your immediate service as a pilot."

"Yes sir, of course. Where are we going?"

"To Miami, as quickly as you can file a flight plan and inspect the plane. We will return as late as you wish on Tuesday or as early on Wednesday. I leave the schedule to you and I must ask you not to call Diego to advise him."

"Now I really don't understand. Why not, Hidalgo?"

"I orchestrated a surprise for him, Diane. Anita is complicit in my mischievousness and therefore equally culpable should you not share the humour which we believe is integral to our deviousness. Anita will also accompany us to Miami, so that you might have a like-minded companion for shopping and for dinner while I attend to matters of business. She would also, for once, like to sit with you in the flight deck, a childhood dream of sorts. That is also your decision, of course. My car will pass by your home in thirty minutes. We can speak of Diego's adventure en route. Though I can tell you that had he not declined Jennie's invitation to dinner his week might have turned out entirely more to his liking. We never know, I suppose, what fate has in store for us?"

"Hidalgo, the one reason I'm not very nervous right now is your tone. Is he in any trouble?"

"His well-being is not a matter of concern, I assure you. I would not mislead my future daughter-in-law, nor would I a valued and dear friend."
*

Diego stepped through the wrought iron gate. He didn't greet the taxi driver. He hated taxis, the way people felt obliged to have a banal conversation with someone they didn't know or care about.

He saw them coming, Del Campo and de la Vega. Cops were cops: their stature, their casual stride, their unsmiling faces, eyes that managed to see in all directions at once, the way the left side of their suit jackets was slightly less fitted than the right. They were coming straight at him with a purpose, branching out in different directions to corral him. He just didn't know why.

"Diego Arquero-Duval," de la Vega said, not asking, coming in from the left.

They knew. "We meet again, detectives? What's up?"

Del Campo answered, approaching from the right. "You're under arrest by order of the Governor of California, Hidalgo Arquero. It seems your old man's sending you to reform school."

"Is this a joke?"

"Yeah, we drove across town to tell you a joke. You know the drill. Drop the luggage. Don't be a hero."

"Guys, I'm a cop for Christ's sake."

"You were a cop. Now you're Joe Nobody. Drop the bags, junior."

"The governor lost his job Friday night. This is bullshit."

He spun around, searching.

"Yeah, he did, after he signed the warrant." Del Campo tossed Diego the cuffs. "Do yourself."

Diego hesitated, uncertain, expecting to see Diane with a camera on the third floor. "This isn't happening. Show me the warrant."

De la Vega dug into the inside pocket of his coat. He passed Diego the sealed envelope. The wording of the warrant left nothing open to interpretation.
*

Diego, my son, once taken from me and now found, please enjoy my hospitality and the company of these good men. I trust you will find your accommodations agreeable. However, should you prefer more modest surroundings, and in any way interfere with what I have asked of these gentlemen, they are instructed to deliver you forthwith to the county facility, a much less agreeable choice.

I do this out of kindness, and for Diane who occupies a special place in my heart. What is in your mind and in your heart is contrary to an oath spoken between men of a common interest years ago. Such oaths do not and should not diminish with time. That you believed he would accept your collusion in place of my own has no merit. Whatever he may be in your mind, he is a man of his word in mine.

This matter is closed and will not be discussed at any time in the future for any reason.

Hidalgo.
*

He slipped the letter into his jacket.

"So, guys, where are we going?"

"To paradise, if you play nice. To a strip search, if you don't."

De la Vega pointed to the unmarked car, which was his own, without the usual police amenities. He and Del Campo were taking a few days off, neither man had ever been to a spa for the rich and famous, all expenses paid.

Diego tossed Del Campo the cuffs. "We don't need these."

The cop caught them. "Yeah, we do, so either you do it, or I will…with your face on the sidewalk and my knee on your neck. I weigh two-eighty, kid. Want to play with that?"

He didn't think so. Message received loud and clear. He caught the steel bracelets.

De la Vega patted him down. He was clean. The twin Berettas and dagger were on Deidre's yacht. Instead they seized his cellular and with his wrists anchored together he preceded them to the car, ignoring the taxi driver while Del Campo carried one suitcase and de la Vega carried the other. They had a 250 mile drive northward, well away from any airport.

Diego was learning about his father.

*

Diane was dressed in her red and white designer uniform, Anita in a cashmere sweater and linen slacks. The tower had warned Diane of a brief delay and she'd gone into the cabin to advise Hidalgo, confessing at the same time to her mounting curiosity.

"He's been arrested, Diane, incarcerated by my order. He will remain in custody until I see fit to release him."

She didn't hear that, she couldn't have.

"Pardon me, you had him arrested, he's in jail?"

"Yes, by virtue of my last official order as governor, for his own good."

Diane began slowly, uncertain, increasing her laughter

until her eyes began to tear and her stomach began cramping. She had to sit.

"He's in jail. You put your own son in jail."

Anita wasn't amused.

"Not quite jail. I would prefer to say that he is undergoing a much needed therapy."

"Cacique, you are being terrible. I have never known you to act this way," Anita broke in. "Diane, don't listen to him. He's teasing you, very badly I might add. Diego is fine. He is at a spa with officers known for their discretion. He was taken at your home this morning, moments after he stepped out."

"You mean Luis and Carlos."

Anita nodded. "I do."

Hidalgo couldn't help himself, smirking. "However he was handcuffed and read the Miranda. Therefore, in point of fact, he was arrested. ¿No es verdad, mi amor?"

Diane bubbled. "Cacique and mi amor, that's so hot, Anita. I'm so happy for you guys. Still, you could have told me before now, given me a heads-up. You didn't think I wanted to see that, my Detective Super Cop brought down with his hands cuffed behind his back, being read his rights, his super ego busted? Thanks a lot."

"Diane, you are talking of the young man who loves you."

Diane was wiping her eyes, catching her breath. "You're right, I'm sorry."

"I was told, however, by the arresting officers, that he took his predicament in stride once presented with the alternative," Hidalgo went on.

"Hidalgo, por favor." Anita tried. "Es bastante. Really, the girl has had enough to deal with lately. And, Diane, don't encourage him."

She was trying to be disgusted with both of them, preoccupied with trying to cool her face. She wasn't accustomed to being called by endearments in public, especially by Hidalgo.

Diane leaned forward, her arms crossed over her knees, clearing her throat. "Meaning what, Hidalgo...a chain gang?"

"Meaning that on a more serious note, I could not allow him to revisit Key West," Hidalgo continued. "And that he had his choice of detention. His job in Florida is done. He would have created certain and intolerable difficulties despite his best intentions."

Diane looked to Anita, from Anita to Hidalgo. The women shared a synergy. They shared a single purpose and motive. Anita nodded again, clasping her hands together.

"You mean Scott Gibson. Diego was going there to kill him, the guy who calls himself Dan Adams. The same guy you're meeting tomorrow."

Hidalgo paled. "Very unexpected honesty indeed, although I should not be surprised after the month we have all lived...or survived. You are well informed, Diane. Should I conclude that my son...?"

"No, Hidalgo, you shouldn't. It was me. I phoned Enrique Mendoza. I spoke with him. I phoned him to beg him not to let you or Diego do something stupid. I don't want anything bad to happen to you. I'm telling you this, not that I expected to, so that you will never have to pretend with me or Anita, or Diego with me."

"What Diane is saying is half true, Hidalgo. I share the responsibility of what has been done, as I do the blame. We don't want anything bad to happen to you, or to Diego. We did what we must without any regret, for our men. We called Mendoza together, to speak with one voice. He has made us promises."

"What promises, Anita?"

"That he is a man of his word, and we believe him. Diane and I will spend our time in Miami knowing that you are as safe as Diego is now and that you are in the care of someone who can do what you cannot."

Diane broke in. "I know the history, Hidalgo. I'm good with it. I saw the man, he made my skin crawl. I'm only worried for you and your son. I have the highest regard for you, Hidalgo. I love you, you know that. I won't let anything happen to you."

"So once again I find myself at the heart of a conspiracy. Am I now to understand that I will live my life wondering each time you are together what is formulating in your devious minds?"

"A conspiracy more by fortunate coincidence than by design, Hidalgo," Anita added. "And all you must know is what has already formulated in our hearts. What is in our minds is ours alone, for you to discover when we feel the time is right."

He spoke to Diane. "Knowing what you do, what you have known for however long, can you fly this aircraft safely, without the least distraction? Or should I perhaps call…"

"No one else flies my plane, Señor Arquero. ¿Comprendes lo que digo? I'm perfectly fine and very capable. Thank you very much. " She glanced at Anita. "Besides, we girls have shopping to do."

"Yes Captain, understood. I meant no disparagement. I would trust no one else at the controls." He slouched into his seat, taking a moment. "That I am telling you this crushes my heart. But I feel now that I must. Gibson is an evil being, not a man or worthwhile creature belonging to this earth. There is none worse and his sentence will be carried out with specific precision so that he will, without the slightest doubt, realize the horror of his abominable crime. I have promised Francine that the horror of his passing will surpass her own, though I believe and I hope that in his final moments he will be sufficiently preoccupied with the manner of his death to forego any consideration of the significance attached to our choice. My sincerest wish is that in his very final moments his mind will fail him, that he will perish on the verge of insanity. Not so quickly, however, that our justice is lost on him. That is what I wish. What I now promise you Anita, and you Diane, is that my participation in his passing will appease me and lighten my heart, that Francine will at last find peace in the universe and that neither of you will have cause to despise me or loathe me for what I am about to do with the assistance of Señor Mendoza and Mrs. Claire Gibson."

"I would never marry a man whom I loathe or despise, Cacique. You have no reason to speak such words."

"Anita's right, Hidalgo," Diane agreed. "We don't envy you, though we will always love and respect you." She giggled and went to sit on his lap, wrapping her arms around his neck, leaving an imprint of her red lips on his cheek. "You're going to be my new daddy. How strange is that?"

Anita was taken completely off guard, chortling at seeing her great cacique blushing deep crimson.

Hidalgo studied each woman in turn.

"As I have requested of my son, this matter is closed. Never again to be broached. You lovely ladies, you think you know all that I do. Let me assure you that you do not. Nevertheless, allow me to give you something to gaggle about in the flight deck as I sit here alone throughout the entire flight to ponder my new life and to enjoy a glass of Canyon Estates finest yield later in the day. First, however, I must hear your separate oaths not to breathe a word of what you are about to hear to any of my children until they are told by me in my own words and in my own time."

"Cacique, what expression is that on your face? You have my word, you know that you do."

"Yes, daddy, ditto for me." She pinched his cheek.

535

"What's up?"

Diane wiggled from his lap into her own seat. Hidalgo was seeing another side of her, one that warmed his heart and, he was certain, Diego's.

"A few days ago I was given a substantial gift with instructions as to its proper use. I have since decided to modify those instructions in order to meet the current situation which, heretofore, was not anticipated. By this I mean the happy expansion of my family. For that reason I have brought you ladies into the equation, which I believe would please the person whose anonymity I would prefer to maintain. What I can tell you is that I am not that person. This morning, before leaving home, sitting in an office which is entirely too feminine for my personal taste, I transferred sixty million dollars into each of your accounts. Upon my return I will do likewise for each of my children. In addition, one stipulation must prevail, a dying wish that you achieve some degree of good with your windfalls and not place avarice before kindness."

He remained as he was.

Anita knew, not that she wasn't flabbergasted. She remembered Claire Gibson's promise that she would do something good to benefit the world before her death. However Diane did think he was joking and began another burst of giggles.

"Hidalgo, such a gift is beyond words. I cannot think of what to say, my mind is blank. She did not know me."

"On the contrary, mi amor. I believe that she did. I have met very few people, Anita, as kind as you and Diane. She would be pleased with my decision. She would want you included in the goodness she intended."

"What! No! No way. Shit! Hidalgo, is this for real?"

Hidalgo snorted a laugh, standing to refill his cup. "Yes, Captain Diane, this is real, which does not obviate your current responsibilities to your passengers. Please deliver me and my lovely bride safely to our destination and your subsequent shopping spree, which I must now assume has taken on a somewhat different dimension." He sat eyeing them, sipping his coffee, appearing quite satisfied with himself. "I trust I have given you sufficient cause to wag your tongues, ladies."

Diane didn't reply. She stood, leaned over him and coloured his other cheek, returning to the flight deck to answer the traffic controller: fifteen minutes to take-off. She signalled Anita in with her, not breaking eye contact with Hidalgo until the lock snapped the door closed.

74
Monday, January 03rd, of this Year

He enjoyed their company during dinner, later strolling with them, holding their hands under a clear sky and bright moon along the calm shore of South Beach to end their evening. He spoke very little, preferring to hear the women speak together, to hear their soft voices, to hear them talking of Gabriella, Francesca, Diego and weddings.

It appeared that father and son would marry their brides on the same day. However when Diane mentioned Valentine's Day once again, unaware, Anita squeezed Hidalgo's hand, peering into his eyes. She knew not to let that happen. That was Francine's special day, not hers, not Diane's.

When they began speaking of brides' maids, however, flowers and honeymoons, he wisely slowed his pace, released their hands and walked behind them. Watching them strolling arm in arm, he thought they might have been sisters in another life.

At the hotel he and Anita made certain Diane was locked safely into her suite. In their suite Hidalgo put Anita to bed, advising her more matter-of-factly than as a confession that he had transferred seventy million into her account, not sixty, which she was not to argue.

She didn't. She acquiesced. Hidalgo was now her man, proving that he was by doing what Anita believed was entirely characteristic of her cacique. He left her. He went to his own suite. He didn't want her to see him waking before dawn, dressing and leaving her to participate in a killing which, to her, now, was no worse than sitting in the viewing room at the end of death row with a dozen or so other witnesses to a deserved execution. Throughout his two terms as Governor of California he had denied clemency to a dozen or more residents of death row. This was no different, she believed. Gibson was being denied what he had no reason or right to expect.

In his room he sat on the edge of his bed. He didn't pray. He hadn't prayed or attended church in years. Instead he spoke to Francine in quiet tones and whispered words of love to Anita that she would not hear. He set his alarm and called the Reception Desk for a wake-up call, not trusting himself. He eased under the covers and slept well for the first time in years.

*

He woke in the dark, the constitution of seventeen-hour days undiminished. He left the hotel at 5:00, two hours before sunrise. He would drive the distance in less than three hours and meet Mendoza at eight.

He stopped in Key Largo at a coffee shop for a coffee and a half-dozen glazed doughnuts. He stood in the parking lot, beyond sight of the main road. He didn't want to meet with Mendoza before the allotted time. He wanted time alone to see the sun rise over the sea, to smell the air. He'd missed so much during his time in office, so much more since his wife and his children were taken from him. And now his life was recaptured.

He'd spoken again with Virginia Meadows. He would re-join the firm on March 01st. Anita had also called her new employer to dissolve her contract with them. They understood. With all that had happened to her over the past few days, with what lay ahead of her, she couldn't possibly focus on a career that would likely deprive her of a private life and family.

He was unaccustomed to having free time to think of personal matters. He was getting married, quite possibly alongside his son. The women had decided that Fernando would stand for the men and that John Canyon would give away the brides. The issue was the honeymoon. Who would fly him to where he wanted to go? How could he expect his son's 'munchkin' to fly him and Anita to the South Seas or Europe when Diane would be a bride herself? And Diane would never allow any other pilot, including the captain of the state's official jet, to fly her baby.

He had a dilemma. He considered himself an easy going person, adaptable to most situations, but one thing he would never do is fly commercial. He chuckled. She was indeed a little munchkin, aptly named and as light as a feather in his lap. She and Anita were already as close as sisters, which he thought was better put from his mind. He was certain, that together, they would soon become worrisome adversaries in matters of heart and hearth.

He tossed the empty cup into the garbage with the three remaining doughnuts and took to the road. Arriving in Key West he called Mendoza, pulling into the designated roadside parking area with access to the beach minutes before eight. Mendoza was waiting.

They hadn't seen each other or spoken since the day Hidalgo sat sedated in a place that could no longer be his home, though throughout his years at Arquero-Duval, and as governor, Hidalgo had not lost track of the man or his burgeoning career.

He hadn't given any thought at all to what he should expect. Photos of Mendoza on the front pages of newspapers or thumbnails squeezed into corners of glossy magazine pages were always shot from behind, the side, or with his face cloaked by the raised collar of his coat or the

lowered brim of a fedora. He certainly wasn't expecting to see the man wearing a cable sweater, Dockers, canvas shoes, a Tilley Outback and Serengeti sunglasses tinted yellow.
*

"We meet again, Señor Arquero, at last."

They shook hands.

"A day I let myself believe would never come."

Mendoza smiled widely. "But for a mother's love. Is that not so? And have we not chosen an ideal day. Despite my lack of knowledge in things culinary, I am an excellent chef when presented with a barbeque. And today, I will prepare an excellent roast."

Hidalgo chuckled in spite of himself, watching Mendoza's goons dragging a large box from the rear of the rented SUV, carrying it several car lengths ahead of them.

"I'm afraid to ask."

"That is our barbeque, one sized to accommodate a large pig. Let yourself be surprised. I assure you, you will not be disappointed in the manner of his departure." Mendoza lit a cigarillo, inhaling deeply. "I have made promises regarding your mental health, Hidalgo." Smoke wafted from his mouth and his nose. "Formality should have no place between us for the long-awaited pleasure we are about to share. I would prefer Enrique. So let me speak plainly. At no time did I intend to let your son take part in our business. As for Miss Diane Quinn, she will remember me as a man of my word. She was brave to call me. The girl has guts and, might I add, she is very attractive. This, of course, is confidential. She has no need to know that I am betraying her confidence. Your son has done well, despite himself. She was not pleased with him, nor was I. You will strike the match, nothing more. I will roast the pig. We last met in your home, Hidalgo. Let us not repeat history. Are we clear?"

"We are. I have also made promises, Enrique, in keeping with the wishes of Claire Gibson and the fears of both my bride-to-be and Diane."

They shook hands once more. They understood each other and joined the others, calling the cab company whose number was posted on a billboard by the boardwalk. The van arrived inside of five minutes, delivering them to the marina at eight-thirty where Hidalgo identified himself to the office over the intercom as Drew Carling. He explained that he'd misplaced his guest pass and wanted to pay in advance for another week's dockage of Deidre Commons' yacht. Moments later the gate rose.

The four men went directly to Life's Compensation, smiling, swaggering without purpose in keeping with the demeanour of privileged yachtsmen, all four openly impressed by what they saw. The man who was to pilot the yacht leapt over the gunwale, searching for the key where instructed by Hidalgo. He was anxious to turn over the engine, more anxious to test the boat on open water than to kill Gibson. The box remained on the dock.

Mendoza's men left them to meet Dan Adams for a day of deep sea fishing. They waited from a distance, watching until they saw him disappear into the lower cabin, boarding within seconds, gently rocking the boat. Gibson called out a greeting, not expecting an expert foot crashing into his throat, hurling him backward onto the cabin floor.

Meanwhile, onboard Life's Compensation, Mendoza was outlining the day. Gibson would die at noon, with the sun at its zenith when most eyes would be blinded by the glitter of a calm sea. The conditions could not be better.

"We will join my associates at nine and cast off at 9:05, Hidalgo. We want nothing to appear unusual. I will cruise first with one man to somewhere ten miles offshore between here and Key Largo where we will cast our lines as a precaution. You will spend the morning with my other associate. He is good company, educated and well-travelled. Not all my men have remained in the barrio. He will keep you within sight of us and communicate with me by his phone which is untraceable and soon to rest on the ocean floor with what remains of Gibson. The end of his day will begin at noon, at which time you will receive an invitation to come alongside us for five minutes, no longer, provided the airspace above us is clear. As for boaters, there is none to see. We are alone here. The sea will be as deserted as this marina on a Monday in January when most will be returning to work with more regrets for the previous year than hope for the coming twelve months. From the time you step onboard I estimate five minutes of extreme discomfort before he is well done and his heart explodes, the first three in preheat if I may say so. After which he will be cooked on HI so that we can be certain. Not that I have the slightest doubt now. I do not."

"What is in the box?" Hidalgo asked.

"A barbeque, as I have told you, which has the appearance of a fifty gallon drum. I would have preferred a bath to enhance the experience, though I believe the drum will do nicely."

"And what if he attempts to jump out? He will certainly attempt to prolong his life."

"He will not. I assure you."

"Five minutes," Hidalgo repeated.

Mendoza nodded. "The heat trapped by the metal will serve to intensify the agony of his final minutes. Thirty more and he will have the consistency of burnt toast crumpled in your hands, charred pieces. By which time his boat will be fifteen miles closer to the horizon, while we are closer to shore watching in comfort as his brittle bones and his boat are blown into hell. By the time anyone cares to search for him, if they do, a few splintered pieces of fibreglass will remain, if that."

Hidalgo checked his watch. "Then we should not keep him waiting. Should we?"

Together they carried the heavy box to the Burnt Out, stopping briefly near the office for Hidalgo to pay the weekly fee in cash, the receipt made out to Drew Carling. The clerk did her job without acknowledging him. She didn't care. Clerks never did.

75

At the Burnt Out with their heads covered, wearing new leather gloves, they first put the box onboard, removing the drum along with four one-gallon jerry cans of gasoline and a large bag of briquettes. When they were done they hid the empty carton in the boat's dockside locker.

Onboard once again Hidalgo went first into the lower cabin, his breathing unaffected by anxiety, his hands and voice steady. Scott Gibson was lying on his back, face-up, his hands bound behind him with tie-wraps, his mouth stuffed with a towel.

"We meet again, Scott Gibson, at last. Or would you prefer that I call you, Dan Adams?"

At first Gibson didn't understand, until seeing Enrique Mendoza's bright smile.

"Hola, amigo. Tell me, you do not recognize this man? No? I must believe that you do. He is Hidalgo Arquero. We have come to join you for lunch, amigo."

Gibson was squirming, trying to cough, the skin at his throat broken.

"We won't waste time talking, Gibson," began Hidalgo. "We have come here with a dual purpose, the first of which is to express our gratitude to your mother. Claire is the one who led us to you before her recent passing. And because of her belated kindness to me I am once again reunited with my children, one of whom you recently encountered. Not once in all these years were they absent from my dreams, as you were never absent from my nightmares. Today is your day of atonement, Gibson. We have come here, Señor Mendoza and I, to ensure you a place in hell."

Gibson was too panic-stricken to cry. His mind not allowing him to accept what was happening.

"Do you recall exactly how you murdered my wife and Mario Mendoza? Do you think of them from time to time or how you killed innocent Navarra Carrera at the very beginning of her existence?" He nodded to one of Mendoza's men. "Would you be so kind as to free his mouth?' He waited. "Do you, think of them?"

"I didn't do it. I was running from him. I swear. I was into him big time. I heard about it, sure, but I didn't do it. And the girl, she wanted to come with me. She begged me. Then she got lost. She used me to get away from him. I swear."

"The girl's name was Navarra, not 'the girl', and you killed her in Virginia after you killed my wife and stole my children to abandon them across three cities. The question is why, for what reason. You shot Francine in the head, after which you exacerbated your cruelty by incinerating her body. She was twenty-nine and beautiful, the mother of three children. What was in your mind to do such a thing to them? And what of the blood on the couch, or that she was put into the car naked?"

Gibson's head was shaking wildly sideways. He was blubbering.

"Enrique, I swear. I did not kill Navarra. She left me."

"Sí, hombre, you did. And now we will kill you as you killed this man's young wife. Hidalgo, talking like this does no good." He nodded to his men. "Stuff his mouth."

Mendoza went to the bar, tossing each of his men a can of beer. "It is noon somewhere, amigos. Hidalgo, will you join us, to properly begin our day of relaxation upon the open sea?"

"A mild vodka, please, with soda."

He poured the same for himself. "Not much time remains before our day begins and his ends." He raised his glass to Hidalgo. "Before you leave us, for a short while, keep your promise to your wife."

Hidalgo leaned against the navigation table.

"You shot her in the head, after what we know was a violent confrontation. Signs of her clothing were found at her feet. As I cannot re-enact what I believe happened, I have decided to compensate myself by way of precluding the bullet from your passing. Do you remember the words I once spoke to you when we first met, Gibson? I said 'don't fuck up, amigo'. Well you did. As I understand the process you are about to experience, you will be placed into a drum. At your feet will be a quantity of briquettes sufficient to make our point, yet not kill you. When you are still able to appreciate the full extent of our hate for you, we will add an ample quantity of gasoline for a roast of your size, to ensure your eventual and complete disappearance. What concerns me, however, is your natural inclination to escape. I am assured that won't happen, though I confess to harbouring certain doubts."

Gibson was already on the verge of insanity, groaning, choking on his coughs.

Mendoza nodded to one of his men who produced a stiletto, pressing his thumb to the tiny button at the base of the pearl handle. The thin blade appeared as though from nowhere, thrust with cool precision deep into the cartilage of Gibson's kneecaps and twisted, then into his groin and twisted.

"That," Mendoza told Hidalgo, "is for what we know this pig did to your wife before her death, my gift to you." He glanced at his watch, and to the man he'd assigned to pilot Life's Compensation. "Now you must go. We are behind schedule. Let him imagine on his own the smell and

the feel of his sizzling flesh, not that he will not know soon enough. Three hours is not a long time at the end of one's life."
*

The Burnt Out left the marina without fanfare for another day at sea. Life's Compensation trailed behind, both boats cruising at 3000 rpm to their respective locations

Onboard the Burnt Out, Mendoza began his preparations as his man stood at the helm. They were ready for a day of fishing while under the Bimini top the fifty gallon drum was prepared with a thick floor of charcoal cubes soaked with a half a gallon of gasoline. What remained would be added each hour to prevent unwanted flashpoint.

In the lower cabin Gibson was wailing, his face distorted with pain, his eyes wild with fear, his puncture wounds effectively meant to torture not kill.

Nothing was happening in the air, or on the sea. Cruise ships had disappeared to wherever they were sailing and tour boat operators had no reason to cruise that far out. They were alone; the buildings dotting the distant shoreline were virtually invisible to them as they would be to anyone peering out to sea and into the glare of the sun from any one of them. From that perspective they were already close to the edge of the horizon and the Burnt Out would soon disappear well beyond.

At 11:30 Mendoza and his man pulled Gibson to the afterdeck by his shoeless feet that were tied together. With spare lines found in a locker they roped his feet to the back of his legs, his elbows to his torso. They hauled him up with some difficulty and dropped him into the drum knees first. His head barely reached the top rim.

Mendoza went about his business. He located the ship's log tossing the binder into the drum. He returned to the cabin to find the keys to Gibson's vehicle and his house. Satisfied, he returned to the man of the hour. He needed the code to Gibson's home, promising Gibson a bullet in exchange, a bullet between friends who once were. All was forgiven. Gibson was wailing, blind with hysterical tears, Mendoza convincing him that one-tenth of one second was much better than 300 seconds, if not more, of melting flesh and a heart that would explode from searing heat which would quickly exceed 500° Fahrenheit, but not before his legs disintegrated before his bowels, his torso and finally his head.

He removed the towel, noting 1-3-6-4-7-9. He thanked Gibson, showing him the gun with an assuring nod, soaking the towel with gasoline and once again stuffing his mouth with a more telling grin.

No more fuel was added. At 11:45 he called Life's Compensation. At twelve noon the boats were side by side, rafting, floating in calm seas, their engines purring at idle.

There was no reason to waste time, Mendoza warned. They had come to kill, not to gloat and put them in harm's way. They would celebrate later, alone or together. Neither would words make a difference. Words at such a time were useless. Dead men had no memory.

He was pathetic, slumped in the drum, his mouth stuffed, his nose dripping loose mucus, his neck craning upwards, his head twitching, his eyes red from a torrent of tears, choking from the dryness in his throat, whimpering from the pain in his knees and in his groin. Hidalgo could not have asked for more.

He struck his match, leaning forward. "This is for Francine, and for Navarra."

"Arquero! Do not make me into a liar. Or yourself into a man who your new wife will despise." His wrist was gripped with a firmness that jolted him backward. "Do not break our agreement, amigo."

"You're right, of course, an impulsive reaction to seeing him after all these years. Take the match."

Mendoza did, carefully from between Hidalgo's gloved fingers, not relinquishing his grip. "We have no time for a moment of weakness that would bring a lifetime of shame, Hidalgo. Grip my hand, amigo. We will do this as one, one body, one man. You shall be absolved with a clear conscience and I will have kept my word." He sniggered. "That, I did not promise."

Hidalgo gripped Mendoza's free hand. "I will not leave here, Gibson, until I hear your screams and see that you are dead."

Mendoza added, "Gibson. We leave you in five minutes, though you should not begin to die before three. First your legs will go, then the rest of you. Five minutes I believe is the longest you should expect to live. Within the half hour you will be cremated, unrecognizable as you sail alone to the horizon where your boat will at last give credence to its name, exploding your cinders into the sky along with her." He tossed the match, gripping Hidalgo's hand all the tighter. "Your promise is kept, Hidalgo. I hope now that you may sleep well each night with the loving arms of your wife around you. Your demon is dying before your eyes. See his expression as he begins his passage into hell. He is not doing well, not quite the man his mother once hoped he would become. You have no need to see the skin melt from his bones, amigo. He will burn just as well if you watch and listen to his screams from a distance. You have done what you have come to do. You must go."

He pulled his hand away, signalling his men who wasted no time ushering Hidalgo from the deck of the Burnt Out onto Life's Compensation.

Gibson was a hysterical blur. His pants and his socks were ignited. He wanted to jump free, but he couldn't, his torso twisting and jerking, his shoulders and arms banging against the drum, searing, his eyes bulging to the point of launching from their sockets.

Hidalgo looked down from the much larger yacht, which his unlikely companion was beginning to untie as Mendoza worked quickly in the lower cabin with the second and third gallons of gasoline while his man stood ready at the helm. He was the smaller of the associates, the most agile and had volunteered to remain onboard alone until he'd set Gibson's course.

Three minutes had passed. On deck Mendoza waited a moment longer. Gibson was near dead and several inches shorter in the makeshift furnace. His shirt was gone. What little hair was left on his head flickered and smoked as his shoulders and arms slumped against the steel walls of his coffin, much of his flesh burnt away.

Mendoza pushed the fourth jerry can into the drum as deeply as he could, grinding his teeth against the scorching heat, crossing the deck quickly, bounding with surprising agility across the gunwales of the two boats. At some point the fumes from the cabin would meld with the heat of the flames and Gibson would be forgotten, his remains crumpled amidst the fury of flames that would not die out before being dissipated by the explosion.

The boats separated in opposite directions, engines groaning, pushing hard against the reluctant water, the Burnt Out commencing its final voyage, cruising onto a plane, the throttle set at 4000 rpm, the auto-pilot set on a northeast course. A minute later Mendoza's man hurled himself from the fly bridge into the sea, not much caring about how he might appear sprawled in midair.

The brilliant flare from Gibson's tomb happened seconds later as the man was pulled from the sea and Life's Compensation altered course hard to starboard.

Retuning halfway to shore they cut the engines, idling. Mendoza and his men toasted their success with Deidre's Johnnie Walker Blue, Hidalgo with red wine. Twenty minutes later the explosion was barely audible, the midday glare of Scott Gibson's flight into hell all the brighter for Hidalgo who stood with his feet apart on the forward deck with Deidre's scope held firmly against his eyes.

The three men let him be. They knew that at certain times a man needed to be alone.

*

The four remained at sea monitoring Channel 16. Nothing they might have expected to hear was being reported and sunset would darken the sea in a few short hours. For all intents and purposes Dan Adams was a missing person, presumably lost at sea, if anyone cared, and Donna Simpson was out ten grand.

They enjoyed a third round of drinks, returning to the marina. Onboard were four garbage bags: one filled with deck shoes, another with pants, a third with shirts or sweaters and a fourth with gloves and hats. They would be disposed of by Mendoza's associates at various stops en route to Miami after they first searched Adams' home to clear out whatever reference existed to the Burnt Out including his guest registry.

Mendoza suggested dinner, not expecting that the ex-governor would accept. Of course, he understood, out of the blue asking whether he might drive with Hidalgo to Miami while his men went their own way to enjoy a night on the town when their work was done.

"I would like that we do, Hidalgo. We can stop for some good Mexican food along the way and eat as we drive. After all, are we not young at heart, you and I? Please, do this for me after so long a time."

Hidalgo accepted, once again stopping at Key Largo for take-out. Mendoza was interesting to talk with, surprising Hidalgo with knowledge of the stock market, international trade, travel and literature. In fact, he solved Hidalgo's dilemma regarding the upcoming honeymoons.

The glittering Miami skyline was thirty minutes away.

"We come to the end of our day, amigo, a day I did not expect to turn out this way. I will remember our time together always. We chose different paths, you and I; otherwise I believe we might have been good friends."

"Suffice it to say we have each other's respect."

"Yes, we do. And on that note I would leave you with a final piece of good news."

"Which is what, exactly?"

"There is a man, or was, in Los Angeles, a drug dealer, a very good one. I have never met the man, although I know a great deal about him. He has always refused to meet with me, preferring to work through, shall we say, my middlemen. I am told, and I believe, that he never wanted to meet me so that he might remain independent. He is extremely good at what he does."

"Aren't all of them independent?"

"Pimps or amateurs, not professionals, which this man is. He's different, was different. And I have recently discovered to what extent. He is, or was, an undercover cop in L.A. until he very recently resigned from the force. Those were the phone calls I made from inside your daughter's yacht earlier today. His name is Drew Carling."

Hidalgo had no reason to hesitate or pause. They each knew.

"And now you are searching for him, as we searched for Gibson, for the same reason."

"No, I know where he is, because of Gibson. This morning he greeted Drew Carling onboard from inside his cabin, not my men whose names he did not know. Carling's name was also entered into the ship's log, which makes me assume that Drew Carling has recently found a good reason to change his name, to live a better life. Why else would he be in the Florida Keys and not L.A.? The men with us today, Hidalgo, as I told you, are not from the barrio. Like me, they do not soil their hands with day to day business.

What they did today was an exception, keeping them active as it were. They are executives with yachts of their own and loving families. They have no idea who or what Drew Carling is. They mentioned the name to me in passing. For that reason I searched for Gibson's log and put it into his tomb to help fuel the fire. No connection remains onboard, not at 500 degrees Fahrenheit or more, not to mention the way the boat blew apart, and as we speak my men are en route to Gibson's home. They will leave with anything pertaining to his boat and his clients. They are the best I have."

"If I were Mr. Carling, I would be worried, Enrique, that you know so much about him."

"Yes, with good reason, the man has cost me serious losses. But that is business, profit and loss, not entirely acceptable however to be expected in any line of work." He chortled. "I have some good years, and some not so good years. More importantly, I have a lovely home, a beautiful wife who has never been a victim of a cheating husband and I have children who are studying dentistry and medicine. Not bad for a kid from the barrio, Hidalgo. We are not so different, you and I."

"He must have been very good at what he did, this Carling."

"Yes, much like his father whom I respect above all others. He was a good cop, a brave cop." Mendoza smiled, peering straight ahead through the windshield. "Not many could do what he did. Not many could do what his father has done. ¿Comprendes lo que digo, amigo?"

"I believe you know that I do understand."

"You have lived a sad life, a difficult life, amigo, great success mixed with incredible sorrow. At the airport, when I first met with Diego, he was certainly more the cop than any other I might see on the streets of L.A. As he said, it must have been the suit. But it was more than that. We are what we are. Are we not?"

"He's a good man. He is engaged to Diane Quinn. They deserve a good life together."

"They do, as do you and Anita. I hope they will be happy flying to their paradise onboard your jet, while you and your bride cruise the frigid shores of Alaska. You must send me a postcard, amigo, and not take credit for my idea." He pointed. "Pull over, Hidalgo, right here. This is where we say goodbye."

Hidalgo swerved easily into the curb, Enrique Mendoza extending his hand.

"Enrique, what of Drew Carling?"

"Most of the contacts he knew in L.A. will believe he was killed, ODed or chose to leave because of certain legal problems. No one knows he was a cop. I have no interest in what he does in the future or where he goes. Diego, on the other hand, I would prefer to imagine raising a family, being with his sisters and his grandparents, Maria and Fernando. Diane crossed the line for him, Hidalgo. She was very brave to do so, to call the notorious Enrique Mendoza who is really a simple family man. They will have a good and happy life together, with such strength to share."

The men shook hands.

"I suppose, were Carling to know, he would be relieved."

"Carling should be proud of the job he did, as should his bride. No one can fault such dedication, speaking as a competitor of course." Mendoza paused, half in, half out of the car. "Gracias, amigo, without you and your son today would not have taken place. Let me thank you the one way I know that you will allow. Let me extend my best wishes to your entire family for long and happy lives."

"And best wishes to your family, Enrique, with much gratitude from me and Francine."

"You make me cry, amigo, not a good thing in my business." Mendoza slapped Hidalgo's knees. "Ah, you see, I almost forgot as we sit here talking like young women. This is for you, your father and Señor Canyon."

He tossed a thick envelope onto the dashboard.

"What is this?" Hidalgo asked.

"Two million in treasury bills, your one million plus interest. The money was not mine to spend. Adios, amigo."

Mendoza stepped out and walked away.

76

Hidalgo remained parked for a few minutes, wiping his eyes and catching his breath. He put aside the envelope. He trusted the man.

Anita was waiting for him in their suite. When he came through the door, she stood, her arms by her side, her face unsmiling, her eyes searching his for regret and self-loathing. Instead she saw relief. She saw a younger, happier man with hope in his eyes standing before her with open arms.

He said simply, "I have kept my promise to Francine, Anita. Gibson is dead. He died badly, more so than you can imagine and beyond my ability or desire to describe his passing. He now resides in hell where he belongs. I have also kept my pledge to you. He did not die by my hand, he died by Mendoza's. I did, however, watch as he perished. I felt not the slightest regret by witnessing the agony he endured. As Mendoza once promised, he left this earth as did Francine and his cousin without the comfort of a bullet to ease his passing. My conscience is clear, my heart much less heavy with sorrow."

She went to him, wrapping her arms around him. "All that remains of the past are your memories of Francine, which is how it should be. We will always remember her together. She will always be part of us, which is as it should be. But now a young woman is waiting in her room for news of you, alone. We must go to her."

He showered quickly and changed. Diane was waiting for them at the entrance, dressed for dinner. He'd never seen her so lovely, or afraid.

"Our past is closed, Diane. All that remains are the best of my vivid memories to share with you and Diego of his mother. As for Mendoza, he sends you his greetings. He wishes you and my son a wonderful and very long life together."

She squeezed him tightly.

"And Drew Carling, nothing was said about Drew?"

"No, nothing at all. He is unaware of Drew Carling, as he should be. Detective Carling did his job well, to the extent that no one cares what might have happened to him. He is simply gone. Those who inhabit our streets after dark, it would seem, are not as compassionate as they could be."

"Can we phone him, Hidalgo, please, now that it's all over? He must be fuming."

"Somehow, Diane, I sincerely doubt that he is." He grinned widely. "In fact, we will not. He doesn't deserve such considerate treatment after the appalling way he's treated you. Let him learn his lesson to the fullest extent possible. And let me be selfish for one night. Let me be the envy of all men as I walk with you lovely ladies on my arm. I promise you the most delightful evening."

He had a point. Anita and Diane exchanged silent thoughts, conspiring.

"He can wait," they agreed.

77

The next afternoon, late in the day, Diego Hidalgo Arquero-Duval arrived home escorted by Detectives Carlos Del Campo and Luis de la Vega after three days and nights of massages, aroma therapy, steam baths, sauna, rejuvenation pool and sensory deprivation. They had each survived pedicures and manicures, new haircuts, creams where they had never creamed and they smelled like a fresh spring day.

Del Campo and de la Vega looked and felt twenty years younger, each one returning home to their wives with gift bags and souvenir photographs of themselves with the staff of Swedish beauties.

That day in the governor's office, Del Campo and de la Vega had strongly refused financial consideration for their part in kidnapping Diego Arquero-Duval or for the rescue of Darcy Wilson, which they considered wise not to confess despite the governor's good humour at becoming engaged to La Bonita. Hidalgo accepted, disheartened at not repaying meritorious goodwill and selflessness. Until soon after their return as newly revived men when he spoke casually with his son.

Over the three days of Diego's captivity the cops had come to know Diego and spoke with him over dinners and fruit cocktails about their dream. They knew exactly where they would build and when, how the place would be, anxious to give up their Glocks and to be with their wives who hadn't had much of a married life.

They didn't realize however that Hidalgo Arquero never let kindness go unrewarded or that he had never forgotten the philosophy once shared by Francine's grandparents. Their wives were the solution. Hidalgo had never said that he wouldn't reward their wives who were important in the equation and on the sixth of January, an important date, the women would be invited to lunch by the firm of Arquero-Duval to become the co-owners of their husbands' dream.

Diego, for his part, was already twenty years younger when he arrived home, delivered none the worse for wear in handcuffs to Diane by jovial cops, the real way, with his hands shackled behind his back. She was given the only key along with his gift bag containing necessities for the modern man. What went on after is a matter of speculation.
*

Hidalgo went to his parents' home. He'd called ahead, asking his father to invite John Canyon for a glass of wine. While he, Fernando and John stepped into the garden, Anita, Maria and Jennie remained inside. Between them there was no speculation, merely quiet memories of Francine as they waited for the men to join them with solemn yet contented expressions.
*

Gabriella and Deidre would not see their family for another day. Darcy Wilson was gone forever. She would never come back, nor would Francesca Maria Arquero-Duval, Deidre had decided. Her name would not change who she was or who she now loved, which wasn't her brother at the moment for having left her most prized possession abandoned in Key West.

78
Thursday, El Día de los Reyes of this Year

Thursday morning Hidalgo went to the cemetery. Anita waited by the car, giving him space to think and say what he must, time to be alone with his past, his present and his future.

He went to where she lay and spoke with Francine, to be alone with her, to speak with her from his heart as he had done so often throughout their youth of his dreams and hers: the dreams they would share together. The dreams they never did.

He spoke to her of Anita, all that he could think to say of the woman he loved, as he sat crossed legged on the coarse grass. He told her of the man that he killed and that she should now find peace in the universe for her son was now safe from harm.

Some hours later, from behind, his mind oblivious to the passage of time, "Hidalgo, you have done a good thing. I can only hope that I love you as much as Francine once did and still does from her special place in your heart and in ours. I believe that I do. I know that I do, as Francine knows that I do."

He stood, turning, his face wet, unashamed of his tears, his mouth agape with shock. Standing with Anita was Fernando and Maria with a blanket and many cushions, Deidre and Gabriella each with flowers, Diego and Diane with a huge picnic basket. John Canyon and Jennie stood with them, a full case of wine at their feet.

Francine Elizabeth Arquero-Duval would never be forgotten.

Deferred Prejudice

Other Mystery – Suspense - Thriller Novels

By Doug Booth:

Split Verdict

The 4th Man

The Madam

Family Lies

Mother of Pearl

From Inside Her Bedroom

The Feast of Tombola

Deferred Prejudice

The Hunt for Gilligan Rose

The Fatal Diners' Club

Silent Conviction

A Christmas Killer, Comfort and Joy

Pariah In the Mirror

***

No One to Tell (Creative Non-fiction)

www.ingramcontent.com/pod-product-compliance
Lightning Source LLC
Chambersburg PA
CBHW030536020726
47494CB00005B/1394

* 9 7 8 0 9 9 2 1 3 5 7 9 9 *